HER OWN *LEGACY*

Château de Verzat Series
Book One

DEBRA BORCHERT

LE
VIN
PRESS

Cover design by Lynn Andreozzi
Book designed and typeset by Ampersand Bookery

Map: A map of Paris in 1789 from William R Shepherd's *Historical Atlas*, Henry Holt and Company 1921. *Wikimedia Commons*, public domain in the United States of America. [https://en.wikipedia.org/w/index.php?title=File:Map_of_Paris_in_1789_by_William_R_Shepherd_%28died_1834%29.jpg]

Published by Le Vin Press
Year of Publication 2022

ISBN: 978-0-9894545-4-4 (Ebook)
ISBN: 978-0-9894545-5-1 (Trade paperback)

First Edition

In Loving Memory of

BARBARA J. DICKETT

CLAIRE MCMILLAN HORTON

DEBORAH COVENER MAHER

PLACE DE
LOUIS XV
PALAIS
ROYAL
Garden of the
Tuileries
THE TUILERIES
PLACE DU
CARROUSEL
THE LOU
Quai du
SEINE R.
PALAIS
BOURBON
HÔTEL DES
INVALIDES
ST GERMAIN
DES PRÉS
VERZAT
MANSION
SORB
LUXEMBOURG
PARIS
AT THE TIME OF
Her Own Legacy

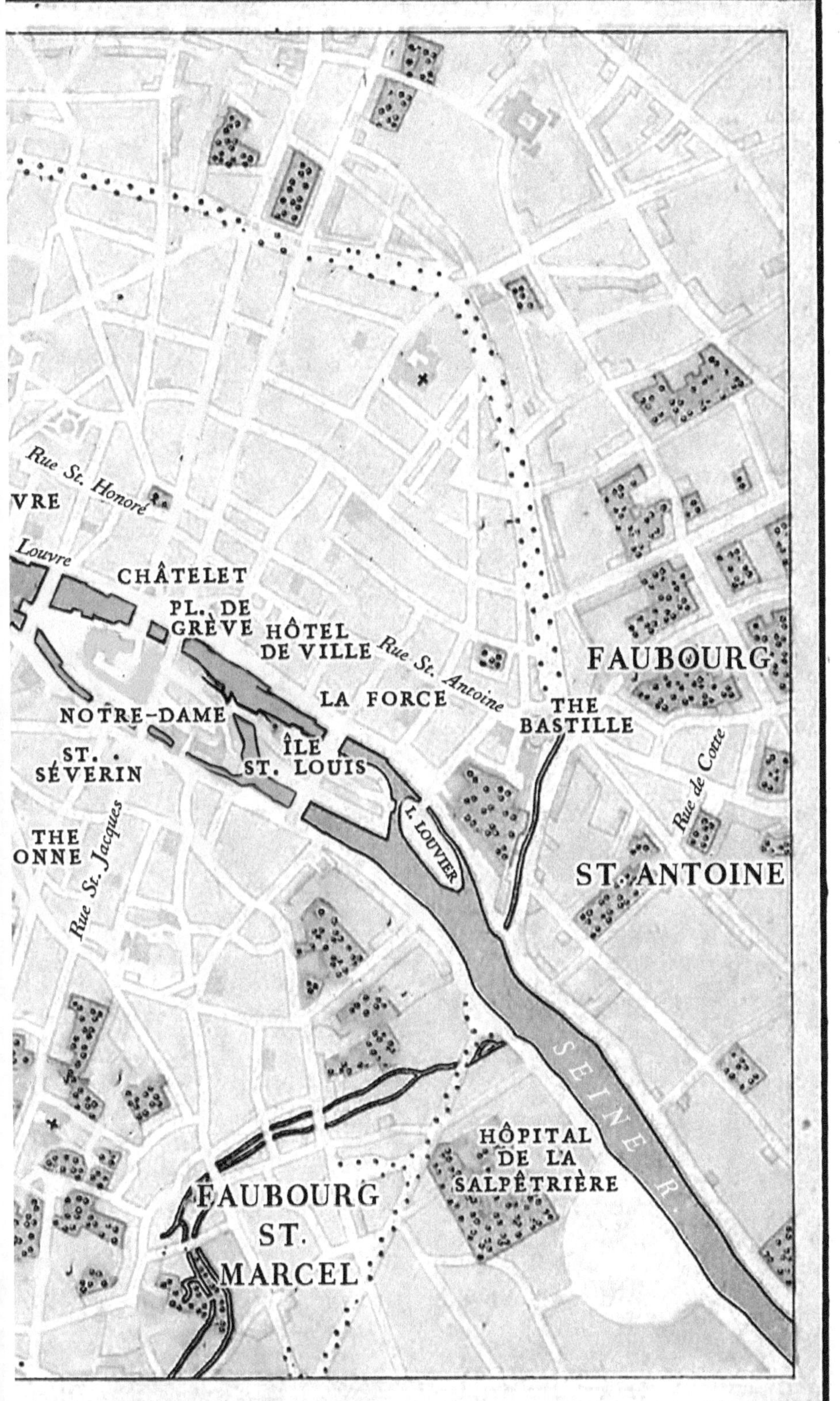

Rue St. Honoré
VRE
Louvre
CHÂTELET
PL. DE GRÈVE
HÔTEL DE VILLE
Rue St. Antoine
LA FORCE
FAUBOURG
NOTRE-DAME
ÎLE ST. LOUIS
THE BASTILLE
ST. SÉVERIN
L. LOUVIER
Rue de Corte
THE ONNE
Rue St. Jacques
ST. ANTOINE
SEINE R.
HÔPITAL DE LA SALPÊTRIÈRE
FAUBOURG ST. MARCEL

AUTHOR'S NOTE

ALL WRITERS OF historical fiction strive for authenticity, but sometimes we may find conflicting facts in our research. Other times, we are faced with using a term a modern reader might not recognize.

Confusing for readers is the evolving names of streets, buildings, people, and locations. Most readers will recognize the Hall of Mirrors at Versailles, but prior to the French Revolution, it was known as: Galerie des Glaces, which is the term my characters use.

Place Louis XV became known as Place de la Révolution, the home of the guillotine at the time of Louis XVI's execution. The Directory named it Place de la Concord, but after the Restoration of the monarchy, Louis's brother wanted to name it Place Louis XVI to honor the beheaded king, but Charles X returned the square to its original name. After France's second

Revolution the name was returned to Place de la Concord, and as of this writing, it remains so. Still with me? The guillotine also moved around a bit, starting at Place de Grève, moving to Place du Carrousel, and on to Place de la Révolution.

All my research confirmed two Gardes Françaises were killed at Versailles in October 1789. However, my research revealed a collection of four names. In this event, I consulted Gallica, the digital library of the Bibliothèque nationale de France and used one of the two names listed as gardes du corps who lost their lives during the assault on the palace.

While incorporating historical fact within the creations of characters and story I sometimes made concessions. In the battle at Versailles, I changed the location of the fight from the bottom of the Queen's staircase to its landing for dramatic effect.

Eagle-eyed readers may find blunders or anachronisms, for which I take responsibility. If so, please let me know through my website. As a thank you, I'll send you a short story leading up to the French Revolution and thank you in my next book in the series. Merci beaucoup.

HER
OWN
LEGACY

PART I

Joliette

1

Joliette

Château de Verzat
August 30, 1786

"**W**INE FLOWS IN your veins." Grandmaman brought her lorgnette to her eyes, examining the underside of a grape leaf.

I walked with her through the undulating hills covered in grapevines. Bees swarmed the grapes' syrupy juices, their humming reverberating in my chest, reassuring me I was home. Ever since I could walk, I accompanied Grandmaman on her daily inspections of the vineyard. I peered over her shoulder at the leaves, but I did not see any mites or cutworms. "My tutor told me blood flows in our veins."

She nodded and brought her arm beneath the leaves, lifted them, and exposed the grapes, round and full and close to ripe. "It does. But you are a Verzat, and wine is in your blood."

"That is silly." A giggle rolled through me. "You know I am allowed only sips—I am just twelve."

"It is not from the drinking of wine." She straightened and dug the tip of her walking stick into the cracked earth, releasing a mineral scent. "It is from the terroir. Everything around you contributes to the wine and your blood."

I laughed. "You are making that up."

"I am not." She lifted her cane, waggling it at me. "You are as rooted to this estate as the vines, and I shall prove it. Close your eyes."

As always, I obeyed her.

"What do you smell?"

A trickle of sweat ran down my neck. I was grateful I was not wearing the tight sleeves or heavy underskirts required at the Court of Versailles. I wanted to give her the correct answer. To her dismay, my papa had no interest in the vineyard, and I often heard him arguing with Grandmaman about it. I could not further disappoint her. A cool breeze brought the scents of mud and fish from the Loire, but they merely influenced the terroir, they were not a part of it, like the earth that rooted the vines.

I turned my back to the wind. Another fruit, besides the grapes. I sniffed again. Peaches? I inhaled a scent so luscious, my mouth watered. "Sun-ripened apricots." I opened my eyes.

Her smile lit up her face and warmed me. She lifted her stick toward the far hill, where an orchard grew. She wobbled, and I reached to steady her until she replanted her stick. "You would not have been able to identify that scent if you did not have wine in your blood."

There was no arguing with her. "Will this year produce as good a vintage as the last?"

She adjusted my bonnet to shade my face. "You have your maman's luminous complexion, and we must protect it, else she will forbid your accompanying me." She pinched my chin. "What else do you smell, child?"

Another scent? My tutor gave fewer tests. I inhaled deeply. A thick aroma shimmered in the heat, as if I had entered a patisserie. "A sweet nectar, like honey."

Her face glowed. "The fruit is smaller globed than most years but bursting with ripeness. Look." She ran a finger along strands of juice trickling from a split grape. "Aging will intensify the ambrosial flavor that accompanies that scent." Her blue eyes sparkled, casting magic, as she searched the vineyard, stopping when she spotted a tall man. "Joseph!" She waved her cane.

Wearing a dilapidated straw hat and blue tunic, Joseph waved and loped through the vines to us. He removed his hat and bowed. "Yes, Madame la Comtesse?"

"Send the pickers here this afternoon."

"Just the southern slope, Madame?"

Her smile broadened. "This is why you are an excellent vigneron, Joseph. You require specifics. Yes, just the southern slope. Will you join us on our walk?"

"Of course, Madame." Joseph followed us at a respectful distance.

"You will see why I am grooming Joseph as my apprentice until you can take over, my dear." Grandmaman cupped her fingers along my cheek, and I leaned into her touch like a puppy nuzzling its maman.

"That will not be for a long time. I have much to learn."

She tapped the tip of my nose. "You have a vintner's sense of smell. That honeylike scent makes the wine robust and gives some wines a hint of caramel, like the caramel in Cook's pastries. It only occurs during years of scant rainfall. I believe this year will be an excellent vintage, better than the last."

I picked a grape and savored the taste, imagining how the flavor would change after fermentation. The cracked dry soil released puffs of chalky dust with our footsteps. If I breathed through my mouth, I tasted the chalk. Like the parched earth, I wanted to soak up every drop of her knowledge. "But if there is little rainfall, will the harvest yield less fruit?"

She planted her walking stick and lifted her face to the sun, her wrinkles slipping away in the golden light. "You are correct. And you have the mind of a viticulturist." She tilted her head, examining me.

I wrapped my tongue around the word, forming it silently and feeling a strange pride growing in me for having the mind of an expert.

"Rather a large word for the growing of grapes. True?" Her lips formed a pink heart. The black lace cascading over her straw bonnet and tied beneath her chin accentuated the heart shape. Leaning on her cane, she wavered a bit.

"Viticulture?"

"Oh, how I wish your father had been as curious at your age. He has the Verzat palate, of course." She stabbed the earth with her walking stick. "But he did not, and still does not, possess the desire for learning how to preserve the Verzat legacy."

A tightness wrapped around my chest—pressing me to not disappoint her. Yet, out of loyalty, I hastened to defend my father. "Papa granted the vassals houses and land on the estate in return for their working the vineyard."

"Yes. That was democratic of him, and he is a good businessman." She twisted her stick in the dirt. "Your father considers himself a student of the Enlightenment. He spent many years studying Locke and Rousseau."

I turned and pretended to examine a leaf. He had encouraged me to read the same, but I did not confess it.

"In recent years he spent much time with that American… the man with the funny fur hat…what is his name?"

I laughed. "Monsieur Benjamin Franklin. He made embarrassing mistakes in French, and Papa had difficulties not laughing at the Ambassador's faux pas."

"That is the man. My son is more interested in the American democracy than the Verzat winery. But should Château de Verzat fail, the land will be sold. And four hundred families will either go back to being vassals or be without homes and work. And it would be the end of the Verzat legacy."

A niggling sensation moved through my stomach. "It will not fail so long as you run the winery, Grandmaman."

"For now. I am nearly sixty and will not be here forever to ensure its success." Her eyes grew moist.

I squinted in the bright light. She could not leave me. I would die without her. I reached out and held her arm. "You are too young to die, Grandmaman."

"Not for a long time. But someday, I will." She gazed out over the Loire River, her eyes unfocused, as if watching the past. "My dear husband taught me nearly everything I know, and it is most fortunate laws allow widows to inherit and run businesses. Still, I made mistakes without him, in the beginning. But I learned from them and survived along with the winery. Otherwise, the legacy would be no more." She pulled me close and wrapped her arm about my waist. Her heart beat rapidly, far faster than mine. "I loved the vineyards so, I never returned to my position as lady-in-waiting to the Queen. You know the legacy?"

Joseph stopped near us and removed his hat, in what seemed like reverence.

"Bien sûr, Grandmaman. Château de Verzat wine is the finest in France. Verzats have held the vineyard and legacy since 1515."

Joseph smiled at me.

My throat grew dry, but I forced myself to speak. "If Papa had a son, would you be training my brother to be vintner?"

Her eyes flashed as her gaze locked with Joseph's. He bowed his head and stepped back, replacing his hat.

She looked at me and pulled at her emerald earring. "Perhaps...but I doubt anyone would be your equal." Her voice brightened. "If your father does have a son, your brother will forever depend upon your nose, palate, and intelligence."

Pride skittered up my backbone. Part of me wanted a brother, so he could inherit the estate and continue the Verzat legacy and name. And although I had often asked my parents for a brother, I was now glad I had none, for I wished more than anything to be like Grandmaman and preserve the legacy, myself. Yet, if Grandmaman and my parents died before I married, a distant cousin would inherit the entire estate and legacy. Everything I treasured and cherished would be lost, and I would be left to the mercy of a man I had never met.

Most girls were thrilled to train as a lady-in-waiting, drinking chocolat chaud, dressing in silks and lace and jewels, and making wealthy nobles fall in love with them. Other girls would be glad their brothers would take over the vineyard and legacy. Although my name would change with marriage, at least I could ensure the winery and estate would always be Château de Verzat, but I would have to find a husband who desired the same.

She placed her hands on my shoulders and looked deeply into me. I was glad I did not lie to her, as I so often lied to fool my parents. I also kept no secrets from her, for her gaze would surely expose them.

"You have your father's eyes—that miss no detail—and his fine mind. Fortunately, that is all of him you have inherited. You have *my* nose and determination." She pinched my chin. "It is time for your first official tasting, ma chérie."

She turned to Joseph. "Please prepare for us."

Joseph hurried down the hill toward the cave's tasting room.

I hiccupped from my excitement. I had been allowed watered-down glasses of wine, but without knowing what I had been drinking. Now I would learn to identify varietals.

She gripped my arm, tightly, and I slowly led her uphill toward the cave entrance. She stopped to rest, and I waved my fan before her, the breeze stirring her gray curls. The hum of cicadas filled the air. She bent and coughed roughly. I patted her back, which was damp.

"Let us continue." She gripped my hand and we climbed and stopped and rested and climbed again until we reached the terrace outside the cave.

I guided her to sit on a silk-covered divan beneath an arbor. On a low table before us stood a silver bowl mounded with clusters of grapes, a pair of crystal wine goblets, sparkling in the dappled light. On a side table sat a green leather-bound book in which I had often seen her writing. Joseph stood holding a carafe, a white serviette draped over his forearm.

My hands jittered, and I smoothed the lace on my sleeve. My glasses of watered-down wine had been served at dinner, never a formal tasting.

"First we shall start with the fruit. Close your eyes, my dear."

I squeezed them shut.

"Taste this grape and tell me the varietal."

I nearly coughed. What a test. The vineyard grew at least five types, perhaps more. I knew them all by sight, but she wanted me to identify one by taste, alone? I swallowed, willing my palate to cleanse itself.

The grape, warm from the sun, trembled against my lips. I opened my mouth and held it with my teeth, sliding my tongue against its shape, which did not give me a clue about variety. I bit. Juice burst in my mouth, tasting sweet, but not overly so; fruity, yet slightly tart; raspberries at the end of the season; ripe plums splitting from an overabundance of juice.

I held the grape in my mouth, inhaling, determined not to disappoint her. I chewed. The Chenin Blanc would be tarter,

Sauvignon Blanc greener, the Gamay and Muscat more floral.
I swallowed. S'il te plait, mon dieu, let me be right, I prayed.
"Cabernet Franc."

"Correct!"

My eyes sprang open.

She dangled a cluster of purple-black grapes and crowed a
laugh.

Joseph's smile was broad.

My face warmed as my success washed through me.

"Are you ready for the next step?"

I nearly jumped up. "Yes!"

"Pour the wine, Joseph."

He poured the bright pale-yellow liquid into two glasses
etched with the Verzat crest of grapevines entwining a fleur-
de-lys. He stepped back, watching me.

Picking one up by the stem, she instructed me to hold the
glass the same way. She swirled the liquid and brought the glass
to her nose, closed her eyes, and inhaled gently. She looked at
me and cupped her other hand, bidding me to do the same.

The scent dizzied me, so intense was the aroma—like a
mélange of all the fragrances of the estate.

Her blue eyes sparked like the wine. "What does your nose
tell you?"

"It smells like home. Like here."

She smiled. "What specifically?"

"Fresh green grass, after a rainstorm."

Her smile deepened the lines that sprang up from the
corners of her eyes.

"The chalky tufa stone." My words surprised me. I had not
expected the taste of rocks to appear in a wine.

She nodded and caressed the emeralds circling her neck.

She wanted me to discover more. I inhaled again and sensed something flowery or herbal, reminding me of my maman, but the fragrance was faint and elusive. I sniffed again.

"Take a tiny sip, hold it in your mouth, and inhale through your mouth."

As the wine touched my tongue, I sipped a breath, and the taste exploded. I swallowed the delicious drop. "Lavender."

"You picked it up!" Grandmaman clapped. She caressed my cheek. "Ma chérie, you do have wine running in your veins. You are a true Verzat. Is she not, Joseph?"

"Indeed, Madame."

Her enthusiasm filled me with such pride my corset pinched as I inhaled.

"If your father does not have a son, this château, the entire estate, and the Verzat legacy will rest in the hands of you and your husband, Joliette. You and I must train our expert vigneron, Joseph, until you can become vintner. As your assistant, he will serve you well."

Joseph bowed and moved back from the table.

Vintner? Me? A prickling crept up my back. What she had said was true. Papa was with the King. He would not be here to oversee the harvest. I did not remember him having anything to do with the vineyard. If I married a man who knew as little as I did, how could we possibly succeed?

She sat watching me, her head bobbing like a sunflower bloom at the top of its stalk, battling a breeze. The oppressive heat made my head pound. The thought of Grandmaman no longer being with me squeezed my chest. I fanned myself. "What will happen if we do not finish training?"

"We *must* find an accomplished vintner should I fall ill before you are vintner. Joseph is an excellent vigneron, but he has neither your nose nor palate." She brushed her fingertips across my forehead. "Do not worry, ma petite princesse. I shall not leave you for a long, long time. I shall dance at your wedding." She pointed to the green leather book.

Joseph hurried over, retrieved it, and placed it upon the table before me.

I picked it up. It was heavy with thick worn pages and smelled musty, as if many drops of wine had splashed upon it over the years. I placed it on her lap.

She caressed the book like it was her most precious memento. "I have kept a diary, of every one of my days in this vineyard. It will explain what to do in any event, a hailstorm, draught, flooding, frost, fungus, pests." She held it out to me. "I give it to you, my dear. For only you can advise the future vintner." Her hands shook, and I rushed to take it from her.

Its weight pulled at my arms, but I hugged the book. "I shall read it every day, Grandmaman." I wanted to be exactly like her, a fearless, knowledgeable keeper of the Verzat legacy, but she had to show me how.

She patted her mouchoir to her face. "As you should. Be prepared for anything, Joliette, then you can make decisions and take actions, quickly. Your wise choices may save a vendanges."

My decision could save an entire harvest? A tightness in my chest trapped my breath. She spoke as if the Verzat legacy would rest upon my shoulders very soon. "I will learn everything to ensure that Château de Verzat produces the finest wines in the *world*." I placed the book on the low table before us. "And I will ensure that wine flows in Verzat blood for another two hundred and seventy years."

"I know you will never abandon the legacy."

I opened my fan, pretending to relieve the heat, but actually hiding my fingers as I tugged at my gown's bodice, loosening the laces, hoping she would not notice. "Joseph knows much about the vineyard and winemaking, but do you not wish to know more so that you might direct him?" Her face was still, but her eyes sparkled.

"Bien sûr." I never wanted anything more in my life. But how would I learn everything? Perspiration collected on the back of my neck. I had tasted but one wine of the six Château de Verzat produced—and every vintage was different. Grandmaman was faltering. Would she have time to teach me everything? I spent most of the year at Versailles, training to become a lady-in-waiting. My parents would not allow me to interrupt those lessons. Only Grandmaman could teach me the Verzat secrets. But she was old and frail. "Do you think I can learn it all?"

"Commoners are apprenticed at thirteen. And they must live up to expectations without the advantage of your fine education."

I grabbed at the challenge. If a commoner could succeed, a Verzat certainly could. The heat dizzied me. I knew nothing.

"If I believe you can, and I do," her eyes cast their magic over me, "then you can believe it, also."

An excited giggle caught in my throat. I pressed my hands below my ribcage and exhaled against my nervous excitement. I had to act as an adult—to ensure the Verzat legacy.

She gripped her cane and stood, looking out over the vine-yard. I thought she was bending to pick up the book, but then her body twisted and slumped. Her stick clattered to the stone.

I caught her in my arms. Staggering, I laid her on the divan. "Joseph!"

His arms were beneath her in an instant. He tenderly lay her back upon the divan.

Grandmaman lay, eyes closed, yet smiling, like she was content and happy.

I shook her. "Grandmaman!" Her eyelids fluttered. I patted her hand and whispered, "I promise, Grandmaman, but you must help me. I have so much to learn and only you can teach me."

She closed her eyes. Her smile grew peaceful.

Joseph picked her up in his arms. I held her hand, not leaving her side, as we hurried toward the château.

I whispered to her. "I will make you proud, Grandmaman. I promise." With every step, I prayed, S'il te plait, mon dieu, let her live.

2

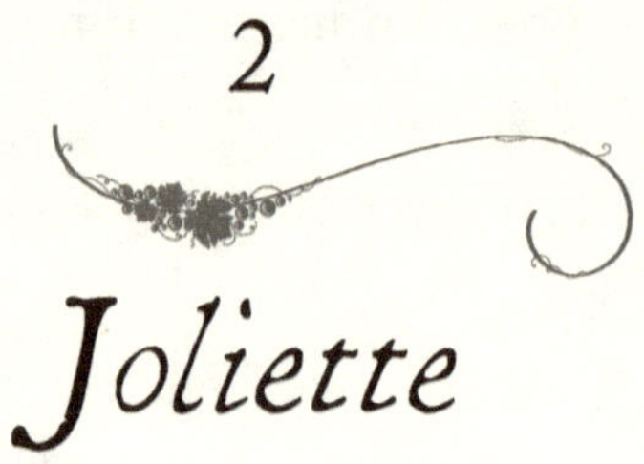

Joliette

Château de Verzat
September 1, 1788

I STOOD IN THE small graveyard overlooking the vineyard, envisioning Grandmaman in her straw bonnet, carrying her cane, bending over the vines, inspecting the grapes. *You were my best friend.* A hollow yawned in me. *How can I live without you?*

I forced myself to inhale—the scents of apricots, lavender, and honey. She had been right. I was as much a part of this vineyard as the rootstock penetrating the chalky soil, the breeze ruffling the leaves from dark to light green, the golden sunlight ripening the grapes to an ambrosial sweetness. She had continued my lessons from her bed, which she had never left after the day she had collapsed, two years earlier. I ran my hand over her white-tufa mausoleum. "I pray I do not disappoint you, Grandmaman."

At the top of the hill, the château glowed like an amber brooch, lit from within. Its future lay within my hands, but only if I could convince my father of my abilities. I had little time to accomplish that miracle. But I might be able to convince Papa to appoint Joseph, who would rely upon me. I would have to make Papa think Joseph was his choice. "Grandmaman, help me."

I returned to the château and stood at the threshold of the salon, Grandmaman's jasmine scent lingering in the warmth of the room. My hands trembled as I plucked her rosary from my hanging pocket and fingered the beads, trying to summon the confidence and calmness she had worked to instill in me. I found a shred of neither. I sipped in a breath, remembering how that tiny act could make a wine's flavor blossom. *Help me convince him, Grandmaman.*

Papa stared up at her portrait above the fireplace. Maman sat on the dark green silk couch, silently praying her rosary. A breeze billowed the white linen curtains, softly dragging them against the parquet floor—the only sound in the room.

I gripped the rosary before my bodice, keeping my grief hostage until I won my case. Only when I controlled the winery would Grandmaman rest. I gazed up at her face, so lovely, so serene, so proud. She held her smiling two-year-old son, my papa, in her arms as if he were the most treasured child in the world. I smiled. He was. How Papa's nose had grown so crooked, I did not know, and I hesitated to ask.

Taking a deep breath, I entered the quiet. "How old was Grandmaman when she sat for that portrait?"

Papa clasped his hands behind his back. "Twenty-five. It was painted just before my father passed."

She learned everything in ten years. I had had less than three for my studies. I pressed my thumb against my stomach, rubbing and pushing the tension down. Grandmaman had not found a vintner. Had she avoided finding him purposely, leaving no one else but me to occupy the position?

I clutched her rosary in my fist. If we did not find a vintner now, the cave, estate, and legacy, were at risk. I was the only one prepared to fight that risk. But how to make Papa think it was his idea? In my mind, I heard Grandmaman whisper: *Surprise. Charm. Plan.*

"You have hired a vintner, Papa?"

His eyes were dull. Deep lines on either side of his mouth drew his lips down. I had never seen him look lost. He appeared a child. I wanted to comfort him. His sigh pulled his shoulders lower. "The châtelain can see to it."

I dropped the rosary. The châtelain had no training. That would be like watching the Loire flood the entire vineyard. I dared not say those words. I pushed my hands together in prayer. "He already has much to do, Papa. And he has not the experience, otherwise Grandmaman would have appointed him."

He picked up my rosary and returned it to me, then walked to the bookcase and ran his finger along the spines as if looking for a vintner there.

"Your maman would be disappointed in you," I whispered.

He turned abruptly, his eyes moist.

I pressed my fingers to my lips. I had been too harsh. I softened my tone. "Unless you have a son, she would want you, the holder of the Verzat legacy, to find an appropriate vintner."

Maman cleared her throat, her eyes aslant as she stared at Papa.

His face reddened. "I suppose I should before we return to Versailles." He nodded. "I will do it tomorrow."

Tomorrow he would say there was no time to find one. I pressed my palm against the knotting in my stomach. He would leave everything in the châtelain's hands—a grave error. I gazed up at Grandmaman. *How can I help him?* The memory of my first wine tasting bloomed in me. Her face, full of wisdom and pride and mischief. She had asked questions. I made my voice sound curious. "What will you ask the potential vintner?"

He turned toward me, his eyebrows rising. "His experience."

"That is important. And what else?"

"Is that not all he needs?"

"He will need to know how to determine the optimal time for the vendanges." I placed my hand on his velvet sleeve. "But you know how to determine that, of course."

"Certainement." He tapped his finger to his thumb. "One pinches the grapes."

I gentled my laugh. "No, Papa. Grapes are not plums. Pinching does not play a part." My heart grew heavy. Grandmaman had not exaggerated. I opened the curtains, letting in the golden light, and looked out over the vineyard. An image of my twelve-year-old self walking with Grandmaman hovered amongst the vines. "He also must know the extra step required when crushing for the white wines." I glanced over my shoulder.

He turned his palms out.

"He should show initiative and ask if Verzat wines are filtered."

His mouth dropped open. "Are they?"

"Yes, Papa." I wanted to shout, yet I made my voice kind. "But by various methods depending upon the wine." I pressed my fingers to my eyes. This was far worse than I imagined. Little wonder Grandmaman was so adamant I learn everything. "Grandmaman taught me everything she knew. Perhaps I could help you interview him—if you like."

Maman looked up from her rosary. "That would be highly inappropriate and unladylike, Joliette."

Heat rushed up my back. "She taught me everything she knew because Papa did not learn it." I pressed my hand to my heart. "Papa needs my expertise."

Maman tucked her rosary in her sleeve and opened her fan. "Should it be known that you are involved in the winery, your reputation at Court will be sullied." She spanked the fan shut.

"A sullied reputation is nothing compared to the loss of the Verzat legacy." I knelt before her and took her hands in mine. "Besides, who would tell if only we know?"

She loosened my grip and pressed her hands along her gown. "Your grandmaman was ostracized from Court because she worked like a commoner in the vineyard."

I sat back. I thought she had lived at the château because she hated Versailles. She told me she never visited us there because the winery could not function without her for even one day.

She may have been ostracized, but I suspected she was happy about it. "But Papa works as a minister to the King, and you work as a lady-in-waiting to the Queen."

"That is not work. Those are our duties. And becoming a lady-in-waiting—if you are fortunate to be chosen as one—will be your duty."

"Yes, Maman." Would they deny my desire if I were a son? I stood and walked to the windows. Clouds gathered from the north. It was too warm for sleet, but hail was always a danger to the vines. My court-duty was as threatening as the weather. Without me here at the estate, who would oversee the vendanges? Joseph could not do it alone.

Papa's heels clacked as he paced the parquet floor. "I have been advising the King to levy a tax on nobles. If he does—and it is inevitable, for funding the Americans' quest for liberty has left the King and France facing bankruptcy—we will need the money the winery generates to pay the taxes."

Maman stood and faced him. "That is very enlightened of you, Henri. But your ancestors fought wars for François I. Your family received this estate as payment for their loyalty." She pressed her fist to her bosom. "We are noblesse d'épée."

He smiled a sad smile. "The privileges of the Nobles of the Sword are not democratic, my dear Catherine. Across the country, peasants have been burning crops and châteaux. If the King does not willingly change taxation, I fear commoners and peasants will force him."

I stood between them, looking from one to the other. "And where will the money come from if we lose the winery?"

"You are a child. These things do not concern you." Maman touched Grandmaman's emeralds circling her neck.

I pressed the rosary to my bodice and inhaled the confidence Grandmaman had instilled in me. "I am fourteen—a woman—and I shall be married within two years. I am a Verzat, and the legacy very much concerns me, as my husband and I will inherit it—unless you and Papa have a son."

Maman flicked her eyes at Papa, who looked away.

"Grandmaman trained me to ensure the legacy, and she would never want you to sell her jewels to pay taxes."

Maman dabbed her mouchoir at her eyes.

I was sorry I made her cry, but I pushed on, as Grandmaman would encourage me. "I vowed to not only protect, but also extend the legacy, and I shall send Cabernet Franc cuttings to Monsieur Thomas Jefferson."

Maman burst into tears. "You, too, shall be ostracized."

I stared at the carpet border, a pattern of grapevines twining around fleurs-de-lis. "I will never embarrass you, Maman."

"How do you know the American Minister?" Papa drummed his fingers on the mantel.

"I played cards with him at Versailles." I picked up my skirts and turned, pretending to examine an enameled box. I could not lie while looking at him, and I had to convince them both of my seriousness. "I won and, rather than accept my winnings, I asked a favor of him: to plant the cuttings and rootstock I shall send." I looked out at the darkening clouds. "We could have Verzat vineyards in America—if they thrive."

"And he agreed?" Papa's tone rose.

"Bien sûr. He has a great interest in viticulture." I could arrange meeting with Jefferson when we returned to Versailles, but winning at cards? That would take more than charm. But how to hire a vintner tomorrow? Joseph had been born on the estate, but as Grandmaman pointed out, he lacked my palate. I could exchange letters with him and oversee him from Versailles. I could suggest the châtelain recommend Joseph, making it look like his idea. "I wonder…" I tapped my chin. "Would the châtelain know of any vintners?"

Papa's eyes lit up. "That is a very good idea. I will ask him for a recommendation."

I looked from Papa to Maman, and back to Papa. My legs shook so that I doubted their support. I had to be a part of that conversation and make it appear as though it was Papa's idea. "Grandmaman taught me much, but I still have much to learn. May I accompany you?" I smiled my sweetest smile.

Maman sank onto the divan, her skirts puffing out around her. Papa rubbed his thumb along his bottom lip.

I extended my hand. "Come, Papa. It would please your maman to know you are teaching me. And it is very democratic of you to discuss viticulture with the châtelain."

His eyes held a glimmer, and I seized it as a sign that he might trust my judgement. But what if I made a grave mistake and the winery and reputation suffered? What if I was not ready to make any decisions?

Papa took my hand and placed it on his arm. "Let us go."

Grandmaman, help me ask the châtelain the right questions so he will volunteer Joseph.

PART II

Henri

3

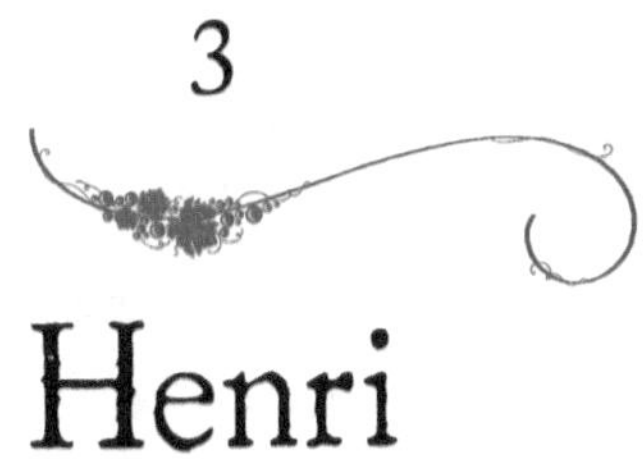

Henri

Eᴠᴇʀ sɪɴᴄᴇ I learned other boys had fathers, I wanted to meet mine. And today was my last chance to find him because tomorrow, I had to begin my apprenticeship with the stinking tanner and would have no time to look for him.

I scuffed my sabots, spraying gravel along the path of the Palais-Royal—a place where anyone could buy anything. As it was the most crowded place in Paris, I figured I'd find my father there one day.

I'd been dreading turning thirteen, because then you had to be apprenticed. I should've been grateful I had any apprentice-ship, for it was all Maman could afford, but being a tanner was the worst job in Paris. I'd have to scrape bristles and rotting meat and fat from the skins and then throw naked hides into a steaming vat of piss and crap. Being a butcher, or chandler, or even a rat catcher would've been better, but those men had sons and didn't need me.

Knowing today had to be the day to find my papa, I raced down a gallery lined with cafés and shops, past ladies smelling of lilies and waving their fans at men carrying silver-topped walking sticks.

I climbed a tree for a view of the stalls lining the garden paths. Bourgeoisie lined up before a fat man selling ribbons. A gangly man blasted a brass trumpet at a few prettily dressed boys. Laughter made me turn toward the central arena where a marionette show played. Since this was my last day for fun, I slid down and peeked behind the stall. Two men and a woman, standing on a platform, worked wooden crosses with strings attached to the marionettes below.

Entranced, I walked to the front of the rickety frame with a painted false roof, surrounding the stage. At its center flounced a marionette wearing a shiny pink gown. Her wig resembled a sailing ship so large it doubled her height—perfectly mocking Queen Marie Antoinette. Others, dressed as peasants not nearly as raggedy as real commoners like me, held strings of glass beads, looking like sapphires, pearls, and rubies. They lined up, bowed before her, and dropped the necklaces around her neck. With each one, she staggered and sank into her skirts. The audience applauded and cheered her descent—inch by inch—before she struggled, rose, and screeched for more.

"She'll drown in her jewels," yelled a flower seller.

I laughed along with the crowd.

"Stop! Thief!" A male voice shouted.

A street urchin ran into me, shoving me into a lady who glared at me. I begged her pardon and turned to grab the little beggar.

A noble, dressed in breeches and waistcoat the color of mustard with lace gushing from his cuffs and a jeweled scabbard hanging at his waist, raised his fist and shouted, "Stop that thief! He stole my purse!"

The urchin dodged through the crowd as the stage curtain dropped and people fled. I stood in the emptying space searching the noble's face, even though my papa couldn't be a noble. The nobleman had brown eyes, but they weren't kind, and they stared—right at me. I turned. Two uniformed guards ran down the arcade—right at me. I held out my open hands. They charged—right at me.

I opened my mouth to yell it wasn't me, but I was nothing compared to a noble. Nobles thought all the poor looked alike, so he figured I must be the thief.

If I were sent to prison, who'd deliver the laundry and carry water for Maman? I'd never meet my papa. I ran for the alley, toppling a lemonade seller and spilling her drink across the cobbles. "Sorry!"

Behind the café, I yanked open a rotting wooden door, flung myself down stone steps, and sprawled at the bottom. The door above bounced shut. I pushed myself up and stood, squinting in the darkness, breathing in dank air, and recalling my mental map of the tunnels. I pressed my hands against the rock wall, forcing myself to calm, then counted twenty-three paces. I felt for and entered the passage on the right, under rue Boucher. A door creaked.

Light slid down the main tunnel. I ran down the side-passage, seventeen paces to the wine merchant's cellar door, and pushed. It didn't budge. My arms shook as I pressed the door. *Merde!* Sweat dripped down my neck.

"He's not here," shouted a man, who I took to be one of the guards, for no nobleman would enter the tunnels and dirty his velvets and silks.

Something snakelike slithered over my ankle. I jumped. It squealed.

"He's here. Hear that? Rats are running from him!"

I crept to the other side of the passage, sliding my hands along the rock wall, searching for a place to hide from the light. An opening! Too shallow. *Merde!*

I slid against the wall as light from the guards' torches flooded the passage I had just left. A sharp rock jabbed my back, but I held my breath.

"He's not here, I tell you," yelled one of the guards.

"We'll lock the door, get more men, and come back." The passage darkened. "A few minutes in this blackness and he'll beg to be taken to La Force."

"What if he gets lost?"

Gruff laughter echoed along with their footsteps. "Then the little thief's skeleton'll be found years from now." Another laugh. "If he's lucky!"

"We'll get more men and come back right away."

Feet climbed the steps. The door slammed. My breath burst. I patted my pouch for my flint, steel, and box of char cloth. No steel. I turned the pouch upside down, feeling flint, box, candle stub, and a few sous spilling into my palm. No steel. It must've fallen out when I fell. They'd be back in a few minutes.

There was no time to search.

Keeping my hand against the cold rock wall, I returned to the main tunnel and, at the corner, I reached up, hoping the street name was not one painted in ink, but etched in the rock. I felt chisel marks, and I laughed with relief. Running my fingers back and forth, I tried to make out the letters. I read the word *rue* just fine, but I couldn't read the letters after *H* and *A*. If I'd taken rue Boucher, this passage should be rue Saint-Honoré. Were there any stores on that street with entrances to the tunnels? What if I wasn't below that street?

I smacked my palm against the wall. The priests promised Maman they'd teach me to read, but they taught their catechism. I'd run in the direction of rue Richelieu, and I could read that one, since it was named after a cardinal, but not this one. Why hadn't they taught me something useful, like street names? I'd heard *Honor thy father and thy mother* hundreds of times. I didn't have a father, and I'd disobeyed my mother. What good was that stupid commandment down here? If I'd a father, I wouldn't be in these tunnels.

I kicked out, my sabot shot off my foot, and I smashed my toe. "Son of a tanner!" I hopped around, cursing until the pain quit. I swept my hands about until I found my shoe.

I shuffled back to the passage, imagining the arcade above. I'd marked this passage on my map but not yet explored it. A draft swept the back of my neck. A bang echoed along the chamber, the sound bouncing like a ball. Did the returning guards take the north entrance? I forced myself to exhale and remember the street above. A boulangerie sat between the café and the wine shop. The baker needed storage for flour and a source of water. There had to be a door to the kitchen, and it would have to be opened often for both necessities. I had to find it—before the guards found me.

I jumped up, pressed my arm against the wall, and counted every shuffle forward. At eighteen paces, my foot struck rock, but my hands felt nothing before me. I crouched down and patted my fingers along a knee-high ledge made of stones about a foot thick. Yes! It had to protect a well. I felt about for a pebble and counted as I dropped it. A distant splash sounded at the count of two. The bakery door had to be nearby.

Crouching down, I held onto the ledge and made my way around it until my foot struck a step. My arms vibrated like when I hooked a fish. Keeping my shoulder against the wall, I climbed. Relief washed through me, only to turn to ice as the door above opened and light filtered down, illuminating the well at the center of a small chamber.

I ducked into a shadow and pressed against the wall. The sound of bare feet slapping the stone steps echoed. A small boy clambered down, dropped a bucket into the well, and lowered it with a rope.

I'd not get a better chance. I tore up the steps and through the doorway, blinking in the bright kitchen as a buttery aroma and a wall of heat hit me. I fell to my hands and knees.

A man wielding a large wooden paddle shoveled rounds of dough into an oven. Steam rose over baked loaves lined up on a long wooden table in the center of the room. The baker, who wore his hat so tight on his head his gray hair stuck out from under it like whiskers on a rat, flung his paddle into the corner, and shouted, "Where's the water?"

I crawled to the table and dropped to my belly. My cheek pressed to the floor, trying not to upset the bowls sitting on the shelf between the floor and the tabletop, I inched under it.

"Where are you?" the baker screamed.

I slithered through spilled flour and grease to the table's end—into the gaze of a scruffy orange cat. It extended its claws and hissed. I backed up, and it jumped up on top of the table. Pushing myself to the end, I looked up to see its tail swaying over the table's edge like it was counting the seconds until it could pounce. I wiggled myself back, watching the door, blinking away sweat, and drooling for a loaf.

The boy grunted as he climbed the stairs, water spilling from the bucket he grasped in both hands. His breeches were tattered and torn. He wore no stockings, but his blue tunic was stained, like mine.

"How many times have I told you to close the door?" The baker cuffed him.

The boy, a few years younger than me, sloshed water over the stone floor, making the flour beneath me into a slippery paste. He rubbed his ear and sniffed. "I can't see without light."

"What's there to see? Fill the bucket and come back. The blind could do such a simple task." The baker's red blistered hand shoved him. "Get that damned cat out of here!"

The cat dropped down and headed along the length of the table toward me. I pulled myself out and crouched low, ready to make a run for it.

The boy dropped to his knees and crawled, stopping and blinking when he saw me. I smiled and put out my hands, like I didn't know how I'd gotten there myself. He laughed. A blue-green bruise mottled his cheek. Not only was this mite working beyond his strength, but he was also regularly beaten. I smiled and brought my finger to my lips, hoping to win his silence.

The baker tripped over the boy's foot and dropped a pile of loaves. They spun across the stone floor. "Pick them up!" His huge foot kicked one.

The boy went after them, collecting them against his chest like a pile of stones. He handed one to me and smiled, showing more gaps than teeth.

I mouthed my thanks and stuffed the warm bread into my tunic.

He pointed toward the door and nodded sharply. With purpose, he walked to the cat and stomped on its tail. The cat yowled and bolted across the kitchen.

The baker screamed.

I ran—out into the alley, down the length of the Palais-Royal, across rue Saint-Honoré, past Place de Grève until I reached the Bastille. Falling against a tree I dragged my sleeve across my forehead. Stupid fat aristocrat. That urchin-thief was smaller than me. I gnawed at the loaf. If they'd caught me, I'd never find my father. If Maman told Papa I was in prison, he'd be ashamed of a son he'd never met. I scuffed my sabot in the dirt. Learning to tan hides was better than being in prison.

Heaving myself up, I headed for home. Tomorrow, I'd be a stinking tanner, but not for long. I didn't know how I'd do it, but I'd stowaway on a ship bound for America. Then, I'd learn to be a captain.

When I reached my street, I brushed the chalky dust and flour from my clothes and squared my shoulders. I gripped the loaf—maybe enough of a surprise to keep Maman from smacking me for being late.

Whistling, I opened the door of our lodging room.

"Where've you been?" Maman hung a dripping sheet over the ropes strung between wooden beams overhead.

Holding out the bread, I kissed her cheek. "A carriage broke down, and they shot the horse, and the crowd blocked the street, and a bread seller dropped his basket, and I got us a loaf at a greatly reduced price." I gave her such a sweet smile she couldn't possibly want to smack me.

She shook her head. "What a tall tale you tell."

I pinched off a chunk of bread and popped it in my mouth. I figured since this was the last day I'd be living with her, she was going easy on me.

She emptied a water bucket into the iron cauldron hanging over the fire. The muscles of her arms were taut and braided, like ropes holding a ship to a dock. "The tanner expects you at sunrise tomorrow. So, you'll get up earlier to haul the twenty buckets before you go, every morning." She dragged the paddle through the steaming liquid.

I chewed the bread. Dozing anywhere near the stench I'd be working in made me want to retch. But not living at the workshop would spoil my plan. I'd no longer be able to escape and stowaway on a barge for Nantes, where I'd board a sailing ship for America and learn to be a captain.

"I'll be sleeping at his workshop." Hunger made my stomach knot. At least tanners got fed well. The day she told me of my apprenticeship, I'd schemed a way to get out of it. I wasn't going to skin dead animals for the rest of my life.

Whenever I went to the river to fish or swim, I watched the bargemen and stevedores. I knew I didn't want to be either of those laborers, for they grew wet with sweat in winter. I heard the sailors at the Palais-Royal, telling tall tales of their adventures. Tall tales because everybody knew fish didn't fly and mermaids didn't exist. Eventually, the job of first mate or captain appealed to me, for I never saw either of them do any work other than shout orders: Hoist the sails! Drop anchor! Flog him!

Maman threw clothes into the pot. "Monsieur Gervet says you can live here."

"But why—"

"Who's going to help me?" She stabbed the laundry with her paddle. "Do you see a husband here?"

"Where *is* my father?" I hoped to anger her, so she would tell me to stay at the tanner's.

She puffed out a stream of air, blowing wisps of hair off her forehead. "I've told you a hundred times. He's far away."

"In America?" I pinched another piece of bread.

"I don't know."

"*Who* is my father?" I jammed the bread in my mouth.

"Monsieur Detré!" She threw down the paddle. Water droplets hissed in the flames. "Who do you think?"

I swallowed. "Is he a tanner? Will I be apprenticing with my papa?"

She frowned. "Would I pay your father?"

I wiped crumbs from my hands. "Is he a sea captain?" I picked up a pair of breeches off the table and folded them. "Do

I look like him?" I looked nothing at all like Maman. So, I had to look like my father, and he'd be tall and have muscled shoulders, like the blacksmith. I put the breeches on the pile and took up a faded child's tunic. He'd speak with a soft low voice, like my neighbor, Bertrand the carpenter, who was like my papa until my real one showed up. The child's tunic was soft and, folded, fit in the palm of my hand. My papa'd have dark blue eyes, like mine. I added the tunic to the pile. "Do I look like him?"

"I don't remember." She balled up a handkerchief and wiped her neck.

I snapped a dry sheet from a rope overhead. "When's he coming home?"

She shoved her cracked red hands on her hips. "What do I always say when you ask that?"

I crumpled the sheet and threw it on the pile. I mocked her stance, imitating her voice to vex her. "You don't know."

"That's right." She kicked the buckets toward the door. "Five more trips. And be quick about it."

"I can deliver all the water you need the night before, so I can sleep at the tanner's. I don't want him to think I'm not a good worker." I smiled.

She laughed. "It will take too long."

"Maman, if I fail, will you get your money back?"

She squinted. "I don't know what you're up to, Henri Detré, but you better not fail."

"Right! And sleeping at the tanner's is the best way to convince him I'm serious about my work." I grabbed the buckets and the wooden yoke from the corner. "You'll see how fast I can fill the pot."

The door closed behind me, and I stood in the Bastille's shadow. When I got a good job, Maman wouldn't have to be a laundress and her hands wouldn't bleed anymore. I lifted the yoke over my shoulders. I'd make her proud of me.

I raced along rue du Faubourg Saint-Antoine and entered the square, passing lace makers twirling their bobbins in the afternoon sun.

I filled the buckets at the fountain and hung them on the yoke, balanced it on my shoulders, and ran until I reached rue du Cotte. I rounded the corner and stopped.

A man, dressed in such finery and wearing so much face paint he resembled one of the marionettes, walked toward me. I slowed. Was he a friend to the noble who mistook me for a thief? His shiny breeches and frock coat, the color of moss and embroidered with gold fleurs-de-lis, caught my attention. A wave of lace rolled down his neck. A dark green cloak hung from his broad shoulders. I'd seen nobles wear powdered wigs, but his was so large it looked like a goose nested between his head and hat.

Maman and I lived in the poorest quartier in Paris. Such a noble wouldn't be there unless looking for a commoner to perform some vile task. If he hired me, I could use the money for passage on a boat. I'd convince Maman of my speed later. I headed toward him.

With his chest puffed like one of the peacocks at the Palais-Royal gardens, he strode along, but as I neared him, he stopped and stared at me—with dark brown eyes.

I stared right back but was so taken by his crooked nose, the most skewed I'd ever seen, I stopped in the middle of the street. "Can I help you?"

He jerked his head toward my lodgings. "You live here?"

For a moment, I feared he *had* been at the Palais-Royal. My legs tensed to run. Sunlight glinted off the bejeweled sword hanging from his waist to ankle. He could slice me in half. I nodded.

"Tanner's apprentice?"

I stepped back, sloshing water onto my sabots. Had the tanner sent him for me? Did he own the tannery?

"Speak, boy!"

The yoke wavered. If he'd come to deliver me to the tanner, all my stowaway plans would be dashed. "Why's it your concern?" My voice rang in my ears. I'd shouted at a noble, who could have me thrown in the Bastille. Sweat ran down my arms.

He drew his thumb along his bottom lip, then he reached into his waistcoat and handed me a paper. Not a speck of dirt stained his fingernails.

I set the yoke and buckets down, unfolded the paper, and acted like I read every word. The paper didn't look official and carried no seal. By the few words I could make out, stupid priests, I suspected it was the contract Maman signed her mark to with the tanner. I returned it. "Yes, Monsieur."

He stuffed the paper in his waistcoat. "Well?"

I shrugged. Was he accusing me of thieving? "Who're you?"

He popped something into his mouth and chewed. "Do you attend school?"

"I did."

He rested his hand on the pommel of his sword. "What do you desire for your future?"

I looked past him. The Bastille's shadow darkened an alleyway where a thin mangy cat lay nursing a parcel of kittens. Did he have a fantasy that commoners had a future other than remaining commoners? Maybe he was making a joke of me, but still, I should've been frightened of his power. I picked up my buckets and looked him in the eye. "I should like to meet my father."

A laugh erupted from his chest. "A most noble desire." He continued to laugh softly and wiped his eyes with a handkerchief more lace than cloth. "And after you meet this man, what then?"

I'd dreamed my papa would teach me to read and take me fishing, but I couldn't say I wanted him to teach me how to be a man. My unknowing must have shown in my face for he barked another laugh. "Come, boy. What is your heart's desire?"

"To be captain of a ship."

"Another noble yearning." He ran his tongue over his teeth. "But why a ship's captain?"

"My father's one." He was far away, so what else could he be?

He arched an eyebrow. "Is he now?" His voice was dark and deep, like the water of the Seine. He ran his finger and thumb in a line on either side of his mouth and stared at me. "How can you command a ship if you cannot read charts?"

The weight of the water pulled on my arms. All I knew of ship captains was that they shouted orders. Charts, like maps, wouldn't have many words. I drew my map of the tunnels without words. Was that why he was here, because I'd stolen paper and ink from the inn where I delivered the laundry? Sweat seeped through my tunic.

His eyebrow still high, he smiled. "I should like to speak to your mother."

My grip tightened on the yoke. I'd probably be sent to a dungeon for not sniveling before a noble—if he could catch me. My arms tensed. I'd throw the buckets at him if he yelled for a gendarme. "Why?"

He flung his arms out. "Ah, protective! A fine and noble quality. I mean her no harm. Tell her Comte de Verzat has arrived."

"You better not hurt her." Keeping my eye on him, I set down the buckets, opened the door, and called out, "Maman, Comte Zat is here."

The wooden paddle hit the floor, and she turned around. Droplets of steam clung to the wisps of her hair like dew on a spider web. She grabbed at the laces of her gown and tightened them, making her bosom bulge.

He followed me into our lodgings. The room shrank around him.

"Madame Detré. Good day to you." He swept off his tricorne and bowed.

Pale as the sudsy water, Maman collapsed into a deep curtsey. "Monsieur le Comte! Good afternoon, Monseigneur." She remained crouched, her hand waving at me. I stepped near her. She grabbed my arm and whispered, "Bow."

"Wh—"

She pulled me down. Her eyes were pinched, like when she was scared. Her grip tightened.

I bent forward. Why was she acting like this man was a priest? If he was taking me to train for the clergy, I would run.

"This is Henri?" Comte asked.

I moved to speak, but she yanked me back. "Yes, Monseigneur. Yes."

He tapped his large green shoe—made of leather, not wood like my sabots. Their buckles looked like silver lace.

"You have not sent him to school."

With each tap, tap, tap of his shoe, Maman shivered into her skirts. "He did learn his alphabet and catechism, and he can cipher, Monseigneur. After that, there was no more money."

He grunted. "Why was I not informed?"

"I'm sorry, Monseigneur. I didn't know…"

"Monsieur Rapineau informed me of the apprenticeship."

I sighed, tired of his questioning what was none of his business and intimidating my maman. "Why're your shoes green and the heels red?"

"Shush!" Maman scrambled to rise and brush her skirts.

"You are observant. Shoes with red heels indicate that one has been presented at Court." He tossed his hat upon the table. "Will you introduce us?"

"Monsieur le Comte, may I present Henri." She shoved me forward.

"And what do you do at Court?" I asked.

He made a little puffing sound I took as a laugh. "I advise the King."

She touched my arm. "Henri, this is Monsieur le Comte de Verzat."

He tilted his head toward her.

"Your…" she squawked like a chicken on a chopping block. "Your…papa."

I jerked around. Cheeks trembling, she clutched her hands and dropped into a curtsey again. I grew dizzy. The floor moved far away, like I was perching on a high tree branch.

"It's true," she whispered. The creases around her eyes deepened. "He's your papa."

The fire cracked and popped, and my face burned like I stood in its flames. I'd imagined my father to be ship's captain or an explorer or a trader. If he was my father and a noble, why did Maman and I live in this tiny room? He treated Maman like a servant. Why did she have to work?

"Henri?" His voice was deep, but not warm like Bertrand's.

I pulled back my shoulders. "Your eyes aren't blue."

His lower lip bulged. "No."

"My papa would have blue eyes, like me."

"Not necessarily."

"Maman told me my father's name is Detré, same as mine." My hands fisted. "You're not my father."

He laughed, a great big laugh that made me feel small. "My name is Henri. Henri Charles Albert de Verzat."

"We *don't* have the same family name."

"We are both Henri, are we not?"

"There's lots of Henris. Doesn't mean they're all my fathers."

"Pah!" His hand waved like a gnat bothered him. "You would have been able to see for yourself that what I say is true, if you could read."

He'd tricked me. Flecks of face powder marred his fancy frock coat. He was a fake. "If you'd been *here*, you could've carried the water, and I could've gone to school."

"Henri!" Maman jerked my arm.

I steeled myself for a whack. Instead, she gripped her apron so tightly I worried it might tear. Why was she calling him *Comte*? If he was my father and she was my mother, didn't they care about each other, like our neighbors, Bertrand and Madame Françoise? They acted like they didn't know each other, like this was the first time they'd met, but that wasn't possible.

The water in the cauldron bubbled furiously, sputtering water into the hissing flames. Maman laundered day and night to buy our bread. If we sold one of his shoes, we'd have bread for a year. If he *was* my father, why had he left us without money? I stood tall and stared him in the eye.

"My son shall not be a tanner."

I started toward him. My toe hit an uneven stone, and I stumbled.

"Get your advance back." He smiled at her. "Henri shall be educated."

My breath left me in a whoosh, like I'd fallen from a high branch.

Maman kissed her praying hands and smiled so sweetly she looked like a young girl. "Yes, Monseigneur."

"I shall arrange for a tutor." His stare was so deep I wanted to run. "You understand, that although I pay for your education, what you do with it is up to you?"

My heart beat fast, like I'd run with ten buckets from the fountain. I'd agree to anything if I could learn to read, because then I'd get a good job and Maman wouldn't have to do laundry anymore. "Yes, Monsieur."

"The wearing of red-heeled shoes must be earned—also up to you."

"Yes, Monsieur. But—"

He drummed his fingers along the hilt of his sword.

If I *was* his son, did that mean I was a noble, too? I knew nothing about being a noble, and I doubted he'd teach me. "Am I a comte, too?"

He dipped his head. "Not at this time."

Heat burned in my face. "Why?"

He might've blushed, but I couldn't see beneath the thick face powder. He was ashamed of me because I couldn't read. Well, I would learn to read so I could get a good job. He wouldn't be ashamed of a ship's captain.

"Expect the tutor." He retrieved his hat and opened the door. "Study every day." He looked back at me. "My son."

He left.

"Wait—" My arm froze, reaching for him. The door closed. He drew the heat away with him, leaving a cold emptiness. I took deep breaths, trying to slow my pounding heart, but it raced faster as I realized I was going to learn to read. I could become anything. I could help my neighbors of Faubourg Saint-Antoine.

Maman collapsed onto the bench and put her hands to her face. Tears ran around her red swollen fingers and plopped onto the table. I put my hand on her shoulder, rising and falling as she gulped in air. Her hands must've hurt, but she never complained. It was my fault. She worked to feed us and pay for my apprenticeship. Why hadn't Papa paid?

This *papa* promised me a tutor. Why hadn't he given her

anything? I'd never seen her look so surprised, like she'd never seen him before. Maman's name was Detré and his Verzat. Were they not married? I was back in Catholic school, standing in the corner, but I didn't know why. Was I a bastard, like the boys at school said? If Papa was real, why didn't he stay and teach me to read?

After a while, Maman patted my hand, rose, smoothed her apron, tidied her cap. "There's laundry to fold."

I looked at my reflection in the shard of mirror I'd found and brought home for Maman when I was little. She'd propped it on the mantel and told me it was the loveliest gift she'd ever received. The more I looked, the more I realized that man and I didn't look alike. Different jaws, chins, mouths. I had a slight bump in my nose, but his was as crooked as the street we lived on. If he wasn't my father, who else would pay for a tutor? Nobles weren't known to be kind-hearted or generous. There had to be something in the bargain for him. Bertrand would say I should be grateful. Other boys would leap with joy.

I kicked the empty bucket, and it spun across the cobbles. "If he's my papa, why didn't he take us with him?"

Maman kept her back to me. "It's time to deliver the laundry, now."

"I have to get water for Bertrand first." He'd help me figure this out.

The Bastille's long dark shadow made me squint in the dusk. I rounded the corner and stopped, the sight making my heart gallop. Stéphan, a water carrier for Réveillon's wallpaper factory, shoved two small boys out of his way and stepped up to the fountain. Nearly as tall as Bertrand, with shoulders as broad as a blacksmith's, he wore no cloak even in the coldest weather. The forked yolk he carried had hooks so he could haul six buckets at a time. He bullied all the carriers because he was so big and strong. None of us stood up to him.

He was cruel to me, but I never insulted him. His crippled maman was too poor to purchase an apprenticeship for him. Two years older than me, he'd be a water carrier for the rest of his life. With the arrival of my Papa, I pitied him more.

Buckets full, he shouldered the yoke and turned toward me. "Detré, you bastard! Tomorrow you'll be a *stinking* bastard!" He laughed.

My shoulders stiffened. I wasn't a bastard. I knew who my father was, and he was paying for a tutor, so I didn't have to be a stinking tanner. But I couldn't tell Stéphan. He wouldn't believe it anyway. I gave him a huge smile. "Good day!"

He walked close, too close. Three of the buckets would hit me if I didn't move. I steadied myself and, when the buckets neared my face, I flung my bucket at his, making him stumble, upsetting his yoke, and splashing water all over him and the square.

I wanted to laugh, but it was too dangerous.

He slammed down the yoke. "You stinking bastard! I'll get you, Detré"

I outran him, but I'd have to avoid his retaliation for weeks. Still, it was worth seeing his fury. I laughed, filled my buckets at the next fountain, and followed the alley to Bertrand's tiny workshop. The door was open, and he stood at his bench, sanding a carved chair. Tall and thin, Bertrand kept his long brown hair tied at the back of his neck with a strip of leather. Despite scarred and callused hands and black fingernails, he ran his fingers over the wood like Madame Françoise caressed Simon.

He glanced at me as I emptied the buckets in his water barrel. "Thank you." He tossed a small chunk of wood at me.

I caught the block—a piece of elm he'd helped me carve into a toy bear.

"All ready to start your apprenticeship tomorrow?" He blew dust off the chair.

"No."

A lock of hair came loose, hiding his eyes. "I know you think it'll be smelly, but you'll learn a trade, right?"

His shop was cold, yet I was hot. "I'm supposed to be tutored instead."

He pushed his hair back. "How'd your maman manage that?"

"She didn't." I scraped my thumbnail along the place where I'd hacked off the bear's ear. "A man claimed to be my papa and said I didn't have to apprentice; he'd send a tutor."

Bertrand wiped his hands on his blue tunic. "Who was this man?"

I bounced the bear in my palm. Laborers hated nobles, and I didn't want Bertrand hating me, so I left off *comte* and *de*. "Name's Henri Verzat."

Bertrand came close and put his knuckle under my chin, lifting my face. I gripped the bear. "You telling the truth?" He stared me in the eye. "Not planning on running away, are you?"

"No. I mean, yes, I'm telling the truth."

He let me go, took the bear, and sat on a bench. "What's your papa like?"

"Tall, like you, but not like you. I mean…" I didn't know what I meant. "He's got the crookedest nose I've ever seen."

He laughed and swiped his finger down my nose. "Not like yours, huh?"

I laughed. "And his eyes are brown." I punched the palm of my hand. "How can he be my father when my eyes are blue? His name's not Detré."

He slapped the bench. I sat next to him. "You think he's lying?"

I shrugged. "Why would a stranger pay for a tutor?" I sat beside him, smelling his fresh-cut-wood scent.

He took a knife and a piece of elm from a shelf and began carving. "So, you think this Verzat man is your father?"

"He said he was. So, I guess he is."

"Don't you want him to be?"

"Sure. But…he left us." I stood and kicked my sabot through the wood shavings. "He shows up thirteen years after I was born, stays for ten minutes, promises to send a tutor, and leaves. What kind of father's that?"

"A father with money." He didn't look up from his carving. "To have money for a tutor means he must work all the time. Perhaps he was traveling; perhaps he's very busy."

"You're not too busy to be Simon's papa." I stared up at the rafters. I didn't want him to see me cry. I wasn't a baby.

"What kind of father do you want?"

I pressed my lips together. I couldn't say, *a father like you.* After all, he was Simon's papa, not mine. "I hoped he'd be around to teach me to read and take me fishing." I picked up a shaving and ripped it in half. "I'm thirteen tomorrow, and I'm supposed to know how to be a man. Who's going to teach me that?"

His knife had a life of its own, notching and cutting the wood so fast it was like a serpent wiggling its way out of the limb. "Papas are all different, Henri. Just like all sons are different. Give your papa some time to show you who he is."

"He had thirteen years. Where was he?"

"In time, you'll know. Why not be happy about your good fortune?" He pinched his nose. "Aren't you glad you don't have to be a stinking tanner?"

We both laughed. Bertrand would think me ungrateful. Most boys would be thrilled. But I wanted my father to spend time with me. Was the tutor going to teach me how to be a man, too? Stéphan had no father, and he was a bully.

Bertrand tossed the finished toy to me. "Simon is practicing the letter *S* for serpent. Would you give this to him? I must finish this chair." He put his arm on my shoulder. It was warm and heavy and sure, like he was proud of me. How I felt right then was exactly how I wanted to feel with my father.

I breathed in the fresh green scent of the wood shavings covering the floor. "I'll take it to him now." Even though Bertrand worked, he'd taken time to talk to me. That's what I wanted my father to do. I didn't know when, or if, I'd see my father again.

I shoved the toy in my tunic, picked up the buckets, and walked out into the cool night. Would the people who'd become my family still feel the same way about me when I was an educated commoner? If I became a noble, then what? I laughed at myself wearing lace and red-heeled shoes, realizing the man who said he was my father might never return.

I sighed. Well, if he didn't come back, it didn't matter. I'd become a ship's captain because I was going to learn to read. Although being a captain would be an exciting adventure, I'd always want to return to Maman, my home, and especially Bertrand, Madame Françoise, and Simon—they were my family.

With or without my father, I'd figure out how to be a man somehow.

4

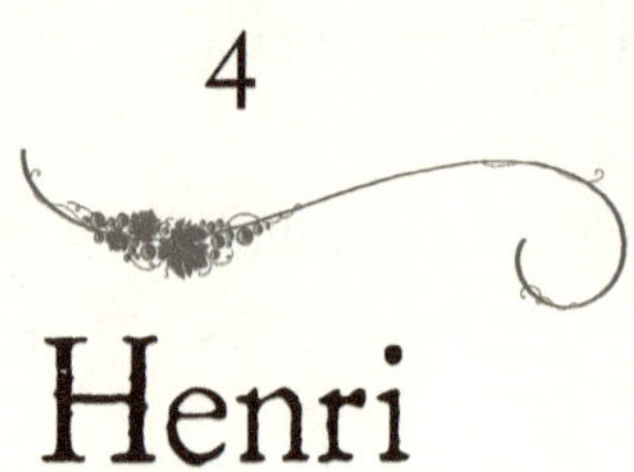

Henri

Paris
August 14, 1786

T HE MEMORY OF my father's arrival the day before was far too intense for it to have been a dream. Besides, I'd never dream my father was a noble, so I guessed he did visit. But what about the tutor?

The wooden yoke dug into my shoulders on my last water trip of the morning for Maman. So narrow was the street, I walked at an angle. Three stories of lodging rooms above hung out over the ground, making it easy for neighbors on upper floors to pass a loaf of bread across the street.

"Attention!" called a woman a floor above. I jumped back as the chamber pot slops spattered on the cobbles.

The stink reminded me how happy I was not to be a tanner.

With the end of the yoke, I shoved open our battered

wooden door. A pale man, bald as a mushroom, sat at the table talking with Maman. He wore a frock coat and breeches of a sturdy gray cloth. Unlike the wave of lace at my father's neck, this man wore a pleated white neckcloth. He clasped his long thin fingers before him, and when I entered, he stood, more unfolded, like a bird with long legs, for he was terribly tall and thin.

I put down the buckets, shoved the yoke in the corner, and yanked my tunic straight.

He gave a slight bow. "I am Monsieur Albert Rapineau, your tutor." He straightened. He would hit his head on one of the beams if he moved sideways.

"You'll teach me to read maps and charts?"

Maman squeezed my hand.

"I am not a geographer, but I *will*."

"You'll teach me to write?"

"I *will*. And many more things." He bowed to Maman. "If I may take leave with your son, Madame?"

Maman blushed like a girl and smiled, bringing her fingers to cover her stained teeth. "Monsieur Rapineau." She curtsied, as deeply as she had to my father, yet this man was not a noble. His heels matched the brown leather of his plain boots, without buckles.

"I'm going with you?"

"You *are* going."

"Why can't you teach me here? Maman needs me to deliver laundry."

"You wish to learn to read?"

"Yes!"

"I have many books at my studio, too many to bring here."

"Oh." I glanced at Maman, holding her hands like she was praying. I had to help her.

"Go with Monsieur, now." Her weak smile told me she'd miss me. I didn't want to leave her alone.

"I'll be back tonight to deliver the laundry." I kissed her and grabbed my hat. "Tell Bertrand I'll bring him water tonight."

The man seemed surprised but bowed. "Good day, Madame."

She would have to pay a water boy to bring ten more buckets. I'd make it up to her. I'd bring home a book and teach her to read.

In silence, I ran after him, for he had a terribly long stride, through the market, past the Bastille, across the river, and through another neighborhood of dyers, weavers, and tanners: Faubourg Saint-Marcel. Taking the tunnels back home would be faster. I'd explore and map them. After I learned to read, I could label them.

He stopped at a narrow building housing a printing shop on the street level. The pounding of the press reverberated as we climbed the rickety wooden steps to the next floor.

He opened the door and handed me the key.

I took it. "What's this for?"

"*What is* this for."

"Well it's the key to the door, but what're you giving it to me for?"

"It *is* the key to the door and *why are* you giving it to me?"

"That's what I said."

He sighed and entered a large room where two desks faced

each other in the center. He opened the brown drapes, and bright sunshine flooded the room and dust motes flurried like ashes from a fire. Shelves of books covered every wall, from floor to ceiling. My eyes ached. I'd learn to read 'em all.

"You a book seller?" I ran my fingers down some spines. A curl of dust the size of a chestnut stuck to my hand. Odd-sized books lay atop those standing upright, filling every crack of space. I'd never seen such a beautiful room.

He shook his head. "I purchased all these books."

"And you've read 'em all?" I turned in a circle. On the far wall, a window opened to the south. In the distance, I saw the barrier of the city. Did the tunnels extend beyond the barrier?

"You *have* read *them* all."

"I can't read, how could I've read 'em all?"

He steepled his hands. "I was not disagreeing with you. I was correcting your grammar."

A tingling ran down my back. Would he punish me? Like the priest who whacked me for a wrong answer. "What's… grammar?" I steeled myself for a blow.

He looked at me with such pity in his eyes I wanted to cry. "What *is* grammar."

"If you don't know, how can I know?" My head itched like it was on fire.

"Grammar is the body of rules that governs the correct usage of language."

"Oh." I hung my head, dumb as a fish on a line. No wonder my father was ashamed and left me. "Is my father coming here?"

He opened a door leading to a small hallway with two doors facing one another. He opened the one on the right. "This shall be your lodgings."

As big as the room I lived in with Maman! A small table and two chairs in the center. A palliasse, supported by a wooden platform and covered with a woolen blanket, sat to the left of the fireplace. To the right sat a chair and desk with a brass candleholder upon it. More books packed the shelves lining the side wall. A small chaise longue, with a pillow, sat before the fireplace. Maman and I never had a pillow. I smiled. She would think this room a palace. I thought it a palace. "I'm supposed to live with you?"

His eyebrows lifted. "I *am*..."

"I *am* living with you?"

He nodded. "You may move your things here whenever you like."

"That's..." Speaking was never so tiresome. "That is why you gave me the key?"

He nodded.

"Does my father live here?"

He shook his head.

Even if I didn't see my father again, I smelled freedom. Maman would no longer order me to haul water or fold sheets or deliver laundry. But I already missed her telling me to eat my bread. Who would help her? She couldn't carry the water, do the laundry, and deliver it—all by herself.

"Do I *have* to live here?"

"You are thirteen. Do you not wish your independence?"

I stood tall. "Of course." I could come and go as I pleased. I could explore the tunnels, every day. But I had to find a way to help Maman. And Bertrand. "Will I also learn to use a sword?"

He nodded. "And a pistol. Your father asked me to train

you in weaponry and to be an equestrian."

"Eq..."

"How to ride a horse."

"Truly!" I clapped. "Will you teach me how to be a noble?"

He waved his fingers for me to join him.

I followed him to the main room where he walked to the far wall and wedged his hand behind a bookcase. A click sounded, and the case pulled away from the wall on hinges, like a door. This was more exciting than the tunnels.

He pointed. "Light those candles and bring them."

I ran and pulled two from the desk and fumbled with the flint until I got a flame. He took one and pointed to a narrow ladder going up into darkness. Holding my candle high, I climbed through cobwebs for what felt like two floors. When I reached the last rung, I circled the candle about. The room was a quarter the size of the studio below and entirely lined from floor to rafters with books. Small holes below the roof line let in shafts of sunshine that glinted off the gold letters on the book spines. I ran my hand over them, warm from the light. I smelled dust and leather, what reading smelled like, and I loved it.

Beyond the ladder stood a small wooden table and chair. A brass candleholder sat on the table along with a towering stack of pamphlets, grouped with strips of paper. I whistled. Pamphlets were illegal. My hand trembled as I lighted the candle on the table. This was much more exciting than the tunnels.

Monsieur gave me his candle. I took it and helped him up.

He clapped the dust from his hands, took the candle from the table, and held it close to the shelves. "Let us see if you recognize any titles: Voltaire's *Candide*, Jean-Jacques Rousseau's

Social Contract, Diderot's *Letter on the Blind* and *L'Encyclopédie?*"

My arm jerked, and the candleflame guttered. The priests ensured we could read not only God's words, but also the titles of forbidden books, so we could recognize those we shouldn't read. "They're banned!"

"Correct."

"But my father works for the King!"

"Yes. Your father has read them and wishes you to read them as well."

"All of 'em?"

He nodded. "All of *them.*"

"So I can be sent to the Bastille? That's what education'll do for me?"

He closed his eyes, and I imagined him praying for patience, but I didn't care, I wasn't going to prison, especially for reading. He shelved the book. "Did you suspect this room was here?"

"No."

"Your father read these books in this room when he was your age. You will be as safe now as he was then. He is an enlightened man and has never been imprisoned."

"Have you?"

"Been imprisoned? Certainly not." He caressed the spines. "But I have read all of these…" he gave me a hint of a smile, "and many more."

Education could help me to do something forbidden *and* illegal. But read every single book? It'd take a lifetime.

He blew out his candle and put his hand out for help down the ladder. "You are behind in learning. We will study every day, beginning now."

Words stuck in my mouth like three-day-old bread. I had

to help Maman, every morning and evening. I promised to bring water to Bertrand. I had to tell Madame Françoise her soup was the best I ever tasted. And play with Simon.

"Come. You must learn other things before reading those."

The candleflame wavered in my grip. I peered down into the darkness at his bald head reflecting a puddle of candlelight. I wiped my sweaty hand down my breeches. I would learn to read and make maps and charts. And I'd become anything I wanted. And I'd help Maman and Bertrand's family. And if Monsieur Rapineau didn't teach me how to be a noble and a man, I'd read about it and figure it out myself. I didn't know how I'd do it all, but I'd figure it out.

"Yes!" I flung my leg over the ladder. I had a plan.

PART III

Revolution

5

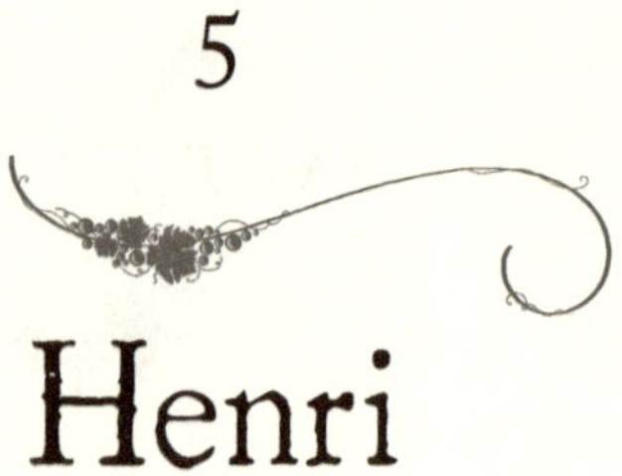

Henri

Paris
June 8, 1788

Nearly everywhere in Paris the possession of one banned pamphlet could get you thrown into the Bastille, except at the Palais-Royal. But I figured the King had to have spies, so I'd be careful. Although Rapineau had overwhelmed me with history, he never voiced his opinions, and I had to learn how to support mine—to be a minister to the King or even a lawyer. So, I went where everyone was eager to tell you their opinions and why yours were wrong.

I stopped at an arcade lined with shops and snatched a pamphlet from a news crier. A tall thin man in gray breeches and waistcoat climbed atop a café table and shouted at people strolling in the center courtyard. "We must demand the return of the Estates-General, so the King will hear our grievances." He punched his fist into his hand. "We must demand it."

The arcade magnified his shouts, making the strollers stop and stare. A great way to get people to pay attention. Could I be as brave?

An old man, sitting at a table, folded his paper and stood. "Should the Estates-General meet, things would remain the same." He steadied himself on his cane. "The combined votes of the clergy and nobility always override the vote of commoners."

Smart old man. Why couldn't other people see that?

"The Estates-General is our only way!" a rat catcher cried out. People near him moved back from the string of dead rats dangling from his pole.

Why did people put their faith in something that was proven not to work? I didn't care if the King *did* have spies. I couldn't hold my tongue against such ignorance. "The old man is right," I shouted. "We're all members of the Third Estate." I pointed to the tall fellow in gray. "Surely you know how many we are?"

He shrugged.

"We are twenty-eight million in all of France." I nodded at him. "How many clergy members in the First Estate?" His face reddened. I turned to the crowd. "There are one hundred and thirty thousand clergy members. And the Second Estate, the nobility, how many do you think? You, sir!" I pointed at a mustachioed man wearing a blue tunic and sabots, just like I used to wear. He worked his mouth, making his moustache wriggle like a caterpillar, but no words came out.

"You shake your head in embarrassment. As you should. There are only one hundred and forty thousand nobles! The first two Estates—add them up—that's two hundred and seventy thousand. One of them counts for one hundred of us. That seem fair to you?"

"But the King is chosen by the Divine." The rat catcher stomped his pole, making his string of rats jump. "We cannot go against the King—we'd be disobeying God!"

"The Americans didn't think it against God to fight the King of England! A fight that we financed!" I hopped up on a chair and spread my arms wide. "That's right. We paid for America's freedom from one king while we're slaves to another!" I looked into the eyes of the rat catcher. "And paying for America's freedom bankrupted France."

He stepped away, the rats swinging and bumping his back.

I leaned toward him. "That's why we pay taxes. Why we starve." I shouted at the crowd, "In America, everyone has one vote and every vote counts the same! If we paid for their privilege, shouldn't we enjoy it ourselves?" I raised my arms. "Our twenty-eight million votes are far more than two hundred and seventy thousand."

The tall man whacked his pamphlet against his thigh. "We must petition the King to listen to our grievances."

Was he ignoring me and my argument, or just incredibly stupid? "You still want to reconvene the Estates-General? I say, it's time for our votes to weigh more than the other two estates! Petition the King for that!"

As I looked at the confused faces of laundresses like Maman and carpenters like Bertrand, I saw these poor souls could neither read nor think for themselves. If I'd not studied and learned to read, would I have thought the Estates-General was our only hope?

"How do we force the King to change?" cried a woman wearing a gown with more patches than skirt.

"Protest at the Hôtel de Ville," called the tall man. "In his May Edicts, King Louis abolished local governments, so he can collect the taxes to pay for more of his wife's jewels and gowns—while common people go hungry!"

"The Hôtel de Ville is a government office subject to the King." I pointed in the direction of the city hall. "The people there can't change anything. They're loyal to the King."

Shouts of anger erupted. Pamphlets flew. The tall man yelled, "To the Hôtel de Ville." People followed him out of the courtyard.

I jumped down. My arms were as useless as my words. This was like a marionette show. People still thought the financial problems of France were due to the Queen's desires. There was some truth to it, but their ignorance saddened me.

I crumpled the pamphlet. What good would it be to write informative articles if commoners couldn't read them? I needed to get back to my studies but stopped and turned.

A news crier crossed the garden waving pamphlets, shouting headlines.

That was it! I'd write articles and hire news criers to read them aloud, not just at the Palais-Royal, but also in secret— anywhere in the Faubourgs Marcel and Sainte-Antoine. I'd hire criers to read to anyone who asked.

Rapineau's studio was above a printer's shop. I'd ask Monsieur Pierre to print my own pamphlets once I got paid by others. I'd write the first on the inequity of votes per numbers of people in each of the three Estates. That's how I could help my old neighbors.

Someone called my name, and I turned. Bertrand elbowed his way toward me, his brown hair flapping about his shoulders as he darted around knots of people.

My heart pinched at the sight of him. He'd not had any carpentry work in the past year, nor been paid for work already done. He'd lost his workshop. He insisted his wife teach him to sew, and they both worked late into the night darning clothes to pay rent. I hated seeing the family grow thin and wished he'd accept the money I offered instead of my sneaking bread to Madame Françoise.

I waved. He grabbed my arm and pulled me along. "I've got to get back to my studies."

He pushed me into an alley. Across from us, a feasting rat looked up then went back to his dinner of rotting cabbage. Bertrand pressed a pamphlet into my hand. "Read."

I read over the warm page, sticky with ink. He jabbed me. "Out loud."

"Oh." I read: "'Freedom for Grenoble. Yesterday, the people of Grenoble rioted before the house of the governor and the Palais de Justice.'"

"They did it!"

"Where'd you get this?"

He pointed at the paper. "Continue."

"'Soldiers, bayonets drawn, marched through the town, threatening the rebels. With no other weapons available, citizens climbed on the roofs, dislodged the tiles, and dropped them on the soldiers below.'"

"Brilliant!" he exclaimed. "Continue."

"'The King's regiment opened fire…killing many…'" My breath caught. "'Including a boy of twelve years.'"

"Damn them." He kicked the wall.

"'The tocsin sounded, and the alarm brought reinforcements.'" I didn't want to continue, but then a trembling spread down my arms.

"What? What is it?"

"'But *not* for the guards...'" I reread the phrase. "'For the citizens!'"

He jumped. "Hurrah!"

"'Friends of Grenoble flooded the city. Troops evacuated. Townspeople paraded Parlement members upon their shoulders to the Palais de Justice.'" Incredible.

"They did it. They defied the King. His troops fled." He clapped. "Do you know what this means?"

I wanted to say, chaos and more violence, yet they'd taken action.

"We can fight the monarchy. We can be like the Americans." Tears rose in his eyes. He grasped my hand. "Show me the word, freedom."

My chest expanded at the thought of being like Americans. I pointed at liberté. Could my writing have such an impact on other people?

He wiped his eyes. "It's a pretty one, isn't it?" He covered my hand. "Can you teach me to read?"

"You can't read at all?"

"Church words. I can write my name." He inhaled, staring at the paper.

Same as I was...before tutoring. "I teach Simon every Sunday. You can join us."

"No." A lock of hair fell over his eyes. "He thinks I can already read."

The paper grew sticky. When could I help him? I already studied late into the night, and I had to map all the tunnels. In Bertrand's dark eyes, I saw his hungry family. Perhaps if he could read, he could get a clerking job. I gave him the paper. "Meet me outside my tutor's studio at dawn."

He grinned so widely his ears rose. "I promise."

"When you can read as well as your son, you must help me teach him."

Bertrand clapped me on the back and left. I stood in the alley watching the rat sniff a pile of dog crap.

Would teaching Bertrand to read help him get a job? Or endanger him? At least Bertrand would be reading my articles. I'd start today.

6

Joliette

Versailles Gardens
September 30, 1788

PARASOL POISED TO shadow my face, I stood next to my dearest friend, Cécile, in the Versailles Gardens, listening to Maman's instructions. I could not bear to disappointment Maman or embarrass her by making the slightest mistake.

Our official Court presentation was soon, and I lagged far behind in my lessons due to the past spring and summer at the château, mourning Grandmaman. At the presentation ball, I had to find an appropriate husband, one who would allow me to be vintner. Finding a man who would encourage my ensuring the Verzat legacy was far more than I could hope for.

Maman looked at us. "I promised your maman, Cécile, that I would train you for your lady-in-waiting duties as she would have. I want you both to follow me and the other ladies-in-waiting closely and *silently* and imitate every one of our gestures."

Cécile's gray gown shimmered in the sunlight. Her eyebrows were powdered to match her tall gray wig, festooned with pearls and an ostrich plume. A lace hat perched precariously at the top. Everything on her head had to weigh more than my gown. How did she keep the whole thing from slipping? In my stiff white gown of mourning, without accoutrements, I was a common pigeon next to her.

I smiled at my friend, thinking how inseparable we had grown since her mother passed, years earlier, except for the summers when I returned to the château, and she accompanied her father to attend the royal family at Saint-Cloud. Though Maman forewarned me about telling anyone at Versailles about my involvement with the winery, I knew she could not have meant Cécile—she was like my sister. I tingled with accomplishment, and I wanted to share my success.

Maman caressed Cécile's cheek. "I will look back upon you both, frequently."

Cécile and I dipped a curtsey.

Maman hurried down the path, joining the other ladies-in-waiting who followed the Queen like a bevy of swans.

I sighed. I had hoped to share my news before our lessons.

Cécile placed her fingertips upon my arm. "I have seen my future husband."

"Shush." I gaped at her. She, unlike me, had always been so obedient.

She giggled and quickly brought her fan to cover her mouth. "He has sky-blue eyes, the color of the King's frock coat."

"How fashionable of him." One of the ladies at the edge of the group ahead gave a slight tilt of her head as she passed a woman below her station. I practiced it before we reached the woman and imitated the lady-in-waiting. Maman turned in time to nod at me, and glare at Cécile. "Tilt your head," I hissed.

Cécile nodded at the woman and smiled, which brought Maman hurrying.

"My dear, we will practice the degrees to which you nod in direct relationship to the status of the other person. Your smile belittled your station." Her parasol vibrated in her clutch. "Fortunately, the Queen did not see it. Please, Cécile, pay attention."

"Yes, Madame la Comtesse." She dipped another curtsey as she pursed her lips.

I dug my fingernails into the parasol's ivory handle. Why was she not taking this seriously?

As soon as Maman rejoined the ladies, Cécile smacked her fan against my arm. "He is a duc, has a château in Saint-Cloud, and he is as wealthy as the King."

That was not very much money, according to my father. "How old?" I whispered, my eyes on the ladies ahead.

She stumbled but quickly righted herself before Maman could notice. "Fifty."

My breath caught. "That is older than my father...and yours." I lowered my voice. "Forty-eight is more than triple your fourteen."

"Age matters not. Only two things are required for marriage."

The ladies stopped in a shady area, circled the Queen, and

fluttered their fans to cool her. I looked to Maman. Were we expected to join them? She gave a slight shake of her head. I put out my hand and stopped Cécile, brought up my fan to cool myself and, with a shift of my eyes, urged her to do the same.

She fluttered her fan like a lunatic.

Sweat dampened my back at the thought of the lecture on proper fan etiquette I would endure.

"You do know the two requirements?" Despite her frenzied fluttering, her curls remained still as stone.

"Love and devotion," I replied.

Her high, sharp laugh launched a wave of dread. I looked up for Maman's ire, but the ladies had started walking toward the Grand Canal and not heard Cécile's outburst.

"Joliette, you surprise me. The only things that matter are status and wealth."

"My parents love each other. I, too, shall marry for love."

She trilled another laugh. "You are a ridiculous romantic. It is not practical. The duc has both wealth and prestigious rank, and I shall be secure forever."

"What if you hate him?"

"How could I? He is a duc!"

"And if you are not compatible?"

"That is not possible. I told you, he is a duc."

I sighed. When did we grow apart? We had read Rousseau's *Julie* in secret together. "You loved reading about the passionate love between Héloïse and Abelard."

She waved me away. "He was much older than Héloïse." She caressed her neck—the same gesture ladies-in-waiting used when flirting. "Besides, that was just a story."

"Your parents loved each other."

"Maman despised Papa, thought him an old goat, but he did not know. She loved his money and title he bestowed. Those made her happy, but he did not. Her lover, on the other hand…" She giggled.

A heaviness crept into my chest. I had never asked Grandmaman if she loved her husband. I hoped she had. Maman's eyes filled with adoration every time she saw Papa across a room. Papa's smile was never as broad as when he looked at Maman. I wanted to share the same kind of affection with my husband. It did not matter if he had title or riches. I had both and would share them. And I would teach him about the winery.

"Truly, Joliette." She scattered gravel along the path with her slipper, and I quickly looked at Maman, praying she had not heard. "Do you wish to become an a vieille fille?"

I snapped my fan shut. "I have plenty of time to fall in love."

She stopped and faced me. I panicked. What if Maman saw? I reached for her arm, and she stepped back.

"I have no brother, nor do you. In the event my papa dies, I will have nothing, for a single woman is forbidden by law to inherit what is rightly hers." Her blue eyes flashed like shards of ice. "You could find yourself in the same predicament. I urge you to rethink your priorities—before you lose your precious winery." She turned. "The sooner we finish these boring lessons, the sooner I can get married." She stomped toward the ladies.

Her words stung like a slap. Cécile had only one parent. I had two. I had time and the luxury for falling in love. She did not. I should show more compassion.

I hurried after Cécile, eager to apologize and congratulate her on her good fortune. I hoped it would be good fortune. I prayed the duc would be kind to her.

The parasol handle grew damp in my grasp. I could only inherit the Verzat estate and legacy as a widow, as Grand-maman had. But was marrying a man I did not love worth it? If the legacy were at risk, I supposed I would. But if I married the wrong man, he could ruin the winery and the legacy. My parents would also arrange my marriage, and my husband's title and wealth would matter very much to them. I shuddered imagining Maman's lecture. I might be able to charm Papa into thinking he had arranged my marriage, but not Maman.

Two years was plenty enough time to fall in love. Was it not? My slipper struck a rock at the edge of the path, and I nearly tripped. I straightened and exhaled. Regardless of romance, I had to start looking for a husband—who loved the making of wine.

7

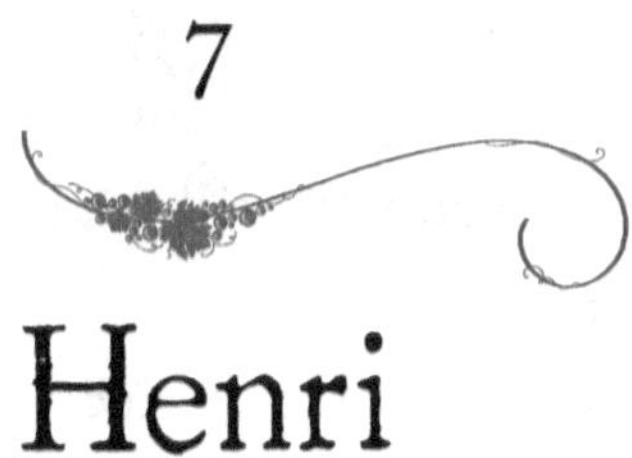

Henri

Paris
October 30, 1788

MY HEAD THROBBED with the beat of the printing presses below. Not only was I learning to read, but also speak the English language, which put me in the foulest of moods. Wrapping my mouth around the blocky words made me want to punch the book. Worse, I'd promised Maman I'd deliver the laundry before dusk, and I had to get these verbs right within the hour. I still wanted to go to America, and I'd need to speak their language.

I paced the room and tried again. "I is. You is."

Monsieur Rapineau cleared his throat.

My ears grew hot. "He is. We is. They is."

His eyes bulged like a raptor's. That's it. I'd call him *Rap*. But never to his face.

"The verb is conjugated differently for first, second, and third person in French, why should it not be in English, also?" Rap cocked his head. "Associating English to our way of speaking will make it easier for you. Do we say, 'Il suis?'"

I laughed. It was a good thing I didn't stowaway. I bent over the desk, dipped the quill, and wrote: *I am. He is. You am? You is?* Damn.

He stood at my side. "Do we say, 'Vous suis?'"

A sharp knock at the door stopped his torture.

Rap opened the door. "Comte, how good it is to see you."

"And you."

I didn't need to look up to recognize my father's voice.

A walking stick jabbed the floorboards. "Ah, you are taller."

My father rubbed his thumb over a silver-topped walking stick. His jaw line had softened. He wore a dark green frock coat and breeches, little powder, and no wig. He removed his matching hat, revealing graying brown hair. He was old.

Heat itched up my back. He was as much a stranger to me as he was when I met him. Every day for the past two years of my studies I longed to be with him. Longed for him to take me fishing. Longed for him, not Rap, to teach me to ride a horse, wield a sword, and shoot a gun. My father had abandoned me a second time, and I was certain he'd do it again. "It's been more than two years. I'm taller. You're heavier."

His laugh shook his jowls. "You are almost as tall as I. You are fifteen?'

How did a father forget the date of his son's birth? He wasn't there, why *would* he remember?

"Please sit down, Comte." Rap whipped his handkerchief about, dusting off his chair. "A glass of wine, perhaps?"

"Merci, but no. Would you excuse Henri from his studies?"

Rap nodded. "Certainement."

"I must finish within the hour and then depart to help my maman. Remember her?" I wanted to add that I preferred to read, as books were more a comfort to me than my father, but the risk of losing Rap and returning to one room in Faubourg Saint-Antoine made me shut my mouth.

Rap walked in front of me and frowned. I mirrored his grimace. He shook his head and left us.

"Come, Henri, I wish to show you something." My father sounded like he spoke to a five-year-old.

"Oh? And what's that?" I spoke poorly to disappoint him. Maybe he'd realize he should check up on his investment more frequently. Maybe he'd realize he needed to teach me to be a good son.

"Ah, it is a surprise."

"Ah, you've plenty of those." I dipped my quill. "Can't wait to see the surprise you'll have in another two years, as I'm sure you won't be visiting again any time soon." I hated sounding like a petulant child, but I couldn't help myself.

"Henri..." His voice dulled. "It is important for you to know what I wish to share with you."

Why did he bother with me at all? Yet, he did pay for every-thing, except taking care of Maman. "You've had two years to visit me. Why's it so important right now?"

"You are my son."

I tossed the quill on the desk. "I was your son when I was born." I grabbed my English book and slumped in the chair waiting for a smack. "I've been your son for nearly fifteen years." I turned a page.

He walked to me, yanked the book from my hands, and threw it on the floor. He towered above, staring at me.

I stared right back, fully expecting him to whack me, but I didn't care.

He reached beneath the pile of lace at his neck and pulled out a locket dangling from a fine gold chain. He brought it over his head, pressed the edge, popping it open, and held it out to me.

I glanced at a fine portrait of a beautiful young woman.

"What do you notice?" he asked.

"She has flowers in her hair."

"What else?" His hand wavered.

"She's holding a bird. Is this a game? I need to get back to my studies."

He grabbed my arm and pulled me to the mirror. "Look at yourself."

I shook him off. "I am." My face was flushed.

He held the locket to the mirror. "Do you notice any similarity?"

"She's a woman. I don't see any flowers or doves around me. Do you?"

"Look…carefully." He brought the locket close to my face.

She wore a white gown, held a white dove. White flowers dressed her powdered hair. The only bit of color was her eyes— her dark blue eyes. My throat tightened. I took the locket and walked to a patch of sunlight. She had large dark-blue eyes.

I faced him. "You're playing a joke?"

"No." His voice was soft. His eyes had lost their glint.

Was this woman my mother? Then who was Madame Detré?

I snapped the locket closed and returned it. "I guess when I was born, she spurned you and left us both, huh?"

With reverence, he brought the necklace over his head and tucked the locket next to his heart. He rolled his thumb over the silver horsehead on his walking stick. "Come with me, now."

"I must finish my work before delivering the laundry for Maman." I picked up the book and slumped into the chair. I was acting like a spoiled child, and I liked it.

The stick slammed upon the desk with a loud thwack. I dropped the book. Jumped to my feet.

"You have the blood of a noblesse d'épée." His voice was soft, and I felt its heat all the more for it. "And as a noble of the sword, I expect you to behave as one."

I stared at the floor. "Yes, Monsieur le Comte."

"Please honor me and call me, 'Papa.'"

I didn't want to pay him the compliment. He abandoned me twice, but he was still my father. If I didn't do as he asked, I could lose my education. I lifted my head. "Let us go…Papa."

He put his arm about my shoulder. I wanted to back away. It didn't feel good like when Bertrand did it. My chest tightened and my eyes burned. I squeezed my eyes until the crying feeling passed.

He patted my back and walked ahead of me. I didn't want to go with him, but I did want to know if the blue-eyed woman was my maman. And, if she was, why she abandoned me, too.

Two white horses hitched to a dark green carriage trimmed in gold waited at the square. A crest of grape leaves entwined around a château and crowned by a fleur-de-lys decorated the door. If it was the Verzat family crest, was it mine, too?

A dark green silk brocade—the cleanest thing I'd ever touched—covered the interior walls and seat cushions. The smell of lavender reminded me of Maman sprinkling the flowers over the fire to scent the laundry. He was accustomed to such finery. The blue-eyed woman was the reason he didn't share this luxury with Maman, but why did he not share it with me?

When Papa got in and sat opposite, the smell of cloves filled the carriage. He was so tall, he had to remove his hat. I sat up straight, but nearly fell when the coach lurched. Gripping the cushion, I watched out the wavy glass as laborers scurried out of our way. I hoped the driver wouldn't run them over.

"Where're we going?" I tried to sound like I didn't care.

"La Comédie Française." He touched his chest where the locket rested beneath his waistcoat. "It is where she worked."

"A cleaning woman?"

He pushed his tongue against the inside of his mouth, making his cheek bulge.

"Sewed costumes?"

He stared blankly at me.

"Actress?"

He nodded.

I leaned over my knees and stared at the thick green carpet. She abandoned me so she could continue acting. But she didn't know me. I straightened. "She doesn't work there anymore?"

He stared out the window at something far beyond the coach, not noticing the beggars with outstretched hands.

My leg bounced, and I pressed my hand along my thigh, trying to still it. I had to get back to carry the water. Maman was always at the laundry pot, always cooking, always cleaning. Knowing a blue-eyed actress gave birth to me would never change my love for Maman—because she was the only one who wanted me.

When we arrived at the old Tuileries palace, he hurried me under an arched gallery that ran along the outside wall. La Comédie Française was carved in the stone above gilded doors that were fancier than Sainte-Marguerite's.

We entered an empty vestibule where guttering candles made the afternoon into twilight. Candles flickered from the wall sconces as we climbed a winding stairway. When we reached a quilted red velvet door, Papa opened it, and silent darkness wrapped around me, like in the tunnels, but thick and muffled. He walked a few steps and separated a velvet curtain, letting in a stream of golden light.

Three huge chandeliers hanging high above cast light upon a stage larger than Sainte-Marguerite's altar. Three carpenters measured a table and moved it to different spots. If she worked here, she must have lived in a palace.

Papa led me to two cushioned chairs on a small balcony surrounded by a waist-high wall. I squinted at the stage that looked like an expensively decorated home.

"This was my box. I sat here, in this seat, the first night I saw her," he whispered. "Every night she performed, I sat right here."

"Were you not bored by seeing the same thing every time?"

"That first night, Abrielle wore all white, including the ostrich feathers in her powdered wig and pearls at her neck and ears. She played a young woman who tricks her papa. She made me laugh so." He wiped his eyes. "At her curtain call, she held her arms wide as she strode across the stage, and when she approached the audience, she looked up at me—for I was sitting exactly as I am now—held my gaze and curtsied to me. Applauding harder, I stood. She remained in her curtsey until the crowd rose to their feet and cheered her name. She kissed her fingertips and raised them to me."

I looked to the stage, expecting to see her. "How could she see you from way down there? Why just you?"

His lower lip protruded, and he shrugged. "I wondered that, too. But I did not stop to think about it. I raced to purchase the largest bouquet of white roses I could find before she emerged from her dressing room." His laugh was sad. "More than a few gentlemen, holding bouquets and bottles of champagne, awaited her. She looked among them, smiling away their compliments and gifts, until she saw me. 'You, Monsieur.' She extended her lovely arm toward me. 'You, with the great laugh, come to me, please.'" He patted my arm. "I needed no encouragement."

I smiled. He let me see how surprised he was by her attentions, how he adored her, loved her. He let me see him. Although I was a result of their love, I wasn't a part of it. I sighed. I had to deliver Maman's laundry. "Where is she?"

He grasped my arm. "Come, you shall see for yourself."

I vibrated. I would meet my mother? Would she still hate me? I'd ask her what I'd done to make her leave me. I jumped up.

He led me out of the box, down the twisting steps, and out into a hall of chandeliers, all empty of candles. Windows above the entrance let in a watery pale light. I slowed. Gilt-framed, larger-than-life-size portraits lined the walls. I slowed, hesitated. He meant I would see her image. The one of a lady, dressed all in white, drew me closer.

Her eyes sparkled like sapphires. My nose burned, like I was going to cry. "Where is she now?" My heart pounded, waiting for an answer I didn't want to hear.

He stood with trembling fingers pressing his lips, his eyes glassy. I placed my hand on his back, like Maman did for me so many times, and felt him struggle to breathe. A tenderness I'd not felt before settled in me.

When his breath calmed, he led me out the door. Neither of us spoke as we returned to the carriage. I pressed my feet into the floor and my back against the bench to steady myself. If my mother left, why tell me about her and take me to the place she performed? This explanation and excursion—both were for him, not me. He missed her. Couldn't he understand I missed him?

What had I done to make the beautiful delicate woman with blue eyes leave me? But she didn't leave. She gave me away. Like the mothers who pushed their infants through the baby-wheels of churches, she abandoned me. Neither of my parents wanted me.

The carriage jolted. Was he taking me to meet her? I didn't want to meet the woman who didn't love me enough to keep me. I gripped the door handle. We passed a gated entrance to the tunnels, but it was too late to jump out and disappear into the darkness. I was sick of people abandoning me, and I didn't want to experience her doing it again. I tried to get my bearings, to be ready for the next opportunity, but the carriage sped across a bridge, I wasn't sure which one.

We were in a quartier I hadn't yet explored, but I searched for something familiar as we bounced over cobbles, past mansions with blue-slate roofs, and iron picketed fences topped with fleurs-de-lis. I had to get away. I didn't want to meet a woman who didn't want me. Even with brown eyes, Madame Detré was my maman.

Papa sat in the corner, staring again at something far in the distance.

I clung to the cushion and forced my voice. "You taking me to see her? Where is she?" My throat was raw.

"I am sorry, my son." He bowed his head. "She died."

I stared at him, his clutched hands resting on his lap. I bunched the seat cushion. "So why tell me about her?"

"It is important for you to know who you are."

"Knowing she's my mother has changed nothing." I punched the cushion. "Madame Detré is my maman."

"Madame Detré has been most kind to you. She was your wet-nurse, your milk-mother. Yet, it is important to know where you came from."

"I come from Faubourg Saint-Antoine." I folded my arms and stared out the window at shoeless grubby children, running after us, begging for coins. I'd been one of them.

I drummed my fingers. I still was one of those children. But I wouldn't be if I could become a captain. Or if I became a lawyer, I could help people I grew up with. I had to deliver the laundry so I could get back to Rap and my studies.

The carriage slowed in front of a church of stone bricks, towering spires, and arched stained glass windows. The footman jumped down, opened the door, bowed, and held out his hand to my father. Papa must have sensed I wanted to flee, for he gripped my arm and didn't release me until we entered the church through large carved wooden doors.

He didn't dip his fingers into the holy water. I splashed my hand into the basin, crossed myself, and let him drag me along the center aisle. The vaulted ceiling stretched so high its walls blurred. Spots of colors splashed the stone floor. Sainte-Marguerite was a doll house compared to this place.

Before I could genuflect, he steered me around to a chapel. A statue of a Virgin holding the Christ Child stood above rows of flickering candles.

"This was your mother's favorite church. She visited this chapel every day she carried you."

The Virgin's fingers caressed the baby's foot. If my mother gazed upon this statue every day, how could she abandon her child? I turned away.

He grabbed my arm.

"I have to help my maman with the laundry." I shook him off, but he didn't let me go.

He pulled out the locket once again and ran his thumb around the edge of the portrait. "I had you delivered to Madame Detré, your milk-mother, so she could nurse you, when …" He wiped his eyes. "Your real maman died soon after you were born."

A roaring rushed through me. The stone floor rose like a wave. I leaned against a column. "I killed her?"

"No! Of course not."

"Yes, I did. She died when I was born." The roaring grew louder, filling my head.

He grabbed my wrist. My legs tensed to run. "No, my son." His grip tightened. "It was not your fault."

"You're lying." The chapel darkened. He loosened his grip.

My arm dropped to my side. The roaring dimmed. How could I be so sad over someone I never knew? The stone at my foot was cracked, and the break ran beneath the statue.

I dropped onto my knees. Was the crack there when my mother knelt here? I dragged my fingers along the edge, like it might connect me to her. "What was her name?"

He knelt beside me. "Abrielle Renée Lenogue Saulnier."

Her name shimmered in the quiet like the tinkling of a bell. "Sounds like a song."

"She was music itself." He wiped his eyes. "She could not be buried in the cemetery nearby."

"Why not?"

"She was an actress."

God doesn't love actresses? It was probably the stupid priests' rule. "Where's she…her body…now?"

His shoulders rounded forward. "She was taken to a mass grave at Les Innocents." He dragged his thumb over his upper lip. "There is no place else to visit her, but I like to think her spirit is here."

The candles flickered in the silence. I imagined her next to me, kneeling before the statue, wrapping her arms about her swollen belly. I squeezed my eyes. Why hadn't Maman told me I wasn't her son? I stood. I would run all the way to Faubourg Saint-Antoine and ask her.

Papa stood and clapped his hands as if to scare away his grief. "Saint Séverin is my favorite church, as well. Do you wish to know why?"

I couldn't imagine, as he'd not crossed himself or genuflected.

He reached into his waistcoat pocket. "I have a special gift for you." He pulled out a long iron key. "My grand-père gave this to me, his grand-père before him, and on and on for at least eight generations." He offered it.

I wrapped my fingers about the sharp flecks of rust. Its cold weight sent a shiver through me.

"This key saved my great-great-great-great-great-grand-père's life. It may someday save yours." His eyes darkened with seriousness. "Let me show you." He plucked up two burning candles from the row below the Virgin's feet and handed them to me.

The tick-tack of his walking stick rang out along the corridors of stone. In the corner at the back of the church, chilly damp air flowed from the depths of an old well. Curious, I quickened my step. Hidden in the shadows stood a battered wooden door. He took the key and pushed it into the rust-covered lock. The door opened onto stone steps. A cold current of air rushed me, making the hairs on the back of my neck prickle.

He took one of the candles and held it out. "You may go first." His eyes sparkled, like he couldn't wait to reveal the surprise.

This key unlocked the tunnel I'd not yet explored. I raised the candle above my head and pretended to be reluctant, not to spoil his excitement. The winding staircase spiraled down beyond the reach of the light. He nudged me and closed the door behind us.

I kept my shoulder pressed against the wall in the meager light and descended for a few moments until I arrived in a small chamber. Cold air drifted through a coarsely hewn stone archway and a gate of ornate black bars tipped with fleurs-de-lis. I'd discovered this place from the other side months earlier. My breathing quickened. We were below rue Saint Jacques. But I wouldn't disappoint him by letting him know.

Papa pointed toward the gate lock and nodded. I slid the key in and turned, enjoying the screech of grating metal. The gate creaked on its hinges as it swung open. I stepped through, and darkness fell around me like a heavy cloak.

With the candle held high, I walked the perimeter of the stone room, about the size of my bedchamber, and stopped before a gaping hole opposite the stairwell. Papa felt about the thick wall and, from a stone ledge above the opening, pulled down a torch, which he lighted with his candle—a brilliant strategy. I would hide a few well-placed flints, candles, and torches and mark their locations on my map.

After lighting the torch, he pinched the candle's wick and slipped the taper into his waistcoat pocket. "Have a spare candle and a flint and steel with you at all times." *All times, all times, all times* echoed as he turned and strode forth into the hole. In one step, the pitch dark devoured the torch flames, and I hurried to keep up with him.

After a few minutes, he stopped, turned, and placed his hand on the back of my neck. I wanted my father to be proud of me, like Bertrand's grip told me he was, but Papa's touch felt different. Hoping to please him, I worked at appearing awed. "Where are we?"

He raised the torch toward the opposite wall. Above him, the letters forming Saint Séverin were marked with soot on a smoothed surface of the rock wall. "Quarries run beneath the entire city, extending beyond the boundary walls. The limestone was excavated for building the Louvre, Hôtel de Ville, Notre-Dame—all the magnificent structures of Paris."

He waved the torch to the right, illuminating a jagged wall of chalk-white rock. "Nearly every intersection will be marked and correspond to the streets above, but you must learn the ways, and you must leave clues for yourself to follow should you need to retrace your steps."

"What kind of clues?"

"Place stones in shapes you will remember. Familiarize yourself with unusual rock formations. This chamber can be particularly confusing."

Another brilliant idea. I picked up pebbles, and placed them into an *H*.

He smiled. "You are aware that peasants have attacked châteaux, burned crops? In Paris, people riot and hang bakers."

"Bakers can't bake bread because they can't get flour. So why do people burn wheat fields and kill bakers when it's their fault there's no flour?"

He nodded. "There is no predicting when these rioters will strike. Never be caught in a mob, Henri. You could be killed."

"I should escape through the tunnels?"

He nodded. "Monsieur Rapineau is also teaching you swordsmanship, how to ride, and how to shoot a pistol."

Rap was teaching me all sorts of illegal things. I stepped toward him. "Even though law forbids anyone but nobles to carry swords?"

He grinned. "The dagger and pistol you will carry can be

hidden, unlike a sword. And it is legal for you to ride a horse."

My arms jittered, but I was late, and Maman would worry. I had to race there soon.

"Today, you must learn to feel the inscriptions to find your way, like our ancestors. Heaven help you if the tunnels are marked with soot rather than chisels, like this one."

I laughed recalling the day I'd been chased by the Palais-Royal guards. I couldn't read even the chiseled names. I lifted my eyebrows and opened my mouth, acting like this was fascinating news. "Why?"

He wrapped his arm around my shoulders. His muscles were firm, his grip strong. I'd wanted this all my life. I leaned into his warmth. "You will not be able to read those marked with soot without light." His chest expanded as he drew a breath. "Do you know of the Huguenots?"

"Yes." I looked up at him. "I have learned of the Edict of Nantes, the revocation by Louis XIV, and the massacre of Saint Bartholomew, when thousands were slaughtered—"

"On that day, your ancestors hid in these tunnels, lived here for days, and escaped the city and their enemies through them." He stepped back.

Cold air rushed over my shoulders where his arm had rested. "They were Protestants? You? Are a Protestant?" Was I?

"No, I am of no religion beyond that of our King."

A strange thrill jumped through me. "Does that mean I'm not a Catholic?"

His great laugh ricocheted around us like a disturbed colony of bats, making him laugh louder, until I feared the racket might wake the dead. He held the torch closer, warming my face. "You may believe in whatever you wish. But you may not wish to share your beliefs with others." He cleared his throat. "Especially if your beliefs should put you out of favor with the King."

Was he warning me? The King could have me thrown in the Bastille. I tightened my grip on the key. I thought I was a Catholic, the same as the King. Would my father be a noble if the Court discovered he was a Huguenot? "Could your ancestors be Huguenots *and* nobles?"

"*Our* ancestors became nobles during the reign of François I."

"Do you attend the Catholic church at Versailles?"

"Of course. I bless myself with holy water." He crossed himself haphazardly. "And genuflect."

"And what do you believe? Are you a Huguenot or a Catholic?"

"I believe in God, but I am neither."

"So, you are *acting* at Versailles?"

The corner of his mouth jumped. "You have read Molière!" He laughed. "Yes, and you must learn to act as well. These times are unpredictable, dangerous, without conscience. You may need acting skills as much as mathematics, reading, and English. Especially English."

Those blocky words. "Why English?"

"We are often at war with England. You must know your enemy. Most important, it is the language of America and Benjamin Franklin."

I nodded. How stupid I'd been, thinking I'd sail to America without speaking English. I'd conjugate those stupid verbs tonight. I'd make Papa proud of me.

"Franklin has told me many wonderful things of his country, of vast farms that belong to commoners. Every man may hunt

and fish to feed his family, without the permission of a seigneur. There is no droit du seigneur, because there are no men
whose rights are greater than others."

"Does the King listen to Franklin?"

He ran his tongue along the inside of his cheek. "I have asked
His Majesté to consider making those changes in France."

"Would you be a noble in America? Would I?"

"There are many opportunities in America, whether or
not you have a title." He turned and led the way through
narrow, curving passages, past sharp boulders, and into a
large chamber. Stacks of rocks formed columns—so unstable
I doubted they would support the ceiling much longer. Like a
crossroads resembling an un-shining star, five tunnels led to
eternities of black.

"This is the star chamber, and it can be confusing without
light. You choose. If you wish to go to the Palais-Royal, there
are thirty-seven tunnels that cross beneath the Seine. You will
need to know them all, like you know the bridges that cross
over the river."

I blinked, stunned at the number. I counted only twenty-
three crossing under the river. Drops of water plink-plunked.
A drop hit my neck and slid down my back. I shivered, glad
my woolens were warmer than my old tunic.

Taking the torch, I brought it up to each corner. Only three
were etched; the other two, *Saint Danté* and *Saint Séverin*, were
marked with black soot—unreadable without light. I climbed
upon rocks and ran my fingers over *Saint Michel*, *Saint Jacques*,
Saint Julien le Pauvre.

I pretended not to know. "Will Saint Jacques take us to the
university?"

"Indeed…Henri?"

I turned toward him.

"Would you like to continue your studies at Université?"

He couldn't be ashamed of me to ask such a question. I gripped the wall. "Even though I'm not a noble?" I could barely hear my voice.

"One day I hope to recognize you at Court as my son, and until then—" he patted the leather purse that hung from his belt, "I have many livres that can open the doors." He turned to walk down another corridor.

Université? The torch wavered. I never dared hoped, but now it was a possibility. I *could* help my neighbors, and Maman could stop doing laundry. I shook a tingling from my hands. "Perhaps with an education I could become a minister, like you, and counsel the King about the laborers of Faubourg Saint-Antoine."

"Being a minister is a most noble profession."

We both laughed.

I wanted to stay with him there, forever.

He led the way through the curving tunnels and straight to another gate, each picket topped with a fleur-de-lys. He motioned for me to unlock it.

"Does this key fit all the tunnel locks?"

"All but one."

"Which one?"

He climbed another spiral staircase. Not sure if he ignored me or not heard me, I followed. We left the tunnels and walked into a huge garden sparkling in frost. The old Luxembourg palais, surrounded by towering trees and a gate, stood in the distance.

I squinted and breathed in the frigid air. The tension in my shoulders eased in the light. I would explore this area tomorrow. "Which—"

"Never be caught in the tunnels. There are workmen repairing collapsed areas, and you must avoid them. Should you be discovered by a gendarme, you could be sent to prison." He looked up at a tall man crossing the street and pulled me behind him.

I tripped and steadied myself, pulling back, not touching him. Did he not want that man to see me?

He watched the man until he turned a corner. "I must leave now." He took an écu from his purse and gave it to me. "Buy flint, steel, and torches. Hide the torches where you can find them. Get to know the tunnels like the inside of your purse." He began to walk away. "Remember, avoid the workmen."

I grabbed his sleeve, not wanting him to leave. "Which—"

"Continue your studies. Even with as many livres as I can pay, you must prove your intellect and knowledge." He shook me off and hurried away.

I shouted, "But which lock does the key not open?"

He was already far away.

The key, cold from our excursion, grew warm in my hand—all I had of my father. Once again, he swept in and out of my life, leaving me to guess when he might return. I shoved the key in my pocket and vowed to know the tunnels like the inside of my purse by the next time I saw him.

First, I'd find out why Maman lied to me.

8

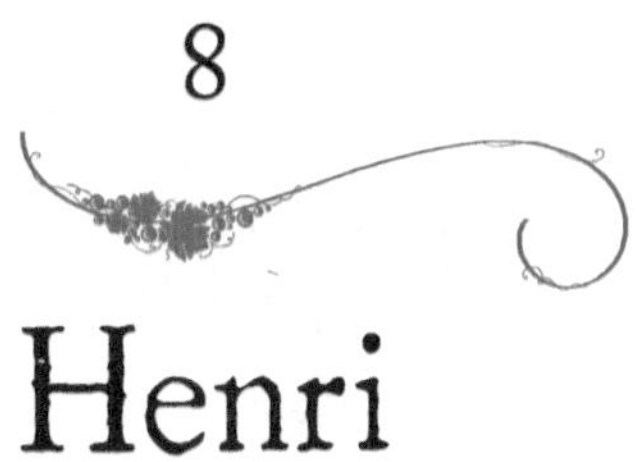

Henri

Paris
October 30, 1788

As BLACK CLOUDS gathered over the Bastille, I crossed the bridge. I was glad I no longer lived beneath its shadow, but I wanted to pay for new and better lodgings, nowhere near the prison, for Maman. Why had she never told me I wasn't her son? No wonder she was surprised when Papa first arrived. She'd never met him. I understood why he left me with her, but why hadn't he paid her more to care for me? He paid Rap more just to tutor me. Did Papa still give her money?

Gritty ice pellets stung my face and bounced along the cobbles. I tilted my hat against the building storm.

No matter the reason, I'd get her to tell me why she'd lied every time I asked her about my father. Was she afraid of him? All commoners feared nobles, but he trusted her with his son.

After he showed up, she could've told me the truth. A gust of wind snapped my cloak open, and I yanked it back around me.

She opened the door wearing a new white bonnet, its ruffle starched and crisp. "What a nice surprise." Her breath escaped with a puff of vapor. She hugged me. "You don't need to knock."

"I'm sorry I'm late. Do you need water?"

She shook her head. "Bertrand and Simon brought it. Simon was so sweet. When I gave him a sou, he kissed me."

I laughed. "That a new bonnet?"

She blushed and ran her fingers along the ruffle. "A gift."

"From?"

She giggled and picked up the iron. The table was so close to the fireplace, she kept her back warm as she pressed the sheets.

I breathed in the scent of rosemary she added to the soap she made. I'd ask her for a piece to take with me. "It's not much warmer in here than outside." In the corners, patches of ice formed between the cobbles from the laundry dripping from the rafters. The whole room was smaller than the one I studied in. I'd get a job soon so I could afford to move her.

"Warm yourself by the fire." She folded a chemise and placed it on a pile.

I picked up the fire poker. "Was it this cold, the year I was born?" I smashed the ice.

Her hands stilled. "Colder."

I swept the ice into a bucket. "How did you keep me warm?"

She looked up at me. Deep lines stretched from her eyes across her cheek bones. "He has told you." Her eyes glistened.

I placed the bucket near the fireplace. "Why didn't you?"

"Wasn't for me to tell."

My hands jittered against my legs. "So, you both betrayed me."

"I? Never!" She gripped my arm. "I nursed you from the moment you were brought to me." She placed her hand on her bosom. "I kept you right here, all the time, to warm and calm you." A tear slipped down her cheek. "I tied a sheet around my chest to keep you ever close and warm."

I wiped her tear. "Did he make you promise not to tell when he brought me to you?"

She shook her head. "Monsieur Rapineau brought you."

I stepped back. Rap knew who I was long before he became my tutor. They all knew, and no one bothered to tell me? I was back at the fountain with Stéphan and the other boys ganging up against me.

"I never met your father before that day he arrived." She stiffened. "Your mother wants you back. Is that what you've come to tell me?"

"She's dead."

"Uh!" Her hand flew to her mouth. "I'm sorry. When?"

"Long time ago." I shoved the fire poker into the corner. "I killed her."

"Don't say such a thing!" she shouted.

"It's true. She died giving birth to me."

She put her hand on my arm. "You didn't kill her, Henri."

"Oh no? What did Rapineau tell you when he brought me here?"

She held onto the table and lowered herself onto the bench. "Only…you were illegitimate, and that I'd be paid to keep you until he returned for you."

I sat on the bench. Papa wasn't married to my birth mother?

Stéphan's voice rang in my head, *Stinking bastard!* I truly was one. I pressed my palms to my eyes, hoping to clear the fog of confusion. Why the fuss over my knowing who she was if he wasn't married to her?

I sighed. "Well, you weren't paid enough." I smacked my hand against a hanging sheet. It slid to the floor. "Papa's carriage is warmer than this room."

"No one needed to pay me to love you," she whispered.

I was so ungrateful. I bent to hide my burning face and grabbed the sheet. I shook it out and smoothed it back over the rafter. I was yelling at her like my father's betrayal was her fault. I sat next to her and held her red, rough, chafed hand. "When he showed me my birth-mother's portrait, I told him you were my maman and always would be."

Both a laugh and cry burst from her. She embraced me so tightly I couldn't breathe. "I am your maman. I am." She buried her face into my chest and laughed and sobbed. "You are my Henri. I am so proud of you, my son."

I squeezed my eyes. She was so fragile. Her arms were strong, but she was tiny, like a starving cat. Would my birth mother have shown this tenderness to me?

Why hadn't Papa taken me with him? Plenty of illegitimate children were acknowledged, titled, and living at Versailles. I was glad I was here, in this tiny room, loving the only person who wasn't ashamed of me. The only person who was proud of me. The only person who loved me and never abandoned me.

I patted her back as her breaths deepened. Papa said she was my milk-mother. That meant she would have had to have had a child. Where was it? I was dumb...and selfish not to have even wondered. I cupped her chin, bringing her face up. "You nursed me?"

She nodded.

"Then, you had a baby before I came here."

She closed her eyes, tears sliding down her cheeks. "My husband died before our child was born. Run over by a horse. The nobleman stopped and threw coins to neighbors to move him out of the way." She dragged her apron across her face. "They brought his mangled body to me. I spent every sou we saved to bury him." She grunted an exhale. "I wouldn't send him to Les Innocents. He was a good and decent man, deserved to be buried in his own grave in consecrated ground." She looked up at me. "My son was born early. He struggled to live and died two days before you arrived."

My chest ached. I'd become her son, for thirteen years, until Papa returned. My bringing her water every day before my lessons had nothing to do with helping her with the laundry. I wanted to be with her, if only for a few moments every day. I rubbed little circles on her back, like she'd done so many times for me.

She patted my hand. "I had to earn money to feed myself, and with your arrival, I fed us both."

"I'm sorry."

"You were a blessing. Alone, I would've starved." She wiped her hands on her apron. "And alone, I didn't want to live."

She stood, walked to the fireplace, and scuffed the toe of her sabot in the ashes. "Sometimes it was so hard—" she looked up and struggled for a breath, "for even then I knew your papa would be back and take you away from me." Her voice faltered.

"But I never knew when." She turned, and her words exploded. "Sometimes I thought I should've taken the money and left you at the baby-wheel." Fingers smashing her cheeks, she cried, "But I couldn't! I pretended you were my Gaston. My son."

I pulled her against me and held her tight. "I am your son, Maman."

"I cannot lose another son," she whispered. "Please come home."

My arms grew heavy. "I can't live with you now, but someday..."

"I should've left you at the baby-wheel." She sobbed, covered her face, and dropped to the floor, her skirts tangling around her.

I knelt and rubbed her back.

She breathed in broken jagged gasps. "But you're too big now."

I laughed at the image of her trying to fit a fully grown me through a baby-wheel. "Yes, I'm too big now." I kissed the top of her head.

She laughed, brought up her face, shiny with tears. "Much too big."

She calmed. I helped her up. She ladled some liquid into a wooden bowl. "Have some soup."

"I have to deliver the laundry."

"First, eat."

I sat, breathing in the aroma of garlic, onions, turnips. "Maman, can you give me some of the rosemary soap you make?"

Her smile lit up the room like a flaming torch. "I'll give you some for Monsieur Rapineau, too."

I'd bring her some meat and bread. I'd buy her a lace-trimmed handkerchief. I'd show her she was the only maman I ever wanted and would ever need. I'd convince her she'd never lose me. I'd try to tell her I loved her.

9

Joliette

Versailles
November 20, 1788

THE DAY OF my official Court presentation arrived. I held my back rigid to keep the colossal wig from slipping down my forehead and checked my appearance in the mirror. The grape-vine, I had insisted upon, woven amongst the curls of my wig complemented the sage green of my gown and slippers. The corset gave me a bountiful bosom that protruded from the lace-trimmed décolletage, but the corset laces were so tight I could sip only small breaths. My official presentation would allow me to attend the Queen's fêtes and give me more oppor-tunities to meet Monsieur Jefferson.

Maman's reflection smiled behind me. "Your father began courting me the day I became a lady-in-waiting." She waved her fan before her, blushing.

"You have not told me that story."

She caressed the diamonds at her neck. "He gave these to me the day you were born."

"But what about the days in between, Maman?"

She giggled. It was the first time I had heard her do so. "You know how he raises his eyebrow and looks directly into you when he means mischief?"

I laughed. "Of course."

"I did not know it meant that at the time, but I soon discovered he was incorrigible. I think I fell in love with him at that moment." She smiled and looked out the window as if watching her younger self and Papa. "He told me he fell in love with me the moment I tripped up the Queen's staircase!" She bent over laughing. "He caught me. It was coup de foudre for us both."

I laughed at their literally *falling* in love at first sight. Cécile was wrong. Love did not happen *only* in fairy tales. I brought my hand to my heart, knowing I wanted to feel the same one day, but also knowing I had a legacy to continue.

She fanned herself. "Do not worry. You are too poised, my dear, to commit such a faux pas."

I smiled, not as certain as she. Because Cécile needed extra tutoring in the simplest of skills, Maman had rushed over others in which I was not as confident.

She kissed my cheek. "I know you will make us proud, ma princesse."

By the time we crossed the black and white marble squares and ascended the winding steps of the Queen's Staircase, I was perspiring, from pressure to make my parents proud, or to find

Monsieur Jefferson or the right husband, I was not certain. But I was determined not to fail before the Queen.

All young women were thrilled to be officially presented at Court and prepared as much for it as they did marriage, perhaps more. Although wishing for love, I would be using the position to find a husband who would join me in running the winery. Shrugging off my guilt over putting love after the winery, I pushed myself up the steps.

"Do you know why Louis XIV built this staircase, balustrade, pilasters, walls, and arches of marble?" Maman brought her arm out into a lovely arc.

I had climbed these steps hundreds of times, and I stifled a giggle remembering Papa helping the Dauphin, Dauphine, and me slide down the banisters when we were little. Yet I never noticed that everything was of green, red, violet, ivory, and black veined stone. "So it will last forever?"

She lowered her arm. "To prove French marble is as beautiful and colorful as that of Italy, and the rest of the world will desire it and buy it."

"That explains why foreign visitors are ushered into Court through this staircase." I ran my palm along the black balustrade, its coolness penetrating my glove. The beautifully carved columns supporting it were yet another type of marble. "Where do the red balusters come from?"

"That is Rouge Breccia. From Languedoc."

"A region known for Chenin Blanc grapes."

"Most often served as an apéritif." She lowered her voice. "That is all you need know about wine, as a lady-in-waiting."

I returned her smile, but my legs grew heavy. Nothing but

becoming a lady-in-waiting to the Queen would make Maman happier. I wondered if Grandmaman had done some specific thing to be ostracized. So far, I had kept my letters of instructions to Joseph a secret.

Morning sunshine flooded through tall paned windows and shimmered off the polished stone, radiating an intense heat. My chemise clung to my sweating back. I climbed the second flight to the landing, where a golden sculpture of cupids tucked into a marble arched alcove supported the King's shield, making me feel like I had grown backward—into a three-year-old.

Two of the Queen's Gardes opened the double doors. My breath stuck in my chest. Maman walked ahead as if she floated on air. My feet felt numb, yet I forced them to follow her through the antechamber and ornately carved and gilded doors into the Salon des Nobles.

The Queen's valet announced us. Maman left me. I stood alone.

Sky-blue silk damask covered the walls. Paintings, separated by elaborately carved golden frames, covered the vaulted ceiling. My neck ached from the weight of the wig. My legs trembled even though I had stood in Her Majesté's presence often. When I was a child, she had played with me at her hamlet, where her children and I milked the goats at her idyllic farm. I wished I was back with the goats.

Cécile stood amongst the audience, smiling so broadly, I knew she had already been accepted by the Queen. She winked and mouthed, *bonne chance.*

Ladies-in-waiting flanked the Queen, making a colorful arc

around her, like a pastel rainbow. The Queen's white opalescent gown glimmered with silver vines connecting flowers of precious gems that sparkled when she moved.

Maman curtsied. The Queen nodded. Maman stepped aside and smiled.

I froze. If I did not perform correctly, I would displease the Queen.

Urging me with her eyes, Maman tipped her head and gripped her fan.

I dropped into a deep curtsey. *Grandmaman, guide me.* I remembered walking with her in the vineyard, inspecting the vines, hearing the insects, inhaling the sweet scent.

Maman inhaled sharply. Tittering moved through the ladies-in-waiting.

I still crouched. Four counts too long. The mistake of a novice. *I am so sorry, Maman.* I had curtsied more properly as a toddler. I straightened and, with head still bowed, stared at the red marble floor. *Please forgive me.*

Fingertips cupped my chin, lifting it.

I looked into the Queen's blue eyes. Maman's skirts rustled. My face grew hot, and I prayed the maquillage was thick enough to hide the redness that surely bloomed on my cheeks.

Her Majesté smiled kindly. "I look forward to the day you shall join my ladies-in-waiting, Mademoiselle de Verzat. Welcome to Court."

I wanted to kiss her. Instead, I pressed my hands against my bodice and backed away, taking my place in the audience as the Queen greeted other aspiring ladies-in-waiting.

I dared not look at Maman. I would endure curtseying lessons every day for a week.

Instead, I gazed out at the Gardens, realizing my acceptance at Court eased my way of meeting Thomas Jefferson. I would learn when he would be visiting next and plan how to be introduced to him. He would be very helpful in extending the Verzat legacy.

10

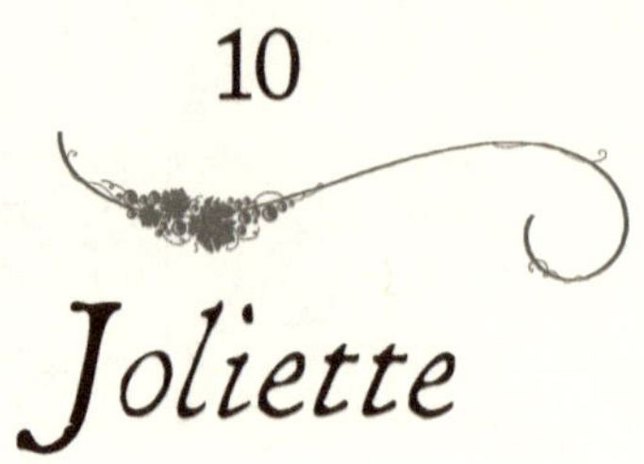

Joliette

Versailles
November 21, 1788

I CURTSIED BEFORE MAMAN in her chamber. The sooner I finished these time-consuming exercises in Court etiquette, the sooner I could return to the Master Gardener and learn more about grafting. The process could extend the Verzat legacy.

"Perfect. Again."

"Maman, this is the tenth time!"

She plunged her needle into the embroidery. "Rest. Then ten more."

The Master Gardener would have to wait. I knelt at her feet and bowed my head. "I am sorry I did not curtsey properly."

"I wonder if you stayed on your knee for so long on purpose."

She pulled the thread taut.

She would forbid my going to l'Orangerie if I admitted I had been dreaming of the vineyard. "Of course, I did not. Please grow angry with me. You do not leave our apartment. You do not wear your diamonds or Grandmaman's emeralds. You are as white as your embroidery cloth. You look so sad."

"I am disappointed."

That was worse. I folded my hands across the ache in my chest. "Please forgive me."

She knotted the red silk thread and clipped it. "You have been seen in l'Orangerie, flirting with a man."

I laughed. "Flirting? With the Master Gardener? Whomever told you that is an imaginative gossip." I stilled her hands with mine. "We have been discussing grafting. It is amazing. He grows limes on lemon trees."

"Whatever for?"

"If the lime tree is failing and could die, you graft a lime branch to a lemon tree, which will produce limes."

She removed her hands from mine and rethreaded her needle. "Why not plant another lime tree?"

"Time. It would take nine years for a sapling to yield fruit. But a grafted branch will produce the next season. Can you imagine what we could do with grapes? If a delicate grape does not do well on its own, we could graft that vine to rootstock that thrives." My fingers trembled. "We could make more complex wines, which would command a higher price, and increase production with this technique!" I willed her to be as thrilled as I was.

She set aside her hoop. "How nice for the vintner. Joseph is his name?"

I wanted to growl: *I am the vintner.* Instead, I smiled sweetly. "Are you not proud that I wish to extend the legacy?"

"That will be your husband's job." She pulled her rosary from her sleeve.

I collapsed upon a pouffe. *You better pray for me, Maman, to help me find the right man.*

She blessed herself with the rosary's crucifix. "And what of your progress learning the Queen's preferred contredanse allemande?"

I sighed, stood, and moved into starting position. "I have learned every one of the complicated steps and intertwining hand movements." I danced across the room with an invisible partner. Finished, I curtsied and awaited her applause, which she always bestowed. I wavered. When I could hold the position no longer, I straightened. The silence was stifling.

She kissed her rosary. "If not for the Queen's kindness of ignoring your faux pas, you would not be presented at Court."

A more devoted daughter would not have embarrassed her parents. A more devoted daughter would excel at Court. A more devoted daughter would be thrilled to be a courtier for life. I bowed my head. I wanted to be truly sorry, but I was a devoted granddaughter and I truly wanted to be a vintner.

She wrapped the rosary so tightly around her fingers I thought it would break. "Your father and I are disappointed in you."

"I am truly sorry. I will do everything to make you proud of me." I would burn in hell for lying, and I was sorry I hurt her, but I longed to get back to the Gardener.

"The Queen is having a ball, where you will be introduced to many gentlemen—potential husbands. I will not be wearing your grandmaman's emeralds. You will."

My throat closed as if the necklace were choking me. "But they are yours. My wearing your jewels will bring you bad fortune."

She laughed. "Nonsense. They will complement your pale green gown."

In my mind, the necklace turned into a noose. The jewels an unmarried woman wore represented the amount of her dowry. Every potential suitor would demand my hand in marriage for those jewels, alone. I supposed that would be good, but if they all wanted the gems, how would I determine if they loved me? I gripped my mouchoir. "But Papa gave them to you."

"He gave them to me to keep them for you until your wedding day, when they become yours. Wearing them at the ball gives suitors a preview of what is to come." She caressed her neck, as if she were wearing the cold sharp stones.

I twisted my mouchoir. "I cannot."

Her face tightened. "You can. And you will." She tucked the rosary into her sleeve. "You may wear grape leaves in your wig. And that is the only thing about wine you are to discuss that evening. Do you understand?"

I shoved the mouchoir into my hanging pocket. "Yes."

"Do not be late for your appointment with the Ballet Master."

"Yes, Maman." Before I was out the door, I searched for words to charm the Ballet Master into excusing me.

11

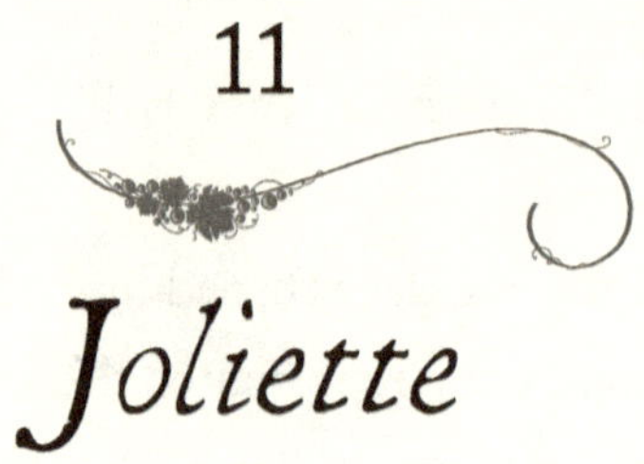

Joliette

Versailles
December 13, 1788

THE EVENING OF the ball my legs trembled, making my feet totter on the steps as if I were walking on pebbles. I gripped the balustrade. Maman accompanied me to the entrance of the Grande Galerie. Gilded chandeliers sparked candleflames, reflecting like stars in the floor-to-ceiling gilded mirrors covering the length of the wall. Music, voices, footsteps made the glass prisms hanging from sconces tinkle like tiny silver bells. Scents of pomades and perfumes thickened the air.

Maman left me and walked down the center of a double line of courtiers, all awaiting my entrance. I spotted Cécile, glowing in a gown of white silk and triangles of stiff white lace circling her neckline protruding upward like the picket fence protecting Versailles. Were the lace chevrons protecting or bringing attention to her virginal décolletage?

A white plume stuck up from Cécile's wig like a frightened dog's tail. The wig alone was twice as tall as mine. I gripped my fan. The warmth from thousands of burning candles made my scalp sweat beneath my wig. I closed my fan and walked to an elaborately decorated servant.

The herald bowed deeply, rose, and turned to the guests. "Mademoiselle Joliette Catherine Alisson Baumere de Verzat!" His voice was clear and bright as a brass horn.

All the ladies-in-waiting had witnessed my failed curtsey to the Queen, and I did not wish to endure their laughter again. I was a Verzat, and I had to show the courage of one, even if I did not possess it. This time I would give them nothing to mock, for I could not disappoint my parents again.

I inhaled, forced a smile, and proceeded down the gauntlet of pastel-colored silk gowns. The ladies eyed my every step, waiting for me to falter. Titters ran behind their fans, until I neared. When they saw Grandmaman's emeralds, they buzzed like a horde of wasps.

A chubby man, more a boy, dressed in shades of rose trimmed in more lace than I wore, scampered out from behind the line of gowns and came to a halt, forcing me to stop.

Puppies had more grace. His breach of etiquette eliminated him as a potential suitor in Maman's eyes. He pointed at the emeralds and giggled.

Imbécile. I fluttered my fan and smiled, as Maman would have.

Maman was by my side in an instant. She cleared her throat.

He looked at her necklace. Pearls were not to his liking, for his gaze returned to my neck. Despite his silks and satins, he had to be a jewel thief.

"Monsieur?" Maman said.

He stared—mouth open.

I hid my laughter behind my open fan. Perhaps he was a jester.

Maman put out her hand, far more grace than he deserved. "You are?"

"Vicomte Richepin, Madame." He pecked her hand and bowed.

Her smile soured. His title was the lowest of the lowly. "Comtesse de Verzat, Monsieur."

"Comtesse." He let out a titter.

"Excuse us, Monsieur, the Duc de Lillers is expecting us." She pulled me away.

She had not introduced me. "Maman, have you not violated protocol?" I did not care if Richepin loved wine. He was severely lacking in intelligence. I suspected Maman's violation was to save time for more suitable courtiers, for which I was grateful.

"Protocol does not apply to such riffraff." She guided me toward a man so old, he could be my grandpapa.

My arms tensed. She could not possibly think him appropriate. Papa strode toward us. "May I have your first dance, ma princesse?"

Relief washed through me.

Maman frowned. "Bring her right back. She has many introductions."

He took my hand and led me toward a group of dancers.

"Merci, Papa," I whispered.

He winked, led me to the lead position, and danced me about the Galerie. As the lead couple, we whirled with and between the dancers. Papa's warm smile and strong leading steps relaxed me, and I enjoyed myself. He led me to greet the last couple. I turned to offer my hand to the next gentleman and his green eyes—bright as grapevines during bud break—startled me.

I forgot the movement and faltered. I searched to locate Maman. Had she seen? She would have me dancing twelve hours a day after this.

Without missing a beat, he rescued my wayward hand and adroitly led it to its next position. My hands grew moist inside my gloves. His steps and arms were strong, like Papa's, but dancing with Papa had not made me breathless. The mirrors spun shards of light as he led me through the twisting rosettes. I dizzied as he returned me to Papa. Perspiration coated my face, and I fluttered my fan to dry it.

The man wore a frock coat and breeches of pale lavender silk with tiny bouquets of violets—so delicate and fine I expected them to have a scent—embroidered along his cuffs and hem. His ensemble resembled that of our King, yet the silk puckered beneath the embroidery—the fabric was inferior. He was working hard to fit in at Court, yet every courtier would notice his black shoes—without red heels. He had not been presented.

The allemande at an end, he turned to my father and bowed deeply. He unfurled from his bow and straightened to Papa's height. "Comte de Verzat, I believe you are acquainted with my father, the Baron Pricaud?"

Papa's eyebrow rose. "Ah…oh, yes, you are…?"

"Guillaume Pricaud." He bowed, again. "It is an honor to meet the man who produces the finest wines in France, if not the world, Monsieur le Comte."

Finest in the world? I leaned closer. The sounds of conversations, laughter, music all faded. His eau de Cologne smelled woodsy with a hint of lime.

Papa gave a tight smile. "May I present my daughter, Mademoiselle Joliette de Verzat?"

He bowed. My hand, of its own accord, sought his. As he held my fingers, his lips brushed my hand ever so gently. Damned protocol requiring gloves.

"Your mother's beauty shines from within you, Mademoiselle."

Words sat in my mouth like melting chocolate. I was supposed to thank him, but I could not summon a word. I held the fingers his lips had caressed.

"You remember my father, Comte?"

"We knew each other many years ago, when we were your age."

Pricaud reached into his frock coat and withdrew a thick blue leather purse. "He asked me to deliver this." With both his hands, he held it out to Papa. "My father wishes me to express his humble gratitude for your patience."

Papa put up his hands. "Eh…that was so long ago. All is forgotten."

"Not by my father." He continued to present the purse.

Why did Papa refuse him? Pricaud's demeanor, his manners, his tenacity, all impeccable. Neither of my parents could find fault with Pricaud. Nor could I. He never glanced at the emeralds. He knew of the Verzat legacy. Why had I not seen him at Court before?

"There is no need." Papa shook his head.

Maman's skirts brushed against mine. "Pardon, Monsieur."

He withdrew the purse and dropped into a deep bow.

Maman inserted herself between me and Monsieur Pricaud, but she did not extend her hand. "My daughter and I have been summoned by the Queen." She held my elbow and drew me away. "Forgive us, please."

His smile was a bit lopsided. Was he feeling embarrassed, slighted, disappointed? I took a tiny step and looked back at him. Maman pulled at my arm, but I resisted. He saved me embarrassment over my missed steps. I should have thanked him.

"Come." She pulled me through a concealed door and along a servants' passage. I kept seeing Pricaud's bright eyes. His kiss was as gentle as a whisper. I brought my fingers to my lips. I never noticed such a thing when other men kissed my hand; his was…tender. Despite Court protocol, I would never wear gloves again.

"Will we return to the ball, soon?"

Maman quickened her step.

Even more, Pricaud congratulated Papa for the Verzat legacy and extended it to the world! I was the only person who held that belief, that hope. I pressed my bodice. The dance had been over long ago, yet my heart beat like a hummingbird's wings. But he was the son of a baron. Maman would never consider him an appropriate suitor. Barons were a lower station than comte but still of noble blood.

I stumbled. Maman caught my arm and hurried me.

"Merci." I was being ridiculous. I wanted to marry for love. I had a legacy to continue. Yet I wanted to discuss viniculture with him. "The ball will go on all evening. I would like to return soon."

Maman slowed before the Queen's apartments. She pressed her fingers to her lips and a tear spilled.

I dabbed her cheek. "What is it?"

"The Dauphin." She wiped her eyes. "He is terribly ill. Coughing wracks his body, and he bleeds from the mouth."

I gripped my fan. The Queen shut herself away for months after his sister died. Now the Dauphin, the next King of France, might die. She would go mad with grief. Yet, I could not help her. If I could return to the ball for a few moments, I could arrange to meet Pricaud at l'Orangerie and return to my duty. "Should I not return to inform Papa?"

She shook her head. "He attends the King. We must be strong for our Queen."

I nodded, not wanting the memory of Pricaud's eyes to fade.

Maman held her head high as she entered the room.

Clutching a lace mouchoir, Her Majesté sat on a chaise longue in the center of the room. Her ladies-in-waiting stood surrounding her, every one of them with silent tears slipping down their faces.

I curtsied and rose. Maman's lectures did not include protocol for this. I stepped back, stood behind the ladies-in-waiting, and watched for some signal, but Pricaud's green eyes wavered in my mind. I squeezed my eyes to banish the image. A better lady-in-waiting would be concerned for the Dauphin. I looked about. Where was Cécile? Her absence was a huge breach of etiquette.

Maman curtsied deeply before the Queen, and then she swept her skirts aside, sat next to Her Majesté, and patted the Queen's back, encouraging the Queen to lean upon her—totally violating Court protocol. The Queen surrendered onto Maman and sobbed like a little girl.

I wobbled in the heavily perfumed air. On a particularly hot day years earlier, I had been walking with the Dauphin in the Gardens. He jumped into a fountain, which terrified the ladies-in-waiting but made me laugh and laugh as he surfaced and spouted water from his mouth just like the marble frogs surrounding him. How could that daring sweet little boy be dying? My breath lodged in my chest. I was totally inappropriate as a lady-in-waiting. I had laughed at his antics instead of being concerned.

My mother rocked the Queen in her arms, caressing the Queen's cheek and wiping away her tears, just like Maman comforted me. She rubbed the Queens' back as Her Majesté cried, "He is six years. Only six."

I knelt alongside the circle of ladies and tried to pray. I was not fit to be a lady-in-waiting, but I was glad I was there with Maman, so kind and comforting. I would tell her how proud I was of her the moment we were alone. Her devotion made me ashamed of my curtseying faux pas and my goal of *not* becoming a lady-in-waiting. I still longed to be a vintner. Like Grandmaman, I could not be both.

I could not complete a prayer—Pricaud's green eyes made me lose my place. I pressed my hands tighter and forced myself to pray for the Dauphin.

After a while, Maman drew her rosary from her sleeve

and began reciting prayers while still holding the Queen. The ladies-in-waiting and I joined her, and the soft murmur of *Ave Marias* filled the room until the mauve light of dawn crept over us. Our prayers calmed me, yet I swayed with fatigue when the Queen regained her composure.

She kissed my mother's cheek and thanked her, then stood.

I curtsied and remained there until she and my mother returned to the Queen's bedchamber and servants closed the door behind them.

Sorrow for my young friend weighed on me like the heat of August. How could his mother bear it?

The ladies and I filed out into the empty Grande Galerie, but I crossed it and walked out onto the balcony overlooking the Gardens. The Dauphin's illness tore a hollow in me that all the beauty, splashing fountains, and marble sculptures could not fill.

I closed my eyes and breathed in the fresh air, remembering l'Orangerie and the scents of lemon, orange, lime. Lime, the scent Pricaud wore. Why did my heart beat so wildly every time I thought of him? It could not be his knowledge of the legacy alone. But what? I had to find him.

12

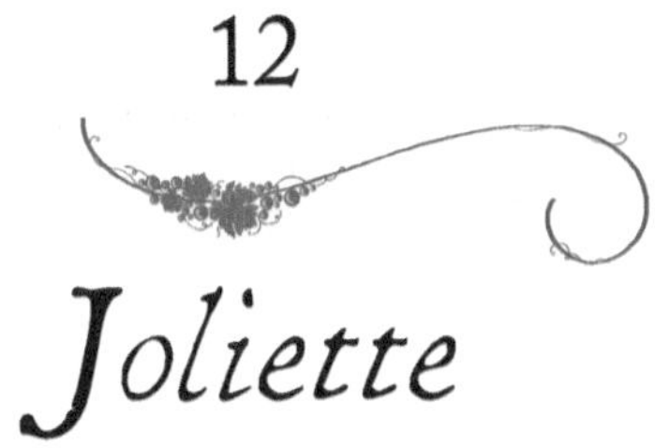

*J*oliette

Versailles
December 14, 1788

THE FOLLOWING AFTERNOON, I sent a note to the
Master Gardner, asking him to meet me near the lime trees.

I found Maman in her chamber. Everything—walls, drapes,
furniture, bedclothes, her gown—was white. She rested against
a hill of pillows, each trimmed with lace and pearls. Her hands
held a needle and thread and a square of fabric stretched across
a hoop. She wore a silver thimble, the edge filigreed like lace.

Throughout my childhood, my mother made pictures with
silk threads the colors of jewels. I loved sitting next to her,
selecting the strands when she requested the colors, watching her as she fed them through her needle, and listening to
her stories of the pictures she embroidered. I wanted to climb

up next to her and listen again, but she did not welcome me to her side.

"Let us stroll in l'Orangerie, Maman." I was eager to embrace her and tell her how proud I was of her break with protocol. I gripped my hands and stood silently as she pulled a yellow thread through the center of a blue flower.

"Every courtier notices with whom you dance and speak." She pricked the fabric with the needle.

I nodded. "Yes, I know this."

"It is customary to speak and dance with only those of a higher rank."

"How can I do that if those people can only dance and speak to those who are of a higher rank than *their* own?"

"Joliette." She laid the hoop on her lap and pressed her hands together. "We are Nobles of the Sword. And as one, you may speak to and dance with a comte, marquis, prince, and duc, but not a lowly vicomte or a baron and never a son of a baron, who will not inherit his title until his father dies."

"In the contredanse, one dances with all participants." I lifted my arms and turned from one imaginary partner to another. "It cannot be avoided."

"I understand the tradition." She resumed her sewing. "However, you must *not* allow yourself to be approached by someone of a lesser rank."

Heat washed up my face. Pricaud had made up for my missed steps. "To walk away from the Baron's son would be a breach of etiquette."

"Yes, it would be, and I am pleased you understand this. But you must learn ways to avoid such circumstances altogether in the future."

I stared at the threads of her embroidery and saw only his bright eyes, felt the ever-so-soft touch of his lips upon my fingers, heard his rich-as-velvet voice—complimenting my father about Verzat wine—the finest in the *world*. He said, the *world*!

"For example, after a dance, you can immediately approach another woman, not leaving an opening for a lesser gentleman to approach you." She yanked at a knot and appraised what I knew was skepticism upon my face. "There is yet another reason the Baron's son is to be avoided completely."

I stepped back, my heartbeat thudding. "Whatever might that be?"

"Neither your father, nor I, like to participate in Court gossip. Therefore, you must swear you will not repeat this. Do you?"

She could find fault with the King himself, but I pressed my hand over my heart. "I swear."

"The Baron is a gambler and is greatly in debt to everyone at Court, including the Queen. He is no longer accepted at Court and, even if he should repay his debts, he will continue to be ostracized."

"But that does not mean his son is a gambler. He attempted to give Papa a purse that likely contained the Baron's repayment."

She shook her head. "Ten of those purses could not repay the amount he owes your father." She stabbed the needle. "And he did not give it to your father; he offered it."

"He did not have the opportunity. You interrupted the conversation."

"To spare your father the embarrassment." She yanked the

thread and knotted it. "It is a game of etiquette, you see. The Baron's son makes an effort and the courtier objects, as did your father. That way, the courtier is saved from accepting a pittance toward the debt owed, and the son is saved from the embarrassment of the courtier demanding his full due."

My chest tightened as if she had twisted her thread around it. "He seemed to be eager for Papa to accept the purse."

"All part of the game at Court."

"Your explanation makes no sense. Is a partial amount not better than no payment at all?"

"It is not honorable for either party."

I tapped my fingers together. "Why blame the son for his father's faults?"

"The son has the same blood."

Was his blood a convenient excuse to further eliminate Pricaud as a suitor? His title was already inappropriate. But why could I not get the Baron's son out of my mind? Was my thumping heart and inability to see anything but his eyes proof I was attracted to him? No matter. He was the wrong court-ier, and I had to marry an appropriate one. I had no time for such foolishness. I would forget him. I would learn grafting techniques.

"Let us walk in l'Orangerie, Maman. It is a lovely day."

13

Joliette

Versailles
January 3, 1789

MAMAN LAY IN her bed, white as the pillows upon which she rested. Blue-black circles beneath her closed eyes bruised her pallor. Her once golden hair now matched the bedclothes.

A sinking sensation pulled at me, and I reached for the chair to steady myself.

The surgeon handed a bowl of my mother's blood to the maid, who covered it with a serviette and left. He tied a cloth about the cut in Maman's arm and looked at me. "She must rest."

I picked up the embroidery she had been working on. Not a stitch had been added in months. "She *has* been resting. How soon will she recover?" The stitches were so tiny, so precise, so perfect. I looked up at him.

He shook his head.

Stupid man. "You do not know?"

He picked up his satchel. "Recovery," he cleared his throat, "is not possible, Mademoiselle. I am sorry."

I dropped the embroidery. I wanted to make him look at me. "But the Dauphin has had the wasting disease for three years, and still he lives. She has been ill only a few months. We should take her to the château. The air is better near the Loire."

"She would not survive the trip. We must make her comfortable." He bowed and left.

Something inside me shrank. What was he saying? I knelt next to her. Had I hastened her illness with my protocol mistakes? Was her disappointment in me weakening her?

Her breath was shallow. I held her pale, birdlike hand. "Forgive me, Maman." My throat tightened. "I am sorry I argued with you about the winery. I should have spent every moment making you happy." I wiped my tears.

I picked up the embroidery hoop and ran my fingers over a chain of knots. She had shown me dozens of times how to make knots and feather stitches, and I could sew neither. Why had I not paid attention? I would ask her tomorrow, when she was stronger. I would help her hold the needle.

She moaned.

"I am here." I helped her to sit up, but her body bucked with her coughs. Droplets of crimson blood spattered the duvet. The color whirled around me. I steadied myself and held out my mouchoir, the one she helped me embroider with my initials. Too weak to hold it, she wheezed and collapsed back upon the pillows.

I patted the mouchoir over her face, wiping away perspiration and blood. "I am here."

She grew still. I bent closer, fearing her coughing had spent all her breath. I placed my hand over her heart. Her chest rose then fell deeply. Her face calmed.

She smiled then, her face taking on a glow, like the luster of a pearl. The surgeon was wrong. She would recover. I would spend every moment helping her regain her strength.

14

Joliette

Versailles
January 4, 1789

THE FOLLOWING DAY, a gray light filled her chamber and, although the fire snapped robustly, I was chilled. Where was the golden sunlight when Maman needed its warmth the most? A mound of white duvets covered her, making her look tiny and helpless.

"The Queen gave me this rose for you after Mass this morning. She wishes you good health." I brought the flower to her cheek for her to feel the velvety petals. Her lips opened, but no words emerged. The rose's intense fragrance nauseated me. I pushed it to the floor.

"Maman, will you show me how to make the feather stitch?" I caressed her fingers until her eyelids fluttered.

She opened her eyes. "Come…close." Her voice was as quiet as a breeze.

I knelt beside the bed, careful not to jostle her, and lay my cheek next to hers. "I sat close to you like this when I was a little girl. Remember?"

She blinked.

"I loved the stories you told me as you embroidered." I made my voice light. "My favorite was about the kid goat. Would you tell it, again?"

She rasped for breath. I put my arms around her. "Please, Maman, you must get better. Please."

Her body convulsed. I wiped the blood from her chin with my mouchoir.

She opened her eyes. "The Queen requests you…as a lady-in-waiting." Her lips trembled as she tried to smile. "Could not…be happier."

My stomach hardened, as if a stone sat in me. "But you have not finished training me in court etiquette." I willed my tears to stop. "I have no confidence without you. I am not ready."

She smiled. "You…happy, too?"

I would say anything to keep her with me. "Yes. So happy." I wiped my eyes and tucked my fingers into my fist. "You must guide me. We will be ladies-in-waiting together. Papa will be so proud of us."

Her eyelids closed.

My heart pounded. Her body fell calm, too calm. I pressed my cheek to hers. "Be strong, Maman. I need you."

Papa entered, his eyes dark and dull, shoulders rounded forward, chest deflated. "How are you feeling, my dearest?"

She opened her eyes a bit and smiled.

He bowed deeply, kissed her cheek, and knelt at her side. He took a rosary from his waistcoat pocket, blessed himself, mumbled a prayer, blessed himself again. Maman looked at me, back to Papa, and gave him a nod. He smiled. "You have accepted the Queen's gift, Joliette?"

Gift? Au contraire. To wait upon Her Majesté was not a gift to me, but it was the greatest gift my mother could hope for. The title would catapult me to one of the highest rungs of marriageability.

I twisted the mouchoir. Papa was staging this moment to comfort Maman. She wanted my position secured because I would marry a man of higher rank and be forever provided for. I nodded and bowed my head as if in prayer. This could not happen. She had to get better. She could not leave me.

She lifted her trembling fingers. I cupped them around my cheek and kissed her palm. "Serve Her Majesté well…ma princesse."

Papa looked at me and arched a brow.

"I will always honor your wishes, Maman." The lie burned my throat like sour wine.

Papa closed his eyes.

"We will serve Her Majesté, together." I caressed her cheek. Her face shone with so much love, it warmed me.

Papa stood. "Please, we must be alone for a little while."

I found myself in the hall, not knowing how I got there. Silence roared in and around me. I could not breathe without her.

I ran through the Grande Galerie, down the Queen's staircase, into the chapel. I dropped to my knees before the altar and begged before the crucifix. "Please, please let her live. I will excel at being a lady-in-waiting. I will stop going to l'Or-angerie. I will give up the Verzat legacy. I will marry whom-ever Maman selects. I do not have to love him. He does not have to love wine."

The lingering aroma of incense dizzied me. I lay on the floor, my face pressed against the cold hard marble. I wanted a stiff wind to blow away the incense and the ache in me. I wanted to smell the lavender Maman loved.

In my mind, I saw the day I had identified the lavender in the wine. Grandmaman's laughter echoed as she stood in the vineyard, a soft breeze rippling the leaves. She opened her arms and smiled.

Sunlight flooded the chapel, warming me like Maman did when she comforted me. It was a sign. She was better. I will give anything and everything to keep her. S'il te plait, mon dieu, allow my mother to live, and I will serve the Queen with selflessness. I lay there on the cold marble, soaking in the sun's warmth, imagining Maman's arms around me.

A soft rustling of skirts broke the silence. She was coming. "Maman!" I pushed myself onto my knees.

The Queen knelt next to me, startling me with her kind blue eyes. She caressed my cheek.

I stumbled to rise and execute a proper curtsey, but she held my hands. A tear slid down her powdered cheek. "Your maman was the kindest person at Court. I shall miss her."

Was? The room closed in around me, dimming the light, making me shrink in my own skin.

"I am so very sorry for your loss, Comtesse."

Maman's title—was now mine. I fell into the Queen and wept.

15

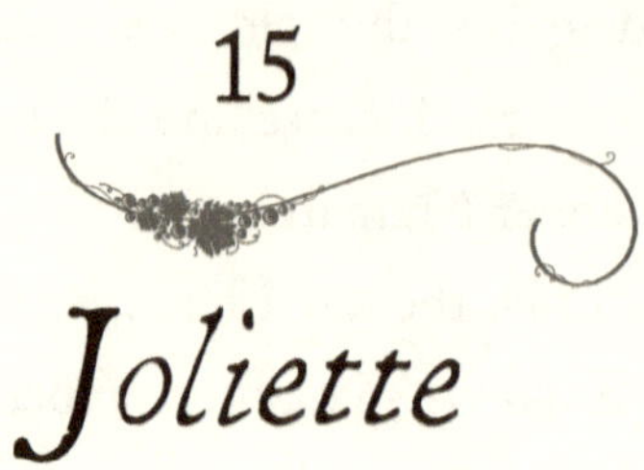

Joliette

Château de Verzat
January 9, 1789

Sunshine sparkled off the thick hoarfrost, covering the barren ground like the white satin duvets that had
graced Maman's bed. I stood numb and cold before a tufa-
stone mausoleum in the family cemetery at the Château de
Verzat. Pressing her favorite white shawl to my face, I inhaled
her lavender scent.

The wasting disease had taken so much of Maman only four
men were needed to bear her coffin. Joseph, two vassals, and
the châtelain, men Papa had selected for the honor, carried
her wooden box inside the mausoleum. A bier of carved white
angels, their wings supporting a square marble slab, stood in
the center. The men placed her coffin atop the marble, bowed

their heads, and folded their hands in prayer as they left her.

Papa caressed her coffin. His face was gray. Laughter lines curved down his cheeks. I gave him the edge of her shawl, and together, we draped it over the coffin as a pall. Papa brought the fabric to his lips and kissed it. He closed the rusted gate behind us. It screeched like a thieving crow. He stroked my hair, and I rested my head on his chest. He wrapped his arms around me but, for the first time, I did not feel safe.

I reached around him, pulling him close. "Do not ever leave me, Papa."

"Never, ma princesse." He patted my back and released me. He walked away into the icy wind, wandering among the barren vines.

I pulled the ribbon from my hair and tied it around an iron picket of the gate. The bow struggled in the stiff breeze. Half of the marble slab was bare, awaiting Papa's coffin. I shivered and wrapped my cloak tighter. She would be alone for many years.

Holding onto the gate, I knelt. "I miss you, Maman. You were as kind as an angel. I want to believe in God so I can believe you are in heaven with him. But I am angry with God. I believe you are here, among the people and things you loved."

I ran my hand over the weathered stone of Grandmaman's mausoleum. "I know you both are watching over Papa and me." I placed my hands on each gate. "Send me a husband who will help me grow the Verzat legacy."

I looked out over the valley. Most people would notice brown vines, not the waiting pale green buds sparkling under the frost. It was late in the season for such cold. Grandmaman would talk to Joseph about how the unusual temperature might affect the harvest and the vintage. The book would contain her notes, and I would read them before talking to him.

I imagined my mother lounging among the brilliant white clouds scudding over the vineyard and across the river. "I will return to Versailles and begin my duties as lady-in-waiting as I promised, Maman." In my mind, I added: To not only find a husband, but also to meet Monsieur Jefferson and convince him to help me export wine to America.

I turned and walked toward the château. I no longer possessed the luxury of falling in love. If something should happen to Papa, I would lose the legacy and be left in poverty. No doubt Maman had thought of this and had instructed Papa to find me a husband—without delay. I ran for my chamber to read Grandmaman's notes before Papa insisted we return to Versailles.

16

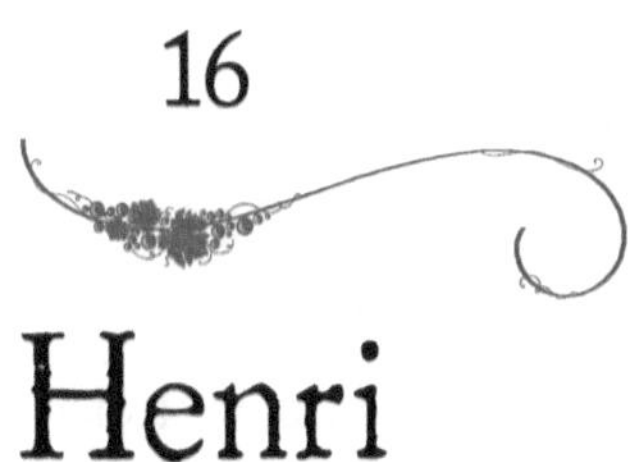

Henri

Paris
January 21, 1789

Despite the sleet, I sweated in my new woolen clothes as I made my way to Université. My father had passed under the same carved stone arches, walked between the same columns, ascended the same steps. Rap assured me my entrance exam grades were better than my father's, but I didn't belong here.

I looked back at the gate, Papa's voice loud in my mind. *You have the blood of a noblesse d'épée. And as a noble of the sword, I expect you to behave as one.* But my father wore a sword. He had the Verzat name and a title. I was an illegitimate bastard. Perspiration leaked into my neckcloth, and I loosened its knot. This was no worse than leaving Maman, and I'd been a boy then. I wanted to learn others' opinions and discuss law, so I headed for the entrance.

Students thronged through the arches. Their jewel-encrusted scabbards clanged. A law forbade all but nobles to wear swords, one of the many laws I hoped to change. I patted the sheath beneath my frock coat that held my pistol and dagger, both illegal for a commoner to own and carry. Were these students as accomplished with weapons as I? I hoped not to find out.

My legs tense, I climbed pale stone steps, worn smooth from thousands of noble boots, to the lecture hall, a noisy echoing chamber with rows of benches tiered down to the center where a lectern stood. Scattered among the benches were noblemen, yelling and joking. Each wore a silk frock coat, breeches, and plumed hat the color of a flower. I thought my new dark green woolen frock coat, waistcoat, and breeches would help me fit in, but my lack of embroidery, lace, and feathers, along with my missing saber would mark me as a commoner. I rolled the brim of my featherless tricorne and held it behind me.

Thirty other students pushed and taunted one another, shouting obscenities, throwing fruit. One stood on the ledge and urinated out an open window. My fellow students at the priests' school never behaved like pigs. Although untrained in etiquette, they respected the schooling they'd received.

I slid onto a bench in the last row and wiped sweat from my forehead. Would I be thrown out if they discovered I was an untitled bastard? I rubbed my hands on my thighs. It didn't matter. I was here to learn how to debate and support my arguments. I figured I'd have plenty of opportunities.

A door at the front slammed against the wall. Students raced to sit down. A gaunt clergyman dressed in black, entered. He held a stick, probably used more for punishment than emphasis. His nose was as narrow as an axe blade. Curling wires of gray hair stuck out from under his hat.

He placed his stick on the lectern and faced us, eyeing the few men who had yet to sit down. "Allow me to present myself, I am Père Sébastien. Messieurs, two new students have joined this class, and you will welcome them. Please stand and tell us where you are from and your course of study, Monsieur Detré."

The nobles swiveled about.

"Detré?" yelled Père Sébastien.

I jumped up. My legs shook so hard my purse banged against my thigh. "I am—"

"Louder!"

I cleared my throat. "I am Henri Detré." I fell back onto the bench.

"It was a three-part question, Monsieur."

Laughter burst like flames on a torch.

I gripped the bench and pushed myself up, too forcefully. I swayed forward and caught myself by gripping a pink shoulder. Guffaws erupted. The man shrugged me off, glaring at me. "Sorry." I stood tall, as Papa would. "From Faubourg Saint-Antoine, law."

Hisses moved through the crowd.

"Studying law. Merci." Père Sébastien nodded. "Monsieur Fouquier?"

A pale man with small hands and no sword stood. "I am Pierre Fouquier, from Les Halles, also studying law." His voice was unusually high, perhaps because of his shortness.

Boos followed. At least I had a commoner for company, even if Fouquier was half my size.

A well-fed noble dressed in silver-embroidered sky-blue silks leaned back and slid a glance at me. "Paysan bâtard," he whispered.

I smiled at his correctness.

Père whacked his stick on a bench. "Comte de LaGarde, you have something to contribute?"

LaGarde smoothed his lace neckcloth. "No, mon Père."

LaGarde would be waiting for me at the end of the day. I raked my hair. For the next hour, I heard nothing besides the pounding of my heart, my voice telling me I didn't belong here, and, finally, class dismissed.

I rushed out into the courtyard and nearly collided with Fouquier. I stuck out my hand. "Detré."

He smiled and shook my hand. "Fouquier. The nobles go to Café Procope to bore one another with their boasts. Shall we go to the Palais-Royal for pamphlets?"

"You read the pamphlets?"

"Don't you?"

I nodded and quickened my step. "I think we'll learn more there."

He laughed. "Absolutely."

We hurried out the gates and ran down rue Saint Jacques to the river. I turned down a street, right into a wall of flesh. I bounced back, stumbling. LaGarde stood before me, six students behind him—all standing like blossoming flowers, all holding the hilts of their swords, all blocking the street from building to building. Seven of them, two of us. Hopeless odds.

My arms tensed. Père had chastised LaGarde because of me, and now the bully was going to retaliate.

"Bonjour." Fouquier smiled, his hands jittering next to his legs, and stood opposite LaGarde. "How do you like Père Sébastien?"

I acted like I was interested in his answer. Horse droppings were everywhere—our only defense. I slid a look at Fouquier. He toed a horse turd, and it rolled into the gutter in the center of the street.

"What are you two doing at Université?" LaGarde arranged the waves of lace at his wrist.

I brought my palms up. "My papa has nothing better to do with his money."

"Such a waste." He tsked.

I picked up a few chunks of dung. "Commoners use dried horse manure to burn when they cannot afford wood." I held them out. "What do nobles do with them?"

LaGarde quirked an eyebrow.

Fouquier grabbed a few and offered them to the bully.

LaGarde and the other students backed up, but only Fouquier and I saw they were about to be standing ankle-deep in chamber pot slops and horse piss. Their silver-buckled shoes would never be the same. I pressed my lips together to keep from laughing.

Our hands outstretched, we advanced. The nobles backed up.

I lowered my hands. "Oh. Looks like you don't need any more."

LaGarde looked down and let out a scream.

Fouquier and I dropped the crap, turned, and bolted.

By the time we reached the Palais-Royal, we were out of breath, more from laughing than running.

I bent over and sucked in air. "He's going to kill us tomorrow."

"Yeah. Too bad we can't wear swords."

"Humor is mightier than the sword…I hope."

Fouquier laughed, grabbed a broadsheet, and skimmed it. Another of my articles was in it. I held my breath.

"Have you read this piece on the inequity of the Estates-General?"

I nodded.

"You agree with it?"

I wanted his friendship. I'd need it against LaGarde. "Do you?"

He laughed. "I asked you first."

I wiped the back of my neck. "The voting system is inequitable, feudal. Convening the Estates-General won't change that."

"You're right. Maybe if everyone had a vote, like this Detré fellow says…You any relation to this writer?" He pointed to my article.

My mouth dried. Could I trust him? LaGarde was already out for my blood. If word got around that I wrote for the pamphlets—against the First and Second Estates—I'd be expelled. I shook my head.

"Pity. He makes excellent arguments for commoners."

I'd find the courage to tell him the truth, so long as LaGarde didn't figure it out.

17

Joliette

Versailles
March 20, 1789

MY PRETENDING ENTHUSIASM for my lady-in-waiting duties not only put Papa at ease, but the charade also helped me obtain my real goal: a husband with a love for wine. Since our return from the château, nothing seemed familiar to me, not the palais, not our apartments, not my body. Remembering Maman everywhere I went, I grew dizzy and walked down corridors I did not recognize.

Outside the Royal Chapel, I awaited Her Majesté and accompanying entourage for morning Mass. Swishing silks and footsteps heralded their arrival. I sank into a deep curtsey.

The Queen stopped before me, and, with the lightest touch

of her fingers, caressed my shoulder. "You attend me so soon, Comtesse?"

I remained in my curtsey, focusing on the tiny rosebuds sewn onto the Queen's delicate pink slippers. "It was her wish, Your Majesté." I stood, as contained and proper as Maman had trained me.

"You are as kind as she was." She brushed my cheek with the backs of her fingers. "You must miss her so."

I gripped the beads of Maman's rosary. I would not cry.

"Comtesse Soubrier?"

I froze. Maman's warning echoed: *At all costs, avoid the Comtesse Soubrier—she is the most vicious and cunning gossip at Court.*

Petite, about ten years older than I, with hair the blue-black of a rook's wing, Comtesse Soubrier glided forward. She was slender, with the breast of a pigeon protruding above the swell of her bosom. Fine lines crept around the corners of her mouth and eyes, more noticeable due to the thick powder she wore. Ribbons the color of aubergine accented her lilac gown. A necklace of amethyst covered her décolletage. Matching stones dripped from her earlobes.

I looked past her at Cécile, whose face held such pity I blinked back tears.

"Ensure Comtesse de Verzat is welcomed by all." The Queen caressed my cheek. "Guide and protect her as her dear mother would want you to care for her only daughter."

Soubrier dipped a curtsey. "With pleasure, Your Majesté."

The Queen plucked her rosary from the extended hand of another lady-in-waiting and entered the Royal Gallery. I wanted to run after Cécile, but the great pale blue doors, decorated with golden wreathes and cherubs, closed behind her.

My breath sat in my chest like a chunk of ice. I was as alone at that moment as when I stood before my mother's mausoleum.

The Comtesse's mole-like eyes examined me. "This shall be fun."

I bit the inside of my lip and followed her into a side gallery.

I gazed at the altar and felt as cold as the marble floor the day I sprawled before it. I knelt. Maman used my lessons to shelter and protect me from vipers like Soubrier and trained me to survive Court. I kept my back as straight as a picket. I would make certain Soubrier would not be around when I spoke to Jefferson.

18

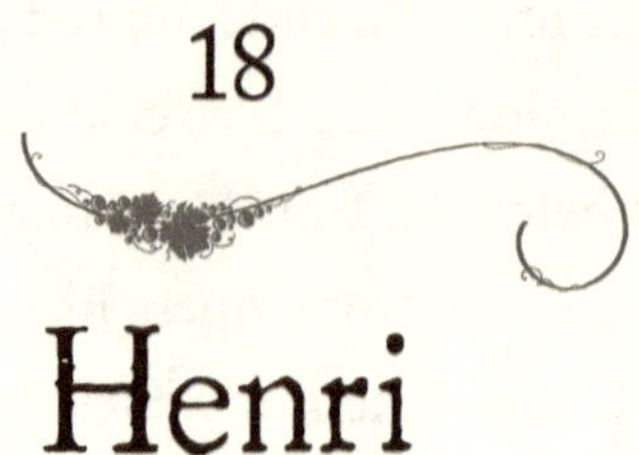

Henri

Paris
April 28, 1789

Sʜᴏᴜᴛs ᴏғ "Dᴇᴀᴛʜ to the rich!" echoed along the Seine.

I blew out a breath. A blank page had never made me anxious. The day before, rioters destroyed the home of the saltpeter factory owner, near my old lodgings. Now, another riot brewed. Would the people of Faubourg Saint-Antoine, my former neighbors, turn on me, too?

I steadied my hand and scratched the quill across the paper: *Laborers think factory owners are against them. But these men, despite their wealth, are valuable employers. Now that rioters have destroyed Henriot's saltpeter factory, where will the people he employed find work? Yes, workers have the right to protest low wages, but destruction means more people will starve, not fewer.*

I dropped the quill and dragged my hands through my hair.

"Hang the rich!" resounded from the street.

I ran to the window. Across the river, towering clouds of smoke rose above Faubourg Saint-Antoine and wound around the Bastille's towers.

A rumbling crossed the river. Thunder? No, gunfire of the Gardes Française defending the factories. The bread and cheese I'd eaten sat hard in my stomach. Being caught up in a mob was dangerous. I'd promised Papa and myself never to join. But how could I write about destruction if I didn't witness it? I grabbed my hat and ran out.

The chill air was swollen, like a dirty rag in need of wringing. The stevedores unloading a barge loosed their hooks from crates, waved them above their heads, and ran up the embankment. I lost my footing as they rushed around me, dragging me into a crowd of laborers carrying poles, hammers, and hatchets, chanting, "Death to Réveillon!" I ducked a swaying hook, the gleaming edge a breath from my cheek. Was writing about this worth risking my life?

A tattoo of gunfire rang out in the distance. The day before, Gardes Française shot into the mob and killed people. I shoved against the sweating men toward a tunnel gate off the quai, but more men joined, swarming and dragging me, my hat flying, my hands clawing, my feet scrabbling, across the bridge. The press of sweating bodies from all directions and a stink like lathered horses made me pant. I pushed and shoved. Calloused hands yanked and slammed and pushed me down rue Saint Antoine. I was fighting an undertow.

A muscled dockworker shook a pike above his head. "Hang the rich!"

My lungs ached with the sharp caustic stink of glue. Réveillon's wallpaper factory was burning. I shoved myself between arms and backs slick with sweat. A huge butcher, stinking of wine, swung a bloodied cleaver and screamed, "We'll drink the blood of Réveillon *and* his family!"

I had to get away before he chopped my head off. He roared a laugh and lurched, falling onto his face. Feet stomped around him.

I threw myself down onto the cobbles, crawled between people, scrabbled into the square, heaved for breath. Market women scattered, banging on doors, begging to be let in. I climbed up on a window ledge, gripped a street lantern, and pulled myself up above the crowd, searching for the alley with the tunnel entrance.

On rue du Montreuil, smoke poured from Réveillon's factory on the ground floor of his mansion, where his family lived on the higher floors. A chair tumbled from a balcony into the street. A line of porters emerged from a cellar and passed bottles of wine to anyone who would take them. A tanner, his hands the color of his scarred leather apron, smashed the neck of a bottle against a building and poured the wine over the crowd. Men opened their mouths. I wanted to smash the bottles over their heads. They thought they were destroying Réveillon's wine cellar. But they were destroying jobs—their jobs. The idiots would blame the rich Réveillon for their starvation, not themselves.

Books sailed out of Réveillon's window. A smithy, stumbling across a roof opposite, caught them. Why were they stealing books they couldn't read?

From surrounding rooftops, people hurled rocks toward the

smoking factory. I dropped down from the streetlamp as a brick hit a woman. She crumpled before me. I crawled to help her. Blood poured from the poissarde's mouth. Her eyes were open and lifeless like the fish she sold. I pressed my hand to her chest. Nothing. My hand shook. A rioter killed her, not a Garde Française. I shoved myself up.

Windows exploded, spewing glass everywhere. I flung my arms over my head and crouched down against a building and picked shards of glass from my hair. The thick smoke burned my eyes. I couldn't open them, but I heard splashing. Crawling away from the sounds of gunfire, I reached through cinders until I felt the rim of a fountain and dipped my hand in the water—so cool. But as I sipped it, gritty ash filled my mouth.

I spat and splashed water on my face, then shook my head and forced my eyes open. The tunnel entrance was three alleys away. I raced to the wooden door, yanked it open, and threw myself down into the darkness.

Running through the tunnels until I reached the café cellar on rue du Cotte, I climbed the steps and stumbled out into smokey sunlight.

In the distance came a chant, "Hang Réveillon!"

A cracking split the air like lightening—another explosion.

I ran into the square. Flaming sheets of wallpaper, the size of carpets, floated in the breeze and shrank down to the size of book pages, turning to ash as they drifted. They stained roofs, walls, people with a fine, gritty soot. With every breath, I smelled the acrid cinders of Réveillon's empire, now lost— along with hundreds of jobs. Flurries of ashes spun and swirled like dingy snowflakes.

I'd never join a mob. But would studying law truly help

my neighbors of Faubourg Saint-Antoine? Would my writing be different if I lived amongst the people I hoped to help? I doubted any other writers were a part of this chaos, so how could they tell the truth? Rioters died *not* from the gunfire of the Gardes Française but from the violence of their own neighbors. I'd be my own news crier for my next article and hope they wouldn't hang me.

19

Joliette

Versailles Gardens
May 24, 1789

Not wanting to spend a minute with Soubrier yet, having been commanded by the Queen to do so, I would make the best of the torment and glean information about Jefferson from her.

During our foray together into the Gardens, Soubrier spewed Court gossip. "You know Comte Axel von Fersen is the Queen's lover."

Despite the sunshine, I was chilled. Etiquette rules tumbled in my mind with the conversation I had had with Joseph. He gave me a list of questions regarding grafting for the Master Gardner, and I wanted to speak with him. I had no idea what Soubrier was talking about.

"Of course, von Fersen has affairs whenever he travels." She trailed her fingers along a bush.

"And Monsieur Jefferson? It is rumored he is well liked by the ladies," I asked.

She stopped and raised her eyebrows. "He is totally inappropriate for you."

"I did not say he *was* appropriate." I fanned my face. This was far more difficult than I expected. "It would be cooler in l'Orangerie. Shall we walk there?"

"We will not be seen there, Comtesse. The reason we are strolling in the Garden is to be seen, no?"

Seen and not heard. I wished she would bite her viper tongue.

As we rounded a corner, I nearly bumped into a flash of turquoise.

"Comtesse Soubrier! I beg your pardon." A tall young man hurriedly stepped back and bowed, leaving his foot extended, pointing toward Soubrier. He then straightened and looked to me.

A little laugh spilled out of me. "Monsieur Pricaud!" His green eyes lit up. He dipped into a deeper bow and began to rise, yet he remained slightly crouched, hat in hand, and looked up at me. "I am so deeply sorry for your loss, Comtesse."

I pressed my lips together. Not one courtier had expressed condolences. Except for the Queen's sympathy, grief was not acceptable at Versailles.

"Although you are not a member of Court, Monsieur," Soubrier looked down her thin sharp nose, "you should know that protocol requires even a commoner to wear a sword in the Gardens of Versailles."

I often wondered who created the protocol of requiring all men to wear weapons at a place where one might find oneself in the presence of the King. The rule facilitated regicide.

Pricaud blushed. "Excusez-moi, Comtesse, I—"

"One of pot-metal—the poorest quality, without ornament, and the cheapest—can be rented at the gate."

"Yes, I—"

"Excuse us." She lifted her skirts as if they would be dirtied by his presence and swept down the path.

He smiled at me in his lopsided way. "Forgive my blunder, Comtesse." He dropped into another bow.

I wanted to tell him a sword mattered not to me, but my mother's warning about his father rang in my head. I nodded and hurried after Soubrier.

"The wearing of swords is supposed to keep out the riff-raff." She yanked her parasol closed. "He probably had a rendezvous, and his lover let him in."

I stepped on a large stone, rolled my ankle, and stumbled. She turned. "Clumsy of you, my dear."

I took a cautious step. Did she know he had a lover, or was she speculating? Her eyes roved from left to right, like an animal stalking prey.

I followed her yet, in my mind, I saw Pricaud's smile. The garden blurred as his words echoed, *I am so deeply sorry for your loss*. Not one of the male courtiers who sought the emeralds I wore expressed his condolences since our return from the château. In this regard, Pricaud stood far above the highest ranks.

Soubrier resumed our stroll amongst the topiary trees in

the Petit Trianon's Gardens. "You know you must be married within a year or risk being une vieille fille?"

I snapped open my fan and cooled my face. "Marriage is of little importance to me."

"It will be when your father dies."

I pressed my hand to my stomach. I wished my fan were a dagger. "I will continue the Verzat legacy, regardless." *Damn!* I promised myself I would tell her nothing.

"Not if your distant cousin, or another man, inherits your precious estate, my dear."

The sound of buzzing bees surrounded me. My mind vibrated with them. "Will Monsieur Jefferson attend the Queen's fête next week?"

"Forget Jefferson." She pointed her parasol at me. "Duc de Lillers?"

"What of him?"

"My dear, he owns three châteaux."

"He has no interest in me. Besides, he is older than my father."

"Both of those facts are exactly why I know he *is* interested."

I held my laugh and smiled. Papa would so enjoy this amusement.

She poked the parasol at the gravel. "I believe the Duc would have been your mother's first choice."

The shaded path darkened. "I believe my mother would choose a man who cares for me." I pressed my palm over my heart. "The Duc de Lillers reveals no such behavior."

She whacked the tip of her parasol at the foliage. "That matters not. His money will provide for you."

"I hardly know him. I do not love him, nor he me."

Her laughter trilled like a mockingbird's call. "Oh, my dear, you are under the mistaken belief that marriage requires l'amour." She shook her head. "Quelle folie. Marriage is a business arrangement—much like that of our King and Queen." She bent over a rose and inhaled deeply. "L'amour is for affairs. And even if it were part of a marriage, it would die as quickly as this bloom." She straightened. "Such a waste. It is far wiser to marry well and save your heart for affairs."

I stiffened. "I shall be faithful to my husband and expect the same." I looked about for the color of turquoise.

"Is anyone at Court faithful?" She shook with laughter.

"My mother adored my father. They loved each other *and* were married."

She pursed her lips and ran her tongue along the inside of her cheek, as if to prevent a laugh. "I forgot." She smoothed her bodice. "Your mother was perhaps the only faithful wife at Court. I apologize." She opened the parasol and twirled it over her shoulder as she strolled away, her shoulders shaking.

Did she find my parents' fidelity amusing? I was back at the vineyard, watching my parents walk arm-in-arm, and Maman laughing at Papa's stories. Their love wrapped around me like a quilt.

She abruptly turned. "I have noticed you attract the attentions of the Baron Pricaud's son. Is he the object of your desire?"

My foot faltered in the gravel path. "Despite his lack of title, he is the only man who has expressed his condolences for my loss, a most noble quality."

She plucked a flower. "If you must love Pricaud, do so as a dalliance." She tossed the bloom at me. "Your father will not allow you to marry a man without fortune or title."

The bloom landed at my feet. "A rose may die within a few days, but my parents' love lasted for twenty years. And so will mine."

She covered her mouth and began slinking away.

I stabbed the tip of my parasol into the dirt. Beyond a row of hedges, I heard her exclaim, "Duc de Lillers, how nice to see you."

I picked up my skirts, turned, and ran. My reputation would be sullied for being without a chaperone but being alone was better than enduring the company of the poisonous Comtesse Soubrier and the ancient Duc.

I headed for the Grande Galerie in search of Jefferson, hoping to see another flash of turquoise along the way.

20

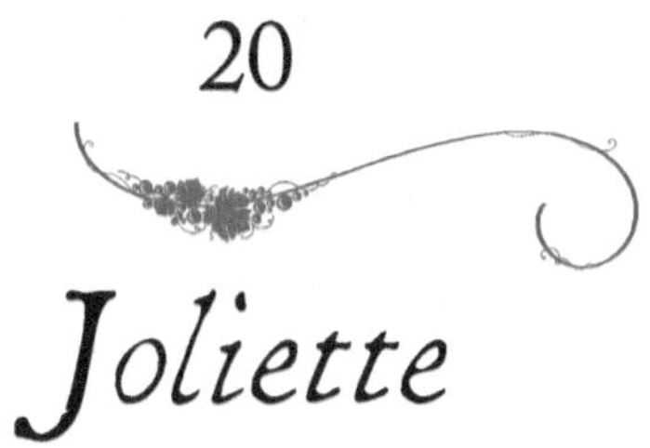

*J*oliette

Versailles
May 25 1789

A DAY LATER, I checked the grape leaves entwined in my wig before entering the Salon de l'Abondance. Soubrier's alleged purpose in attending fêtes was finding a suitable husband for me, but her real purpose was to find dalliances for herself. My express purpose was finding Thomas Jefferson and introducing him to Verzat wines. Then I would ask him to recommend a distributor in America. The other ladies-in-waiting tittered about him all week. They would laugh at me, but I would give him the leaves from my wig as a memento of the greatest wines in France.

I followed Soubrier into the salon and stared up at Neptune, reaching out from the trompe l'oeil ceiling surrounded by gilded cornices. Tables around the perimeter of the hall overflowed with liqueurs, gâteaux, and fruits glacés. Flames snapped in the huge fireplaces, unnecessary for the warm evening. The wig so itched my scalp I wanted to fling it into the fire. I looked about for Cécile but did not see her. Who was her chaperone now that Maman was no longer?

"This was an antechamber for Louis XIV's cabinet of rarities." Dressed in sky-blue satin, Duc de Lillers stepped before me, forcing me to stop. "And you, my dear, are a rarity." He shouted as if *I* were hard of hearing. His breath stank of chamber pot slops.

I lifted my fan as if to cool myself, wafting the fragrance of pomades and perfumes of the other courtiers.

The Duc gripped my elbow. Soubrier smiled at the Duc, slid her arm around me, and prodded me into a smaller room. Captured by a tortoise and a viper, I longed for l'Orangerie.

Fifty or more courtiers, dressed gaily as peacocks, bet on games of chess, backgammon, and trick-track in the salon du jeux. The American Minister would stand out, as Jefferson wore somber colors, but I did not spy him.

The air pressed on me. Three crystal chandeliers bathed the gilded room like a sunset, but myriad candles also made the atmosphere thick and muggy. Was he late? Should I search for him at the Galerie?

A wave of laughter caused Duc de Lillers to turn, and I darted away. A tall man, dressed in shades of turquoise, entered. My heartbeat quickened. Monsieur Pricaud.

I stepped forward, wanting to greet him, even though I had been warned against him. My fingers tingled—anticipating his kiss—I was not wearing gloves.

His sword did not appear to be rented, but he did not know

that swords were required for Gardens and inappropriate for salons. He could not enter unless someone had sponsored him. Had he purchased a brevet d'affaires to gain entry? I admired his tenacity.

He gazed about, and his bright green eyes caught mine.

My heart raced, like the first time I saw him at the ball. But he looked past me and continued to search the room. My heartbeat slowed.

Deciding he must not have seen me, I made my way toward him. Maman's warning rang in my mind, and I assured her, *I'm just going to greet him as the lady-in-waiting you trained.*

Pricaud's smile grew lopsided. Was he embarrassed? He approached an elderly widow, whom other courtiers called a toothless old toad, and bowed deeply. "Excuse me, but are you the Marquise de Bourran?"

She brought her fan to her chin and nodded slowly.

I neared her.

"You may not remember, but you were most kind to me when you attended a summer party at the château of my father, Baron Pricaud." His voice was loud enough for all to hear.

"Was I, Monsieur?"

He blushed. "My mother took away my book and told me to join the other children. I was distraught, for I was most interested in the story. You took me by the hand and said, 'If it is stories you like, let me introduce you to the greatest storyteller you shall ever meet.' Your husband recounted a hunt and his encounter with…what was it…?"

"A porcupine!" She brought her hands to her bosom, and her mouth twisted into what I feared was a sob, then she let loose a roar of laughter. She grasped his hand in both of hers.

"I have not thought of that story in years!"

He patted her hand tenderly. "I have thought of it often."

Another wave of laughter shook the wrinkles from her face. "Do you know…my husband could not sit down for three weeks because of that beast?" She wiped her eyes. "But Philipe did not mind the pain because he told that story for years and years! He loved to make people laugh." She patted Pricaud's cheek. "Merci, Monsieur. You brought my dear husband back to life for a few moments, and I am most grateful."

"It is I who am grateful, Marquise. You are as beautiful as I remember."

Her hooded eyes sparkled like the Queen's jewels.

Pricaud's attention to the Marquise warmed me. He was kinder and more gentlemanly than any courtier I ever met.

Pricaud turned and looked about, past me, then swept out his arm and bowed. "Comtesse Soubrier, may I engage you in a game of Quadrille?"

Why did he pass me by? Was I looking peaked? I bit my lips.

Soubrier languidly fanned herself. "Truly, Monsieur. Is that your attempt at seduction? It takes more than a card game to woo *this* lady."

I gripped a chairback, steadying myself. Soubrier played the game of infidelity at every opportunity.

"I wish to play at cards, Madame, not l'amour." Pricaud straightened. "L'amour is *not* something I play at. I take it most seriously."

Something in my chest shifted. Did he value fidelity as I did? Pricaud appeared taller when he spoke of love. He showed courage dueling with Soubrier—she had cut him to shreds in the Garden. I searched the crowd for Jefferson. Many ladies-in-waiting were also absent, as well as Cécile. Were they with the Queen?

Vicomte Richepin, still acting the jester and mincing like a girl, rushed to Soubrier's side.

"Quadrille is no longer fashionable, Monsieur." Soubrier tickled Richepin's face with her feathered fan. "The game now played is Médiateur." Richepin fell upon a chaise longue giggling.

"I am a quick study. If you would not mind revealing the rules?" Pricaud bowed.

My corset was laced so tight, I struggled to inhale. He had no idea how Soubrier played to win—at all costs. She would bankrupt him.

"Forgive my reluctance, Monsieur. Your father has lost a great deal to me. I should not wish to throw good money...." A laugh rumbled in her throat.

Richepin sniggered and made to touch Soubrier's décolletage. She whapped him with her fan. He rubbed his fingers and pouted.

Maman had dismissed Richepin at the ball. She could have been as imperious to him as Soubrier, yet she had been kind. Maman, how can I be kind to this foolish jester, Richepin, when I wish to twist off his nose?

At that moment, ladies-in-waiting thronged to the end of the room. The tall American Minister nodded as each lady curtsied. Cécile walked next to him, her fingers resting upon his arm. My fingers trembled as I adjusted the leaves in my wig.

"Ah, I shall not require a marker." Pricaud reached into his waistcoat and rippled a thick packet of money. "I have livres I can afford to lose. Shall I exchange them for jetons?"

"We will need a banker." Soubrier flicked her fan at me. "I

appoint Comtesse de Verzat." She pulled me to her. "You are good with numbers, no?"

Did she know I managed the winery's accounts? "Excuse me, I must greet Monsieur Jefferson." I picked up my skirts.

"He is such a bore. Speaks only of politics and wine." The Comtesse clutched my arm. "You shall be only too happy to be banker."

I resisted. Her nails dug into my flesh. I gripped my fan to stop myself from hitting her with it. "I am not good with numbers," I snarled.

"And my partner, Comtesse de Verzat?" Pricaud bowed to me.

The room swirled like I had just finished dancing.

Soubrier yanked me to her side. "No. She will be *my* partner." Her smile was broad, too broad. If I stomped on her foot, she might release me, but I would pay dearly for it.

"Comtesse Soubrier, you must wish to lose. I am very bad at cards." I forced a honey-sweet smile.

"Then I will ask the most beautiful woman in the room to be my partner." Pricaud looked about.

My mouth trembled as I tried to keep my smile.

Soubrier straightened, as did many of the other women in the salon not clustered about Monsieur Jefferson. Pricaud bowed deeply to the Marquise de Bourran. "Would you do me the honor of being my partner, Marquise?"

She tilted her head. "It would be *my* honor, Monsieur." Servants helped her to the gaming table.

I wanted to thank him for his kindness to the Marquise, but Soubrier would interpret it as flattery. She did not release her grip on me until I sat at the polished dark wood gaming table with the Marquise on my right, Pricaud to my left.

Across from me, Soubrier flicked her hand, making her bracelets click. At this command, the servants brought porcelain baskets filled with a complement of playing pieces, those belonging to nobles sporting coats of arms and decorative edges painted specifically for family members.

Jefferson walked toward us. I began to stand, but Soubrier pinned my hand onto the table.

I fell back into my chair, crossed my leg, and kicked her. She shrieked.

"Excusé-moi." I gave her my honey-sweet smile.

Cécile led Jefferson to a nearby gaming table. Why had she not told me she knew him? My stays pinched. When I caught his eye, I smiled and adjusted the leaves in my wig. He took no notice.

The servant distributed our baskets. I reached but stopped. The decorative edge was not mine of tiny pink roses but white camellias against a dark green vine—my mother's. A fresh pain stabbed me. I withdrew my hand.

"Is it not yours?" Pricaud asked.

I shook my head.

"Please bring Comtesse de Verzat's basket and some wine."

The servant delivered both. He turned and offered wine to Jefferson's table.

Jefferson accepted a glass. I gripped my chair to stop myself from running to him and asking how he liked it. No matter the consequences, I would convince him to plant Verzat rootstock in America.

I pressed the wineglass to my lips to stop their trembling.

The wine was viscous, but I sipped a tiny bit to be polite. I hoped they had not served this ordure to Jefferson.

Pricaud frowned. "Is it not to your liking?"

My hand trembled as I set the glass down. "It is fine."

He sipped. "It is too sweet, too thick."

He had a palate! I brought up my fan to hide my grin.

"Are we going to drink or gamble, Monsieur?" Soubrier picked through her jetons.

Pricaud smiled. "Shall we bid for naming the trump suit? Or tourné?"

Soubrier fanned her pigeon breast. "Oh, what does it matter?"

"Madame le Marquise, would you do us the honor of naming a favorite suit?" He smiled as if deeply in love with her.

The Marquise pushed her tongue through her lips, back and forth, and because of her worn-down teeth she looked a bit like a rabbit munching clover. I wanted to hug the dear sweet woman. "Diamonds! They are my favorite gem."

"Diamonds," he replied. "Are they *your* favorite, Comtesse Soubrier?"

She bristled. "Only if they are on the cards in my hands."

Pricaud held the deck out to Soubrier. She languidly picked up a few cards, dropped them on the table, and adjusted the gold hoops at her wrist.

He shuffled the cards as if born to the task.

I blinked at his speed. Soubrier might pay dearly for not noticing his legerdemain. My parents ruled that I never lose more than the jetons in my basket, a rule I honored. But tonight, it might be worth breaking it—to watch Soubrier fall from her noble perch at the hands of a son of a baron.

I stole a glance at the nearby table, where Jefferson had amassed a large pile of jetons. He seemed in no hurry to depart. I had to lose quickly so I would be free to approach him when he finished his game.

Soubrier settled the rings on her fingers and barked out the rules. "Bids made in the favorite beat bids of any other suit. A forced spadille is doubled. The Médiateur, or roi rendu, in favorite is worth two...."

Although I had played the game many times, tracking her rapid recitation was difficult. The Marquise sat munching away until Soubrier finished with, "Now deal, Monsieur."

His long fingers spun the cards to each player. Like those of an artist, his hands were sensitive to the bending of the cards. Had he lied about not knowing this game?

I placed my bid. "Spadille." The lowest possible, as I held no diamonds. I glanced at Jefferson who won another pile of jetons. My feet tapped the parquet.

An impish smile spread across the Marquise's face. She upped the bid by one hundred livres. Did she understand the rules? Pricaud *and* his father would be grossly indebted to Soubrier.

"Grandissimo." Soubrier tossed her jetons in the center of the table.

Pricaud met the bid and raised it by another hundred. "When you hold all favorites, is it Misère?"

He was pretending to not understand. Holding all favorites was the winning hand.

Soubrier's smile hardened, deepening the lines about her lips. This would be a short game.

I put down my cards. Soubrier mouthed, *He's bluffing.* I met the bid.

We both lost to Pricaud and the Marquise, who held all diamonds.

Monsieur Jefferson began to rise and bow to the ladies at his table.

I jumped up. "I apologize. I have lost all my jetons and must leave the game."

Soubrier lunged across the table. I backed away.

The Marquise grasped my arm. "You must continue." She waved her hand, and a servant brought another basket. "No need to repay me, Comtesse. I have not had this much fun in years, and I intend to continue having it. Deal!"

I crumpled into my chair. I would have scratched Soubrier's eyes out, for I cared not a fig about her, but I could not disappoint this dear old woman. She reminded me of Grandmaman.

Monsieur Jefferson left with Cécile clinging to his arm. I had to be introduced, and it had to be tonight. I picked up my cards but did not see them. I felt like a spent candle, my hope drowning in a puddle of wax.

"I understand the Minister is returning to America soon." Soubrier tossed her bid.

"Comtesse, you seem to have a drop of wine on your chin." I lied.

She scraped her chin with a card. "You shall not have time to sell him your precious Verzat wine."

How did she know? Heat raced through me. It could only have been Cécile who had told her.

"Verzat wine is the finest in France, if not the world." Pricaud picked up his glass. "I hope they did not serve this swill to the American Minister."

I wanted to thank him profusely, but my gesture would have revealed my desire. And Soubrier would warn Papa that I was in love with Pricaud, which was absolutely absurd. How could I leave the game? I could search for Monsieur Jefferson in the Gardens—at the risk of my reputation. Cécile was promised to a duc. Had she intentions for Jefferson?

"Château de Verzat should be the only wine served at Versailles." The Marquise drew a finger across her eyebrow and looked to him.

"I agree," said Pricaud.

Was she giving him some sort of sign? He seemed not to notice. If the Marquise knew Jefferson, I would ask her to introduce me. But I would ask when we were alone.

At the next deal, the Marquise drummed four fingers along her jaw. And the next, she ran her fingers along her three bracelets.

She was giving Pricaud imperceptible hints on the number of diamonds she held in each hand. Although she was adroit at cheating, Pricaud took pains *not* to notice her signals.

I sat stone-faced, fearing Soubrier would notice my astonishment. But she never paid the dowager the slightest bit of attention. As I was playing with the Marquise's money, I did not take advantage of her hints, which would have helped Soubrier win. Each time Soubrier lost more money, keeping my amusement hidden grew more difficult. I squirmed from the pressing of my stays.

I longed to participate in the folly, and, by pretending not to notice, I was, which filled me with glee. I dutifully followed Soubrier's lead, which assisted her losing streak. I wanted to clap with delight at her imminent losses, and, at the same time, weep in frustration that I missed Jefferson.

The pink-mauve light of dawn filled the room. Servants extinguished the candles. Jester Richepin snored on the chaise longue.

"Banker, what do I owe?" Soubrier asked.

Perspiration collected at my temples. "You owe the Marquise and Monsieur Pricaud three thousand, five hundred livres—each."

"Fini!" Soubrier's face, neck, and bosom blazed crimson. She snapped her fingers at a servant for quill, ink, and cards. She signed the markers with a flourish and waved them to dry the ink. "What a chicanery, Monsieur."

"What about mine?" The Marquise's eyes glittered like a child's.

I laughed, covering it with a cough.

Soubrier leaned forward, giving Pricaud a perfect view of her overflowing bosom. She flipped the card at him. "Beginner's luck?"

"The rules may change. The skill does not." He picked up the marker.

The Marquise placed her bejeweled hand on Soubrier's. "You must learn to be more observant, my dear."

I bit my lip to stop laughing.

Soubrier yanked away her hand and dropped the other marker.

Pricaud stood. "Madame, how much is my father's marker you hold?"

"Ha!" She did not laugh. "Five hundred less than I owe you."

He held the card, as if to tear it. "Would you exchange them?"

She raised her eyebrows. "You would lose five hundred livres?"

"And my father would no longer be indebted to you." Pricaud held the card higher, his fingers tensed to destroy it.

I clapped and immediately gripped my fingers to hide my delight. He found a way to pay off his father's debt *with* the biggest gossip at Court. Other courtiers would no longer avoid him. Pricaud's business acumen might impress even Papa.

"I do not have it with me."

"I will destroy this marker, if you destroy my father's."

"I prefer to exchange markers, Monsieur." Soubrier rose. "Come to my apartments tonight." Her fingers caressed the flesh bulging from her low-cut neckline. "And I do not like to be kept waiting." She swept her skirts and left.

Jester Richepin snorted awake and raced after Soubrier.

"I told you we could do it." The Marquise leaned over the table and patted Pricaud's hand. "But you did not pay any attention to my signals!"

"We won fairly, Madame." He kissed her hand and held it tenderly. Though without title, Pricaud was more honorable than those with them. I longed to have been a part of their ruse.

"You will need a chaperone when you meet with Soubrier and her earwigging Richepin." Her laughter bubbled. "The Comtesse de Verzat and I shall accompany you."

I wanted to kiss the Marquise. She created an opportunity

for us all to be together and continue the fun—at Soubrier's expense.

Bright morning light fractured in the prisms of the chandeliers, spinning tiny rainbows upon the walls and carpets. I was caught up in the Marquise and Pricaud's magic, laughing, reliving their planning, and executing their scheme.

My delight made me miss Maman. She had been my best friend, my confidante, my guide. I had no camaraderie with Soubrier, no trust, no fondness. She had taunted and been cruel to Pricaud and the Marquise, and she had mocked me, the Verzat legacy, and love. I was glad I had contributed to her losses.

I had been betrayed and undermined by the very person the Queen asked to protect me. And Cécile had aided her by disclosing my secret. A chill ran through me. I had an enemy, maybe two, at Court. The very thing Maman trained me to avoid at all costs.

An idea heartened me. Perhaps Papa might agree to an older chaperone, one with years more experience, like the Marquise de Bourran, who hated Soubrier as much as I.

Soubrier's malfeasance was nothing compared to my determination to make Monsieur Jefferson's acquaintance. And I would manage both—no matter what the cost.

21

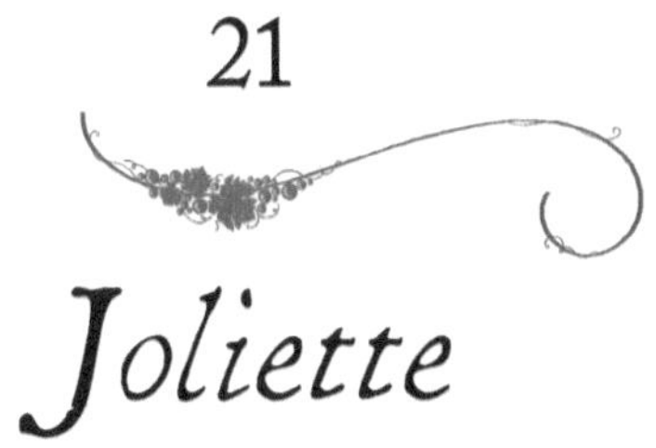

Joliette

Versailles
June 1, 1789

"DID YOU MEET with Monsieur Jefferson when he was last at Versailles?" Papa paced before the fireplace.

"No." I looked up from the account books. Soubrier had told him I wanted to meet Jefferson. I had no secrets from the viper.

He tapped a folded letter on his chin. "Strange, I thought you were the one responsible."

I dipped the quill. Was she blaming her losses on me? Had she told him about Monsieur Pricaud? My shaking hand spat ink on the figures. "Papa. Please. Joseph needs my recommendations tomorrow. I must finish."

"But you *did* play cards with him?"

A year earlier, I had boasted I had, when there had been

plenty of time to arrange it. Monsieur Jefferson was preparing to go home now, and there was no more time to make my lie a truth. The lie sat like a stone in my stomach. I patted the ink with a cloth. I was a Verzat and, as one, I had to uphold the Verzat honor. "No." I faced him. "Is there anything you wish to add to my report?"

"You lied?" His voice screeched like a poorly played violin.

He would marry me off within the week. I gripped my shaking hands before me and stared at the carpet. "I wrote to Monsieur Jefferson."

"Is that all?" His eyebrows rose.

Drowning must make one struggle like this. Against sinking down, down, down into cold dark, dark, water, unable to breathe. "I...sent him some wine."

"Ah ha!" He slapped the paper on the desk. "I knew it!"

My nails dug into my palms. "I am advising the vintner about casking the wine. My monthly duty to the Queen ends tomorrow night and will resume in ten days. I would like to be at the château before we re-cask it."

He leaned toward me, his face a breath from mine. "Which vintage did you send?"

"Our best," I squeaked. "The seventy-two."

He cupped my chin.

My face burned.

"Fantastique!" He kissed my forehead. "Fantastique!"

I steadied myself on the desk.

He waved the letter before Maman's portrait hanging above the fireplace. "We cannot deny it! Our daughter is formidable!" He burst into laughter.

I laughed. For the first time since her death, Papa and I laughed together. Though mine came from relief, I wondered what was so funny to him. "I sent wine and a letter to Monsieur Jefferson. What is so formidable?"

He pointed at me. "That is the mystery." I gripped the chairback. His eyes held mischief. "What did you say in the letter?"

I knew it by heart, but the words came in spurts. If Soubrier told Papa anything, I would no longer be formidable. "Hope you like the Cabernet Franc…Verzat, finest wines in France… wishing to extend the legacy to the finest in the world."

He beckoned for more.

"Ah…would you be so kind to assist our Château…exporting our wine to America?" My voice quivered.

He roared a laugh. "Well, he did!"

A ringing in my head dulled my hearing. Did what?

"A wine merchant in New York has ordered fifty barrels upon Jefferson's recommendation!"

I grabbed the accounts book, flipped the pages, ran my finger down a column. "We have more than two hundred barrels of the seventy-two at the cave."

He rocked from his heels to his toes, laughing.

I clapped. "We did it!"

"*You* did it, ma princesse." He grabbed my hand and waltzed me about the salon.

"This is formidable!" I came to a halt. "We have never shipped to America."

"No?" He splayed open his hands and tapped his fingers together.

"Normally, the vintner arranges all the shipping with a firm in Paris. But, terms for a new contract must be negotiated." I straightened my back and looked him in the eye. "I should like to negotiate and sign that contract."

"Unless widowed, unmarried women's signatures are not valid."

A prickling sensation ran down my arms. "I should not have written or sent wine to Jefferson, but I did. You consider that formidable. It is imperative to make my signature valid since the Verzat legacy rests in my hands!"

"Your duties as lady-in-waiting are here, with the Queen."

"As I said, this month's duty ends tomorrow evening. I will have ten free days."

He glanced at Maman's portrait. "Remember your promise?"

The room spun. I was back on the floor of the chapel, begging God to let Maman live. If anyone at Court learned of my business activities, I would be an embarrassment to the Queen, and worse, my mother. I was risking being ostracized. By honoring my promise to Grandmaman, I was being the very best granddaughter and ensuring the Verzat legacy—my legacy. A better daughter would honor her promise. A better lady-in-waiting never would have contacted Jefferson. But a better God would not have taken Maman.

I blew out a breath. I would have to pray a rosary for that blaspheme, but I would not take it back. I tried, but I cared not a fig about Court, other than using it to gain what I wanted.

"And what of our legacy, Papa? Every summer, at the first glimpse of our château, I begged you to tell the story of our ancestor. You told me he assisted François I in capturing Milan. It is due to him that we are noblesse d'épée. The estate has been Verzat land since 1515, and it is *my* heritage." I pressed my hand upon my heart. "Would you have me lose that?"

Lines deepened in his face. His sadness made me want to take back my words. But I would not. The Verzat legacy was my life.

Our butler gently knocked on the doorframe and bowed. "The Marquise de Bourran and Monsieur Pricaud, Monseigneur."

Papa glanced at me.

I retrieved the accounts book. Soubrier told him. Damn her. "Send them in."

I replaced the book and smoothed my skirts.

The rustle of the Marquise de Bourran's satin skirts preceded her. She had traded her mourning dress for a gown of robin's egg blue. "Comte, lovely to see you. It has been too long."

"Indeed, Marquise, but one day without seeing you is too long." Papa bowed and kissed her hand.

She tapped her fan upon his arm. "Oh, you flatter me." She laughed. "And I enjoy it immensely. Do continue."

We all laughed.

I squinted at the bright yellow of Pricaud's frock coat and breeches. He resembled a daffodil, but I was relieved that he wore no sword. "Monsieur le Comte." He bowed deeply to Papa, and then turned to me and bowed. Taking my hand, his lips brushed my fingers. My heartbeat pounded so loudly I could not hear, but I saw his lips form the words, "Enchanté, Comtesse."

My throat was so tight I squawked. "Merci, Monsieur."

Papa led the Marquise to the chaise longue before the fire.

She settled herself. "Comtesse, I am in need of your kisses."

I pecked both her cheeks and sat next to her, inhaling her

lilac scent. Now was the time to convince Papa I needed an older and wiser chaperone.

She held my hand. "Comte de Verzat, I have accompanied this gentleman because you have rejected his offer four times." Her voice boomed. "Monsieur Pricaud is a man of honor. He has come to settle his father's debts."

I stared at the carpet. My voice begging in my mind, *Please do not tell Papa of our game.*

Pricaud pulled out a blue leather purse.

It bulged so, it must have contained the entire debt. *Maman, let Papa accept it,* I prayed.

"Monseigneur, you are the last courtier to whom my father is indebted. If you accept his payment, my father can begin to rebuild his reputation." Pricaud offered it with both his hands.

"It is not necessary. I forgive your father's debt."

The Marquise leaned forward, rapped her fan on Papa's leg, and glared at him.

"That is most kind." Pricaud extended the packet. "But your acceptance is necessary to my father's honor."

"Very well. Please thank the Baron for me."

Pricaud's smile brightened the room more than his ensemble. "Merci! Merci, mille fois!"

The Marquise clapped so hard her diamond earrings swayed. "You were the last and the most difficult, Comte. After Monsieur Pricuad beat Comtesse Soubrier at cards, courtiers preferred to accept payment to losing to his son."

I smiled and patted her elbow, hoping she would not mention the part I had played in the coup.

She extended her hand to Papa. "I think you shall have to make it up to me by playing cards with us."

"Alas, I learned my gambling lesson long ago." He arched an eyebrow. I studied the carpet. He placed the purse on the desk. "I must decline."

"Then supper tonight in my apartments, the four of us." She grasped my hand.

I arranged my skirts. Papa would never agree to this. I knew he heard my mother's lecture in his head as loudly as I heard her in mine.

Pricaud brought his hands together as if in prayer.

"Alas, we have time only for a celebratory glass of wine." Papa rang for Jacques to bring a decanter, and then turned to the Marquise. "Early tomorrow, Joliette and I must travel to Paris to negotiate a contract."

I leapt to my feet, my heart galloping. I was going to negotiate the contract. I did not know how, but I would insist the shipper accept my signature.

"Quelle dommage." The Marquise smiled. "But what are we celebrating?"

"Thanks to Joliette, we are exporting Verzat wine to America!"

Pricaud's eyes brightened. "Verzat wine will be known not only as the finest wine in France but also the world."

For the first time since Maman's death, I was hopeful, happy.

"You must be proud of your daughter, Comte." The Marquise boasted as if I were *her* child.

Papa pushed his bottom lip out, as if disappointed. When his laugh boomed, I realized he was teasing me. "Bien sûr."

Pricaud stood next to me as we brought our glasses together in a toast. His kind gaze lingered as I sipped. At first, I could not look away. But I grew dizzy and looked up at Maman's portrait. *Regardless of his title, he is a man of honor. And, he understands the Verzat legacy.* I turned back, smiled at Pricaud, and took a sip of the finest wine in the world. I would develop a plan to make that boast true, no matter whom I had to charm, convince, or connive.

22

Joliette

Paris
June 2, 1789

Early the next morning, our carriage awaited beyond the iron-picket gate surrounding Versailles. The gilded roof ornaments gleamed in the sun's rays, and the entire palais shimmered like the King's crown.

Was I doing the right thing? I had sent a note to the Queen claiming an illness and begging her forgiveness. I was abandoning that day's duties to travel to Paris and, the next day, force a shipper to accept my signature on a contract that wouldn't be legal. Would he take that risk for the finest wine in France?

A lady-in-waiting to the Queen of France was one of the most coveted positions in all of Europe. If Soubrier came looking for me, and she learned I traveled to Paris, she would cause problems even Papa could not solve. I pressed my hands into my lap and tried to calm my nerves for the next hour as we traveled the main road.

When we arrived in the city, the carriage shook and rattled along the cobbles, making me appreciate the gardeners who constantly raked and pampered Versailles's gravel paths. We passed a laundress wearing a basket, twice her height and stuffed with clothes, strapped to her back. How did she manage such a load? A passel of hogs trotted around the carriage and into a lane. I shook my head. The city was filthier than I remembered.

"Before we go to the mansion, may we stop at Saint Séverin? I wish to light a candle for Maman." I hoped to feel her presence there, and I also wanted to light candles for my negotiations tomorrow and beg God's forgiveness for my lies.

"Certainement." Papa wore an amused smile.

We trundled through a warren of lanes lined with narrow houses until we came to a square and stopped before the church. Its pinnacles soared above fierce gargoyles that gazed down at us. I pointed. "Maman told me a wizard cast a spell upon the gargoyles, so they would not harm anyone."

"Seems the spell is still cast." Papa laughed.

The footman opened the carriage door and assisted us.

Before the church, a small girl stood, clutching a bouquet of violets. Open sores oozed around her mouth. She looked to be four years and was terribly thin. I wished I had food to give her. I reached into the pouch I kept in my hanging pocket and extracted an écu, far too much for a bouquet, but enough money to feed her family for a week.

"Are your flowers for sale?" I held out the coin and, quick as a rabbit, a boy dressed in rags captured it and ran like one of the King's hounds. I yanked back my hand as if he had bitten me. "He took my money!"

Papa turned. "What? Who?"

The footman called out, "Stop that thief!" He ran in pursuit.

"Do not give money to beggars. It is dangerous, as you just witnessed."

"But Papa, this girl is starving, so, probably, is her family."

"We cannot feed all the starving in Paris."

"She is also ill."

He sighed. "Very well." He approached the child's mother.

"Allow me, please." I bent toward the girl. Her lips were cracked, her eyes crusty. "Are you selling your flowers?"

She bit her fingers. Her mother wrapped her arm around the child's shoulders. The woman's face was the color of hickory nuts and as dried and wrinkled as a fallen autumn leaf. "Curtsey for the lady."

The child nearly toppled over, and she grasped at her mother's skirts. "Don't bother the lady now." The woman began to push the child behind her.

"I wanted to give her money for her flowers, if she is selling them."

"They're wild." She patted her daughter's head. "Give the flowers to the lady."

The child, one hand in her mouth, held up the bouquet.

I took them. "They are beautiful. Did you pick them?"

She nodded.

"May I buy them?" I pulled out another écu.

The mother's hand guided her daughter's and gripped the

coin. The woman's eyes glistened. "Merci, Mademoiselle. You are most generous." She curtsied deeply.

I took Papa's arm and hurried to the church before she saw my tears.

Unlike the chapel at Versailles, no gold or marble decorated this church. Maman loved Saint Séverin because of its pillars—twisting stone columns chiseled to resemble palm trees with fronds unfurling as they reached heavenward.

The tower bell pealed the hour, the deep tones resonating. The reverberations had moved my mother to tears. Now, they shook my heart. The last rumble died away. Papa squeezed my hand. I blessed myself, brought the flowers to my cheek, remembered Maman had loved embroidering violets.

Papa gestured for me to lead him down the main aisle of the nave. Before we reached the altar, I stood in the warm golden light filtering through the fine stained-glass windows, feeling Maman next to me, smelling her lavender perfume, hearing her soft voice, seeing her fingers holding her pearl rosary beads.

"Papa?" A male voice called out.

I turned. A tall young man with broad shoulders, proud posture, and deep blue eyes stood in a side aisle. White dust streaked his brown hair, frock coat, and neckcloth. He was not dressed as a courtier, yet he was familiar.

He waved. "Papa! I thought it was you." He took another step forward.

I gripped the violets. Why was he calling *my* father, *Papa?*

My father placed his hand on the hilt of his sword. The young man stopped and cocked his head. "It's me." He put his hand on his chest. "Henri."

"Who—" But Papa yanked my arm. I jerked my head around to look at him.

His jaw tightened. "Be off with you, beggar!" His tone pierced me.

The young man's mouth dropped open. He shut it, his lips forming a straight line. He lifted his chin. His bright eyes dulled.

"Be off!" Papa shouted.

I reached for Papa's elbow, but he shook me away

The young man bowed. "Pardon, Monsieur. I mistook you for a noble." His voice was familiar. He turned and strode away. His sharp steps echoed along the stone.

His gait was familiar. He did not look like a beggar. He looked like a bourgeois. He turned into a side chapel. A door slammed.

"Papa, was it necessary to be so cruel?"

His eyes were pinched. The muscles in his neck taut. "The city is teeming with beggars."

A cloud must have passed before the sun, darkening the chapel. I wrapped my cloak tightly. Unable to move, I stared at the space the young man had occupied. Had I imagined him?

"Let us go now." Papa tugged at my arm.

I stood paralyzed. "Who was that young man?"

"No one I know."

"But he called you, 'Papa.'"

"I am a Noble of the Sword. Of course, I am known." His voice was low, as if he did not wish to be heard.

He tugged, but I resisted. "Why would he call a noble, 'Papa?'"

"Beggars call all men, 'Papa.' It is a ruse to get money. Have you so quickly forgotten the thief outside?"

"He did not ask for money."

"The thief outside the church did not ask, either." He took a clove from his snuffbox and chewed, staring at the stained-glass window behind me.

I shivered. "I wish to light a candle and pray."

"Very well."

I knelt in the chapel. The meager flame wavered in the draft. I could no longer sense Maman. Papa had always been honest with me, yet I could tell he knew that young man. I squeezed my eyes, seeing the young man's face—so familiar.

I pulled Maman's rosary from my réticule and prayed, but I kept seeing the young man's deep blue eyes, his broad shoulders, his confident strides. What was Papa hiding?

If he was Papa's son, the Verzat legacy would rest in his hands.

A draft extinguished the candleflame.

I shoved the rosary into my sleeve. Regardless of what Papa told me, I would learn the truth. For if that young man did inherit the Verzat legacy, I would have to convince him that it was *my* legacy. And I would run the business with or without him.

23

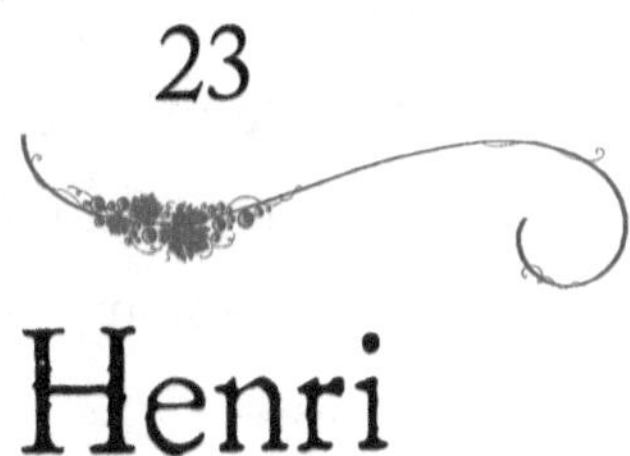

Henri

Paris
June 2, 1789

BEGGAR! MY FATHER'S words clanged inside my head with my every step down the aisle and through the back chapel. *Beggar?* I flung open the wooden door to the tunnels and tore down the steps. The door banged behind me. I wished it'd slammed on my father's face.

Beggar. I lighted my hidden torch, unlocked the gate, made my way to the star chamber, slipped behind a column of stones, collapsed against a stone wall. The stink of church incense lingered in my frock coat. I ripped it off.

It was my own fault. I should never have approached him. I *made* him deny me. Made him betray me. Made him ashamed of me.

I punched my fist into the column and yelped. Pain flared

up my arm. Tears burned. I would not cry. I would never cry. Damn him. I rubbed my hand. The trembling torch light cast wavering shadows.

I got up and paced. How was I a beggar? I never asked him for anything. Never asked him into my life. Never asked to be born. Never asked to cause my mother's death.

Past kings bestowed noble titles to their illegitimate sons and daughters. Was I, the son of a noble, not due the same honor? The same courtesy? His smug answer: *I cannot acknowledge you at this time.* Would he ever?

He needn't worry. I'd never acknowledge him again. I'd quit wasting time trying to make him proud. I'd study for me, Henri Detré, and *my* future, not to impress the Comte de Verzat. I'd write articles as me, Henri Detré, that would embarrass my father.

The torch died out. I flung it into the darkness. It clattered along the floor. Would he have denied knowing me if he'd not been with that woman? Who was she? I squeezed my eyes so tightly shards of light pierced the darkness.

If nobles betrayed their sons, I didn't want to be one. I saved much of the allowance my father provided. Enough to buy passage to America.

This time, I'd abandon him.

24

Joliette

Paris
June 2, 1789

DARK CLOUDS ROLLED toward the Seine as we rode home in silence. The carriage wheels pulsed. A whisper throbbed in my mind, *Papa knows that young man.* Heavy raindrops turned into torrents within minutes. When we arrived at the mansion, Papa shut himself in his library.

Jacques took my dripping cloak, but I refused his offer of a tisane. I wound my way up the grand staircase and entered Maman's chamber. White cloths covered the furniture. Her pearl-trimmed pillows sat awaiting her on the bed. A hoop of embroidery and her sewing basket lay on her bedside table. I placed her silver thimble on my finger. "Maman, I miss you so."

I stood in a silence as empty as the hollow in my chest. Her lavender scent surrounded me as I opened her armoire and found my favorite of her shawls, the white one she had embroidered with pale green leaves. I wrapped it around me, remembering her wearing it one summer evening as she and Papa walked hand-in-hand through the vineyards. I never doubted their love.

But if that young man was Papa's son, my parents' marriage had not been the perfect union I thought it was. Soubrier's words burned. *Your mother was perhaps the only wife at Versailles who was faithful.* She had not said the same of Papa.

I left, closed the door, crossed the hall, and stood outside Papa's chamber, listening. Odd that I visited Maman in her room every day, but I never entered Papa's room. I pressed the latch, and it clicked. Slipping into the scent of cloves and leather, I closed the door.

A fire snapped in the grate, and I brought a candle to it. Rain spattered the windows, and pale light cast mottled gray shadows over the room. Atop the mantle stood a portrait of Maman at about my age. She smiled down at me. Her face had glowed when she told me they fell in love at first sight, and this portrait must have been painted about that time.

I turned to the mirror and saw my father's eyes in mine. The young man had deep blue eyes. Papa could have had a child with another woman before he met Maman. But the young man looked to be my age, perhaps a year older. I was born five years after my parents married.

I tied Maman's shawl about me, placed the candle in the holder atop Papa's bedside table, and opened the drawer. A dark green ribbon bound a silver folding frame. I pulled the ribbon. A beautiful woman smiled. Her powdered white hair was interwoven with blue ribbons, and her dark blue eyes held mischief, like the mischief I found in Papa's eyes. I snapped the frame closed. The young man had dark blue eyes but no mischief in them. I retied the ribbon and returned the frame.

If that young man was Papa's son, did Maman know? My mother's adoration of my father was my most vivid memory. If she knew, she forgave his infidelity. Would I forgive my husband? I rubbed my temples. Infidelity. Commonplace, according to Soubrier.

What did truth matter now that Maman was no longer with us? Her kind smile and patient face warmed me, gave me courage. There was nothing left to prevent my father from telling the truth. I thought no less of Papa for the indiscretion, but I did think less of him for not acknowledging the young man—if he was his son. I descended the stairs and knocked on the library door.

Papa opened the door. "Come in."

Larger than other rooms of the mansion, this was the warmest because of the flames roaring in the immense fireplace. I stood before it, rubbing my hands, searching my heart for words I never imagined I would need.

"Joliette."

I turned to face him. "Yes?"

"You are never to leave this house without my knowledge, a chaperone, or your pistolet." His voice was stern. "You must defend yourself at all times."

"My pistolet?" What was he thinking? "To defend myself against what? Little street urchins, like the one today?" I opened my arms. "She was harmless."

"Peasants have rioted all over the countryside. They have set fire to many châteaux. Last month rioters destroyed Réveillon's wallpaper factory, and twenty-five people died, hundreds were wounded. You could be caught in a mob at any time. You could be killed simply for the gown you wear."

I picked up my skirts. "This is an old silk."

"You are of the privileged class, Joliette, and therefore hated by many."

At Versailles, courtiers gossiped about burning châteaux. I swallowed a bitter taste. "I promise."

"Let us not speak of it again." He poured a bottle of wine into a decanter.

I sat on the dark green velvet pouffe, watching flames devour the logs. Was his warning an attempt to keep me from questioning him? If so, it was up to me to uncover whatever he was hiding. I forced myself to inhale. "Who was that young man?"

He ran his tongue over his teeth, contemplating his answer when Jacques entered and presented a note upon a silver tray. Papa accepted it and dismissed him.

I looked up at my father's portrait hanging above the fireplace. His presence was strong, similar to the young man's confidence. "How old were you when you posed for that painting?"

"Seventeen, eighteen, perhaps." He folded the message. "We meet with the shipper at ten tomorrow."

"Bonne." A tremor moved through my chest. "Who *was* that young man who seemed to know you?"

"Whatever do you speak of?" He tucked the message in his waistcoat and studied me, the lines in his forehead deepening.

He knew exactly. I walked to the painting. "Henri. The young man at Saint Séverin. He greeted you and called you, 'Papa,' and he bears a strong resemblance to you at the same age."

He shrugged. "Shadows play tricks. Any tall man could resemble me."

"Yes, he is as tall, and he has your broad shoulders." I stood before him, but he did not look at me. "He also has your nose, Papa. And *that* is unique."

"You think he is my son?" He barked a laugh.

His tone mocked me. I pressed my hands against my bodice. "Did Maman know of him?"

He jerked his head to look at me. Sorrow filled his eyes.

I regretted paining him, but I pushed on. "He is about my age."

"Enough, Joliette. I do not know the beggar."

I winced. How could he call his flesh and blood a *beggar*?

He held out a glass of wine. I clasped my hands before me. He cocked his head. "Joliette, have I ever lied to you?"

My arms trembled. I had never seen such pleading in his eyes. I would regret this. "Not until now, Papa."

His smile faded. The flames flickered. The lines in his face deepened.

I stared, awaiting confirmation, inhaling to calm a clawing in my chest.

He sat, leaned over his knees, and clasped his hands behind his neck.

I knelt before him. "Do you remember how often I asked you and Maman for a brother or sister?"

He closed his eyes.

The image of my grandmother in the vineyard looking at Joseph flashed in my mind. They had held a secret. "Grand-maman knew."

His head dropped so his chin touched the flounce of his lace jabot.

"Did she not?" My voice tightened. "Did Maman know?"

He shook his head. "There were rumors at Versailles, but your mother, being the lady she was, never questioned me."

"All these years you and Maman lectured that I must find an appropriate husband or risk losing the estate to a distant cousin." My throat tightened. "A cousin I have never met. Does he actually exist? Or were you referring to that young man, Henri?" My voice wavered. "I have a brother. Regardless of his legitimacy, he is the rightful heir to the Verzat estate *and* legacy." I stood, wanting to stamp my foot, but knew it would be immature.

Papa's eyes were pinched, red-rimmed.

Heat raced up my back. "Why have you never told me? Have you thought of what would happen to me if you should join Maman?" My voice flared like a torch.

He reached for me, but I backed away.

"If Grandmaman knew, why did she train me?" I gripped my hands as overwhelming helplessness swirled inside me. Our conversation, the look that had passed between Grandmaman and Joseph when I had asked about a brother, her reassurance that if I had a brother, he would rely upon my palate, played in my mind. "She trained me to train him," I whispered. My mind whirring, I sat on a pouffe.

I forced words through my throat, tight from keeping tears from spilling. "The Verzat legacy never rested with me."

Papa grabbed my shoulders and pressed me to him. His chest shuddered with his breath.

I stood rigid. "And it never will." I pressed my hands against him and pushed back.

Fear gripped his face. His hands dropped limply before him.

"I have a brother. And I wish to meet him."

"I am sorry, ma chérie." His eyes were glassy. "Knowing him would endanger your life."

"Endanger? He will save the Verzat legacy! I already know he exists. I want to meet my brother, Papa."

His feet shuffled along the carpet. He opened the door and closed it behind him.

I stood in the now cold room. I would meet my brother with or without my father's assistance. And the Marquise, old enough to remember Court gossip, would help me.

25

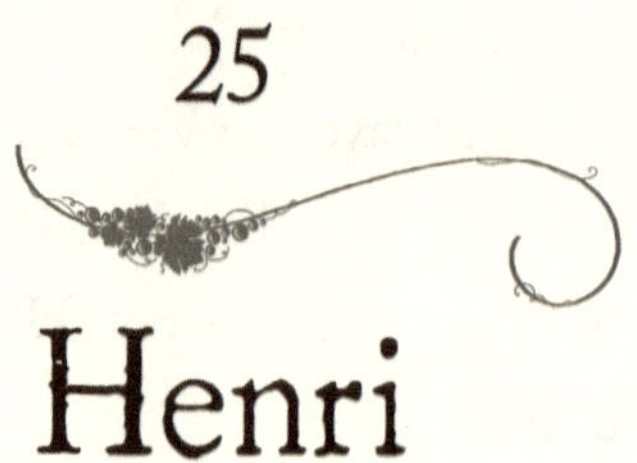

Henri

I RETURNED TO MY lodgings, did not acknowledge Rap, slammed the door, and threw myself on the pallet. Rain pounded against the window. When I rose to draw the curtains, a note slid under my door. The dark green wax seal made me want to throw it in the fire, but I tore it open.

> *My Son,*
>
> *Please meet me at the crossroads this evening. I must explain.*
>
> *Your Papa*

"Ha." I crumpled it, opened the window, and threw it. He'd denied me in daylight. Of course, he would be ashamed to meet me anywhere but the tunnels. He'd never bring the young woman there. I slammed the window shut.

I'd let him know I was leaving and abandon him.

The key Papa had given me lay cold against my chest as I made my way through the tunnels to the crossroads. I yanked it from the leather string around my neck. I'd give it back. After extinguishing my torch, I climbed up on top of a pile of boulders and rested on my haunches. The plinking of water no longer frightened me, nor the squeaks and scratches of rats. I breathed into my hands and rubbed them. Why would he want to meet a beggar? This was the first time he'd requested a visit. The other two were unannounced. This time, I would surprise him. I would make him regret calling me a beggar.

All the workmen had left. I had only thieves to worry about, and they didn't venture this far from an unlocked entrance. The sounds of scuffles and crunching gravel ricocheted among the caverns. His heavy breathing reached me before his light.

With one hand trailing along the rough-hewn walls, his other thrusting the torch above, he waved it about. "Henri?"

The resounding *Henri...Henri...Henri...*filled me with a strange joy, like something I imagined Stéphan, the water carrier, had relished when taunting a younger me at the fountain. I pressed my hand over my mouth to keep from laughing, but I was powerless against the cruelty skulking inside me.

Only a few steps away, he shouted, "Henri, can you hear me?"

I dropped down from the boulder right in front of him. He

yelped. His torch knocked against the wall and spewed embers. He grabbed the hilt of his sword and drew it.

I straightened. "Yes. I can hear you."

The makeup outlining his eyes streaked his powdered and rouged face, making him look like a tragic marionette.

"I could have harmed you." He sheathed the weapon. "A childish game."

I pulled back into the shadows. "Too ashamed of me to meet in public?"

He pressed his chest. "You are my son. I could never be ashamed of you."

"Calling me a *beggar* is a compliment?" I pinched my lips not to spit.

He placed the torch in an iron ring protruding from the wall, then sat on a boulder and patted the rock beside him. "Please, my son. I would like to explain why I denied you."

"You admit it?"

"Yes. Sometimes lying is the noble thing to do." He patted the rock.

My breath left me. Did admitting a lie make it a truth? I leaned back against the wall opposite him and crossed my arms over my chest.

He waited a moment, stood, and walked to me. "I had hoped to tell you when you were older, when you understood the ways between men and women." He pressed his palms together. "It seems that time is now."

I understood long ago, but I didn't want him thinking I was ignoble, so I kept quiet.

He rubbed his hands. "I met your mother one night at the Comédie. You remember the story?"

That day in the theater filled me with joy, but it dissolved like a trail of smoke remembering him calling me a beggar. I kicked at the gravel. "Yes."

He sat on the bolder. "Her voice was bird song, and I heard it in my dreams. I woke each day, giddy with anticipation of seeing her." He gazed into the distance. "When we entered a café, everyone, not only the men, turned to look at her. She graciously accepted their applause and curtsied. But when we sat together, she looked only at me, as if I were the only person in the world." He chuckled. "She was not without a temper. I still have the scar from when she threw her slipper at me." He rubbed his eyebrow.

"Brava for her."

He wiped his forehead. "When she was on stage, she enthralled me. When we were alone, she enchanted me." He looked up. "I fell in love with your maman. It was a feeling I had never known before." He pressed his hand to his heart. "Nor since."

He appeared weak, not like the thunderous man I had come to know. I didn't want to see him so distressed, but something wrapping my chest was coiled tight against him.

"When your mother told me of your impending birth, I was alarmed. She confessed she was secretly married, and I was also married." He looked up, his hand outstretched, waiting for my acknowledgement. I didn't give him a blink.

"But then joy filled me. My wife had not conceived, and I thought, since she was Catholic, we might have the marriage annulled, and I could marry your mother, if her husband also agreed to an annulment. I would then have an heir. I nearly burst with happiness. Nothing gave me greater joy."

I bit the inside of my cheek. "I gave you the greatest joy in your life, and yet you left me with Madame Detré? Called me a beggar!"

He reached for me, but I slid away. "Please, I know you are angry. I would be also. May I explain?"

My jaw was as tight as my fists.

"Your mother's husband had traveled to London months before I met her. He returned, unexpectedly, a month before your birth. He demanded to know whose child she carried. She refused to tell him, but gossips informed him." He dabbed his handkerchief across his brow. "I went to him and proposed we annul our marriages. He looked down his thin nose and shouted, 'You will never see her again.' After throwing me out, he took his dagger," Papa said, drawing a line along his cheek, "and scarred her—so she could never again appear on the stage."

My fists grew hard as rocks, rocks I wanted to pummel into her husband. "The bastard should've been thrown in the Bastille."

Papa gazed far beyond me. "He was too ignorant to know her beauty emanated from within." He wiped his eyes. "He vowed to kill her child the minute you were born."

I jolted, held onto the wall. "Double bastard."

"I challenged the cur to a duel. The coward fled before dawn." Papa rose and began to pace. "I immediately moved your mother to rooms in Faubourg Saint-Antoine, not far from where you lived with Madam Detré. Your maman made me promise two things. First, I would not go after her husband. She had hurt him and felt he had suffered quite enough. And second, I would hide you, protect you from her husband for the rest of my life, or until the coward died."

I stepped close to him. "He lives?"

Papa nodded and walked to the flickering torch. His fingers smudged the soot labeling Saint Séverin.

"The day you were born, I hastened to be with your mother. I was there when she birthed you and suckled you. And when she drew her last breath." He rubbed the soot between his fingertips. "I could not leave her." His voice cracked.

I longed to comfort him, but I stood, my arms useless.

"I held you until Monsieur Rapineau took you to Madame Detré." A tear streaked through the white powder on his cheek. "I am so sorry, my son." His chin trembled.

I breathed against the pounding of my heart. I wanted to go to him, but my feet were stuck. I was afraid to move.

He wiped the soot from his hands. "Your mother's maid assisted in delivering you, and your mother made her swear to keep your birth a secret. The maid told your mother's husband that you died, too. But there was no body, so the bastard took his dagger to the maid. The poor creature admitted that you lived, but she did not know where I took you."

The knave bullied helpless creatures and ran from danger like a frightened mouse. I made myself exhale. "This man's name?"

"Cassard. Comte André de Cassard, a gambler without funds. He has not the courage to threaten me, for he knows I will challenge him to a duel he is too cowardly to fight, but he does not know the promise I made to your maman. I learned he was in a London debtors' prison before your thirteenth birthday, and so I presented myself to you."

"He is still abroad?"

He shook his head. "Returned soon after you and I met. He has been asking about you at the Palais-Royal, I suspect because you will soon be of age. I fear he also may try to harm my daughter."

"Daughter?" My heartbeat galloped.

"She was with me at Saint Séverin."

"That beautiful woman is my sister?"

He smiled.

I had a sister. I wanted to meet her. But she was in danger because of me. I wiped my sweating hands along my breeches. "Why would he harm *her*?"

"He blames me for taking his wife, and he is determined to exact revenge. As you are nearly a man, able to protect yourself, he may do the cowardly thing and go after someone whom he thinks cannot protect herself."

"Does your daughter know she may be in danger?"

"I do not wish to alarm her. She has recently lost her mother, and although Joliette is resilient, she is also vulnerable. I have taught her to shoot—she is an excellent markswoman." His chest expanded with his smile. "And, I have forbidden her to leave the mansion without my knowledge. Of course, she is never without a chaperone."

"Good. What does this Cassard look like?"

"Back then, he was tall, thin as an asparagus spear—I never trust people who do not eat—struts like a *coq*." He dragged his hand across his brow. "He wore powdered wigs, but I think he had light hair." He brought his hand to his ear. "He is no better a fencer than gambler. A Marquis sliced off the top of his ear."

"Distinctive characteristic."

He smiled a sad smile.

"And he still asks about me?"

He nodded. "The only other person who knows your mother's identity is Monsieur Rapineau."

"Is he in danger, too?"

Papa shook his head. "Cassard does not know him."

"Even though no one knows of me besides Monsieur Rapineau, Cassard still asks?"

He nodded. "He plays cards for high stakes at the Palais-Royal. I have it on excellent authority that he inquires about you, regularly. That is why Monsieur Rapineau warned you against going there." He smiled. "We do resemble one another, you know."

I inhaled deeply, my chest expanding as I imagined having my father's build, his noble carriage, his proud posture. How intimidated I'd been when we met. How much I longed to be like him. And now, I was? "Do we?"

He nodded. "My daughter certainly thinks so."

I already liked my sister. I hoped she liked me.

"Until this man dies, or you can protect yourself, I am honor-bound to your mother to keep you hidden and protect you. That is why I could not send you to a school and why Monsieur Rapineau tutored you. That is why you lived in one room with Madam Detré and have her name. The knave would never look for a noble's son in the poorest faubourg in Paris."

"Brilliant plan."

The torch sputtered, flickering light over my father's face. He looked old. There was nothing I could do to change my life or my birthright. I'd spent only five hours with my father in my lifetime. How much more time would there be to spend together?

I inhaled the cold dank air. It sat like a rock in my chest. But now, I had a sister—who I could not meet. "Why did you not ask the King for a lettre de cachet? Have him thrown in the Bastille?"

He stared at the scattered gravel. His broad shoulders hunched forward. "It is my fault he lost his wife. I have caused him great anguish." He looked at me, his eyes so sad. His compassion took my breath. Could I ever be as kind?

"You would have been in danger had I taken you with me to Versailles. Cassard could have paid someone to poison you." He rubbed his jaw. "I may have done the wrong thing for the right reason." He sighed. "Your baptismal certificate at Sainte-Marguerite, the one with Monsieur and Madame Detré's names and Madame's mark, is public. I paid the Bishop at Saint Séverin to sign another baptismal certificate, which was blank. I have written upon it your mother's name and mine, my signature, and what will be your title upon my death: Comte. Monsieur Rapineau holds it for you. You will need it to prove your inheritance."

The silence pressed on me like I was under water. I wanted to hug him and feel his arms around me, but I feared I would cry. I pushed my back against the cold stone.

He brought his hands together, like he was praying. "I have provided for you in my will, Henri, but you are to be recognized as my heir and take my name and title, *only* after I die— for I cannot endanger your life—I promised your mother. It is the best that I can do."

"Does your daughter know of this?"

"She suspects. I admitted knowing you could endanger her. But I have not told her what you now know." He smiled. "She thinks you have my nose."

My hand flew to my face. "Truly?"

He laughed. "She thinks it handsome, although crooked. She wants to meet you."

I rubbed my nose. "You'll have to bring her to the tunnels."

His laugh caromed around the chamber.

"This is why Monsieur Rapineau taught me swordsmanship? Why I learned to ride and fire a pistol?"

His chest expanded. "He says you excel at both these arts and your studies."

"Yes, I do. I'll wear my dagger and carry my pistol, always. I'll defend myself and my sister and my father against this bastard, Cassard."

He removed his hat. "I am sorry I denied you, my son." He bowed to me and rose. "Please, forgive me."

The pressure building in my chest burst. I stumbled into him. He wrapped his arms around me and held me, his heat and strength filling an emptiness I'd carried in me ever since I could remember.

He wrapped his hand around my neck, rubbing his finger along my head. "I am so proud of you…my son." He shuddered.

My body trembled. My chest could have burst from the love that rushed through me. I gulped air to calm myself and breathed in his scent of cloves.

I clung to my father until the torch expired.

26

Joliette

Paris
June 3, 1789

Wearing my dark green silk gown, I examined myself in the mirror as I put on Grandmaman's emerald earrings. My hands trembled as I spoke to her. *You gave me confidence in being a vintner, but we did not speak of distribution. At least Papa understands business and has instructed me. But what if I do not negotiate a fair price? What if I forget the terms we agreed upon?* My eyes must have been playing tricks because I thought she tilted her head, as if to give me courage.

I positioned my bonnet, relieved I did not need to wear the powdered wig of a lady-in-waiting. But would my upswept blonde curls be as elegant? I had not yet schemed a way to convince the shipper to accept my signature. I hoped my ensemble conveyed a commanding presence. I had to discover a weakness in the shipper that I could turn to my advantage when he resisted my will. *Grandmaman, this will require more than charm.*

We had rehearsed my bargaining skills, but would Papa allow me to make a mistake? A brisk wind whipped my skirts about as we left the carriage and crossed the Quai de la Tournelle to a dilapidated narrow building, yet perspiration collected under my bonnet. I fingered Maman's rosary, nestled with my pistolet in my réticule.

Our groomsman opened the building's door to a dark hallway. How much should I dare pay for the shipping, beyond what Papa and I had agreed upon? I stomped my feet before entering, hoping to stop the trembling in my legs. The steps were so narrow my skirts collected dust as we climbed them. Would I feel more confident if the surroundings were more like Versailles?

A squat man with heavy jowls and a chest the circumference of a small wine barrel stood at the landing. His bow to Papa was overdone and his gray waistcoat gapped, exposing a crumb-encrusted jabot. "Comte, how good of you to visit."

Papa nodded. "Monsieur Jaupart. May I introduce my daughter, la Comtesse?"

Keeping my hands close to my bodice, I nodded to the man.

"Enchanté, Comtesse." He made to kiss my hand, but his lips did not graze it. I was relieved his greasy lips did not stain my gloves.

He led us into a small salon lit only by tallow candles sputtering in their brass dishes on a side table. The smell of burning animal fat thickened the stale air.

I swallowed against a tightening in my throat. The squalor

demonstrated his lack of success, yet he had shipped our wines to other European countries.

"Would the lady care to wait in the salon while we conduct business?" He pointed to a rough wooden bench as he released the curtain that swaged across a doorway. A cloud of dust erupted, making me sneeze.

I dabbed my mouchoir. "I will be conducting business. My father will join us."

Jaupart blew out a breath and, with it, spittle landed upon his sleeve.

Papa smiled and opened his arm toward the next room.

I swept past Jaupart.

"Most unusual," he muttered.

At the center of the office sat a large, battered desk. On the wall behind it hung maps of Europe, North Africa, and Caribbean Islands. None of America.

I sat in one of the two armless chairs on the far side of the desk. Papa sat next to me. To my side, a dirty window let in a trickle of light. Stacks of papers towered upon tables, and dark blue ledgers lined an entire wall. The ragged conditions of his establishment made me wonder if we had received premium payment for the wines he had shipped throughout Europe for years. My heart thumped. I could not identify exactly what I did not trust about him. If Grandmaman had trusted him, had she ever met him?

"Now then, you wish to ship wine to America, Comte?" He sat across from Papa.

My corset stays dug into me as I inhaled. "I and my business partner, the Comte, wish to ship wine to America."

Looking at Papa, he drummed his fingers on the desk. "How much wine?"

I gripped my hands and waited until he looked at me. "Fifty barrels."

He nodded, watching Papa. "And where in America?"

My patience frayed like an overused tassel. "Have you shipped wine, brandy, or rum before, Monsieur?"

He swiveled in his chair toward me. "Of course." He looked at Papa. "Verzat wines."

"And to what ports?" I asked.

Still looking to Papa, he replied, "Denmark, Holland, Britain."

Did he think me invisible? "Which ports in America?"

He jerked his face to me. "America? You do not understand the trade routes, Comtesse. Goods are transferred at Saint-Domingue and shipped to ports up and down the American coast from there." His jowls shook.

"Which ones, specifically?" I made my voice sweet as freshly squeezed grape juice.

He tucked his dirty jabot into his waistcoat. "Comte, you must be familiar with our reputation?"

Papa nodded.

I raised my voice. "We wish to know your shipping routes to America."

Jaupart's mouth opened and closed. "Our history—"

"Have you shipped directly to American ports?" I leaned forward.

"Goods are shipped to Saint-Domingue and transferred to ships bound for America." His face reddened. "It is a common practice."

I sighed. This was like pinning a butterfly's wings to the sky.

"You have *not* shipped from Saint-Domingue to New York or arranged such shipments?"

He snapped open a snuffbox, took a pinch, and shoved a wad into his nostril. "We contract another firm that ships from Saint-Domingue." He sniffed loudly.

My insides jangled. "Would you be able to arrange transport from the ship to the merchant in New York and guarantee a date of delivery?"

"As well as anyone can, depending upon the weather, the ships, and the other firm."

I smoothed the fingers of my gloves. He had no experience shipping to America. If we hired him, we would be at the mercy of people and shipping routes he did not know. Grandmaman would say there was too much risk, but would Papa agree?

Jaupart sneezed into a rag and shoved it into his pocket.

France traded many goods with America. There had to be plenty of shippers with those connections. I looked to Papa for some sign. He studied his fingernails. A small clock chimed the hour. I adjusted my earring as I heard Grandmaman's voice: *Rely on your nobility. Intimidate him.* "As this is our first shipment to New York, I am sure you can appreciate its importance."

He huffed and pushed out his chest. "My delivery of Verzat wine has been flawless for more than thirty years. You will not find another with such a fine reputation."

I was certain Grandmaman had never met this man. "That may be, but unless you can guarantee delivery to New York, I am afraid we will not be able to hire your firm." I pressed my palms to my bodice.

He jumped up. "Comte, I have been shipping Verzat wine

since before the Comtesse was born. Surely you must trust me."

The image of Comtesse Soubrier humiliating Pricaud at the Gardens of Versailles came to mind. Perhaps this bourgeois would understand the power of my nobility. I stood to my full height and stared at him. "You are negotiating with me, Monsieur."

"But you are a…woman!"

"Kind of you to notice. When I hire a distributor to ship Verzat wine to America, I will be bringing the European business to that firm as well. I will not be renewing your contract. Good day to you, Monsieur."

"Comte!"

I lifted the hem of my skirts and swept out the door. My feet pounded the stairs. Did he think me daft? I shook the dust from my skirts. My corset was no longer tight. I wanted to growl. I wanted to bite his head off—but not defile myself in the process.

Jaupart sputtered after us all the way to the carriage door. The groom shut it after us.

I blew out a breath. Not only had I not negotiated a contract, but I also lost the one we had. *Grandmaman, forgive me.* Would she be ashamed of me? Sunlight sparkled across the waves of the Seine. She would be proud of me. I felt hopeful. I had not failed. I had gotten rid of an inferior shipper.

"If he wanted our business, he should have had, at the very least, a map of America on his wall, no?"

"Formidable!" Papa's laugh thundered. "'You are a woman— Kind of you to notice!'" He imitated me. "Ha!"

"I released the man from our present contract, and I am formidable?"

"I could not have negotiated better. I might not have demanded proof, as you did! That would have been a grave error."

I felt taller, lighter, older. "I wish to meet another as soon as possible. But where does one find a distributor?"

"I shall arrange it."

Another thing I had to learn. I breathed in the bracing scent of the river. The leafy chestnut trees reminded me of our vineyard. I would distribute Verzat wine around the world, and the Verzat legacy would blossom like the leaves on those trees. If the next shipper did not have a map of America in his office, I would walk out. No point in wasting time.

27

Joliette

Paris
June 4, 1789

T HE NEXT MORNING, my legs did not shake as we ascended the steps to Monsieur Taradeau's offices. Maps of Europe, Africa, the East, the Caribbean, and America lined his office walls. Papa and I exchanged approving smiles.

A tall man, older than I by at least ten years but young to be a successful distributor, strode toward us. He wore a dark blue woolen frock coat and breeches, and a blue-and-white-striped silk waistcoat. Nestled among folds of his pleated jabot sparked a tiny diamond. A dark blue ribbon gathered his chestnut hair at the back of his muscular neck.

"Good day!" His smile emphasized a dimple in his cheek and made tiny lines spring up at the corners of his dark eyes. He opened his arms wide. "I am Pierre Taradeau. Monsieur le

Comte de Verzat?" He bowed formally and deeply to Papa. He then turned to me. "You must be Comtesse de Verzat, lady-in-waiting to our Queen."

Papa would not mention my position. A squirming in my stomach made me wonder how he knew.

He bowed deeply. "Enchanté. It is my honor to make your acquaintance." His lips brushed my fingertips, and my heart beat faster. He continued to hold them. "You probably do not remember, but we met briefly about two years ago when you attended the Queen at the Opera."

I had no such recollection. Had I met him? Or was he using familiarity to bolster his negotiation? The squirming intensified, and I withdrew my hand.

"I am so very sorry for your loss."

I smoothed my bodice. "Merci, Monsieur."

He nodded. "You wish to discuss shipping to America?" His eyes sparkled like the diamond in his jabot.

He asked me, not Papa. Excellent. "Yes."

He escorted us into his office. Had Papa mentioned something about my being his business partner in his message?

At the room's center, four armchairs surrounded a low table. He invited me to sit in one facing a wall covered in maps of shipping routes drawn in vermillion between the Caribbean Islands and the American coast. Ports were labeled in gold ink. A buzz of excitement shot through me as I read *New York*.

Fantastical sea creatures floated amidst the seas' waves. A group of slaves toiled in fields on one of the islands at the bottom. Vermillion lines emanated from Saint-Domingue and reached Charleston, Philadelphia, New York, and Boston. The maps could have been decorative paintings. I would hang similar ones in my office at the château so I could track our shipments.

Taradeau picked up a decanter of wine and poured some in an etched crystal glass. "Would you care for a bit of wine, Comtesse?"

I accepted to be polite and waited until he and Papa each held a glass.

Taradeau toasted. "To the success of the Comtesse de Verzat in exporting Château de Verzat wine around the world."

My mouth dropped open. Papa informed him of our partnership, yet Taradeau respected it. "We wish to ship only to America right now."

"Such a shame the finest wine of France shall leave our country." He sipped again. "Yet, once it is tasted by the Americans, its reputation will no doubt travel around the world." His eyes did not leave mine as he drank.

I grew warm and forced myself to sip. Full bodied, redolent of dark cherries, a hint of earthiness. It was one of our vintages, the seventy-two. Coincidence? Or flattery to gain a negotiation point? Taradeau attempted to impress us. He was handsome and charming and confident. What was his weakness?

He sat next to me, leaned back, and crossed his legs. "Which American ports would you like to ship to, Comtesse?"

I set down the glass. "New York."

"We ship to New York, as well as Charleston, Philadelphia, and Boston—through Saint-Domingue." He pointed at the maps. "We arrange full shipment from both Nantes and Marseille."

His directness made my mouth grow too dry to form words.

"How many barrels, Comtesse?" His eyes shone.

"Fi-fifty."

"Fifty! That is quite an order. Félicitations!"

"Merci." The word exploded from my mouth. Maman would have frowned at such unladylike behavior. Grandmaman would have told me to hold back. I appeared too eager.

"I wonder if we would be safer dividing it." He walked to the map and pointed. "We have two vessels departing, one from Marseille the other from Nantes, within a week of each other. They would arrive at Saint-Domingue about the same time, and from there we could send them on to New York."

"As insurance, do you mean?"

"Exactly." He returned to my side. "In the unlikely event that one ship is lost, your entire lot would not be."

"Is there a surcharge for this insurance?"

"No. As this is your first export, I am certain you wish to establish a superior delivery reputation the quality of Verzat wine deserves. Am I right?"

Papa and I had not discussed this. I was without words. I nodded.

"The price would be the same to you. Once in port, all the wine can be sent on to the merchant in one delivery." He stood straight as a courtier.

Did he not have space for fifty barrels on one ship and was capitalizing on this? If so, he made a persuasive argument. I rubbed my jittery fingers along the velvet upholstery. "The merchant requests the wine be delivered within two months. Is that possible?"

He ran his fingers down a ledger page, then bit his lip. "It is possible, but I do not want to guarantee a date because I cannot predict the weather, winds, or currents—which can sometimes delay a ship by as much as three weeks at this time of year."

Honesty. Still…was his gracious demeanor a cover for actual possibilities he listed, or was he so driven to get the Verzat business he would promise anything? I regarded Papa. He nodded at the question that must have lingered on my face.

I twisted the cords of my réticule. I was caught in a cross-current. Papa and I had not discussed this possibility. I had so much to learn, and I wanted to negotiate—but that included failure as well as success. I had not considered the possibility of failure. Did any Verzat?

I let go my reticule cords and turned to Monsieur Taradeau, whose smile shone bright as the sun. I forced myself to not respond in kind. "What is the proposed cost to Verzat?"

"Should anything happen to either shipment, Verzat will be responsible only for the amount of wine successfully delivered." His eyebrows lifted.

"Yes, I—we—understand this."

"The sum for fifty barrels." He wrote and slid the paper across the table.

I picked it up, but before reading it, I looked to Papa, who sat gazing at the maps. He wanted me to make the decision on my own. Please let it be within the range Papa and I discussed. *One thousand, two hundred and fifty livres.* Exactly the amount we estimated. I pressed my lips. Had Papa outlined the deal in his message to Taradeau? Was Taradeau merely going through the motions of an agreement he already made with Papa to make me think I was a good negotiator? Papa was protective, but I wanted to succeed on my own merits.

I smoothed the paper upon the table. "We were expecting a slightly lower figure. Perhaps one thousand livres?"

Papa leaned in, his eyebrows arched.

Taradeau's smile froze. He leaned back. "If time is not of the essence, Comtesse, I could give a better price."

I examined the maps. It seemed that ships leaving Saint-Domingue stopped at many American ports before reaching New York. "Do the ships you propose take the most direct route?"

"In order to deliver the wine at the earliest date, I must remove previously contracted cargo. Therefore, the discount for later transportation goes to that cargo. Do you wish me to give you a price for a later delivery date?"

My father took his enameled box from his waistcoat, extracted a clove, popped it into his mouth, and chewed.

The réticule's silk cords were damp. Maman would remind me to be still. "This is your best price for that delivery date?"

"Bien sûr, Comtesse."

I stood. "Monsieur Taradeau, we accept your terms. Please have the contract drawn up for my signature."

Taradeau jumped to his feet and bowed deeply. "I will deliver the contract this afternoon, personally, Comtesse."

"Merci, Monsieur." I extended my hand, and he kissed it, but I did not feel it. I pulled my hand away, turned, and walked out.

My feet flew down the steps and out into the sunshine. Bright white clouds piled over the Seine, and I imagined Grandmaman's smile. *Merci. I know you were watching over me.* I wanted to drink champagne with Papa, the Marquise, and Monsieur Pricaud. I wanted to dance.

A stiff breeze caught the sail of an empty barge, hastening it downstream. Had the meeting gone too smoothly? Had Papa previously arranged this deal? The thought dulled my elation.

I gazed again at the sky. Taradeau would accept my signature or lose the contract. If so, we would have to find another shipper. I dared not allow myself to celebrate, yet.

28

Joliette

Paris
June 4, 1789

WHEN WE ARRIVED at the mansion, I followed Papa into the library. The floor to ceiling shelves of books had always comforted me, now they towered, insurmountable as a mountain.

I stood behind the chair Papa had sat in and read to me when I was a child. I ran my fingers back and forth against the velvet's nap—rough, smooth, rough, smooth. "In your message to Taradeau, did you tell him to negotiate only with me?"

Papa pushed out his bottom lip and lifted his palms. "It matters not. You, not I, negotiated the deal, a very fine deal." He removed a lid from a dish on his desk, picked up a clove, and chewed it.

I pulled the heavy drapes aside, letting in a wedge of sunlight. "But if you arranged it, I did not negotiate it at all."

He poured some wine. "I told him you were taking over the business. That is all." The laugh lines about his eyes softened.

The scent of cloves grew overpowering. I dropped the lid over the dish.

"The negotiation is *your* success, not mine." He held out a glass. "Let us drink to that."

I accepted the glass and brought it to his, but I did not drink. I could not celebrate until I was convinced I, and only I, had negotiated the deal. The wine was darker than it should have been. I sipped. Sediment tainted the wine's berry flavors, making the wine slightly ferrous. How had Papa missed it? I would write to Joseph about it. "And if Taradeau does not accept my signature?"

"Then we shall interview other distributors." He smiled.

"That will delay delivery. I have made a commitment." I set down the glass.

Jacques knocked at the door. His usually serene face, pinched. He bowed. "A message from Versailles, Monseigneur."

Papa tore open the paper. "The Dauphin has died." The paper floated to the rug. He rubbed his face and pressed his eyes. "We must return immediately."

Feeling lightheaded, I gripped the chairback. The Dauphin, my little friend, only seven years old, dead? The room pressed in on me. I sat, trying to breathe against the shaking moving through my chest and down my legs. In my mind, I saw him handing his mother a bouquet of wildflowers he had picked at the Queen's Hamlet. He had the sweetest smile and his mother's blue eyes and blonde curls. Tears dropped on my hands.

The thunk of a log breaking in the fireplace made me look up at the flames as they devoured the wood. I would miss the deadline. "Papa, the contract." I whispered.

"It is your duty to attend the Queen. You are a noblesse d'épée." His voice was sharp. "Jacques, tell the groomsman to prepare the carriage and the servants to pack. We leave within the hour."

He expected me to take Maman's place. But I could never be as kind and loving as she was. How could I possibly comfort the Queen? I must try. I wiped my face. "The shipment will be delayed."

Papa placed papers into a leather case, slapped the buckle, and tucked it under his arm. "Come." He beckoned.

I stumbled to his desk and pulled paper from a drawer. "I will write to Taradeau and have him deliver the contract to me at Versailles. Have Jacques call a messenger."

29

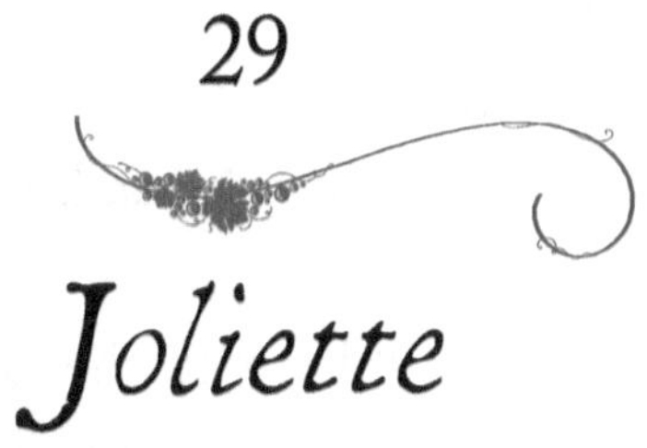

Joliette

Versailles
June 4, 1789

I PULLED THE SHADES in the carriage and prayed Maman's rosary. Papa chewed his cloves. It was dusk when we arrived at Versailles.

Papa opened the door himself and jumped down. "I attend the King. Go to the Queen as soon as you have changed."

Even for death, I should be dressed appropriately. The halls, normally lit by sconces, were dark and empty. The Grande Galerie, too, was empty, its candles guttering. I plucked up a stub and made my way to our apartments. Muffled cries and prayers hung in the passages like cobwebs.

I unlocked our door to find Marie standing on a ladder, lighting the salon's chandelier. A dizzying sweet fragrance permeated the room. A vase of white roses, Maman's favorite flower, which had covered her coffin, sat on the table. I pressed my eyes so hard, sparks swirled.

I wiped my face. "When you are done with the candles, Marie, please remove the flowers."

"Yes, Comtesse."

Before I reached my chamber, a rapid knock fell on our door. Was it Taradeau already?

Jacques bowed. "The Marquise de Bourran and Monsieur Pricaud."

The Marquise should be with the Queen. I patted my mouchoir at my eyes. "Show them into the salon."

The Marquise's black silk rustled as she hurried toward me, her arms outstretched. Pricaud, also dressed in black, remained at the door, standing straight as a pike. Black, required for royal mourning. I had no black gown. I had worn the traditional white to mourn Maman and Grandmaman. Perspiration collected on my face and neck. Damned protocol.

I led the Marquise to the chaise longue and sat next to her.

Her eyes were swollen and red. "The Queen has gone into seclusion."

I gripped her hands. "Without anyone to attend her?"

She dabbed her mouchoir at her eyes. "Before she dismissed me, she told me to tell you how she wished your maman were with her."

My heart curled into itself, opening a fresh ache in my chest.

"The Queen said her only consolation is knowing your maman is in heaven…holding the Dauphin in her loving arms." Her voice trembled.

I lifted an embroidered pillow and caressed Maman's silk

couching stitches, her bullion knots, her feather stitches. I imagined my mother, sitting next to me, comforting me as she had the Queen.

The Marquise shuddered. "The Queen," her voice rose, "is forbidden to attend the funeral ceremonies."

I nearly dropped the pillow. "She cannot see her son laid to rest?"

The Marquise shook her head.

"It is cruel to deprive a mother of her farewell. Why?"

"Court protocol." Her expression soured.

"The Queen could go mad with grief, all for the sake of *protocol*." I gazed up at Maman's portrait. *What would you do? What should I do?* She always smiled at me. Perhaps it was the candlelight, but she appeared aloof, distanced. I had to do something for the Queen.

I wiped my mouchoir across my eyes. "Then we shall be with Louis Joseph—for her—until he is laid to rest."

"I knew you would say that." She half-smiled. "Guillaume will accompany us. Your father is no doubt with the King."

"Forgive me, Comtesse." Jacques stood at the door his hands folded before him. His eyes, too, were red. "A visitor insists upon seeing you and your father...a Monsieur Taradeau."

I could not put off signing the contract. Just one day could delay the wine's arrival by months. I tucked the mouchoir into my sash. "Show him in, please."

"Surely he has not heard the news." Pricaud offered his hand.

I waved him off. "It is necessary."

Taradeau entered and bowed. "Forgive my intrusion at this most inopportune time, Comtesse, but I am honor-bound to deliver that which I have promised." He held a rolled document before him.

"Of course." My voice quivered. I inhaled and willed myself to sound authoritative. "I will sign it now."

He brought the document behind his back. "The Comte's signature is required, also, Comtesse."

Just as I had feared. Papa's voice echoed, *I told him you were taking over the business. That is all.* Tears threatened, and I blinked at them furiously. In my mind, I saw our entire meeting as the farce it was. Nonetheless, I had to uphold my half of the agreement and sign the contract. "We are business partners. Each of our signatures binds us both to the contract." Legs trembling, I walked to him and held out my hand.

"Nonetheless, I must have the Comte's signature as well, Comtesse."

Pricaud stepped toward him. "Did you not hear the lady? The Comtesse was most clear in her instructions."

Taradeau pulled his shoulders back. "I always listen, Monsieur—?"

"I am Guillaume Pricaud. You are dismissed, Monsieur. I will accompany you."

"Merci," I snapped at Pricaud, "but I am fully capable of handling my own affairs." I thrust my hand toward Taradeau. "The contract."

Pricaud bowed his head and stepped back.

Taradeau tapped the document on his hand. "Women's signatures are not binding. Your father is where, Comtesse?"

There it was. Proof Papa orchestrated the deal not me. I should have trusted myself. I would in the future. I straightened my posture. "If my signature is not enough for you, you do not deserve the privilege of shipping the finest wines in all of France. Good day to you, Monsieur."

He bowed, turned, and walked out.

My arms ached as if I had been holding a cask of wine. I had destroyed the only opportunity to ship in time. I was just another ornament at Court. My title put me near the top of a pile of invisible, unimportant, powerless women. I should have agreed to his terms and taken the contract to my father. Papa would never trust me to negotiate. The memory of the young man in the church stopped my breath. Papa's son. He would have the privilege.

I looked to the Marquise, whose eyes bulged.

Pricaud stood stiffly, his hands fisted at his sides. "I apologize, Comtesse. I was out of turn. As a gentleman, I wanted to shield you. I would do anything to protect your honor."

"Merci, Monsieur. I hope that I shall not need your protection."

I looked up at Maman's portrait. Was her serenity because she accepted her fate as a woman? I would make an opportunity to speak to the Marquise in private and learn all she knew about my brother, after the funeral. Right now, I was honor-bound to act as a lady-in-waiting. I rubbed Maman's pearl rosary beads in my hanging pocket. Protocol could be damned. I would not leave the poor boy alone while I had a gown made of black silk.

"Let us go to the Dauphin, now."

30

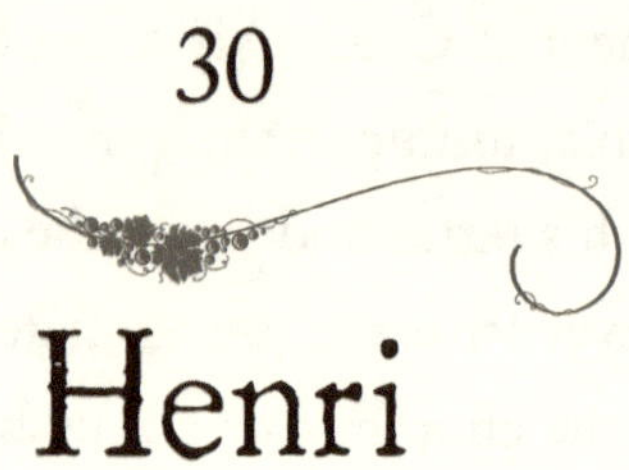

Henri

Paris
June 20, 1789

From the back of the lecture hall, Père Sébastien boomed, "Define les lettres de cachet."

Beyond the open window, pink bloomed on the trellises lining the garden wall. I imagined myself a minister, like my father, counseling the King. The first thing I'd advise is equal voting. A breeze shook the blossoms, and I brought my thoughts back to my next article. Maybe lettre de cachet was the arcane law I'd tackle this week. I tapped the quill.

Pierre Fouquier, in his usual front row seat, was the only student to raise his hand. Père nodded as he ascended the steps through the rows of students.

"Père Sébastien," he said and jumped up, "why do we learn

ancient laws when they will not be sustained? Why are we not discussing Abbé Sieyès's essay?"

Père tilted his head. "Very well, let us discuss an important point of his essay, 'What is the Third Estate,' Monsieur Fouquier?"

Before Pierre could open his mouth, the bull of a man, Comte de LaGarde, stood. I smirked, remembering him and his cohorts attempting to threaten us and ending up standing ankle-deep in horse crap. He shouted, "Of what possible use can a censored pamphlet be?"

"It has not been censored. It was assigned reading, and therefore it is worthy of discussion." Père stomped his walking stick on the floor. "Sit down, Comte. Monsieur Fouquier, continue."

Pierre faced us. "The Abbé states that privilege is a social crime—"

Noble students jumped up from the benches, shouting and thrusting their fists toward the ceiling. Père pounded his stick until everyone sat and grew silent. "Continue, Monsieur Fouquier."

Pierre inhaled. "Privilege leads to wicked injustices—like lettres de cachet." LaGarde leaped up, but Pierre shouted, "Privilege is not useful—but in fact—weakens and harms the nation."

A collective roar rose. LaGarde's face grew purple.

I pressed my lips against a smile. Pierre had great pluck. I scribbled his statement.

Père Sébastien waved his stick as he walked through the rows of protesting students. When he arrived at the front of the hall, he turned and slammed his stick upon the lectern. A clock ticked in the silence. Père clasped his hands behind his back. "What is a nation, Comte de LaGarde?"

I sat up. Père was taking his questions directly from those the Abbé asked in his essay.

"France," LaGarde barked.

Titters erupted. Père extended his arm, quieting them.

I shouted, "It's a country whose people live under laws that're the same for everyone and where people are represented by their peers."

"Excellent, Detré. And are the people of France represented by their peers? Stand please."

I stood. "No. Well, perhaps in the First and Second Estates, but in the Third, there're no representatives of tanners, or blacksmiths, or laundresses, or stevedores, or lace workers, or—"

"Yes, all commoners and peasants, Detré. But what does that mean for the Third Estate?" Père asked.

"They're not represented." I extended my arms, encompassing everyone. "None of the Estates is aware of the majority of the populace's concerns or needs." I'd include that in my article. I sat down.

LaGarde groaned. "Why has the King not sent Sieyès to the Bastille?"

"Why do you think the essay is so popular, Comte?" Père asked.

LaGarde danced his fat fingers over the silver embroidery of his waistcoat. "The *Gazette de France* is Louis's official newspaper. But people are reading the pamphlets, which are more sensational and banned, outside of the Palais-Royal."

That was astute. Perhaps he wasn't as dumb as he looked.

Père stood before him. "And that fact tells you what, Comte?"

"More people are learning to read in order to read the pamphlets."

"People learning to read. Of which estate do they belong?" Père asked.

LaGarde sighed. "The Third."

"Detré, what does that mean for the Third Estate?" Père asked.

I jumped up. "The Third Estate's representatives, mainly lawyers, doctors, and wealthy merchants, are not, and cannot be, aware of the problems of the common people and cannot speak for them. And without these people—the people who do the manual labor—the country couldn't exist." I sat down and scribbled.

LaGarde jiggled his lace neckcloth like he was clearing it of crumbs. "And who shall represent peasants who are uneducated and cannot read?"

"Excellent question, Comte. Thank you for the suggestion. That is the topic of a five-hundred-word essay you will all write and deliver to me in the morning." Père placed his stick before him and rested his hands atop it. "Class dismissed."

The floor shook with stampeding, cussing students heading for the door. I waited for Pierre and grinned. He tried to cover his smile but lost the battle. We clapped each other on the back and headed outdoors. Sunlight brightened the gray stone walls, but the wind was chilly.

Someday I'd thank LaGarde for the title of my next article. I needed to get some quotes from the common man, first. "Palais-Royal?" I asked Pierre.

He nodded.

"Fouquier!" LaGarde leaned against a column. Two noble students flanked him.

"Careful," I whispered.

Pierre marched straight at him. "Yes?"

"The law states you must address me by my title."

"Class dunce?" Pierre tilted his head.

My hands jittered. Pierre was half the brute's size.

LaGarde withdrew his rapier from its jeweled scabbard and slowly brought the blade above his head. I reached under my waistcoat for my pistol. LaGarde brought the rapier forward, resting its tip at Pierre's jabot. Pierre did not blink. I withdrew my pistol.

With one deliberate swipe, LaGarde sliced through Pierre's waistcoat and tunic, which fell away, revealing two breasts bulging over the edges of a lace corset.

My mouth dropped open. A thin line of blood wandered like a silk thread, trickling down Pierre's chest, detouring over a pale swell of flesh. My breeches grew tight. The wound did not seem deep. But—.

With one hand, Pierre calmly clutched the edges of the waistcoat. His—her face was calm.

LaGarde and his companions stood, jaws dropped, eyes bulging. He—she had fooled us all. What a charade. What nerve.

"You are a…" LaGarde blustered.

"Woman?" Pierre smiled. "Have you not seen one before?"

"Women have no right to enter Université." LaGarde's rapier vibrated. "Salope!"

Like I was in a tunnel, darkness fell around everything but the glinting rapier. He'd called her a whore. "If this woman passed the exams to enter, she deserves the right to attend—the same as any man." My thumb pulsed on the pistol's hammer as I brought it up.

"This is a fight for swords, not guns. Where's yours?" LaGarde spat.

"Even peasants know only nobles may wear them." Pierre spat at LaGarde's feet.

LaGarde's face reddened. "Why don't you go back to the squalor of Saint-Antoine, Detré?"

Pierre—whatever her *real* name was—stood straight and tall. "As you've proven, LaGarde, being a noble does not mean one is a gentleman."

"You going to allow a salope to fight your battles, Detré?" The brute moved to the en garde position.

"Regardless of whether or not I'm entitled to carry a sword, I've no need of such encumbrances." I aimed the pistol at his face. "I'm an expert shot. You'll be dead before your body hits the ground."

He pointed his rapier at me. "I shall deliver your lettre de cachet myself."

"And I shall kill you before your next breath. Sheathe your sword."

"LaGarde, do you know my father's name? It may assist you at the Châtelet." Pierre gave him a coy smile. "My father is prosecutor there."

I broke into a sweat. The torture chambers deep in the bowels of that prison were something I never wanted to see.

Pierre crossed his arms over his...her...breasts. "He has been influential, not only in the courts, but also with tortures and executions."

LaGarde's rapier quivered.

Pierre walked to within a foot of him. "Does the name Antoine Quentin Fouquier de Tinville sound familiar?"

Relief at not being in LaGarde's shoes washed over me like warm water. The two noble students standing behind LaGarde ran.

LaGarde's jaw slackened. "If your father knows you attend Université, why do you dress as a man?"

"To protect myself from idiots like you." She could have the dolt arrested, put in a dungeon, tortured, and left to rot, *if* he survived the torture. "I don't think my father will like the new cut of my waistcoat."

"Excuse me, Mademoiselle, I did not know." LaGarde gawped like a landed fish.

"Unless you'd like to receive a lettre de cachet yourself, I suggest you take Monsieur Detré's advice and sheathe your weapon."

He did so and stood at attention, as if the prosecutor stood before him.

"Monsieur Detré, would you kindly walk me to my father's office?"

LaGarde seemed to shrink as he bowed, stepped back, turned and walked away.

I took off my cloak and put it upon her shoulders. "Is the cut deep?"

"But a scratch." She buttoned my cloak and wrapped her

arms around herself. "Thank you…*and* for standing up to that bully."

She looked like Pierre again. But underneath… "It was nothing." I holstered my pistol and followed her.

"It was everything." She stopped and faced me. Her eyes were gray and bright, and I wanted to stare at them. Her cheekbones were high, and her lips full. Black curls escaped the strip of leather tied at the back of her neck. "You were willing to pull the trigger. That could've sent you to the gallows, Detré."

"I was defending the honor of a lady."

"Not according to ancient law. He is a noble." She sighed. "You'd have been hanged—and that my father couldn't prevent."

I swallowed against the dryness in my throat. Would that be the case if my own nobility were exposed? We walked down rue Saint Jacques toward the river. Think of a question to ask her, I told myself. Think. But all I saw was the gentle rise of her breasts.

She tugged my elbow. "I asked, do you actually believe women's rights should be equal to those of men?" Her voice seemed higher. Was it because I now knew she was a woman, and I should hear it that way?

"Yes, I believe so." I'd not meant for my reply to be so loud.

"Because of the Abbé's pamphlet?" She turned onto the street, running along the river below.

"No, because I think men and women are equal."

"Where'd you learn that?" She stopped and looked deeply at me.

"I see intelligent and smart women, like my maman, in Saint-Antoine working themselves to death. If they had the right to be educated, they wouldn't have to work at such hard labor." *If my birth maman had been an equal, she might have had a proper grave.* "What's your real name?"

"I used my brother's name for entry to Université. I am Geneviève."

"Geneviève's a beautiful name. I'm Henri."

She walked toward the bridge. "I'll not return to University."

She was the best thing about it. "Why?"

She looked down at the stevedores traversing the mudflats, unloading a barge of wool. "My father doesn't know I've been attending."

"But how did you gain entry? His signature is required."

She grinned. "I forged it and used my brother's name."

I whistled. I'd never thought of such a thing.

"If he knew, he'd not allow me to leave the house for years. Worse, my stepmother would marry me off."

"Surely you don't think even one man at University would betray you? Not after that display of raw courage." I put my fists on my hips. "Every man there would be terrified to cross your path, or your father's."

"You think so?"

"I assure you. Your secret is safe. Besides, LaGarde's probably headed for the border. You'll never have to subject yourself to his presence again."

"Hmmm." She smiled and headed down rue de Grenelle. "Then I'll have to purchase a new tunic and waistcoat."

I reached for my money pouch.

She put up her hand. "I'll get one second-hand. Wait here for me?"

"Of course."

She ran across the street to a wooden gate, pulled a bell rope, and was admitted. A cross was etched in the stone archway along with, Abbaye de Penthemont. Why had the sisters of a convent let her in, dressed as a man?

I sat on a log and watched a barge navigate the swells. The river was swift and muddy. If I'd sailed for America, I'd never have met my father or Geneviève. I'd never have attended University nor learned English. I'd never have known who I was. I'd be as lost as the debris in the current.

Someone poked my shoulder. I looked up into the face of a young woman with long black lashes surrounding dove-gray eyes. My chest swelled. I jumped up.

She laughed. "You don't recognize me."

"Geneviève?" I stepped back. She wore a gown of yellow and a blue bonnet trimmed with yellow ribbons. Curls of black hair ran down her swanlike neck.

"Of course." She held out my cloak. "I must hurry and find the second-hand seller if I'm to attend classes tomorrow." She looked out over the river, golden sunlight casting a glow around her face, like an angel.

I wished a breeze would carry away her bonnet. "I'll accompany you."

"No need. We both must write our essays for tomorrow. See you then." A breeze swept up the quai, showering tiny chestnut tree blossoms around her as she hurried away.

The blossoms swirled as I envisioned her pale round breasts. A strength charged through me, making me want to run after her, pull her close, kiss her. I laughed. We'd only just met.

I had noticed her small stature, her high voice, her too big hat, but I'd never guessed. Nor had anyone else. Both Geneviève and I were not who we appeared to be. Both of us would be in danger if exposed. She didn't know my secret. Could she keep quiet about my heritage? Or would she see me like every other noble?

My article would offend every student in class, except Geneviève. I'd argue that women deserved an equal education, to the benefit of our society and our country. Writing the article was the first step I'd take in changing the inequitable laws.

31

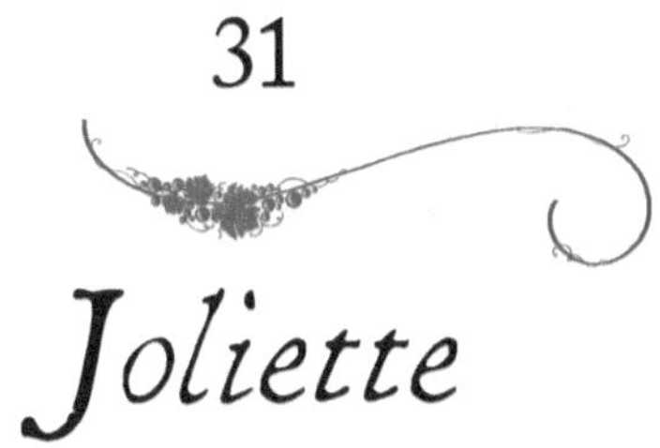

Joliette

Versailles
July 2, 1789

As June bled into the heat of July, cries of sorrow drifted through the hallways of Versailles like tendrils of smoke. Not only did I miss the Dauphin, but also his siblings, due to the Queen's self-imposed solitude for them all.

I wrote to Joseph every day instructing him in searching for signs of pests and rot. I wrote to the wine merchant in New York, apologizing for our delayed shipment. The shame of failure cut deeper with each scratch of the quill, yet Papa considered it a mere setback.

Would my brother consider it such? Whether or not he needed me, I needed him. I needed to know about him, and there was only one person who could tell me. First, I had to convince her I knew of my brother.

I found the Marquise de Bourran, wearing yellow and strumming a lute. Since she had stopped wearing black, she looked younger than her sixty years. "Come, we shall find a cool breeze on the Grand Canal."

The unrelenting sun beat upon the white gravel paths running along the tapis vert, mirroring the heat. Rather than provide shade, my parasol trapped the reflected heat and intensified it, as if I walked in an oven. The carpet of lawn was brown. Fine dust coated the trees, making them more gray than green. Like the Dauphin, rosebuds shriveled before blooming. I would ask the Marquise about the rumors of my brother when we sat in a cooler place, so she was comfortable when she searched her memory.

We sat on a stone bench. Heat shimmered off the still waters of the Latona fountain, distorting the statues of the goddess and her children, the frogs, and toads. I tried to make my voice nonchalant. "Did you know Marquise, that according to the myth, Latona transformed peasants into the slimy creatures because they rioted, refusing to allow her to drink from the pond?"

"Indeed. Even in mythology, peasants revolt." She fanned herself.

Two tall men, wearing the shiny black boots, spotless royal blue frock coats trimmed with crimson collars and cuffs, and pristine white breeches and waistcoats of the Gardes du Corps, walked around the perimeter of the fountain. I squinted from the glint of their brass epaulettes. Instead of continuing down l'Allée royale, they veered toward us, removed their tricornes, and tucked them beneath their arms.

The Gardes bowed deeply and spoke in unison. "Mesdames."

"Guillaume!" Marquise de Bourran stood. "You wear the uniform of the Queen's Gardes?"

In this attire, he was most handsome. My heartbeat quickened as I realized I was not wearing gloves—I would feel his lips against my skin.

"Indeed, Madame la Marquise." The shorter man answered. "I am François Rouph de Varicourt, at your service. Pricaud has joined les Gardes du Corps, and we are two of the privileged twelve bodyguards of Her Majesté."

He turned to me, reached for my hand, and kissed it. "Enchanté, Mademoiselle la Comtesse. My deepest desire is to go to America and, when I arrive, I shall seek out a tavern. I shall drink the wine of Verzat and proclaim it the best in the world." His smile was as bright as the sun.

Quite overwhelmed, I fanned my face. "Merci, Monsieur."

"I shall leave you now." He clapped Pricaud's back and strode away.

As Pricuad looked back to me, sunlight lit up his golden lashes, intensifying his green eyes and making them shine like emeralds.

"What is the meaning...Of. This. Costume?" The Marquise tamped her walking stick upon the ground with each word.

"Not a costume, Marquise. It is my uniform." Pricaud rested his hand upon the pommel of his sword.

I smiled. Soubrier would never dare to embarrass him now.

The Marquise frowned. "But whatever for? You are of noble blood."

A vein pulsed at the side of his neck. He looked past us. A trickle of sweat ran down his cheek and dripped onto his white lapel.

"What is it, Guillaume?" The Marquise tugged at his sleeve.

He swallowed. "You are correct. I am of noble blood, and I am now titled. I am Baron Pricaud."

The title snatched away my breath. "Your father has passed?"

He nodded.

I pressed my hand against the ache in my heart. "I am so deeply sorry."

"As am I." The Marquise gripped his arm. "Was he ill?"

"No. It happened while I was in Paris." His lips quivered, and he swallowed. "I was detained while conducting business on his behalf and departed much later than expected." He stared at the ground. "If only I had not left him. Upon returning, thick black smoke hung over the valley and the château. I raced across fields of blackened stubble, thinking lightning had struck, but the stink!" He tucked his fingers between the buttons of his frock coat.

I pressed my hand to my heart.

"I kept going." His eyes darkened as he looked past us. "As I neared the château, peasants were fleeing, their arms laden with silver, tapestries, chairs."

I wanted to touch him and reached out but remembered protocol and withdrew my hand.

"Forgive me for upsetting you, Mademoiselle."

I shook my head.

"I stopped a farmer blowing a brass hunting horn—in celebration! I demanded my father's whereabouts." He looked at the sky and blinked. "The man pointed to the charred remains of my home. My father's valet stepped forward at that point, telling me my father refused to leave the château, and vassals set fire to it—with him in it."

The Marquise groaned. I held her arm. My own legs grew weak.

"I buried his remains in the family cemetery. I am now with title, but without a château." He dropped his gaze. "I grew up with François. He is my best friend. He urged me to join him in America. I refused. He delayed his trip to help me train for the Queen's Gardes du Corps."

"How very kind of him." I stroked the Marquise's arm. "Have the vassals been imprisoned?"

"They cannot all be hanged. There were so many."

"Why not?" I snapped. "They all participated."

"There are more of them—the entire estate and village—than there are gendarmes." He ran his finger under his collar. "This has been happening all over France. My father should have relinquished his droit du seigneur. The villagers were starving—he should have allowed them to hunt and fish his lands." He looked at me. "As your father urged him."

Papa warned him? When had Papa advised Pricaud? I was glad he did, but sorry it was to no avail. I struggled to inhale the thick, heavy air.

"It is too late for my father." He rested his hand on the pommel of his sword.

I wanted to comfort him, but how? Damned protocol. If I touched him, I would be branded a tart.

The Marquise rested her hand on his arm. "You may live with me in my apartments here at Versailles—they are much too large for me anyway."

"You are most generous." He kissed her hand and replaced his hat. "But I live in the barracks of les Gardes du Corps."

"These are dangerous times," I said.

The Marquise pounded her walking stick. "As you have seen, Guillaume!"

He stepped back, staring at the ground.

She shook out her mouchoir. "Please dampen this in the fountain and bring it back." She looked to me. "Joliette. You are as pale as a church candle. Dip your mouchoir, as well. Go with him."

What sort of chaperone was the Marquise? I gripped my parasol to calm the tingling in my hands.

We walked for a few steps. "It seems we have been exiled into a few moments of privacy." He smiled his lopsided smile. Was he embarrassed?

"I am deeply sorry for your loss." I stopped, which dizzied me, for I was back at the ball, Pricaud rescuing me from my false steps. I tried not to think of that dance, but my heartbeat galloped as it had that night. "Are you certain you want to become a garde?"

"Yes, Comtesse." He offered his arm.

I felt his muscles through the wool of his coat. As if I touched a flame, I wanted to pull back. What was I doing? I kept my fingers barely touching his forearm as we continued to the fountain's rim. I slid my hand away, and he dipped the mouchoir. He pressed the excess water from the delicate fabric so tenderly it resembled a blooming flower. He lifted it. "May I?"

"Yes." My response flew from my mouth in anticipation of his touch. He patted my cheek, so softly I did not want him to stop. I inhaled his scent, like the limes in l'Orangerie.

"I am now titled, but my station is still far beneath yours." The tiny muscles around his mouth quivered.

"My father…he is…democratic…like the Americans."

He dabbed around my temples. The trees and sky spun about, not from the heat but from his nearness.

"He would never consent to my…" He blushed and withdrew the mouchoir.

I guided his fingers back to my cheek.

"Ever since that dance." His eyes sparked. "Do you remember?"

The warmth and excitement of that evening washed over me. I pressed my lips together, yet I smiled.

"Before that night, I dreamed to be accepted at Court. Ever since then, I dream only of loving you." He kissed my fingers.

A tingling charged through me. My breath plunged deep in my body, in places I did not know it could reach.

"Not only because of your beauty, but also because of your kind and intelligent spirit."

I began to pull away, and he dropped my hand.

"I have said too much."

"No, I…" A tremulousness flooded me, as if waves of hot and cold water washed over me at the same time. I could not let this happen. I must discourage him. If Soubrier saw us and told Papa, he would forbid me to see him again.

"I pray you will bestow upon me your friendship. I wish to defend and protect you for as long as I live."

I wanted to cry, to laugh, but my pride burst. "I do not need protection."

"I know." His smile faded. "You wish to continue your family's legacy, in a world where women are not respected as business owners. Indeed, they are rarely allowed into business, under the guise of preserving a lady's virtue. What nonsense." He tilted his head, inviting my affirmation, and I nodded. "It means the world to you, no?"

As if on a runaway horse, I could not slow my heartbeat. I clutched my parasol. He heard one sentence uttered by my father and witnessed my failure with the shipper. Yet he knew my deepest desire. I nodded.

"I can name only two women who run businesses. The Court painter, Vigée Le Brun, and the Queen's dressmaker..."

I smiled. "Rose Bertin is the Queen's couturiere."

He tapped his forehead. "I knew she was named for a flower. They *both* work for the Queen. If not for the patronage of Her Majesté, would they be as successful or have businesses?"

"It would be difficult to stop a force like Madame Bertin."

"Her force is but a trickle compared to your sea of passion for wine, Comtesse." His smile broadened. "Even François knows of the Verzat legacy and wishes to support your efforts. Your success will require defending, for many vintners will be jealous of you and the legacy you are expanding." He released my hand and stood at attention. "Will you call upon me at any time, whether or not you need protection or defending?"

I wanted to fall into his arms, but I stiffened my back. "I would welcome your company at any time, Baron."

He laughed. "I could take flight you have made me so happy."

The Marquise called out to us. Pricaud dipped the mouchoir once again into the fountain and cradled it in his hand as we walked toward her.

I sighed deeply. He knew my secret desire. He listened to me, not only with his ears, but also his mind and heart. A flock of gulls squawked and screeched overhead; they dipped, flew over l' Allée royale, and landed on the Grand Canal. We returned to the Marquise.

"I must take my leave now. I hope that I will see you both soon and often." He bowed deeply, turned, and marched back to the palais.

"What an honorable man. If I were younger..." She twirled her parasol and smiled as if she kept all the secrets of the world. Including mine.

I sat next to her. "Madame la Marquise, I have an intimate question to ask."

She smiled serenely. "Yes?"

"Do you recall any rumors about my father having a son?"

The muscles of her face rippled like a breeze disturbing a pond. She gazed up at the palais, her thumb rubbing her parasol's handle.

Perspiration dripped down my chest. I wanted to speak, but I knew anything I might say would not convince her. She had to decide for herself. The fountain splashed. I closed my eyes, feeling the sensation of Pricaud patting my cheek.

"His mother was a beautiful and famous actress. No man could resist falling in love with her." She turned to me, her eyes moist. "Yet, your father loved your mother with all his heart."

I nodded and gazed at the palais. Heaviness sat in my chest. "Did my mother know?"

She stabbed her parasol's tip into the gravel. "Court vipers ensured she knew." She shook her head. "Why do you ask, my dear?"

I pressed my mouchoir over my face and neck. "I saw him."

"Where?" Her voice rose.

"In Paris."

She grasped my hand. "You must tell no one, Joliette. Speaking of him with anyone could endanger his life."

I placed my hand over hers. "But why?"

"Your father must tell you that, my dear."

I wanted to flee. I stood. The baroque gilded trim around the roof of the palais shimmered like gold lace. I held onto the bench, but the Gardens spun around me, and I sat back down. I did indeed have a brother, and his life was in danger. If only Papa could tell me why…I would insist until he did. I patted my mouchoir over my face and tucked it into my sash. "Let us take a cool refreshment."

32

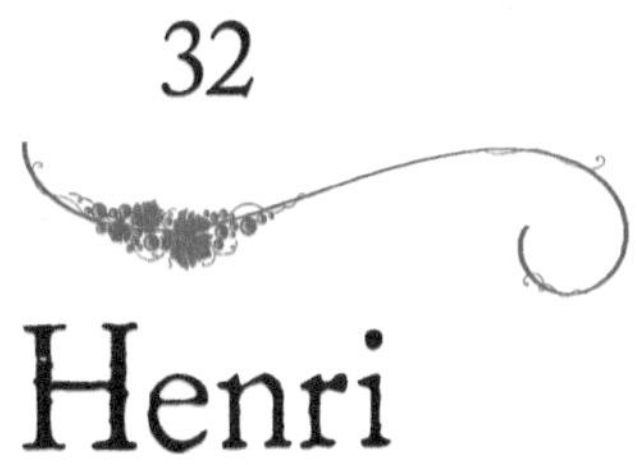

Henri

Paris
July 13, 1789

THE SHARP STINK of smoke swirled across the river from
Faubourg Sainte-Antoine. Not another riot. Bertrand had been
injured at the attack on Réveillon's factory. I wouldn't let him
join this time. I holstered my pistol and sheathed my dagger.

If it was another riot, I'd be there to witness and write about
it. The printer ran out of my article about Réveillon. I'd pay
him to print four times the normal order to print this one. I
rushed through the tunnels to my old neighborhood.

The heat intensified the stench of rotting chamber slops
and animal dung. It was market day and there should've been
crowds, but the streets were empty. I found Bertrand at the

fountain, his eyes red-rimmed, like he'd not slept. "The King dismissed Necker."

"People have hope in the finance minister. Why?" I cupped some water and sipped, frustration pricking my back.

"He was our *only* hope. Necker's the only one sympathetic to the people who're taxed." He splashed water on his head. "The King enforces his authority—and the Third Estate does nothing—declaring themselves the National Assembly—it's gotten us nowhere." Water streaked through the grime on his face. "Have you seen the German and Swiss armies camped on Champs de Mars?"

"They're here to protect the people of Paris."

"You used to be one of us. Now you see with the eyes of a Royalist!"

I pulled at my ear. I wasn't a Royalist, but I wasn't a rioter, either.

He dragged his sleeve across his forehead. "They're not here to protect us. They're here to *control* us. Yesterday, the people battled them with only stones for weapons." He pulled his axe from his belt and shook it. "We've spent the night tearing down the mur des Fermiers généraux and setting the walls afire."

"With the barriers destroyed, people won't have to smuggle, but..."

"We ransacked tax collector offices." He shoved the axe under his belt. "Let 'em try to tax us now."

"They won't be able to, but..."

"Right!"

"Violence won't lead to any good. I don't blame you for the destruction, but…. You're so angry you could get yourself killed."

"My family starves." He raked his fingers through his hair, flicking water. "You've no idea what it's like to see the people you love go hungry."

"I do see the people I love go hungry." I shoved my hand in my pouch and pulled out three écux. "You keep refusing money. Take it now."

"I'm a man, not a beggar."

"Accepting money is not begging. I get the money from my father, who has plenty. I want you to have it." I whispered, "Please."

Slapping his chest, he shouted, "Don't I have the right to work to feed my family?"

"Of course. More than most since you don't join the drunkards at cafés."

"People are forming a citizen militia. They broke the windows of the gun shops and armed themselves. Now, we need ammunition." He sat on the edge of the fountain. "I've no other choice."

"You do have a choice." I swallowed back a bitter taste. "You could be killed. Please don't go."

"At least I'd die trying to feed my family instead of watching them starve."

"If you die, they *will* starve."

"I will be careful, not stupid." He glared at me.

I grabbed his sleeve. "I'll ask my father to get you a job at Versailles."

"I haven't been paid by the King for the work I did there six years ago." His voice sounded like a cry. "For me, it's more honorable to fight."

I let go his tunic.

"Should something happen to me..."

Ash from the fire had landed in the water I'd sipped and sat like grit in my mouth. I spat. How could I get him to see reason?

He wiped his brow. "Continue teaching Simon to read? Look after him?"

My arms hung heavy, limp, useless. Simon would be all alone, like I'd been before Papa arrived, but I'd had Bertrand. "Simon doesn't learn as fast as you." My voice was weak.

He walked away.

"Wait!" I ran after him and shoved the coins at him. "Please feed Simon and Madame Françoise. I don't care if you think me a Royalist."

He put his hand around mine. "It would only delay starvation."

"What'll Simon do without you?" I stomped. "What'll *I* do without you?"

He put his hand on my shoulder. "You're an honorable man, Henri—with or without a papa."

He strode away, his broad shoulders straight, his head held high. I wanted to cry out, Don't go! But Bertrand had to be his own man and make his own way, without my help. I shoved my hand into my pouch and rubbed the bear he'd helped me carve, felt the space where its ear should've been. I'd give the money to Madame Françoise. She'd accept it and not tell him.

I walked to their home and knocked.

Madame Françoise opened her door. "Come in. Have you seen Bertrand?"

I held out the écux. "He told me to give this to you."

"But where is he?"

I shrugged. "I think he's selling his wooden animals at the Palais-Royal."

She pressed the coins to her heart. "It's enough for porridge and many, many soups. Thank you. Would you like some?"

She was like Maman, insisting I eat my bread. "No, merci."

Church bells clanged. The lines around her eyes deepened. "They sound the alarm." She was right. Not another riot. "Please." She grabbed my arm. "Find Bertrand. Bring him home?"

"I'll try. Keep Simon here." I closed the door behind me. I'd search for Bertrand and drag him home if I had to. Shutters and doors slammed. I checked my pistol and dagger. The tocsin pounded in my head along with the need to find Bertrand.

As I headed for the northern bridge, the air grew thick—a low vibration moved through the city like a river current. Fruit and vegetable stalls that had lined the bridge the day before were smoking charred ruins. I kicked a smoldering chunk of roof. The rioters destroyed the little remaining food. Why, when their own families starved? I had to find Bertrand.

33

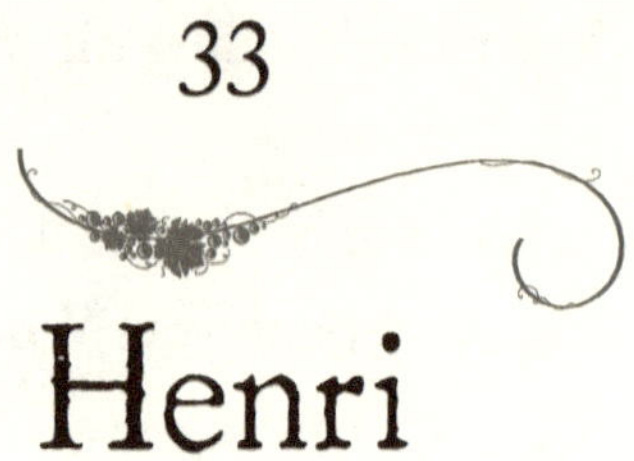

Henri

Paris
July 14, 1789

ALL NIGHT I searched crowds, alleys, and the banks of the Seine until dawn. Hoping Bertrand had gone home, I knocked on his door.

Madame Françoise came out, gripping a rosary. "Did you see him?"

My chest tightened like a fist gripped it. "No."

She hugged herself. "Last night, Bertrand held up his axe and said, 'I go to build a new France.' Then he left. I pray he hasn't joined the militia, but I fear he has."

The tocsin sounded, and we looked toward Sainte-Marguerite.

I fingered the last coins in my pouch. "I'll try to find him.

Don't go out today." My head ached from the alarm, clang-ing without mercy. People had been shouting about guns and ammunition. I raced to the tunnels.

When I emerged at the quai, people swept past me, rushing toward les Invalides. A woman stooped with age waggled a rolling pin my way. "Join us. We get arms."

She could barely lift her rolling pin—how would she wield a weapon? Had starvation caused her insanity? I shoved through sweating men, stinking of wine, and entered the gates of the military hospital.

The veterans, curved and stumped from injuries and age, shouted welcomes. National Guard troops broke the mob apart. But rather than arresting people, the soldiers organized them. Blacksmiths emerged from the hospital cellar pushing a cannon. The guards made a pathway through the crowd for them. A young woman jumped up and straddled the cannon. "To the Bastille for gunpowder!"

Please, God, I prayed, don't give them gunpowder. I ran, calling for Bertrand, through the cellar and hallways and out into the square. A Guardsman thrust a musket equipped with a bayonet at me. I grabbed it, more to keep it from my neigh-bors than to use it myself. "There's no gunpowder," he shouted. At least the bayonet worked.

Another guard waved his arm. "To the Bastille for ammu-nition!"

How did these people—armed with only hatchets and pikes

and impotent muskets—think they'd penetrate a medieval fortress? I joined the crowd out of the gates and across the Pont Marie. No stevedores worked the docks, no flotteurs maneuvered barges, no peddlers shouted their wares. Wiping sweat from my eyes, I searched the faces of hundreds of laborers. Most Parisians had avoided the fracas, and I wished Bertrand was one of them.

The medieval walls loomed. Along the tops of the four turrets, cannons pointed through the embrasures—down at the crowd. The only shelter was the wall of shops surrounding the square, which, if hit by cannon fire, could tumble and crush everyone nearby. I kicked at a loose cobblestone. *Damn, Bertrand. Where are you?*

The massive chains of the first drawbridge had been cut. Still, the portcullis barred the way. The smithy from Saint-Antoine could get through that metal grille, but the guards would shoot him before he finished the job. I stopped, bent over, and heaved for breath. The shouting rose and fell like a river rushing over rocks. Had they already cut the grille?

A laundress with cracked, red hands yanked my sleeve. "People are saying two men are meeting with the governor of the Bastille for gunpowder."

I focused on the prison. Anyone giving gunpowder to this mob would have to be mad. Surely the King's servant would refuse. I'd ask that very question in my article. I shivered in the heat.

The King's guards weren't protecting the Bastille; they had joined the crowd. Violence was madness. But not stopping Bertrand was *my* madness. I collapsed against the wall of a shop.

A white flag hung limply from the top of one of the Bastille towers. Had the governor surrendered? Nausea welled up in me. I steadied myself against the wall and wove among the people, many of whom seemed familiar to me—a basket maker, a baker's boy, a chandler—they all worked in my old faubourg. I stopped a carpenter, whom I'd often seen at Bertrand's workshop. Sweat streaked through the grime on his face. His gray hair was plastered to his head like water had drenched him.

"Monsieur. You know Bertrand Amoulin?"

Heaving for breath, he nodded.

"Have you seen him here?"

He dragged his arm across his forehead. "He's close to the second drawbridge. He'll be one of the first inside once we break through."

And one of the first to be killed. Heat flared in my chest. Images of Simon and Madame Françoise veered wildly in my mind, sending an ache deep inside me. *Bertrand, don't be stupid.*

Gunfire cracked overhead. I dropped back against a wagon. The few people with ammunition fired their muskets in retaliation. Using their hooks, stevedores climbed onto the roof of the surrounding buildings and threw roof tiles at the tower guards. I ran for cover. Bricks crashed to the cobbles. One grazed my shoulder, and I dropped the musket. I snatched it up and joined others cowering in an alley.

A team of men pulled a burning cart of dung near the gate. Smoke billowed over us. A cannon fired. The roar pitched me to my knees. The drawbridge crashed down. People charged over it. My eyes and lungs burned. I lurched to my feet and ran. "Bertrand!"

I pushed through the throng, over the bridge, and grabbed

onto the corner of a stone wall. Guards fired their muskets into the crowd, shattering the cobbles and blasting shards that cut my face and neck. People screamed and smashed into me, knocking me over. I crawled forward, choking through the smoke. Men skirted the fallen, grabbed forsaken muskets, and returned the fire. Guards fell from their stations above and thudded onto the cobbled courtyard.

Blood and offal splattered the stones. I swallowed back vomit. Dying men moaned. I pushed myself up, ran, and stopped. Just beyond the inner gate, a man lay sprawled face down on the cobbles. A large man. Brown hair. A worn sabot on one foot.

Something shattered in me. I pulled my arms in, like I was squeezing myself back together, and stood staring.

Beyond the man's large hand lay an axe. I dropped and crawled to him.

"Bertrand?" I lifted his shoulder and rolled him over and swiped hair from his cheek. He was smiling, peaceful. Thank God. I gently shook him. "Bertrand. Wake up. We'll go home now." He was sleeping so soundly. I placed my palm on his chest. "Bertrand." I pressed down. "Bertrand?" I pushed his chest. It didn't rise or fall. My own chest burned like I'd inhaled fire.

I grabbed his hands and pulled him to sit up. His head lolled. Blood trickled from the back of his head, pooling on the cobbles. I braced his neck, wrapped my arm around him, pulled him to me. *I go to build a new France.* I should've stopped him.

Pressing my face into his shoulder, I longed for his scent of fresh wood shavings but smelled blood and sweat. I should've stopped him.

I gripped his hand, limp and bloodied, and rubbed his shiny scars. His fingers were so strong when he guided the knife as we carved the bear together. Now they curled like he'd never let go of the knife. *One ear's not such a big thing. You'll make him another.* I never had. I should've stopped him.

Someone clasped my shoulder.

"He was one of the first to go." The man squeezed. "An honor."

Darkness dropped. I laid Bertrand down, then jumped to my feet and turned on the man. "It's an honor to die?" I yanked the neck of his tunic. "He leaves a wife and son who'll starve!"

The man brought his arms over his head. Blood dripped from a gash across his forehead. "Please, have mercy."

I released him and spat. "That's what I think of the honor to die." The stench of blood thickened the air. My arms hung, trembling, useless. I should've knocked Bertrand out, dragged him home, tied him up so he couldn't leave his family.

"I'm sorry, Monsieur. Was he your brother?"

I slid down, knelt at Bertrand's side, wiped my neckcloth across his cheek. My brother. I nodded. Bertrand was my brother.

"How can I help you?" The man placed his hand on my back.

I began to shrug him off, but his gesture was like Bertrand's encouraging me when I needed it, before I met my father. "I must...take him home to his wife."

"I know a vinegar seller. He can bring his cart." He left me.

I stood and wiped my face with my sleeve. "Bertrand, you've wasted your life—for what?" I turned and kicked the stone wall. "A dead man cannot build anything." I kicked and kicked and kicked until I couldn't. I coughed against the smoke and spat black. Shouts and gunfire and screams pounded in my head.

A silence, a terrible, deathly quiet sank like a stone inside me. His absence pulled on me like a tide pulls sand from a shore.

I stared at his body. *Look after them?* A squeezing in my throat tightened, choking me.

How was I to look after his family? I didn't know, but I had to be the man Bertrand had been for me, for Simon and Madame Françoise. I'd promised.

A man rolled a one-wheeled cart next to me and bent down. I recognized the vinegar man from my old neighborhood. "Bertrand Amoulin?" He ran his hand over the wood. "He made this cart many years ago."

I held out a coin. He waved it away, removed the cask from the wooden frame, and placed a rag in the bottom where the neck of the cask had rested.

He helped me fit Bertrand in the cart, draping his legs on the long handles. I wrapped my waistcoat into a pillow, cradling his head.

I lifted the handles. The weight pulled my arms taut, sending a pain to lodge between my shoulder blades. Pain was better than helplessness.

"Can I go with you? I know his wife. I'll help you tell her." I nodded. "Please."

Bertrand would've admired how his simple wheelbarrow could carry such a large and heavy load—a fitting bier.

I pushed Bertrand around splayed bodies, through the

hot air, thick with smoke. I breathed in the stench of death, choking on the stupid senseless waste of it all.

Commoners had destroyed a symbol of the monarchy. So what? Even more people would starve. Others would write of the battle; I'd write of the stupid senseless waste. Perhaps in some tiny way my article would help stop the insanity. But nothing would stop the grief. Not Madame Françoise's or Simon's. Nor mine.

34

Joliette

Versailles
July 15, 1789

"PAPA!" I BANGED on his chamber door." We must attend the King and Queen."

Jacques opened it, and I rushed to my father.

He jumped from the bed. "Not Louis-Charles?" Jacques held out Papa's dressing gown.

"No. The Bastille has been taken." I knotted my shawl and brought my candle to another.

"By what army?" Shrugging the gown over his shoulders, he tied a silk rope at his waist.

"Peasants! The Queen sent all her ladies-in-waiting to command everyone to the Grande Galerie. Hurry."

Carrying a torch, Papa led the way down narrow winding servants' passages I had never traveled. The marble chilled my bare feet. When the Queen's maid had entered my chamber, I grabbed only my shawl and dressing gown. As we passed other nobles' apartments whisperings hissed.

We hurried into the Grande Galerie. The wall of mirrors covering the length of the hall from the parquet floor to the vaulted ceiling reflected a moonlight haze that hovered over the Gardens beyond the windowed doors. The chandeliers, empty of candles, glinted like icicles. Papa handed his torch to a servant, who whisked it away. I shivered in the muggy warm night.

The pistolet, so tiny it fit in my palm, sat in my hanging pocket. Should Parisians attack Versailles, I had but one shot. I should have brought powder and bullets. Papa's training ensured I was an excellent shot, but could I kill a person? I longed to release a tight curl caught in my ribbon, but it would be an unladylike gesture, so I stilled.

Courtiers, wearing sleeping attire no less luxurious than their court wardrobe, swarmed into the hall. The courtiers' faces—wan without powder and rouge and shadowed by flickering light—appeared haunted. A specter walked among us, silver nightdress shimmering in the moonlight—Soubrier.

I rubbed my bare foot against my ankle and searched the crowd for Cécile. She and I had opposite duty schedules, I supposed because we were the two newest ladies-in-waiting. I missed her yet kept myself at a distance as I suspected she had betrayed me by telling Soubrier of my plans to send wine to Monsieur Jefferson. Yet, I still missed Cécile.

The doors to the King's antechamber opened. The King and Queen emerged, followed by a dozen servants holding lighted candelabra. The King's sister and two brothers followed. Silence fell. We all bowed and curtsied until the King's gesture released us from our positions.

Rising from my curtsey, my breath caught. Her Majesté was protecting her children, for they were absent. Where were her guards? Where was Baron Pricaud?

The King mumbled. A minister stepped forward and whispered. I leaned around Papa to watch the Queen, her wet cheeks reflecting in the squares of mirrors that broke her face into two misshapen spheres.

"Yesterday," the King's voice faltered, "Parisians attacked the Bastille. They lynched guards and slaughtered Gouverneur de Launay." He shook his head and lifted his hand to his minister.

Had my brother been one? My hands tingled and I rubbed them.

The minister cleared his throat and announced: "A butcher sawed off the Gouverneur's head and paraded it at the end of a pike."

I gripped Papa's arm. No Verzat would be a part of such an attack. Nearby, a lady moaned and sank into her skirts. Overwhelmed by the heat, the hundreds of courtiers, the flickering flames, I wiped perspiration from my neck.

"Peasants seized the prison, *and* all the gunpowder stored there."

The King held up his hand. "Parisians were lost. The exact number?"

"Only about one hundred."

I pressed my heart. My brother? A vein in Papa's neck pulsed.

The King sighed and shook his head. "It is not, *only,* one hundred."

The minister's voice rose. "Crowds continue to riot in Paris."

The King lifted his arms. "There is nothing for me to do but abdicate."

Gasps crashed through the hall. The King had been chosen by God. He could not leave the throne. The hall darkened. Specs of light swirled in my vision. If he abdicated, what would become of the courtiers? Of Papa and me?

"Never..." Princesse Élizabeth raised her voice. "Never in the history of France has a king abdicated. You cannot."

The King's brothers, Princes of the Blood, spat harsh whispers. Louis's shoulders sagged.

The King, chosen by God, was a near deity, yet he was a man, and, despite his royal blood, not a terribly courageous one. His fur-trimmed robe repulsed me.

"We must move closer to the protection of Austria," the Queen cried.

"The King's troops cannot be depended upon to protect the royal family should you leave Versailles," the minister replied.

The Queen's face paled to the white of her robe. More than three thousand people lived at Versailles, but could they defend the palais against thousands of Parisians?

"I must honor the wishes of the National Assembly." The King's voice rasped. "I shall withdraw the foreign troops from Paris." He gripped his hands behind his back and looked at the floor. Defeat rounded his shoulders. "I hope that will calm the Parisians."

His lack of confidence terrified me. I could not take a breath for the tightness gripping my chest. The château and vineyard would be safe. The tenants would protect both. I wished we were there.

The Queen began to weep, and her ladies, shedding their own tears, hurried to comfort her. Unsteady, I moved toward her, but Soubrier intercepted me. "Ladies of your lowly rank are not needed by her Majesté. You are dismissed." She turned and hurried to the Queen.

My mouth dropped open. Was Soubrier telling the truth? Or would she tell the Queen I had abandoned my duties?

We bowed and curtsied until the King and Queen left, followed by the ladies-in-waiting. I started to hurry after them when Papa caught my arm.

He shook his head. "Soubrier is frightened. She will not be kind to you."

I fisted my hands. "She *should* be frightened—of me."

Courtiers and servants rushed from the Grande Galerie.

Papa and I stood in the emptying hall. Candles guttered. The air hung thick with the scents of melted wax, stale perfume, and the sour sweat of fear.

"Come. We shall bear witness to history as it unfolds."

I did not move. "My brother...." Only weeks before, I learned of him, and the Marquise confirmed his existence but did not know of his whereabouts. "I wish to send a message. I wish to know if he is alive. I pray that he is."

Papa nodded.

I wanted to kiss him, but I stopped myself. Papa had not yet agreed to introduce us, and I prayed it was not too late. I hurried after him.

Papa's quick footsteps echoed in the marble halls. When we walked out of the palais, coaches were pulling up beyond the gate. The Gardes Françaises lined the picket fence, a wall of crimson, their swords glinting in the dawn. I spotted Baron

Pricaud, and a tiny thrill bubbled up inside me when he flashed a smile.

Servants carrying sedan chairs, trunks, and boxes hurried after courtiers fleeing across the courtyard. The faint pink light of sunrise lit up terrified faces. I recognized the mole-like eyes, large fleshy lips, and abundant bosom of Soubrier, but she wore a simple gown the color of dirt and a white apron and cap. Why was she not with the Queen? Her maid wore the Comtesse's aubergine-colored gown. The whimpering Vicomte Richepin, also dressed as a maid, followed her. The real maid assisted the fakes into a carriage, climbed in beside them, and shut the door.

A tingling ran down my arms. She prevented me from joining the Queen in order to escape. I ran to the carriage and banged on the door. "You coward! You abandon Her Majesté?"

Soubrier's eyes flashed. She grabbed the curtain and pulled it across the window. The driver snapped a whip, and the horses pulled the carriage out into the red dawn. The tightness in my chest released. She could not be my chaperone from afar.

I turned back and stopped. Duc de Lillers, moving faster than I thought him capable, pulled Cécile by the hand toward a waiting carriage, her father trailing behind.

I called out, "Cécile!" I hurried to her. She broke away from the Duc and ran to me.

We embraced. Her thin frame trembled in my arms. "Where are you going?"

She brought her mouchoir to her mouth. Her eyes were red and swollen. "Papa has accepted the Duc for my husband."

"Duc de Lillers? But he is older than fifty. Is he the duc of whom you spoke?"

She shook her head.

I clasped her shaking hands. "He is your choice?"

"He owns three châteaux." Tears dripped down her cheeks. "I shall be most secure."

"And happy?" I did not mean for my voice to be shrill and regretted it. She was not yet married and already miserable.

I pulled her close, and she sobbed against me. I rubbed her back. "What happened to the man you wanted to marry?"

The Duc rapped his walking stick on the carriage door and called for her.

She pulled back, brought her mouchoir to her eyes, and kissed my cheek. "Be well, Joliette." She inhaled and hiccupped. "I am to be married in Koblenz, where the Duc has an estate. Perhaps you can visit us." Her voice rose, sounding like the call of an anxious bird. She hurried to the carriage.

I stood, my arms reaching. I swallowed against the tightness in my throat, but it did not stop my tears. She had no choice. My arms fell to my sides. Courtiers were fleeing, and that meant fewer eligible bachelors. Cécile knew and feared that. Being married to an old tortoise was better than not being married at all.

At the crack of a whip, the carriage lurched out of the courtyard and swayed, rumbling down the avenue. I could not think her a coward for fleeing, for her future husband had commanded her. Even if she had betrayed me, I was sorry for my childhood friend. At least when she was widowed, she could then marry anyone she wished.

The scene was more like one of the Queen's plays than an actual morning. I swallowed a taste like sour milk and walked back to Papa. "Where are they going?"

The Marquise de Bourran crept up next to us. Her eyes lacked their usual twinkling. Her lilac silk dressing gown shimmered like a dragonfly's wings. I clasped her hand, soft and reassuring, like Maman's.

Papa dragged his hand along his jaw. "Italy, Germany, England."

"Why?" I asked.

"They are afraid." The Marquise tsked. "Things have been so easy for them. They have no idea what is required of a noble. Valliance!"

"Are we leaving?" I looked up at Papa. "We cannot abandon the royal family."

He pushed out his lower lip. "Verzats have been loyal to the monarchy since 1515. Not one of us has abandoned them, nor shall we."

"Nor shall I," said the Marquise.

"Then perhaps you might chaperone me, Marquise?"

"It would be my honor."

As more courtiers fled the gates, I realized fewer of us remained to defend the royal family. My heartbeat thrummed so loudly, I thought Papa and the Marquise could hear it. From the deepest part of my soul, I knew I should be courageous. I was a Verzat. But I longed to be at the château. I reached under my nightcap and untied the ribbon, releasing the taut curl.

Papa took the green silk and tied it around my wrist. "Every time you see or touch this ribbon, remember you are a noblesse d'épée." He looked out past the gilded iron pickets and put his arm about my waist. "Your courage shall keep you strong. It runs in your blood."

I trembled. I had to have courage, whether I felt it or not.

Did the same blood run in my brother's veins? Had Henri attacked the Bastille? Would he attack the palais? If he did, would I shoot my own brother? I wrapped my arms around myself. Never.

Golden light flooded the courtyard and reflected off the gilded gates. The heat dizzied me, and I held onto Papa's arm as I watched more laden carriages flee.

What did this mean for Verzat wines? Further unrest in France would be reason enough to increase exportation. I would send letters to Monsieur Jefferson and the distributor in New York, tempting them with the new vintage. I would worry about a husband later. At least the Duc de Lillers was no longer a threat.

35

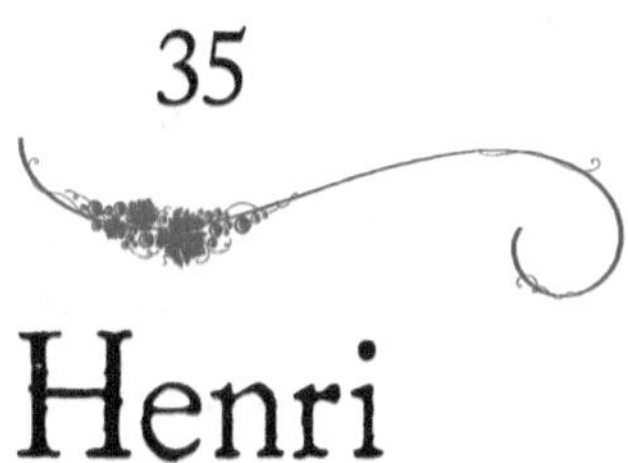

Henri

Paris
July 16, 1789

THE FOOD BASKETS pulled at my arms. The stalls at the market offered little, but I bought all I could find.

When I knocked at Bertrand's rooms, Simon peeked out from around the thin curtain. He usually ran to open the door, but he stared, open mouthed. I smiled. "Open the door." He remained still. I took a piece of barley sugar from my pocket and held it up. His head slid down below the window ledge. Had his grief turned to shock?

I pushed open the door and entered the dark room. A small pile of wood shavings sat at the corner of the fireplace, like Bertrand had been working there. Madame Françoise lay curled on the pallet, her back to me. Simon sat next to her.

I knelt and placed my hand on her arm. "Madame?" She shivered. "I brought food. Can you eat something?"

She pushed herself up. Her face was gray-white like salt. I helped her to stand and walked her to the bench, holding her arm as she lowered herself and sat at the table. I retrieved her shawl and placed it on her shoulders.

She gripped it. "You're so kind, Henri." The sorrow in her eyes made me want to weep.

"Thank you for paying for Bertrand's name to be read at the vainqueurs Mass." Her voice trembled. "And for his burial."

"I am honored to do so." I broke off a piece of bread and handed it to her. "It's dark, but good." Simon sat next to her. "Here's a piece for you, too. Want some cheese?" He shook his head.

"Lafayette is visiting the homes of vainqueurs and their widows in Saint-Antoine, tomorrow. He may visit you, Madame."

"Why?" She stared at something far away. "What does he want?"

"It's rumored widows of vainqueurs will receive a pension. That'd provide for you and Simon."

"If it ever happens." She broke off a piece of bread. "We may starve first."

"Not while I'm here. I promised Bertrand I'd take care of you, and I will." Her shawl slipped, and I replaced it around her shoulders. She patted my hand and let out a moan. Simon laid his head in her lap, his eyes dull and glassy.

I tip-toed out and shut the door behind me.

A heaviness spread to my chest, my arms, my legs. I walked out onto the boulevard and looked up at the cloudless sky.

Already the ramparts were being torn down, and the Bastille no longer cast its shadow over the neighborhood. Bertrand would've loved to see this symbol of the monarchy destroyed. He'd be proud of his efforts. But he'd hate what his revolution was doing to his wife and son. Did a father not have an obligation to fight for the safety of his family instead of his country?

Bertrand wasn't here to show me how to care for them. Papa wasn't around either. I'd have to figure out how to act like a Papa for Simon, even though I was only ten years older. I sloshed through the muck. I'd have to figure out how to be a Papa to myself.

More than a hundred people died at the Bastille. Four times that number would starve because of those deaths. Was my writing not persuasive enough? If I wrote of Simon and Madame Françoise, would it move people to stop the violence? The deputies of the Third Estate weren't reading my articles. If they were, they didn't agree with me. Maybe I should become a deputy and persuade them, and the King, directly. Being a lawyer was of no use. But a deputy could change things. I headed for the tunnels and my quill.

36

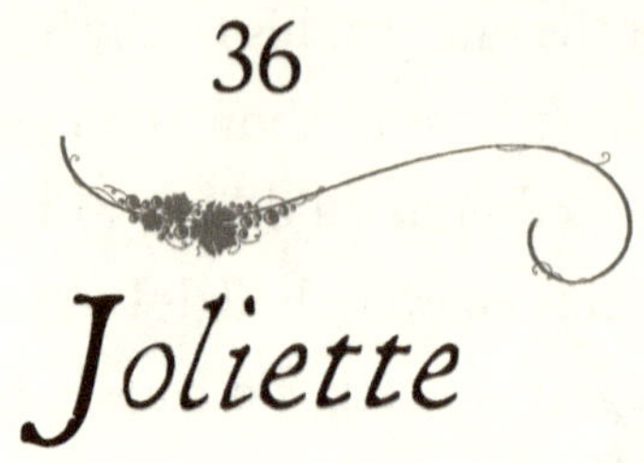

Joliette

Wɪᴛʜ ᴛʜᴇ ᴘᴀᴍᴘʜʟᴇᴛ rolled up in my hand, I marched up the Queen's staircase to her guard room and requested Baron Pricaud.

Guards' jeers of "A Comtesse for Baron Pricaud?" echoed.

The last time I traveled this staircase, Maman accompanied me. She would be more infuriated than I. You were right, Maman. I should never have spoken to a lowly baron. I tapped the rolled sheet and paced the landing.

When Baron Pricaud emerged, embarrassment bloomed on his cheeks. "Comtesse! You are alone?"

"My maid awaits downstairs. I wish a private word with you." I led him around the balustrade and stood next to the windows where we could not be heard by people traveling the steps. "You attended the fête two nights ago?"

He tilted his head. He was too ashamed to admit it. "Well, did you?"

"Certainement. It was my duty."

"Did things actually occur as written?" I slapped the pamphlet on his arm. "And were you a part of it?"

He unrolled it. My hands curled into fists as he read.

He paused, studied the words. "The royal family attended, but—" he jerked his head up, "I can assure you, there was no orgy." He flipped the paper to the title page. "What is this filth?"

My fingers relaxed. "*L'Ami du Peuple*. Continue reading, please." If it were not true, why did the author lie? Who was this Jean-Paul Marat?

He shook his head slowly. "The Queen held up the new Dauphin for everyone to see—such a handsome little prince— he was wearing a tiny uniform of the royal bodyguard. We made toasts to her, we were all so proud of the Queen and her son. That is why an officer said, 'Take the black cockade, that is the fine one!' to compliment the Queen, not to disrespect the tricolor of the people."

Two ladies stood at the opposite end of the hall and giggled behind their fans. I smiled sweetly and glared at them until they descended the steps. "This pamphlet was written to enrage people; Marat is no friend to them." Did my brother read the pamphlets? Did he believe them?

Pricaud's eyebrows hooded his eyes. "Has Her Majesté read this?"

"I do not know. Since Louis Joseph died, she cloisters herself with only her most intimate confidants." I fingered Maman's rosary beads. "My father is at the Assembly, urging the King to sign the *Declaration of the Rights of Man*, but the King demands so many changes, he will infuriate the people."

"Do you think the King should sign them as they are, Comtesse?"

I opened my mouth but had no words. I had not thought of it before. I accepted my father's opinion as my own. Did I agree? I stared at the streaks running through the green marble like grapevines. "My father already runs his estate without honoring the feudal laws that the decrees will abolish, and the tenants do not starve; they thrive and are loyal. The vendanges have never been more plentiful—living proof that what the decrees propose works." I pressed my palms together. "The King requested the cahiers de doléances. But if he does not want to know the people's grievances, why did he make the request? The people expect that he will remedy the complaints if he asked to hear them." I dropped my hands. "But the *Rights of Man* should also apply to women." I lifted my head. "Women should have rights equal to men."

"I agree with you, Comtesse."

Clattering footsteps descending the steps jarred me. "You do?" I squinted as the morning sun streamed around him.

He smiled. "Both your word and signature should command as much respect as any man's." A curl escaped his hat and glinted in the sunlight. The sound of footfalls on the steps faded, and the hall grew silent.

I touched the pearls at my throat. "Merci, Monsieur."

He gave a slight bow. "Please call me Guillaume."

My heartbeat thrummed beneath my fingertips. "Guillaume," I whispered. "Merci."

"I must return to my duties." He bowed and left me.

The marble reflected the sun's heat. I fanned myself. I vowed to marry an appropriate suitor, one of my noble stature or higher. Yet, this man, a lowly baron, believed my rights should be equal to any man's and my signature should count the same.

I ran my fingers along the balustrade. Maman told me that Louis XIV designed this staircase of French marble to show people French marble was superior to Italian.

Like Louis XIV, I would ensure people would find Verzat wine to be the finest in the world. And if Guillaume, a lowly baron, could help me, I would welcome him. Sunshine warmed my back as I descended the steps. In my mind, I saw Grandmaman in the vineyard, smiling, nodding. *You might have to assist me with this, Grandmaman.*

37

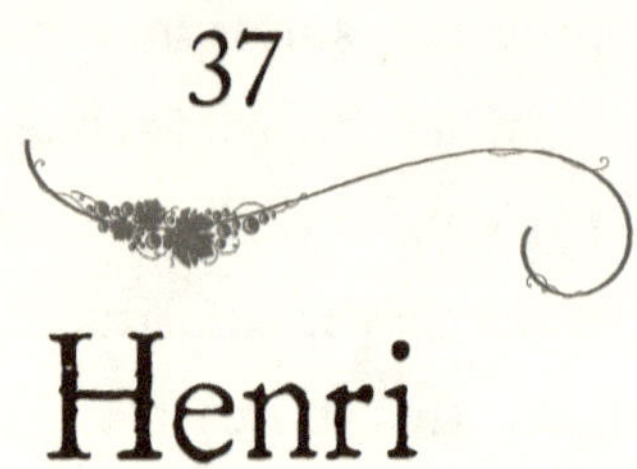

Henri

Paris
October 5, 1789

THE MUFFLED CLANG of the tocsin woke me. Not again. I stumbled to the window and drew back the drapery. Mist hung heavy over the Seine. People scurried in the streets. Shutters and doors slammed. I secured my pistol and slid my dagger into my boot. After filching Rap's hidden purse, I grabbed my hat and cloak and headed for Faubourg Saint-Antoine.

Icy needles of rain pricked my face as I ran down rue de Cotte and rapped furiously at Madame Françoise's window.

Maman's door, next to Madame's, opened a crack, and Maman peered out. "Henri?"

"Where're Madame Françoise and Simon?"

"Simon is here, and Françoise hasn't returned from the market." Simon peeked out from behind her.

I clapped him on the shoulder, and he jerked back. "When did she leave?"

"Hours ago." She squinted in the rain. "Come in and have some soup."

"She went to find my father," Simon shouted.

Simon was acting far younger than his ten years. He was jittery. I feared the shock of Bertrand's death still haunted him. I couldn't leave him without a mother, too. "I'll find her."

I rushed toward the market, following a stream of chattering market women. As I neared the Place de Grève, a steady drumbeat echoed in my chest. I shook my head against images of the crowds at the Bastille.

Determined to avoid the mob, I slogged through puddles and rivulets of debris toward the Hôtel de Ville. At the top of the steps, a young girl, without cloak or shawl, stood banging a drum. Women carrying baskets, milkmaids with pottery jugs strapped to their backs, laundresses balancing bundles on their hips thronged the square, chanting in time with the drumbeat. "We want bread!" they called, reminding me of the chants for gunpowder at les Invalides.

How could there be bread when peasants set wheat fields afire? People swarmed boulangeries, threatening to hang bakers, and bakers closed their shops. I'd close mine, too. Why did people not understand the part they played in their own misery? Did I see this because I was educated, and they weren't? My writings couldn't open their eyes to this not only because they couldn't read, but also because they wanted no blame for the part they played.

From around the corner of the Palais-Royal, a dozen poissardes, fish scales glinting off their aprons and bonnets, pushed a wheeled-cannon. The tallest shouted, "Join us, citizens. We go to the King for bread."

I slipped into an alley. They were going to Versailles? The very warning I'd made at University sent a shiver through me.

The palace was leagues away. By foot, it'd take all day. My wool cloak was already saturated. Most of the women would never make it. Some might die on the way, including Madame Françoise. I had to find her. I wasn't delivering any more corpses. Worse, I couldn't face Simon.

A powerful woman with flowing red hair charged up the steps of the Hôtel de Ville, raised a musket in the air, and cried, "Take arms, citizens!"

I looked twice at another tall figure, too tall and broad-shouldered for a woman, yet the man was dressed as one. His powerful arms clutched a bundle of pikes. What kind of coward dressed as a woman? "We'll bring the King back to Paris," he shouted. Women swarmed around him, grabbing weapons, and joining the makeshift regiment. I wanted to rip his bonnet off, expose him.

His arm shot out, blocking my way with a pike. "Take arms, citizen!"

I reached into my waistcoat and aimed my pistol at his face. "I am armed, Monsieur." A drunken smile spread over his face. He leaned over and guffawed.

I ran to the Palais-Royal, owned by Duc d'Orléans and where pamphlets were *not* illegal. Could the King's cousin be behind this? The drumming and shouting blared, dizzying me. If the people killed Louis and his son and Louis's two brothers—all at Versailles—the Duc d'Orléans was next in line. I leaned against a wall, steadying myself. Papa and my sister lived at Versailles.

As I neared the entrance, the stink of cheap flower-water gagged me. Whores lined either side of the street, shoving pikes at women. Where'd they get all the pikes? Had the Duc hired these whores to force women to join the mob? Had he planned all this to make it look like commoners organized themselves to topple the King?

Two whores cornered a laundress who dropped to her knees, begging to be left alone. One brought the tip of her sword to the woman's throat. I had to help her.

"Ladies!" I aimed the pistol at the sword-wielding woman.

A drop of blood ran down the laundress's throat. Another woman thrust a pike into the pleading woman's hands. The sword-wielding woman grinned. "And after you fire once, Monsieur, what's to stop the rest of us?" The other women pounded the ends of their pikes onto the cobbles.

I wanted to pull the poor woman away, but the madness in the others' eyes warned me they'd force me to march, after ramming a few pikes in me.

"Come with us, Monsieur. Put your pistol to good use." She cackled and rested her sword on her shoulder, shoving the poor laundress ahead.

I holstered my pistol. I was as useless here as I'd been at the Bastille. I climbed an elm tree. Thousands of women clogged the boulevard all the way to the Chaillot city barrier. The Duc d'Orléans was behind this, I was sure of it. And I'd expose him in my next article. But if the mob succeeded in killing the royal family, what would it matter?

I shivered as cold rain trickled down my back. Madame Françoise was soaked and cold and no doubt hungry. I'd never find her in this mess. I jumped down.

My arms, shoulders, and hands ached, but I refused to be helpless. I splashed my way to the stables to hire a horse. I couldn't save her from marching, but I'd find her at Versailles—after I warned my father. This time he might be happy to see me.

38

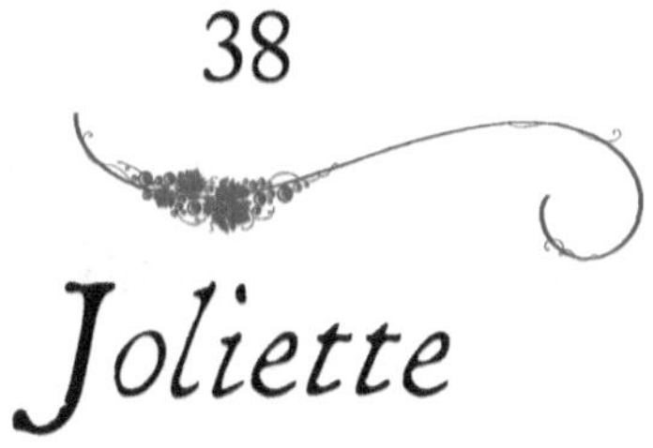

Joliette

Rain pattered on the dried leaves, releasing the first coppery scent of autumn. I longed to be at the cave, checking the crushing, pressing, and fermentation. Joseph sent reports daily, but I needed to discern how the scent of the grape-must would indicate the quality of the harvest. I could do that only by smelling and tasting the juice myself. No matter the argument I made for returning to the château, Papa refused to abandon his post to the King.

Despite the heavy rain, Marquise de Bourran agreed to accompany me to l' Orangerie. Unlike Maman, grafting fascinated her.

"I instructed the vintner to send rootstock and vines to the

Master Gardener, who has grafted them. We will inspect the results." I lifted my skirts and dodged a puddle.

Thunder rolled in the distance. The Marquise gripped my arm, staring beyond me. I turned.

Down l' Allée royale, a horse galloped. The rider's cloak billowed as he passed and shouted, "All of Paris marches with cannon and muskets!"

The pounding of the racing hooves echoed in my chest. If Parisians were on their way, Versailles would be attacked as the Bastille had been. I patted my hanging pocket, ensuring my pistolet was there. The Queen may have secluded herself, but I was honor-bound to defend her.

The Marquise swayed. I gripped her arm. "Come." She staggered as we pushed through the pouring rain back to the palais.

Papa ran across the courtyard, waving us toward him. "Hurry!"

I slid on the wet stone. "They will attack the palais?"

"The Gardes will prevent their entry."

Guillaume was in great danger. I bunched my cloak to my heart. *Please, Grandmaman, protect him.*

Papa held the Marquise's other arm and hurried her along. "We must leave for Paris immediately."

I stopped. "You are Minister to the King."

"I will return after I deliver you both safely to the Paris mansion."

"I have a duty, just as you." The rain stung my face.

The Marquise stopped and shrugged off my father's assistance. "I was born at Versailles. I will not abandon His Majesté."

Papa held her hands. "All your life, you have served the royal family. The Gardes Françaises will protect them, but not you or Joliette. They have sent everyone else dear to them away." He turned to me. "Do you not think that the Queen would want the Marquise and you to be safe, Joliette?"

I saw the Queen's kind blue eyes and felt her soft warm touch the day my mother died. Of course, that is what she would want. I also remembered Guillaume's promise, but his *duty* was as bodyguard to the Queen. Even if we were in danger, Guillaume could not, would not, leave his post to defend us.

My stomach turned the same way it had when Guillaume described the peasants' attack on his château. Did I want to face the same fate, here, at Versailles? I remembered arriving at our château, hearing the honor in Papa's voice as he lifted his sword skyward and told the story of our ancestors. I was a noblesse d'épée. I looked to the Marquise. "It is what Baron Pricaud would want for you, also."

Papa clapped. "Then we leave now."

"No." The Marquise stamped her walking stick. "Versailles is my home."

Papa thrust his arms. "Joliette, please help me to convince her."

I inhaled and pressed my hands in prayer. "Are we not noblesse d'épée? Like the Marquise and you, I shall not abandon my duty to the Queen."

Sadness and regret filled his eyes.

A heaviness settled in me. I wanted to make him happy, but I could not.

"You see, Comte?" The Marquise straightened her back. "It is not only her knowledge of wine that makes her a Verzat, but also her courage."

I had no courage, but I hoped to—I would need it.

The corner of Papa's mouth lifted. "Then I trust you will stay with us in our apartments."

The Marquise patted his arm. "I am happy to chaperone the Comtesse."

"You will be safe there." He raised an eyebrow. "Promise me you will go directly to our apartments and remain until I return."

"Yes, Papa." I reached into my pocket and held the pistolet. I would get more powder and bullets as soon as we returned. I did not believe we would be safe.

I led the Marquise to our apartments and ordered fires to be lighted.

She stood at the window. "Your view of the Gardens is enviable, but all of Paris will be arriving at the opposite side of the palais."

She was right. We would be blind to our demise. "The Ministers' wing faces Avenue de Paris. I have my pistolet."

"And I, mine." Her eyes brightened. "For our own safety, we must know the progress of the marauders. Do you think the Comte will understand our mission?"

"No. His duty is to the King. But our safety is *my* responsibility." I gave Marie instructions to tell my father, should he arrive before we returned, where we had gone. I shoved gunpowder and extra bullets into my hanging pocket, picked up a candelabrum, and led the way.

A cold draft rushed us when I pushed the double doors. Heavy drapes kept out the watery afternoon light, making the salon dark as velvet. I set the candelabrum on the mantel, where once stood Sèvres porcelain figurines and a ticking gold clock in a glass case. Cobwebs were the only adornment, now.

The Marquise lifted her walking stick and drew back the curtains. I coughed as dust clouded the room. Needing air, I opened the glass-paned doors and stepped out onto the balcony. Water dripped from the eaves. Every drop made me shiver. Rain pounded the Ministers' Court, which looked more like a pond.

I searched for Guillaume's face among the Gardes, splashing about and checking the gates that, before this moment, I had never seen closed. Relieved I did not see him, I wondered if guarding the Queen was a safer or more dangerous position. I rubbed my arms. Gardes Suisses followed and took up positions along the pickets.

Mist blurred the main road, stretching into the distance. A flock of geese waddled in the standing water, but as the mist swirled, the white objects became the caps and aprons of women—thousands of women. Steam rose above the column of marchers, moving like a slow, meandering dragon.

I wrapped my arms around myself. "How did these poor women—with shawls as their only warmth and protection—walk all the way to Versailles in this ceaseless downpour? Where are their children?"

The Marquise lifted her chin. "They march for them. A woman will do anything to feed her starving family." She stared out at the arriving throng. "They will kill if necessary. Let us hope they do not."

Would I be able to kill to defend the Queen? Could I kill a woman? My brother? I patted the pistolet in my hanging pocket. I hoped I would not have to use it, but I would be prepared.

39

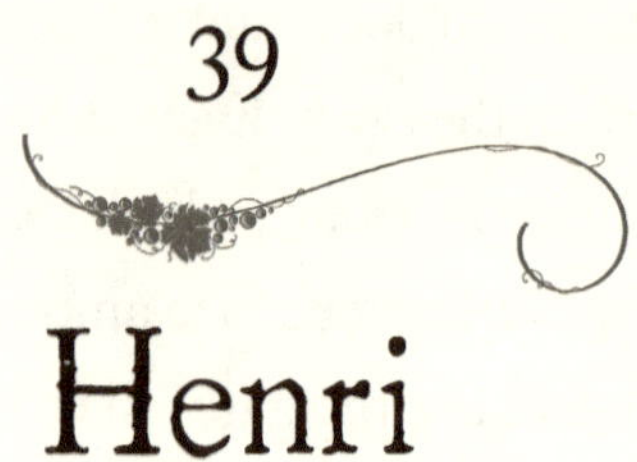

Henri

Versailles
October 5, 1789

FOG SHROUDED THE less-traveled northern route—empty except for a raft of ducks on a growing pool of water. I urged my mount through the torrential downpour, icy water streaming into my tunic. *Bertrand, protect Madame Françoise. Don't let me be too late to warn my father.*

Gray forms appeared in the distance. The mist drifted, and a team of six horses pulling a gilded carriage, tilting and shaking as it rumbled over the rough road, pushed me off it. I squinted to see the crest, but it'd been painted over. Courtiers, not wishing to be recognized, were fleeing.

If Papa and my sister had not left, they were in danger. If the armed women had reached the palace, I might be too late.

I spurred the horse to a gallop, wishing the stables rented faster beasts. If I ever did get to be a noble, I'd buy a stallion.

The rain lessened and rays of sun reached through the clouds. In the distance, the palace's gilded gates, roofline, windows, and balconies all shone. A sheet of water covering the courtyard before the palace shimmered like liquid gold. I halted the horse and let the magnificent splendor shine on me. This was why the country was bankrupt. This was why people were starving. This was the cause of violence.

I looked beyond, searching for a delivery or servants' entrance. The Louvre was large—half the length of the Île de la Cité—but Versailles was huge. I wiped sweat from my neck. Where to begin searching?

Three avenues radiated into town. I rode along Avenue de Paris, lined with shuttered and barred shops. An aristocrat hurried toward me.

"Can you tell me where the National Assembly meets?" I asked.

He dismissed me with a wave.

I spurred the horse into his path and shouted, "Stop!"

He grasped his neckcloth in fright. "What?"

"Where does the Assembly meet?"

He pointed. "La Salle des Menus Plaisirs."

"Thank you." I stabled the horse and approached a National Guardsman, knowing he'd never admit a commoner. When I heard a man ahead of me announce himself, I followed his lead. "Deputy Detré, Faubourg Saint-Antoine."

He didn't glance at me. "You do not wear the black of the Third Estate."

I flicked my hat brim, spraying water on his face. "Have you not noticed the rain, Monsieur? I have ridden in it from Paris. If I were wearing the black, my fine clothes would be soaked and muddied."

"Pardon, Monsieur." He bowed. "Enter."

I stomped past him and shook the tension from my shoulders. A murmur like a swarm of wasps filled the hallway. Inside the double doors, a U-shaped arena opened before me, and loud voices clanged. Rows of columns along either side supported a domed ceiling that amplified the ruckus. The noise confused me. I leaned against a wall, removed my hat, and shook my head to clear it.

At the farthest wall, a raised stage supported an empty throne. A red canopy, looking like a crown trimmed with gilt and white plumes, projected over the stage. Red cloth draped down from it in two arcs, and more cloth covered the far wall. I wanted to spit. The sale of that fabric could buy bread for all of Paris for a month. A thousand men were here. How would I find Papa?

The men sitting under the vaulted ceiling on the left wore the clerical garb of the First Estate. On the right, men wore the luxurious fabrics of the Second Estate. Among them, I looked for Papa's dark green velvet frock coat. I ran my hand through my wet hair. Would he deny me again?

There was little chance of Cassard being here, but any noble could inform him. A draft seeped down the back of my neck, like I was in the tunnels. If Papa did deny me, it would be for my own safety.

Rows of benches stepped down to a central opening. Men sitting beneath the lower ceiling surrounding the main arena wore the drab black of the Third Estate. These men argued amongst themselves, then turned and shouted across the hall.

Noblemen rose and shook their arms in protest. A broad-shouldered, richly dressed man stood—but he didn't have Papa's profile. Stomping shook the floor.

Shouts rang out rapid as gunfire. These men were as loud as the crowd at les Invalides, but a bit more civilized. I steadied myself.

"If the King signed the Decrees, they would not be marching," a black-coated deputy hollered. His wig slipped, and he threw it upon the floor.

"How many?" asked a clergy member.

"Six to seven thousand women march, demanding bread," the black-coated deputy retorted.

"Women?" screeched a clergyman.

A noble dressed in scarlet shouted, "How can the King provide bread?"

Give them his own. Sell the palace gates. Sell your fine clothes. I wanted to spit.

"They have cannons," the black-coated deputy shouted, riling his fellow deputies.

"Muskets, too," yelled another dressed in black.

"Where did fishwives get muskets and cannons?" A noble dressed in gold and white stood in the center of the stage and threw up his hands. I recognized him as the president from the sketches in the pamphlets.

"At Hôtel de Ville," yelled a black-coated deputy.

"Lafayette keeps order in Paris. Where is he?" asked the president.

"Following them." This answer came in unison from the Third Estate.

I jolted. I'd beat Lafayette? Did he travel by mule? A clamminess oozed over me. Or, had he delayed on purpose?

A collective groan rolled through the Assembly.

"We must meet the women and listen to their demands." The black-coated deputy walked down the steps toward the stage.

"Meet poissardes from Saint-Antoine? Who here represents them?" the president asked, scanning the men of the Third Estate.

Grumbling moved through the black-coated men, but no one answered.

I took a deep breath and squared my shoulders. This could be one way of finding my father, and the guard believed me. If these men didn't, they'd throw me out, but Papa would see me. I wiped my hands against my breeches and walked toward the stage. "I am from Faubourg Saint-Antoine."

Silence.

At least what I said was true. I turned slowly, sweating as every man looked at me. The weight of my wet cloak pulled at my shoulders. I wanted to run, but I searched for Papa.

"Your name, Monsieur?" The president motioned me forward.

I walked to the edge of the stage, still scanning the crowd. "Henri Detré."

"And why do you allow these women to march?"

I laughed. "Allow? I do not *control* them."

His eyebrows shot up. "Why not? Is that not your duty, Monsieur?"

I rocked back on my heels, staring at the idiot. I turned and faced the members. "My duty is *not* to control them, but to represent them and their complaints."

More grumbling. Someone wearing dark green dashed behind the curtain. My hopes lifted. If it was Papa, he'd approach me when it was safe.

The president crossed his hands over his protruding stomach. "What are their complaints?"

"I can only say what they want: to feed their children." The memory of Bertrand's lined face propelled my voice. "People starve, gentlemen. Not only in my faubourg. I am amazed these women have the strength to march at all. The poissardes believe the King can feed them. They will not leave without bread and a supply of flour for the bakers of Paris. They look to the King, gentlemen. Why not give them what they need in return for their loyalty?"

Shouts of outrage from the nobles filled the room until the president calmed them.

"Are they dangerous?" the president asked.

Was he joking? "Poissardes filet fish with sharp knives, every day." I faced the crowd. "Their arms are as strong as any blacksmith's. I'd say they are very dangerous."

A roar filled the salon. If Papa were in the room, I'd have heard his laugh by now. That left only the palace. How would I get in there?

"Gentlemen!" I shouted. Quiet fell. "Some of those marching are men—dressed as women—with muskets and cannons. If you wish to avoid Versailles being taken like the Bastille, I recommend you give them bread and flour."

The black-coated men smiled, some laughed. Nobles screamed in rage. The clergy bowed their heads in prayer.

I left the hall, climbed the rear steps, and lurched out the door. I heaved a breath and wiped sweat from my face. Outside, I saw no sign of marching women. I'd no time to wait to see if Madame Françoise was among them. I hurried to the stable.

The mare had been fed and watered, but she ambled along. She would need a good rest before I could rely on her. I had no money to rent another. Along the avenue, guards argued amongst each other, challenging one another's loyalty to the King, sounding like the dark talk the day of the Bastille when some of the King's guards defected. Would they do so again? Sweat, not rain, coursed down my back. They'd defect, and worse, they might allow or encourage the women to enter the palace. I doubted the women could tear it down but aided by the King's own guards…I had to get my father and sister out of Versailles. Madame Françoise was safer amongst the crowd.

40

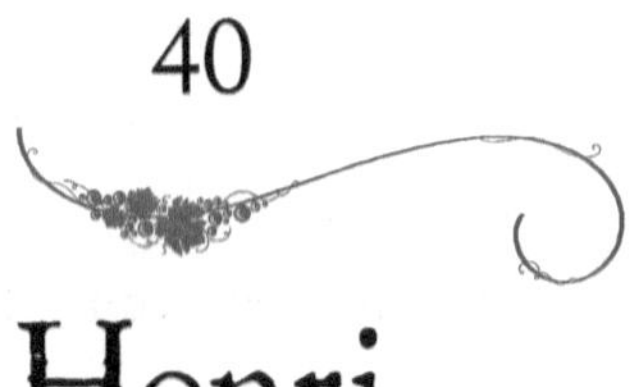

Henri

ACROSS FROM THE palace gates, stood two huge buildings, in the same style as the palace but without the gold: the Grande Écurie du Roi and the Petite Écurie. Surely there was a way from one of these stables to the palace, without going through the gates. I'd use the excuse to stable my horse.

I walked the mare through the gathering crowd across the Place d'Armes. A small group of bedraggled women gathered, but Madame Françoise was not among them. The gates to the Petite Écurie stood open. As I approached, two guards crossed their pikes before me and demanded my name.

I thrust out my chin. "Deputy Henri Detré. I have a meeting with the Comte de Verzat, and I must stable my horse."

"Stalls are in the west section." The guard pointed.

Resisting the urge to thank him, I nodded like an aristocrat would. Stable hands scrambled to harness teams to carriages. Drivers shouted. Groomsmen threw saddles. Walking through the chaos, I searched for my father's crest and a connecting passage to the palace.

I forced myself to exhale slowly as I led the mare to one of the many empty stables. Listening to the panic around me, I removed her saddle and calmed myself by brushing her.

The guards cursed their service to the King and promised to join the marchers. My heartbeat clanged. Carriages loaded with trunks rumbled from the stables.

I found Papa's carriage in a back stall, a brass plaque with the number 117 tacked above it. Was it the same number as Papa's apartments in the palace? I moved two fences and mounded hay in front of the carriage so that it would not be taken by poissardes looking for a drier way back to Paris.

A servant emerged from a hole in the storeroom floor, and I leaped down the steps before the hatch door slammed. At the bottom of the stairway, a metal basket held torches. I grabbed one and caught a flame from a burning torch hanging on the wall.

The tunnel opened to the right and left. I turned to the left, toward the palace. Servants carrying stacks of boxes and trunks passed, paying no attention to me. Some of the *servants* shouted orders at people dressed as *nobles*. Where was their loyalty to the King? I wasn't the only impersonator, but I wasn't a fleeing coward.

When I reached a winding staircase, I snuffed the torch and waited in the shadows until a group of servants hurried down the steps past me, then ran up the stairs into a whitewashed stone vestibule. Trunks and boxes towered against the walls. I ripped through them until I found a waistcoat and breeches of scarlet and a frock coat of black trimmed with red braid. I pulled the servant's clothes over my own and stashed my cape and tricorne behind a trunk.

Entering a marble hall surrounding a grand staircase, I crept up the steps. The corresponding 117 had to be on the first level above the ground floor.

I stole a candle from a sconce and hurried down dark narrow corridors used by servants, finding many apartments padlocked. I saw no sequence to numbering, odds and evens on both sides, some doors without numbers. I crouched and peered at every lock-plate.

A winding passage led me to a grand salon of gilded walls, crystal chandeliers, and marble fireplaces, making me wonder if there was a servants' passage at the other end. As I pondered, running footsteps echoed. I dashed behind a drape, thick with dust.

A group of four guards, swords clattering, ran by. Sweat pooled under my arms. I followed them through a corridor, connecting salon after salon of magnificence. God help the King if the poissardes see this.

41

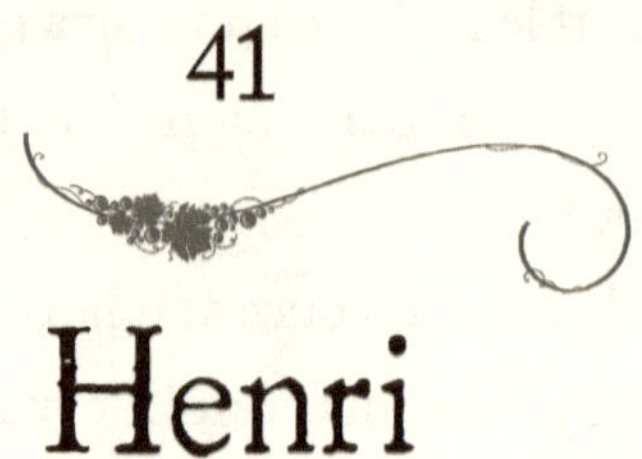

Henri

Versailles
October 6, 1789

A CLOCK CHIMED THREE times. I'd spent most of the night searching. Despite stealing candles, some lock-plates were so worn I had to run my fingers over them to read the numbers. I was about to head toward a hallway that blazed with light, when I ran my thumbnail along the numbers: 117. My shoulders dropped.

Pressing my ear to the door, I heard footsteps. I knocked lightly. The footsteps halted.

"Yes?"

"Deputy Detré has a message for the Comte de Verzat." I whispered.

The door opened. Papa held a pistol aimed at my heart. My arm jerked. The candleflame guttered.

He lowered the gun and embraced me. "My son."

I fell into his strength and warmth.

He pulled away. "How did you get in here?"

I smiled. "Not only Paris has tunnels."

He laughed softly.

"You and Joliette must leave. The National Guards are joining the poissardes, like they did at the Bastille. They will fight the royal bodyguards."

He squinted. "But Louis signed the *August Decrees and the Declaration.*"

"No matter. The Guards are planning to help them attack."

"I was there when Lafayette met with the King and assured him safety. The King has agreed to move to Paris."

I shook my head. "I heard whispers in the stables. I doubt Lafayette knows. The King, you, Joliette—everyone in the palace—is in danger."

He motioned me inside. While he wrote a message, I studied the large room with stripes painted on the walls to look like wallpaper, and the furniture covered in worn green velvet. Were the Verzats not as rich as I'd imagined?

A portrait of a young Joliette, and a woman with the same honey-blonde hair, hung above the fireplace. What would it have been like to grow up here? Despite the glowing hearth, the room felt cold. Maman's steaming laundry pot and fireplace provided more warmth than this room held.

Papa folded the paper, dripped wax, and pressed his seal.

"Deliver it to Lafayette at this address." He handed me the message. "To him and only him, not a servant. Once you have ensured he has read it, leave him. You found my carriage in the stables?"

I nodded.

"Order the groomsmen to prepare it for travel. Wait there for us."

"Yes, Papa."

He unbuckled his sword-belt and held it out to me. "You endangered your life tonight."

My chest swelled, my arm trembled, yet I didn't reach out. "You won't have a sword."

"I have my father's. Wear this and do not take unneeded risks."

I buckled it and ran my hand along the bejeweled scabbard. The gems alone could force me to use it.

"You have a pistol and dagger?"

"Always, Papa."

He pulled me close and wrapped his arms around me. "I am proud of you, my son."

My heart thumped. I clutched him. I needed his strength.

"Henri de Verzat." He patted my back, then released me. "Jacques," he called softly. A male servant appeared at his side. "Show Député Detré the passage to the stable tunnels."

Disappointment sat thick in my throat. I wore my father's sword, yet I was Detré to his servant. I knew Papa loved me, and that was more important than being acknowledged. Still, I was proud to be his son. Cassard be damned.

I hurried after the servant. I had to get my father and sister out of here.

42

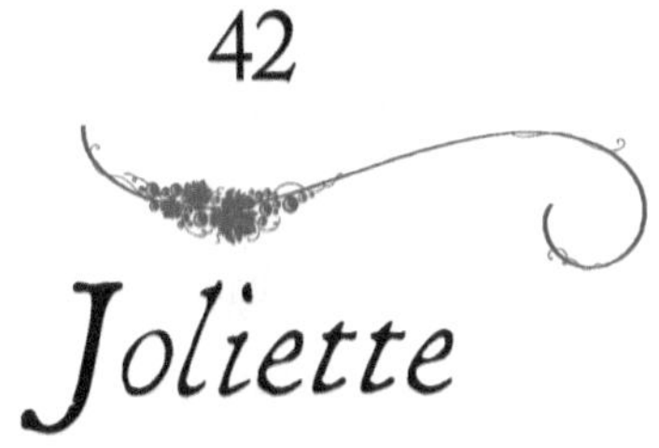

Joliette

Versailles
October 6, 1789

THE HORRID SCREAMS of women jamming the Place d'Armes rang in my mind. I could not sleep. I rose and opened the window to rainwater rushing over the roof tiles. I rubbed my arms, chilled, although I had lain down fully dressed, pistolet loaded and ready. Needing Maman's comfort, I retrieved her shawl.

Running footsteps and the snick of a lock startled me. I tiptoed to the salon. Candles burned. Snoring resonated from the chamber where the Marquise slept.

"Papa?" The ticking clock answered. I knocked at his bedchamber and opened the door. "Papa?" He and Jacques were gone. The clock chimed five times. Papa could not still be at the Assembly. Jacques would not attend him there. Was Papa with the King? If he was, whose footsteps had I heard? Could the women have breached the palais? Their sickening screams blared in my mind. I had to warn the guards and find Papa.

Picking up a candelabrum, I opened the door to a dark hallway. After locking the door behind me and stomping my feet to keep the rats from my path I hurried through corridors to the light spilling from the Grande Galerie. Royal bodyguards stood before the entrance to the King's chambers. François Varicourt hurried to me.

He bowed. "Mademoiselle la Comtesse. How can I be of service?"

"Have you seen my father?"

"No, Comtesse."

"I must speak with Baron Pricaud."

He nodded and whispered, "I leave for America at the end of the month. I will request Verzat wine at every tavern."

I smiled. "Merci. Bon voyage."

He backed away and motioned to Guillaume.

Guillaume appeared before me in an instant. "Comtesse, you are alone?"

"Is my father with the King?"

"I have been here since midnight. No one has entered."

Unease moved through me, making the candelabrum waver. He took it and placed it on a sideboard.

"He left me long ago, but he did not return, and I heard running footsteps outside our apartments. Could someone have broken in?"

"It is doubtful. Perhaps it was a servant?" His eyes avoided mine.

"Jacques would not have left me, but he, too, is gone." I could not fully exhale. "All the corridors are empty."

"Perhaps your father is at la Salle des Menus Plaisirs?"

"I pray not. I watched the mobs this afternoon from the north wing." I pressed my hand to my bodice. "I saw women surround a lieutenant on horseback. Was it a poissarde who screamed so awfully?"

"It was the lieutenant's mount. Five poissardes fell upon the beast with filleting knives." He shook his head. "I had never heard a horse scream."

I drew my shawl close.

"They passed the hunks of flesh, still steaming, and ate it." The muscles in his cheeks flinched.

A chill draft swept through the Galerie, guttering the candle-flames. Melting wax spilled from the bobèches of the chandelier above and splashed upon the parquet next to my slipper. A rumbling moved beneath my feet. The crystals in the chandeliers began tinkling.

Guillaume, his hand on the hilt of his sword, turned in a circle. "You should return to your apartments, Comtesse."

Shouts came from beyond the King's chamber. Guillaume and the other Gardes drew their swords. He pushed me behind him.

A Garde burst through the door. "They've breached the palais. Varicourt, take your men to the Queen's staircase! The King orders: 'Hurt no one!'"

Guillaume shoved me. "Go to your apartments."

I reached for him, but he ran after François and two other Gardes. Stumbling, I turned to follow the King's bodyguards, but they filed into the King's apartments and locked the doors behind them. I was alone, except for the fractured images of myself reflected in the wall of mirrors. Footsteps thundered from both entrances of the Galerie—my only way back. My heartbeat matched their pounding. I pulled out my pistolet and ran after Guillaume.

I followed the Gardes through a warren of passages. The screech of splintering wood ripped through the sound of trampling feet and shouts. I stopped and peeked around the door. Peasant women and two men, armed with swords and axes and knives, charged up the Queen's staircase and swarmed the landing. A woman yelled, "Kill the Austrian bitch!" The others began chanting her command.

François and Guillaume shoved their way through the crowd. A man with the shoulders of an ox hacked at the doors. François pulled at the man, but the attacker turned his axe on him. François backed away. Guillaume drew his sword.

Mon dieu. If they get through those doors and the antechamber, they will reach the Queen's bedchamber. Where were the other guards?

Peasants, men and women, surged up the stairs, wielding blood-stained pikes. The stink of sweat and blood made me gag, but I stepped wide and held my stance.

Guillaume turned and saw me, his eyes wild with alarm. "Go back!"

François shouted, "Save the Queen!" He brandished his sword at a pike-wielding man. Another man with a sword jumped up on the balustrade behind François.

Arms shaking, I pulled back the pistolet's hammer. I took

aim, but the man leaped and brought his sword down, slashing François's neck. Blood sprayed.

I screamed.

François dropped in a heap. Gripping the pistolet, I stumbled out from behind the door. Guillaume shouted, "Go back!"

A bearded man stomped upon François's chest and brought a hatchet up over his head. Guillaume pushed to get to François. "Stop!"

My arms shook so I could not take aim.

The hatchet came down. Blood sprayed as if from a fountain.

Guillaume lunged, slid, and fell on the bloodied marble. "No!"

Bile filled my throat. I fell to my knees. Shoving myself against the wall, I stood up and steadied the pistolet against the door.

Guillaume struggled to stand.

A poissarde grabbed François' sword, raised it, and brought it down, slashing Guillaume's arm.

I fired. She faltered. Blood spread across the woman's bosom. She collapsed. Her bonnet and wig flew. She was a man.

Nausea rushed through me. Mon dieu. I killed him.

On his knees, Guillaume clutched at his arm, crumpled to the floor, and lay on his belly in a spreading pool of blood.

The man with the axe broke through the door to the Queen's antechamber. Peasants pushed and shoved each other through the splintered opening.

I gripped the wall and pushed myself toward Guillaume. Mon dieu, help me.

A man in rags snapped up François's head by his hair and

swung it above, spraying blood over the peasants, the Gardes, me. I dropped to my knees.

A howl, sounding like a wounded animal, filled the hall. Guillaume reached for François and howled again.

I crawled on my stomach to him but stopped as laughing peasants, gripping gowns, shoes, wigs, swarmed out of the antechamber.

I pushed myself against the balustrade. They killed the Queen.

Gardes streamed out of the antechamber, following them, wielding pikes and pushing the peasants from the landing. Peasants jumped over the balustrade and scrambled down the steps. Cheers sounded from the marble hall below. Gardes shouted commands to leave. A musket fired. Their cheers faded. A door slammed.

Quiet, but for the cheers echoing in the courtyard beyond the windows.

Dieu, help me. I dragged myself to Guillaume, my hands slipping in blood. Everything was red. Red. Red.

Guillaume lay on his stomach, his hand outstretched, reaching for François's body. I slid myself next to him and held his arm. Warm blood soaked his sleeve and seeped between my fingers. "Guillaume."

He turned his face to mine. His lips moved, but no sound emerged. He swallowed and closed his eyes. "He…should be…in America."

I pressed my mouchoir to his wound and yelled, "Get a surgeon!"

A Garde rushed to me. "Immediately." He ran toward the Grande Galerie.

"Guillaume, I am here. I will not let you die." The stench of blood and death gagged me, but I kept my hand to his wound and prayed. *Mon dieu. Let him live. Let him live.*

It seemed like hours before a surgeon knelt at my side. "Mademoiselle la Comtesse? Are you hurt?"

"Baron Pricaud—his arm has been slashed."

The surgeon turned Guillaume over. "Remove your hand, Comtesse."

With a thin-bladed knife, he cut Guillaume's sleeve open and poured liquid over the wound. Guillaume gasped for breath. His eyes rolled back.

Do not die. I need you.

The surgeon gave me a clean cloth. "Press this firmly until I ask you to remove it."

"Will he be all right?" My voice, my arm, my body shook violently as I pressed.

"If the wound does not become infected." He threaded a needle. "You may release the cloth now."

I held Guillaume's bloody cloth and prayed all the while the surgeon stitched. Shouts from the crowd in the courtyard rattled the windowpanes.

Guillaume's eyelids fluttered. He struggled to speak. "Why...not return?"

"I had no other escape."

He closed his eyes as a smile came to him. "You are safe, Comtesse."

"I will not leave you." I stroked his cheek.

He caressed my fingers. "I will never leave you, Comtesse."

The surgeon tied a cloth around Guillaume's arm. "You

must rest for at least a month." He turned to a Garde. "Assist the Baron please."

I looked up at the Garde. "We must take him to the Verzat apartments."

He nodded and called for another Garde. I followed them as they carried Guillaume. Waves of cheers from people crowded in the courtyard rang out as we passed windows.

When we arrived at the apartments, the bolt slid open when I turned the key in the lock. "It is me, Joliette."

The door screeched, and Jacques stood pale and trembling. I wanted to hug him but stood still as the room spun around me. He stopped midbow and reached out to help Guillaume. Grasping onto furniture, I hurried into the salon.

The Marquise's hands flew to her face. "Mère de dieu!" She rushed to me. "You are hurt!" She pulled me to her.

"No. Guillaume was injured, but a surgeon has tended to him." I pulled back to look at her. "Where is Papa?"

Jacques and the Gardes placed Guillaume on the chaise longue. The Marquise pressed the back of her hand against his forehead. "You lie still. Joliette will tell me everything." She tucked her shawl around him.

"Where is my father?" I knelt and held Guillaume's hand.

"He went looking for you." Her lips trembled. "He is frantic."

The door banged open. "Joliette!" Papa wielded his father's sword.

"I am here." I stood.

He dropped the sword and ran to me. "Mon dieu!"

"I am not hurt!" I collapsed into his arms.

He heaved a ragged breath. "Your Maman would never

forgive me if anything happened to you." He stroked my hair, kissed my head, as if I were a child.

"I am all right, Papa." I surrendered into him.

He stiffened. "Why did you leave…" His voice was hurt, but his anger broke. "I commanded you to remain here."

"To find you. Why did you leave *me*, Papa?"

"Monsieur le Comte," Guillaume struggled to sit up. "She saved my life."

Papa pulled away, looked at Guillaume and back at me.

"I killed…" I grasped his sleeve and slid to the floor. "I have killed a man."

He knelt beside me. I clutched his arms. "We must protect the royal family." The room spun.

"That is Lafayette's job, now. We leave for Paris."

43

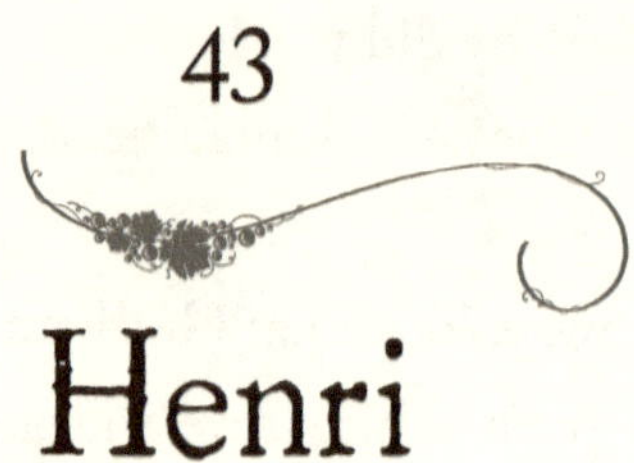

Henri

Versailles
October 6, 1789

I COMMANDED THE SERVANT to wake Lafayette, who lost no time thanking me. He mounted his horse and charged toward the palace. I dug my heels into the mare's sides and followed.

The crowd had increased tenfold from the day before. They clogged the Place d'Armes, all three avenues, and the entrance to the stables. The reins grew slippery in my sweaty hands as I kept close to Lafayette's mount.

Men and women thrust halberds, scythes, and muskets above them, chanting, "To Paris! To Paris! To Paris!" Different words. But the same sickening feeling I'd had at the Bastille rose in me. Was Madame Françoise among them? I pushed away the memory of carrying Bertrand's body to her.

National Guardsmen pushed the crowd back to allow Lafayette through. He did not seem the same hero in France that he was in America.

I turned my mount toward the stables, but a porter in a blue tunic yanked at the bridle. Two other men grabbed at the saddle. The mare faltered.

I reached for my pistol, but I had only one shot. Instead, I grabbed the hilt of Papa's sword. My arm shook with its weight as I brought it aloft. "Away!" The horse jittered and whinnied. I tightened the reins, desperate to control her.

The porter put up his hands. "The sword of a noble. We'll hang!" The other men dropped to the ground.

I urged the horse through the people, who now stared and backed away from my raised weapon. In the stables, my arm vibrated as I sheathed the sword. The gems embedded in the sheath instilled more fear than my pistol. No man should possess the power of nobility. Still, I was glad I had it for that moment.

After asking a groom to ready Papa's carriage, I smeared boot polish over the Verzat crest and gildings of the carriage, hoping it looked like mud.

"Député Detré!"

I jumped at my father's voice. I was beginning to own the title.

A wounded Garde slumped between a servant and Papa. I swallowed cold air. The people *had* breached the palace, as I had warned the Estates General.

The young woman I'd seen in the church, my sister, followed. Supporting the arm of an old woman, my sister hurried, her cape furling open and revealing a blood-stained gown.

She was hurt. I wanted to run to her, pick her up, and carry her to the carriage, but I stopped myself. My actions could embarrass Papa. I threw the cloth into the straw. I'd play the deputy.

I hurried to her. "Are you hurt, Mademoiselle?"

She had Papa's brown eyes. "No." Her smile was rigid, her face pale. She placed her hand on my arm. "Merci."

I patted her hand and smiled. Papa said she suspected, but had he confirmed I was her brother? I wanted to tell her, see her reactions, know her.

Two groomsmen opened the carriage door and bowed to Papa. The wounded Royal Garde grunted as the groomsmen pulled him into the carriage. The old woman climbed in next to him.

Papa offered his hand to my sister, but she did not take it. She closed the carriage door and stood before it, looking from him to me. "Député Detré is my brother, Henri, is he not, Papa?" she whispered.

My chest expanded like my heart had bloomed. She acknowledged me.

Papa's jaw tightened.

"Is it not time to introduce us?" Her tone was sharp.

I pressed my lips together in case Papa saw my smile. No one would stop her. Anyone would be a fool to try.

She curtsied. "I am Joliette, your sister." She extended her hand.

I wanted to jump and clap, but she'd think me an idiot. I

stuttered and found my voice. "Enchanté." I bowed and kissed her hand. Blood encrusted her fingernails. She had more than witnessed the battle. I rose.

"No one else can know this." Papa looked about the empty stable. "It is not safe."

"Safe?" Her eyes were red-rimmed and swollen, but they sparked. "There can be no more danger than that which we have already lived through. I have seen peasants shatter the doors to the Queen's inner sanctum. I have witnessed a man chopping off the head of another." Tears rolled down her face, but she did not wipe them. She pressed her fist to her heart. "And, I have killed a man."

I stepped back, struck by her bravery. What had she lived through this night? I could only hope to have her courage.

"What more danger can there be, if you rightfully acknowledge your son, who risked his life for ours by coming here to warn us, Papa?"

I felt prouder of my sister's acknowledgment of me than if Papa had. My shoulders tensed. Yet she did not know of Cassard.

Papa's jaw muscles twitched. "I will explain when I get to Paris. I must remain here to assist the King's departure."

"Did they kill the Queen?" She grasped the front of her cloak.

"She is safe." Papa opened the carriage door.

"Merci dieu." Her cheeks trembled, but she held her tears. She got in the carriage and drew the curtain.

I looked to my father. "She makes me proud to be a Verzat... should you ever acknowledge me."

"Protect her as I would." His mouth hardened to a grim line.

My chest tightened. I'd taken advantage of my sister's words and hurt my father. There was no time to right my wrong now. I nodded and mounted my horse. "Take the northern route," I shouted to the driver.

I had to expose the Duc d' Orleans and the part he'd played in this debacle. I needed to figure out a way to use my articles to be elected. I liked the sound of Deputy Detré. Even with the threat of Cassard, it would be a far safer name than Verzat.

44

Joliette

Paris
October 6, 1789

W ITH EVERY JOLT of the carriage, the bloodstain on Guillaume's waistcoat spread. I laid my hand on his. "We will arrive soon, and you will be able to sleep."

"You are most kind..." He struggled to smile.

Grandmaman, Maman, protect him. I need him. I prayed Maman's rosary.

The northern route was longer and, every moment, I expected armed peasants to attack. I had neither time to reload my pistolet nor ammunition, but I could aim it as a threat. I pulled it from my hanging pocket and placed it on my lap. The Marquise brought a pistolet from her réticule and laid it on her lap.

I smiled at my brother, riding next to the carriage, one hand on the pommel of our father's sword. Papa giving it to Henri meant something, if not full acknowledgment of his son. I hoped my brother knew that I was proud to acknowledge him. I wondered if he even knew about the Verzat legacy. I would discuss it with him before Papa returned.

At the city gates, Henri commanded the guards, who waved us through. The streets of Paris were empty, but Henri held his pistol at the ready, his eyes sweeping back and forth. He had the courage of a noblesse d'épée.

Mercifully, the rain stopped, though a pond of water stood in the courtyard before the mansion. The groomsman opened the door, but Henri remained on his mount. Would he leave us before I got to know him?

Jacques jumped down, and he and the groomsman carried Guillaume inside. Still Henri sat on his horse, not taking command. Risking offending him, I called out, "Jacques, please help Baron Pricaud to the blue room. Marie, show the Marquise to the yellow chamber." The groomsman reappeared. "Stable Monsieur Detré's horse and the carriage," I shouted to the groomsman.

Henri hesitated. "I must tend to her."

"It is my duty to brush and feed and stable her, Monsieur." The groomsman held the mare and reached up to assist Henri. Not taking the offered hand, Henri jumped down, released the reins, and stared at the house.

"Come, you must be cold and hungry." I led the way into the entry hall where Cook stood, clutching her flour-covered hands. "Please prepare dinner, and broth and a tisane for Baron Pricaud."

Henri took in the marble floors, the chandelier, the gilded

moldings, the portraits, his deep blue eyes shining like sapphires. He craned his neck to view the dome above the spiraling staircase. Did he know he would inherit this? "I apologize. It is not Versailles."

"I'm relieved. It took six hours to find the Verzat apartments."

He had Papa's humor. "How *did* you find them?"

The weak afternoon light accented his strong jawline and his nose, slightly less crooked than Papa's. He swiped at his forehead. "The brass plate above the Verzat carriage stall in the stables."

"You are most intelligent. And brave. I am proud to be your sister." I lowered my voice. "Even if Papa has not yet acknowledged you."

His head jerked up. "I am proud to be your brother. You have the courage of ten men."

Though warmed by the compliment, I tilted my head, not understanding. He pointed to my gown, and my hand flew to my bodice—caked with dried blood. The stink of blood and sweat and gunpowder pushed me back to the Queen's staircase. I fell back and gripped the banister.

Henri guided me to sit on a step. "Take deep breaths. It will pass."

His kind and gentle nature touched me. "Forgive me."

"I've never killed a man." He sat next to me. "Although I'm sure he deserved it. Killing takes tremendous courage."

I coughed a laugh. "I killed more from terror than courage."

He smiled and shook his head, eyes blazing. "Without terror, courage would not be required."

What would it have been like to grow up with him? A vision of us as children, running amongst the vines, laughing and shouting ran through my mind. Tears welled, and I closed my eyes. "Let us warm ourselves by the fire, mon frère."

He helped me stand, and I led him into the salon. He looked down at the silk damask couch and the mud on his wet breeches. I pulled the servants' bell and Marie arrived in an instant. "Please bring some blankets."

I poured a glass of brandy, but my hand shook so the liquid splashed.

He rescued the glass and returned the decanter. "Thank you." He sipped and sputtered. "Sorry…not used to it." He coughed.

I took the blankets from Marie and spread them on the couch. "Please make yourself comfortable." I could no longer stand my bloodied gown. "I must leave you for a few moments."

He perched on the couch's edge and gazed at the fire.

"Do you not wish to rest?"

"Your father asked me to protect you, as he would."

I sighed, hearing longing in his voice. Not having been acknowledged affected his confidence. "He is your father, too."

He rolled the glass between his hands.

"Why has Papa not acknowledged you?" He looked like a hurt six-year-old when he gazed at me. I pressed my hand to my heart. "Forgive me."

He shook his head. "He must tell you that."

Papa's presence sat like a wall between us. Did I dare leave him alone? "Have you slept?"

He rubbed his eyes and shook his head.

Papa would never have asked Henri to accompany us if he had not trusted him. I pulled the pistolet from my reticule, and bullets and powder from a drawer in the table next to him. I offered them. "There is no one left in Paris to endanger us. Rest now."

He accepted them and laughed, not nearly as robustly as Papa, but his laugh was deep and free like our father's.

"I am glad you are my brother," I said and turned to see his chin rest upon his chest, his hands gripping the gun. He snored softly.

Warmth flooded me. He was every bit a Verzat. His initial reaction to the brandy did not bode well, but I would test his palate at the earliest opportunity.

45

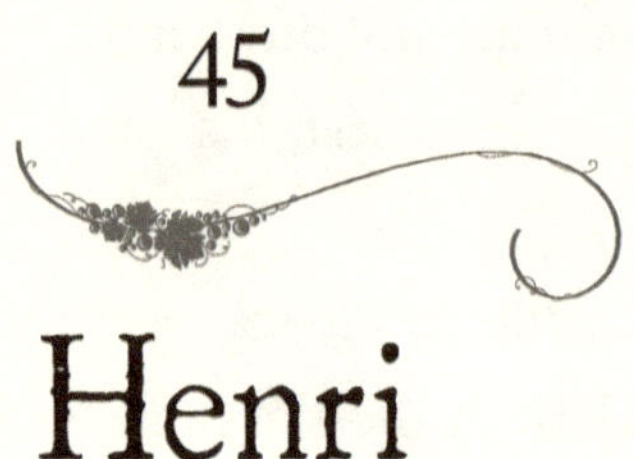

Henri

Paris
October 6, 1789

THE SOUND OF tinkling glass roused me. I had to find Madame Françoise. "Excuse me. I did not mean to fall asleep."

The old lady, wearing a gown the color of lilacs, sat opposite me sipping a glass of wine. "Allow me to present myself. I am the Marquise de Bourran."

I jumped up and bowed.

"Please rest, young man. You have delivered us safely."

Joliette, wearing a pale green gown with dark green ribbons, picked up the pistolet, examined it, and placed it into her hanging pocket. "You have cleaned and loaded it. Merci."

I squeezed my eyes and opened them. I didn't remember doing it. "Is it possible to send a messenger? I am concerned about a neighbor's safety."

"Certainement. I'll have Jacques summon one. You must be hungry after such a long ride in the cold rain. Shall we have supper?" Joliette smiled.

"You must be famished." The Marquise put out her hand to me.

I smoothed my hair back. Was I to kiss it? I glanced at Joliette who cupped her elbow. What did that mean?

The Marquise tapped her fan. "Young man, accompany this old woman to table."

Joliette mimed again, and I took the old lady's extended hand, placed it on my arm, and followed Joliette into the dining room. It was like a garden. Pale green and silver fabric covered the walls. Crystal candelabra held tall white tapers that cast as much light as a summer's afternoon. Flames roared at the end of the room in a fireplace larger than the room Maman and I had lived in.

Joliette swept her arm. "Henri, you shall take Papa's place at the head."

I held the chair for each of them, but I remained standing. If I learned anything from Maman, it was that my muddy clothes would ruin silk.

The manservant placed a blanket on my chair and pulled it out for me.

"Merci, Jacques." Joliette smiled up at me. "Please, sit down."

"Did you find a messenger, Jacques?" I asked.

He stiffened and looked to the floor. "He will arrive soon, Monsieur."

"Thank you." I sat on the edge of the seat. The dark green Verzat crest glinted in the center of the white plates and bowls.

Hanging on the opposite wall was a full-length portrait of Papa at about my age. He appeared far more confident than I ever felt. Was that because he always knew he was Comte de Verzat? If I were not a commoner, would I be as self-assured?

Jacques took my napkin, snapped it open, and placed it on my lap. A grin began, but I squelched it. Bertrand would've howled over anyone needing a servant for such a task.

"You may serve the soup, Jacques." Joliette pointed at the wall to her right. "That is a portrait of my maman."

"She is beautiful." I did not say: not nearly as beautiful as the portrait of my maman at the Comédie Française. "You look like her."

"She was the most beautiful woman at Court," the Marquise exclaimed. "Except for the Queen, of course." She blessed herself. "Merci dieu, the Queen is safe."

Silver spoons and forks and knives lined up like a regiment on either side of my plate. I wrapped the napkin between my fingers. Rap never included so many tools in his etiquette lessons, lessons I wished I'd paid more attention to.

Jacques served us soup and bread. The smell of leeks and potatoes made me want to grab the tureen and gulp it all down. He poured wine into crystal goblets etched with the Verzat crest. "Anything else, Comtesse?"

Joliette flinched. "No. Merci." She might not have heard her title at all, had I not been there. She'd just met me. I was a stranger and a commoner.

Jacques left us and closed the tall double doors.

I picked up the spoon corresponding to the one Joliette took and watched how she dipped it. I doubted I could take so little, but I tried.

"You are terribly young to be a député, Monsieur." The Marquise sipped her wine. "Which section do you represent?"

The rich, savory soup coated my tongue. I swallowed. "Faubourg Saint-Antoine."

Her eyebrows lifted. "Did you rouse the peasants to attack the Bastille?"

The soup hit my empty stomach like a fist. "No."

She sniffed. "But you joined them?"

"No, I...I had to find my friend's body."

"I am so sorry for your loss." She patted her napkin about her lips. "Then I may conclude that you are not a Royalist?"

I tore off a piece of bread, so white and soft and fragrant. I wanted to chomp into the whole loaf, not think up lies. "I represent the people of Saint-Antoine, but that does not mean I am against the King, Madame. Many of my neighbors feel only the King can help them."

"In what way?" She sipped again.

"By regulating the price of bread." I held up a chunk. "By reducing taxes. By passing laws—laws that represent the poor."

"Formidable." The Marquise shivered in the blazingly hot room. "Joliette, would you be a dear and get my shawl? I left it on the dressing table."

I jumped up. "I will get it for you."

"Nonsense, you remain right where you are." The Marquise was as intimidating as Papa. Did such force come with titles?

"I will summon Marie." Joliette reached for a ribbon hanging next to the window.

"Oh, please, allow me a moment alone with this handsome young man."

I looked to Joliette, thinking: *Please don't leave me alone with her.*

The Marquise fingered the necklaces resting on her bosom. "And, you should look in on the Baron."

"Very well." Joliette half smiled. "Please, continue eating. I shall be only a moment." I jumped and pulled out her chair, my heart pounding as she left us.

I sat. Should I not eat until she returned? My stomach rumbled, and I feared the Marquise heard it. I popped a piece of bread in my mouth, hoping I'd not committed a social sin.

"You have your mother's eyes." Her face was calm as a duck pond.

The bread sat in my mouth. I swallowed it whole. "You know my maman?"

"I did." She rested her elbows on the table.

"My maman has brown eyes. How long have you lived at Versailles?"

She waved her jeweled fingers. "My late husband and I never missed her performances."

Where was that messenger? I tilted my head. "My maman's a laundress."

"Your maman was a wonderful actress."

Rain pelted the window. My lips trembled, and I dragged my fist across my mouth. "You have me confused with someone else."

"I think not. She was a star of the Comédie."

For this woman to remember meant my birth maman must have been, as Papa claimed, quite famous. She could tell me what my birth maman was like. I gripped my spoon. "Excuse me, but to whom do you refer?" The formal words were like wooden sticks in my mouth.

She rested her chin on her hand. "Abrielle Renée Lenogue Saulnier." She smiled. "You have her incredibly dark blue eyes."

I reached for my wine glass, nearly toppling it, righting it before it spilled. Stupid clumsy beast. "My maman, a laundress, has the same color eyes." What an idiot. I'd just told her they were brown. I gulped a spoonful of soup.

"Like sapphires." She put her hands in her lap and straightened. "You seem to possess her kindness as well. She assisted the poor. Taught peasant girls to read and sing and dance. She would be most proud of you, risking your life and coming to our aid, Henri de Verzat."

My legs jounced. This woman could tell Cassard. The dishes on the table rattled. I rubbed my hands down my thighs, pressing them against the chair.

"There were many rumors at Versailles. But, do not worry, Monsieur." She smiled. I wasn't sure if it was genuine or out of pity. "No noble worth his title would betray you or your father by identifying you to that half-eared woodlouse, Cassard."

The room darkened, and the day my father told me of my birth-mother's husband rushed me. I gripped the stem of the wineglass. "I do not know of a Cassard, Madame."

"He makes himself known at the Palais-Royal—he is a reckless gambler. Rumor has it he is looking for his late wife's child."

I drank deeply. The wine's heat rushed through me as I gazed up at Papa's smiling portrait. His face no longer held the mischievousness that played in his eyes when the portrait was painted, which had to have been done before he met my maman. His eyes were sadder, his face heavier now—the effects of grief? He'd lost my maman and Joliette's.

A tapping sound forced me to look back at the Marquise. She stopped hitting her fan against the table and flicked it open. "I asked: Does Joliette know that you are her brother?"

"Has Joliette a brother?" I dragged my napkin across my mouth. "I would like to meet him."

"Pity." She sighed deeply. "I believe she is in need of a brother." She waved the fan. "Your secret is safe with me. But I urge you to avoid the Palais-Royal." She sat back and gazed at me like she could see my heart beating inside.

The Palais-Royal was precisely where I'd look for Cassard, right after I found Madame Françoise.

Jacques entered. "The messenger has arrived, Monsieur."

I was never so glad to leave a conversation.

46

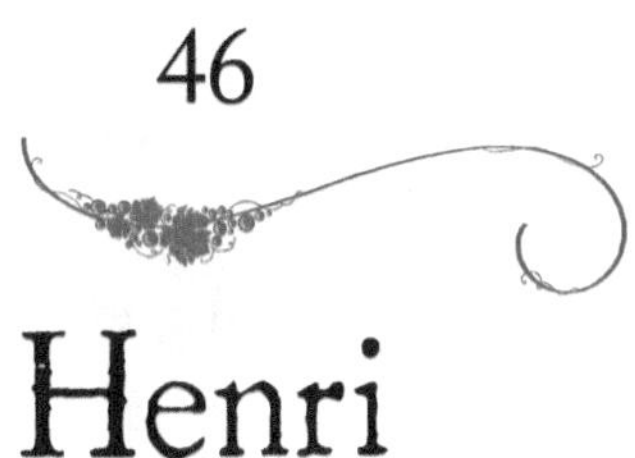

Henri

Paris
October 6, 1789

T HE LADIES RETIRED, and I sat watching a roaring fire, trying to stay awake.

As dusk descended, Jacques took a torch and lighted lanterns on either side of the gate. He shook wet leaves from his cloak when he returned.

"You must be tired riding all the way in the rain. I'll await the Comte." I wanted to speak with my father about Cassard, alone.

He straightened the buttons of his waistcoat. "It is my duty, Monsieur. I would never leave my post."

I was just as loyal to Papa, so I didn't insist. He sat on a bench next to the door, his back straight against the wall. Not once did his head nod.

He lighted all the candles in the candelabras, making the house a shining beacon. And a target for poissardes still thirsty for blood. I didn't have much more strength to defend myself, much less two women, a house full of servants, and a wounded Garde.

I joined Jacques on the bench in the hall and kept watch through the window. If not for the two flickering lanterns, I'd have believed I was in the tunnels, so black was the night. After a clock chimed twelve, I grew light-headed and imagined sounds, but I never released the hilt of my father's sword.

Mist swirled about a lone rider as he passed the lanterns and approached the front door. Jacques jumped up, shot open an umbrella, and picked up a lantern. I followed him, hoping it was Papa. Jacques took the reins. I smiled but bit back my greeting.

Papa dismounted. "Merci, Jacques. I trust you are well?"

"Yes, Monseigneur. I am grateful you are safe."

Papa nodded and strode toward me, his arms outstretched. "Henri."

Jacques tilted his head yet kept his gaze on his feet.

"The King signed the *Declaration of the Rights of Man* and returned to Paris!"

"That *is* progress."

"Thank you for protecting Joliette." He clapped me on the back. "I never once worried with you here."

He embraced me, and I clasped my arms around him. I hung onto him longer than he hugged me. My cheeks warmed as I stepped back. "You trust me to protect her, but you do not introduce me?"

He squeezed my shoulder. "Henri, there was no time to explain."

"It matters not. The Marquise told me she knew my mother. I denied it."

He sighed. "Come, we have much to discuss."

"She thinks Cassard is a half-eared woodlouse."

He barked a laugh. Like pulling a thread unravels knitting, his laughter shook loose the tension that gripped me for days, and I laughed too.

I unbuckled the sword-belt and held it out. "Papa, I must find my neighbor's wife. She was forced to march to the palace, and she has a son who must be terrified without her."

He put his hand on my shoulder. "I am proud of you, Henri. You are a true noblesse d'épée, my son."

The warmth and weight of his hand moved through me. My eyes burned. I nodded, turned, and ran to retrieve the mare.

47

Henri

WHEN I KNOCKED at Bertrand's door, it banged open, as if it hadn't been latched. My chest constricted and then released when I saw her. "Madame."

"Bonsoir, Henri." Madame Françoise, fingers laced before her, stood at the cold fireplace. Mud stained her gown. Simon stood examining a wooden bird. The room was as frigid and empty as the tunnels. I searched for Bertrand's scent of greenwood shavings, but a tallow candle sputtered on the mantel, filling the air with a mutton stink. It was like the room missed Bertrand as much as I did.

"My maman said you'd gone to the market, but when you didn't return, she grew worried. I tried to find you."

Her shoulders hunched like she held heavy buckets. "They forced me to join them."

"You left. Like Papa!" Simon threw the bird, breaking it on the stone hearth.

"Simon!" She grabbed his arm, and he kicked the floor. Heaving for breath, he collapsed before the empty fireplace.

I picked up the wing and body. The scent of fresh wood brought Bertrand back. I sat next to Simon, took his fingers in mine, and ran them over the beak. "Your papa carved beautiful animals, didn't he?"

"I don't want it." He pushed it away.

I grabbed him to me, like Papa had embraced me. He pummeled my chest, his body shaking against me with his sobs. I caught his fists and opened them. "You have the fine strong hands of a carpenter. Like your papa." I pulled him close and rubbed his back and inhaled until I could speak. "Just like your papa." His cries dwindled. I pulled out a sack of sugared almonds Joliette's cook had given me. "Taste one of these."

He shook his head.

"Your maman will save them for later." I stood and gave her the sack.

She pressed it to her bosom. "Thank you," she whispered. "Madame Detré gave me the money. It was most kind of you. Thank you."

"You have enough for food this week?"

"For two weeks. You are most generous."

I put on my hat. "I'm glad you're safe. I'll visit again, soon." I closed the door behind me. Cold rain slid down my neck. Now was not the time to ask what I should do about Simon should something happen to her. I pulled my cloak about myself and strode down the alley.

"Henri!" Madame Françoise ran out the door, wrapping her shawl around her.

I hurried to her. "You must be cold. Take my cloak."

She shook her head. "Thank God, your maman took care of Simon." She turned her face to the rain as she struggled not to cry. "Did you know there are *three* palaces at Versailles?" Her voice grew hoarse. "How many does one family need when thousands have *no* homes? I don't approve of what those women did, but I understand why they did it." She looked down at the muck. "Perhaps one day, I'll have to do something like it— to feed my son."

The rain stung my face. I understood, too. Forcing the King to return to Paris would make him see how most people struggled to survive. I stared across the street at a lamplighter bringing his sputtering torch to a lantern. I turned to tell her she and Simon would never starve.

She placed her fingers over my mouth. "Bertrand asked you to watch over us." A tear ran down her face, and she swiped at it.

I felt weak and empty, and I hated it.

"Promise me, if something should happen to me, you'll care for Simon?" Her eyes became Bertrand's, when he'd asked the same.

The failure of not having saved Bertrand hung over me like a fog. "I promise."

She kissed my cheek and ran home.

Had the Duc d'Orléans organized the women who forced Madame to march? No one in this faubourg had that much power or money. It could only have been a noble. But what noble would want to push the Third Estate toward more violence? If I dared to ask that in my next article, Cassard might not be the only one looking for me.

48

Henri

Paris
October 8, 1789

IF GENEVIÈVE DIDN'T march to Versailles, she might think I had. I prayed she was safe. I wanted to know what she thought of my Duc d'Orléans theory before I put myself in danger. The streets were more crowded with slops, garbage, and people, but few vendors. I wondered if they were too afraid to hawk their wares, or if there was nothing left to peddle.

I found Geneviève dressed as Pierre sitting on the University steps the next morning.

She jumped up and hurried toward me. "We are the only two left. Père canceled the lecture."

"Was there a lecture yesterday?"

Geneviève shook her head. "Were you at Versailles?"

"I rode out there in search of Bertrand's wife. She was forced to march." Her gray eyes were pinched. I wanted to kiss away the lines of worry. "Let's walk." We headed into a chill wind toward the river.

"What do you mean, 'forced to march?'"

I rubbed my forehead. "I saw women and men dressed as women forcing women to march. Rumor is the Duc d'Orléans paid them."

"For what purpose?"

"To get them to riot, kill the royal family, and gain the throne for himself."

"So, he paid starving people? What choice did they have, even if they were loyal to the King?" She kicked at a loose cobble. "Did you find her?"

"Not until last night." A breeze pulled at my tricorne, and I grabbed it. "The violence. It's difficult to imagine people are capable of such horror."

She stopped at the stone wall next to the quai. "Perhaps if you talk about it, you will feel less haunted."

I dug my fingernails into my palms. "I lied to you."

Her eyes darkened to a steel gray, a color I never wanted to see again. "I am Henri Detré. The pamphlet writer."

"I knew that." She grinned.

I exhaled in a slow steady stream.

"You didn't know you could trust me then. Didn't know I was a woman."

Her eyes softened, drawing me closer. I shook my head. "I want to write about what I saw, to expose the Duc, but I fear suggesting such a thing would put me in grave danger."

"True." She tilted her head. "Can you use a pseudonym?"

A woman extended a pole from the roof of a tall building

and tied sheets to it. The laundry snapped in the stiff wind. Using Detré could also put Maman in danger.

"Is it important to you to attach your name to your article?"

I shook my head. "Using a pen name is a good idea. Hiding my identity would also better my chances at becoming a deputy." I leaned over the wall and clasped my hands. "I must learn more about the Assembly. Does your father need another clerk?"

Her face brightened. "Papa needs to know everything that goes on in the Assembly. He agreed to let me clerk in his office, and at least I see laws in the making, but, unlike me, you'd be allowed to attend."

She grabbed my sleeve. "You'd become known at the Assembly, make connections. And when it's time to elect new deputies, you'd already be familiar with the process."

A gust of wind scattered dry leaves over the quai. My presence at the Assembly just might help my election. What other choices did I have? Despite all my efforts to protect Papa at Versailles and Joliette in Paris, Papa still hadn't recognized me, which I was beginning to consider a blessing. But even if he did, what would I do with my life? Becoming a lawyer was as futile as becoming a noble. What did nobles do, anyway? "As a child, I wanted to become a ship's captain. I nearly stowed away for America."

"I'm glad you didn't."

I looked at her hand, wanting to caress it, but then glanced around. I worried what people might think, not knowing Pierre was a woman, and yet, because Geneviève was dressed as a man, we could be together without a chaperone.

She shot me a sly smile. "Come, I'll present you to Papa."

"How will you explain knowing me?"

She laughed. "I forgot. I can't say I met you at University."

"No matter. I'll apply with every lawyer until I gain a position."

"Have you a sister?"

Sunlight reflecting off the water made her eyes sparkle. No wonder she kept her hat on—the brim cast a shadow hiding her high cheekbones and small delicate nose. Did I trust her? If I lied, she'd feel betrayed when she learned the truth. But if she told her papa of my real heritage, I could endanger not only myself, but also Joliette. "Not that I know of."

She tilted her head. "That's an odd answer."

I dragged the back of my hand across my mouth. "I have a benefactor, and my father is unknown to me." I hoped to buy more time.

She nodded. "I help the nuns at a convent where I grew up. Many parents are removing their children from the Abbé. I could tell my father you're the brother of one of the girls."

"Aren't they nobles?"

She shook her head. "Not all. Some are children of merchants and lawyers. Monsieur Jefferson's daughter attended for a while."

I didn't want to create another story to memorize. I didn't want to put myself in a position where I'd risk having to tell the truth. "I don't want to get you in any trouble."

She slapped her leg. "I can take care of myself. Why won't you let me help you? Because I'm a woman? Am I not your equal?"

"No! I mean...of course, you're equal. I...I don't..." I blew out a sigh. Why did women complicate things?

"What?" She stood before me, fists resting on her hips. Her posture was a good imitation of a man's.

"I'd never forgive myself if your father learned your secret through me. What if I accidentally said something, exposing you?"

"You're too smart to do such a thing, Henri. You want me to present you or not?"

She might punch me. Better to face her wrath later. "Yes."

I'd have to conceal my identity in a very public place, but I'd also learn how to be a deputy. I grabbed her hand. "Let's go."

49

Henri

Paris
October 8, 1789

Monsieur Antoine Quentin Fouquier de Tinville's thin lips spread into a straight line. "You have been at Université for a year, and you feel qualified to clerk for le Prosecutor de Châtelet?" His whisper competed with the crackling fire.

I gripped my hat's brim. "I have a broad understanding of the law, a keen ear, and I am a quick writer. I can inform you of the Assembly's every action at the end of every day, Monsieur le Prosecutor."

"What sort of information might you provide?"

I'd no idea. My theory on the Duc d'Orléans was just that, a theory. His eyes darkened. "There were no representatives of Faubourg Saint-Antoine present at the National Assembly the day the women marched on Versailles."

He tapped his quill on the desk. "And?"

"All the other deputies were uninformed and ill prepared to persuade the crowd because of this."

He leaned forward. "And you know this, how?"

Sweat ran down my jaw. I had to admit I'd impersonated a deputy. I'd never become one. "I attended the Assembly that day, Monsieur." I hated my weak voice.

"Why were you not at Université?" He scribbled the quill on a paper.

I shuffled my feet. "I know the ancient laws. I wish to learn laws in-the-making. Doing so will make me a better avocat, Monsieur." I feared I might tear my hat in two. "I arrived before the poissardes, so I conveyed their grievances."

"Did you, now?" He adjusted his ill-fitting wig. "What did you tell them?"

"That everyone doubted the Bastille could be taken, but it was. And the same could happen to the palais. It would be far simpler to give them what they wanted: bread and flour for the bakers of Paris."

He looked over his spectacles. "How do you know my daughter?"

"We were presented at the Abbé, Monsieur." Sweat ran down my chest.

He tossed the quill and took a bit of snuff. "And you wish to assist your family by working while you study?"

I hadn't even thought of the money. A little thrill jumped in me. "Yes, Monsieur."

"The wage is not much, but it prevents starvation." He plucked up the quill. "The Assembly now meets at the Salle du Manège."

"Yes, next to the Tuileries. I have been there, Monsieur."

"Take notes and return here after today's session."

"Thank—"

"It is your trial, Detré." He stood and tossed the quill on the desk. "If I am not satisfied with your report, you will not be hired."

I bowed. "I understand, Monsieur. I will not disappoint. Merci."

He waved his hand like he was shooing a fly.

Outside, I ran along the quai. The Seine sparkled like Geneviève's eyes. I could take her to a café. In case anything happened to Madame Françoise, I could pay Rap to tutor Simon. I'd take copious notes. I'd not make any mistakes. I'd include my observations. I'd become a deputy within a year.

50

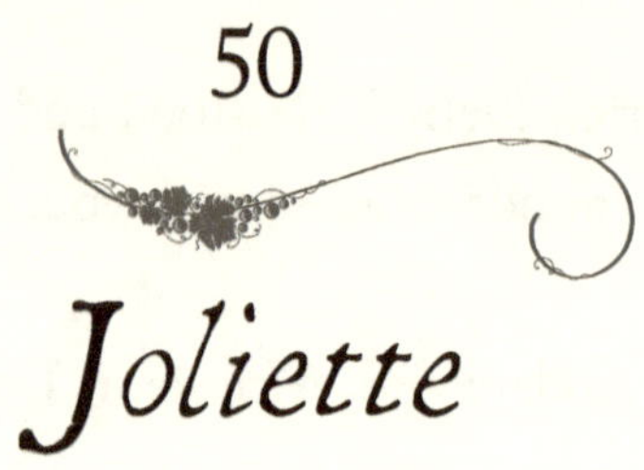

Joliette

Paris
October 8, 1789

THE TALL GAUNT surgeon stood next to Guillaume's bed and opened a leather box. "His humors are out of balance."

I clung to Guillaume's hot hand. "He has lost so much blood already!" Maman died soon after a surgeon bled her.

The surgeon took a tweezers and lifted a leech. Guillaume lay motionless.

A wave of nausea rolled in me, but I pushed it down. "I forbid you to bleed him."

He dropped the leech back in the box. "He may die of fever, Madame."

I bent over Guillaume, soothing his forehead with a cool cloth.

"Have you ever been on a battlefield?" The Marquise turned

from him. "Marie, boil cloths in water and bring them to me."

The surgeon sniffed. "Have you, Madame?"

"I followed my husband to the Battle of Fontenoy—where five thousand were wounded and half as many died." Her sagging neck shook. "But those men whose wounds we treated with maggots did not die."

Nausea rolled again, and I swallowed against it.

The surgeon coughed. "Maggots are not used for fever, Madame."

"They are used on infected wounds that *cause* the fever."

The surgeon buckled his case shut. "I see I am not needed here."

"You are correct," I snapped. "Thank you for coming. Jacques, please show him out."

I turned to Marie. "Send Cook to the nearest abattoir to collect a bowl of maggots she'll find on the rotting carcasses." She paled but nodded and hurried away.

"I am forever indebted to you, Marquise." I entwined my fingers with Guillaume's. "How can I help you?"

"Undress him." She pulled off her lace gloves.

My face grew warm, but I reached under the sheets and unbuttoned Guillaume's nightshirt.

Jacques returned with a basin of water, serviettes, and a carafe of wine. The Marquise nodded. "Excellent, Jacques. Help the Comtesse roll the Baron onto his side and put a pillow behind his back to keep him there."

Guillaume moaned as we positioned him.

Marie brought steaming cloths, a flacon of vinegar, and another basin.

"Pour vinegar over my hands and give me a boiled cloth."

When the Marquise finished cleaning her hands, she unwrapped the stained cloth binding Guillaume's arm. A thick yellow-red pus oozed from the gash.

Flecks of light spun around me. I knelt beside the bed, rested my forehead against it, and gripped Guillaume's hand.

Papa entered and patted my shoulder. "Joliette, are you all right?"

I looked up as he crossed to the other side of the bed and hunched over Guillaume, his hand supporting Guillaume's back. I pushed my face in the coverlet. Papa reached over and ran his finger along my cheek. "He will recover." He lifted my chin. "He is strong."

The candlelight encircled my father—he looked so powerful and yet so helpless. "I am glad you are here, Papa." I rested my head next to Guillaume.

Guillaume thrashed and cried out, "François! No!" He struggled every time Papa wrapped cool cloths around his neck. I willed myself not to cry. It took more courage to face the thought of losing Guillaume than it took to kill a man.

After a little while, Marie brought a porcelain tureen atop a silver tray.

"You may not wish to see this, Joliette. It is quite revolting." The Marquise took a silver spoon from the tray.

"I will not leave him."

She nodded. "Knowing how to do this could save a life." She dipped the spoon into the bowl and placed tiny writhing white things on Guillaume's wound.

I swallowed to release the urge to vomit. "Maggots?"

"They are larvae, which will hatch into flies. They eat dead flesh and clear infection." She scooped the spoon.

The tray rattled as Marie sank to the floor. I grabbed the tray and held it for the Marquise as she dropped more maggots along the gash.

I coughed to cover my gagging. "Jacques, please revive Marie. I think it was too much for her."

Jacques and Papa carried her from the room.

The maggots feasted. "They will not harm him?" I asked as I studied Guillaume's pale face. I replaced the cloth on his forehead with a cool one.

"No, they will cure him of the infection. I am amazed the surgeon did not employ them and instead wanted to use those disgusting leeches. Will these *learned* men never learn?" She smiled. "You should get some rest, my dear. I will attend to him."

Should he die, I would be with him. Tears burned. I shook my head.

"You are almost as stubborn as I am, Comtesse." She rinsed her hands and dried them. "Then I shall get some." She left us.

Papa stood before the window, running his thumb and fingers down the sides of his face and pulling at the skin beneath his chin. "I will remain with him. You should rest, ma princesse."

"You did not leave Maman."

He turned to me. "She was my wife."

"I care for him, Papa. I shall not leave him."

The dawn cast shadows under his eyes, making him look

old and tired. He loosened his jabot. "Your Maman extracted a promise from me before she passed."

I pressed my palm into Guillaume's.

"I am bound not to allow you to marry him."

"Why?" Anger flushed my cheeks, feeling as hot as Guillaume's forehead.

Papa stared out the window.

"You cannot prevent me from loving him." My heart beat faster. Did I love Guillaume? When had it happened? The day at the Latona fountain when he told me he knew my heart's desire? At Versailles, when he told me my word and signature should command as much respect as any man's? He told me he lived to love me. Had I fallen in love with him then? Or long ago, when I first looked into his eyes at the ball? Or this minute?

Papa placed his hand over his heart. He inhaled deeply and then let out a sigh. "No, you cannot ever stop yourself from falling in love. That is true, ma princesse."

I lay my head on the pillow next to Guillaume's cheek and closed my eyes. I vowed I would marry an appropriate noble. How had I allowed myself to love him? I had no choice. I had also vowed to marry for love. Warmth flooded my chest, and I let my tears flow. Guillaume had listened to me, not only with his ears, but also his eyes and his heart.

51

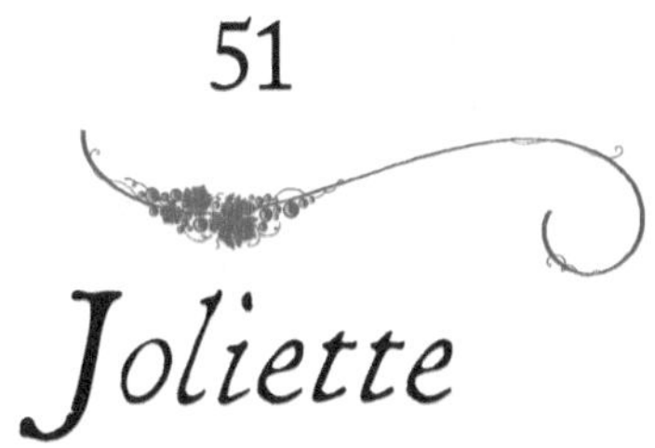

Joliette

Paris
October 9, 1789

I MUST HAVE DOZED, for I jerked awake panting, the sound of gunfire cracking and the sulfur of gunfire stinging my nose. Afternoon light filled the chamber. Guillaume's face was pale and still. My heart thumped. I leaned closer. Relief washed through me as I heard his shallow breathing.

The Marquise stood opposite me, removing the cloth wrapping Guillaume's wound. I wanted to sing at the sight of the skin around the stitches, shiny and pink, and the wound no longer oozing pus.

"You must eat something so you're strong when he wakes."

Within seconds, Marie set down a tray. My stomach contracted when I smelled roast chicken.

"Come, I will hold his hand while you eat." The Marquise gently nudged me off the chair and took my place.

Ravenous, I broke off a piece of bread and savored it. "How did you get on a battlefield?"

"I followed the King's army because I was so in love with the Marquis. Philipe was not my husband, then."

I put down my fork. "Your parents allowed you?"

"Queen Marie lied for me." She smiled, but her eyes held sorrow. "I was younger than you, but not nearly as refined. A few ladies-in-waiting and I hid in a small chapel for three days until the fighting ceased. I searched through acres of dying men and barely recognized Philipe when I found him, his face was so twisted with pain. A surgeon commanded me and the other women to collect maggots from rotting corpses."

She placed her hand on her stomach. "If I had not been intent on saving the Marquis's life, I could not have done it. Most of the men we treated survived." She exhaled deeply. "I wish we could have saved them all."

"You were very brave."

She sighed. "Love makes you brave, my dear."

Guillaume groaned and thrashed. I ran to his side and steadied him. "Comtesse!" he called out. The Marquise looked at me as she helped still him.

My heart thundered. *Please, Grandmaman, help him.*

He began to whimper. "Go back!"

"Marie, brandy!" I yelled.

Marie poured a bit of brandy onto a spoon and tipped it into Guillaume's mouth. He spat and gasped for breath.

My heartbeat pulsed in my throat. *Please, stay here with me.*

His eyes fluttered open. "Comtesse!" He gasped for breath. "You are here." He reached out and pulled me to him. "You are safe."

I pressed my cheek against his. "I will never leave you."

52

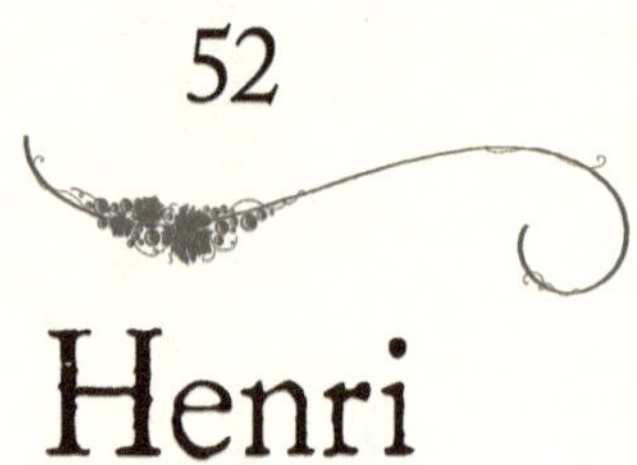

Henri

Paris
October 11, 1789

Prosecutor Fouquier de Tinville paced before the fireplace. "And why is this important, Detré?"

I wanted the position almost as much as I had wanted to meet my father. But my instructions had been to take notes, not to have opinions. "Uh…"

He stopped, punched his fist in his palm. "What is the import?"

I clutched my notes. "It would degrade the monarchy's power?"

"Would it?

I had guessed, now I had to defend it. "Yes."

"Why?"

My report rustled. "Any legislation put into action by the Assembly reduces the power of the King."

He nodded. "In addition to your notes, you are to deliver a summary of events and your assessment of them, every evening within an hour of the session's closure."

"Absolutely, Monsieur Prosecutor." My throat was dry. "Am I hired, Monsieur?"

"For a month. We will evaluate your position then."

I feared my legs would jump and leap of their own accord. "Merci, Monsieur Prosecutor."

Barely able to contain the "whoop" I wanted to scream, I raced to Tinville's clerk room where Geneviève stood writing at a tall desk. I did not stop, but smiled, and ran two fingers along my jaw. She nodded.

I ran from the Châtelet. I had only to wait for her at the Pont Neuf that evening to celebrate. I'd not disappoint her father. I'd leave my rooms at Rap's studio and, with my earnings, I'd rent lodging in Faubourg Saint-Antoine. I'd tell people how I'd work to change their lives and ask them to elect me deputy.

53

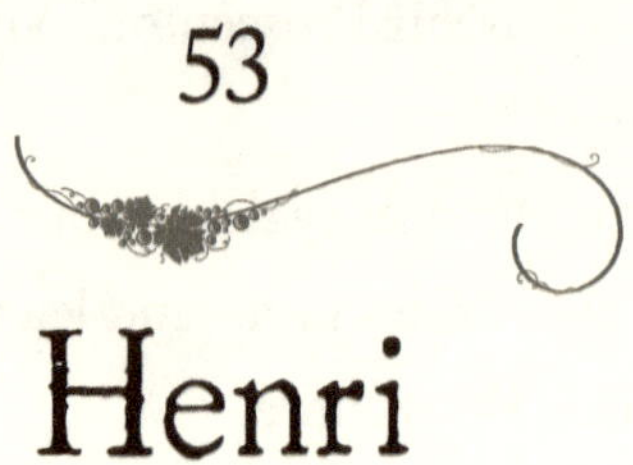

Henri

Paris
November 10, 1789

AN INVITATION TO dine at Maison de Verzat arrived and, like a starving man pounces on bread, I read but stopped at: *For your safety, take the tunnels to the cave de Verzat.* A queasiness moved in my stomach. I sent a reply that the only day I was available to meet was Sunday. I was making my own career. He would have to meet me halfway from now on.

I was half an hour late on purpose. Standing before the cave de Verzat, I smiled, knowing I'd discovered this door long before I knew who it belonged to, and I'd solved my father's puzzle soon after he had gifted me the key. I extinguished my torch and knocked.

The door swung open. I blinked in the bright light.

"Welcome." Papa's voice resounded.

Squinting, I entered. Candles blazed in an iron chandelier. Wooden barrels and casks lined the stone walls. The scent of wine hung heavy.

Candlelight surrounded Joliette like a halo.

Papa reached out. "My son."

His warmth and strength wrapped around me. My arms ached to hold onto him, but I stood stiff, my cheek pressed into his thick velvet frock coat.

"It is about time you presented my brother, Papa."

He sprang back. "Pardon." He bowed his head and brought out his arm. "May I *formally* present Joliette, your sister?" He patted her arm. "And may I *formally* present your brother, Henri."

"You are here, *formally*, at last." Joliette's eyes shone bright. She placed her hand over her necklace and blinked at tears, her face prettier now that fear no longer gripped her. She curtsied and, when she rose, her lips quivered. From nervousness? Anticipation?

I waited three years to be accepted, and I wanted to run and hug them both, but it was like I was caught in a current. I couldn't move closer.

They stood smiling at me. Papa's great laugh rumbled along the stones. I didn't belong here, but I wanted to. I ripped off my hat and bowed.

"Welcome, my brother." She swept her arm toward a long wooden table and chairs with green velvet cushions. Rows of carafes and glasses stood along the length of the table. I stiffened. Were we having dinner in the cellar? Was the cave de Verzat the only place my father would acknowledge me?

Papa opened a leather-bound book laying open at the end of the table. At the top of the page was an elaborately painted Verzat crest in dark greens and gold. He dipped a quill, wrote in the book, looked to me and Joliette, and smiled. "Henri Charles Albert Lenogue Saulnier de Verzat, a noblesse d'épée, is now recorded in the history of la famille de Verzat."

I mouthed the words, *Lenogue Saulnier*, rolling over my tongue. I warmed. My mother's family name was now part of mine.

Joliette let go a little sob and laugh at the same time. I laughed a great big laugh. She clapped.

Papa took a ribbon from around his neck. "The key to Maison de Verzat."

Unlike the rusted iron key to the tunnels, this was smooth, shiny brass with an elegant fleur-de-lys as the bow. "Merci." I placed the ribbon around my neck and held the key to my heart.

"Welcome home, Henri." His eyes shone in the flickering candlelight.

Home? My home? He looked so happy. But I had to live in Faubourg Saint-Antoine. Now that I had a home, I didn't want to live in it, and yet part of me did. I tucked the key behind my neckcloth.

"That key also fits all the locks at the château, your other home in Saint-Étienne-de-Chigny. And only we three possess master keys." Joliette brushed tears away.

I didn't want to disappoint them. I patted the key that lay over my heart. "I shall wear it—always." I did not intend to use it.

"Bien." Joliette picked up a crystal decanter and poured the ruby red wine into three goblets etched with the Verzat crest. "A special vintage: the year you were born, Henri." She handed one to Papa and me.

My face burned, and I hated that they could see it redden. My hand trembled as I accepted the glass.

"A toast to my son, the future Comte de Verzat." Papa lifted his glass.

My arm jerked so hard I thought I'd break all three glasses as we toasted. The ring filled the cave and my heart like the clang of Sainte-Marguerite's bell.

I drank. A flavor, like ripe berries, burst in my mouth. "Mmm..."

"What do you taste?" Joliette leaned toward me, eyes eager and bright.

"Blackberries, currants..." I took another sip and held it in my mouth.

"And?" She clutched her hands before her.

I searched to name a flavor that ebbed and disappeared. I took another sip. It reminded me of the herb Maman sometimes used. "Lavender?"

She clapped. "You have the Verzat palate! Grandmaman would be thrilled! Wine runs in your veins!"

I coughed as the heat of the wine moved down my throat. "Wine is in my blood?"

"Very few people identify the elusive hint of lavender. But

I knew you could not believe it, so you took another sip to confirm it."

Her smile was radiant. She was radiant. I had a sister. And I liked her.

Papa set his glass down and removed a gold fleur-de-lys pinned to his waistcoat. He pinned it to my frock coat lapel, then kissed both my cheeks, held my shoulders, and stood back. "My son." His eyes brimmed.

I looked down at the pin and felt a splitting in me. I should be grateful. I was thrilled he called me his son, in front of Joliette, but this symbol of nobility could get me killed, especially in Saint-Antoine. I couldn't sit with members of the Third Estate wearing this. I wanted to tell him of my clerking for Tinville, but what if he noticed me at the Assembly—without the pin? He'd be hurt.

He clapped his hands. "Now, I have a surprise for you both." He grabbed a torch from an iron ring on the wall. "Come."

Joliette looked to me. I put out my hands.

We followed Papa past huge barrels, lying on their sides—their diameters greater than Joliette's height. He stopped before one of them. "Remember, it is third from the end." He withdrew the dagger at his waist and ran it between the metal hoop and the wood end until a click sounded. He gently pressed the edge of the round head of the barrel, and it swiveled, acting like a door. The circle of wood, held by a rod running through its diameter, was attached at the top and bottom of the barrel's rim. He crouched, stepped through the narrow opening, and motioned us to follow him.

I grinned. How many more surprises awaited?

"I have lived here all my life, and this is the first time you have shown this to me?" Joliette gathered up her skirts. "What is this?"

"Come, my dear." He reached out.

She gripped his hand. I followed. As I exited the barrel, the torchlight revealed a tiny stone-walled chamber—room enough for six people to stand—and a narrow wooden staircase, leading up the wall to a wooden door. Papa bent and pushed against the wooden disk. It swung back into place. "This passage was built after the Saint Bartholomew's Day massacre."

"Because they were Huguenots?" I asked.

"For *everyone's* escape." He took the torch and climbed the steps. At the top, he pulled a lever and the wooden door swung out.

We entered a salon decorated in dark green silks. At the far end, candles flamed in a candelabrum that stood upon a desk to the right of a huge fireplace where a fire snapped. Gilt-framed life-size portraits lined a wall. I scanned them, hoping I might resemble one of my ancestors.

A faint scent of leather and cloves told me this had to be Papa's private library, for I'd not seen it when I brought Joliette back from Versailles. Had he acknowledged me when I was a child, would I have spent evenings studying in this room while he read?

Floor-to-ceiling bookshelves lined two of the walls. How many books could I have read had I lived here? I ran my finger against the gold letters of a spine. Flecks stuck to my skin. I rubbed them between my thumb and finger. I'd be a different person. Would I like that person? I'd not have any friends in

Saint-Antoine. Would I have liked the people at Versailles? An emptiness crept into my heart. I wouldn't have grown up with Maman.

"I have been in your library countless times, and never suspected." Joliette's voice was high.

"I did not believe we needed it, but after Versailles, we *all* may need this escape." He took a clove from a dish on his desk and popped it into his mouth. "Should the peasants attack, gather the servants and use this passage to the chamber. When it is safe, travel the tunnels."

The air grew heavy, thick, smelling of the cloves. My lodgings in Saint-Antoine wouldn't be attacked. I was back with Maman, in our old home, the day I met my father, when I asked if he'd take me to court. When I was a boy, the wearing of red-heeled shoes and plumed hats seemed nearly as exciting as becoming a ship's captain. But the title and clothes of nobility were now dangerous. The room grew hot, and I wiped sweat from my lip.

Papa ran his hand along the books. "Watch." He pulled a lever. With a creaking, the bookshelf swayed back into the wall and closed with a soft thud. "The lever is to the side. See if you can find it."

Joliette lifted it in a few seconds and laughed. "You try."

My fingers were not as sensitive, and it took me longer, but when I did find it, she smiled and said, "You are every bit a Verzat."

A draft shot through the warmth of the room. I longed to become Deputy Detré. Was it wise for me to be a Verzat, now? "Is Cassard out of the country?"

Papa looked away. "We'll discuss that later. Before we join

the Marquise at dinner, I wish to discuss your future, Henri."
He pointed to a chair that looked like a lady's: tiny, spindly,
covered in a shiny pale green cloth. "Please sit down."

I sat but did not lean back, fearing the gilded thing might
break. Joliette sat in the same type of chair next to me, smoothing her gown.

"How are your studies at Université?"

"University is closed."

His smile drooped.

"I have been hired by a lawyer, Antoine Quentin Fouquier
de Tinville, to attend the Assembly, take notes each day, and
report to him each evening."

"Fouquier de Tinville? Of the Châtelet?"

"He is also a member of the Gardes Nationale." I held onto
the chair seat.

He drew his fingers along his jaw. "Should you not continue classes?"

"There are none. But laws are changing—in the Assembly.
What is the sense of studying laws that are destroyed? There
is no time."

He drummed his fingers along his jaw. "By living here, you
will be closer to the Assembly, the Châtelet, and Université,
when it reopens."

Would he never be proud of me, no matter my accomplish-
ments? I shook my head. "I wish to remain in Saint-Antoine."

His fingers stopped.

I stood. "A year ago, the King proclaimed the number of
deputies representing the Third Estate be doubled. Saint-
Antoine lost one at the Bastille and needs three more. I wish
to represent the people I grew up with, so I moved to lodgings

there." My mouth was dry. "I hope to be elected deputy."

"In the most squalid quartier of Paris?" Joliette rose.

"It is my birthplace."

"But this is your home, Henri." She reached out and touched my arm. "I want to know you better, spend time with you. We are a family."

Any other man would be thrilled to live in a mansion and a château. I couldn't allow myself to appear ungrateful.

Papa turned to stare at the fire. "There is much to learn about running the estate and this house. You must meet the châtelain at the château."

I rubbed my palms along my frock coat. "I want to work, here, in Paris." I'd not meant for my voice to be so loud or sharp. "I want to accomplish this—independent of a title." I stilled my hands and gripped my lapels. "Besides, Joliette is making an unprecedented success of the winery."

He huffed. "Joliette is succeeding. But the winery is a small part of a large estate that supports nearly a thousand people."

"I wish to help the people of Faubourg Saint-Antoine, as you have helped those who live on the estate."

Papa picked a few more cloves from the dish on his desk and chewed them.

"May I ask you for more than a favor, brother?" Joliette asked.

"Of course."

"Although I am exporting Verzat wine and negotiating the terms of the contracts, by law, my signature is not binding." She toyed with her necklace. "Would you be willing to sign the contracts for me?"

"Joliette knows the business better than I do. She corresponds with the vigneron at the château, twice a day. She fights for equitable terms and is quite shrewd in her negotiations with clients and distributors as well as shippers." Papa raised his hands. "I sign whatever she puts before me."

My sister's eyes held a hint of Papa's mischievousness. She flicked open her fan, fluttered it, and leaned back into her chair. "And I would appreciate your campaigning for equal rights for women when you are elected député."

I barked a laugh nearly as loud as Papa's. She reminded me of Geneviève.

I looked up at a painting of a man with a profile like my father's. Joliette could not ensure the Verzat legacy, nor could she inherit the estate—despite her wine success. Was Papa acknowledging me to protect Joliette? If not for me, when she married, everything would be inherited by her husband. What would my position be? Things were much simpler for commoners.

I plucked up the quill from the desk and scribbled in the air. "It will be my honor to do both, my sister."

"Merci." Joliette clapped her fan shut and kissed my cheek.

I hated to disappoint her and Papa, but I could not live here. I could not run a château. I didn't want to.

Papa's eyes glittered. "Then I shall plan a visit to the estate for all of us. Surely, Tinville can spare you for a few weeks."

I felt like a marionette resisting its strings. Should I refuse my heritage and remain Henri Detré for my own safety? If I accepted my title—would I be risking my life? Remaining a commoner could help me protect Joliette and Papa but also insult them. I felt as if the strings had torn me in half, leaving me in scattered pieces.

Joliette stood. "I shall see if the Marquise is ready to join us for dinner. Perhaps she can persuade Henri to consider this his home." She left us.

I wished I had my glass of wine. "You have been so cautious, for so many years. Has something happened to Cassard?"

"I have not told Joliette of him, that is why I avoided your question earlier. A noble wrote me that Cassard lost so heavily at the gaming tables in London that he will never be able to return to France."

"Malefactors hire such desperate persons to commit crimes."

He arched an eyebrow. "You have already learned something at the Châtelet."

I laughed. Wouldn't Geneviève be surprised? She'd never trust me again if I told her the truth. Cassard could reappear at any moment. I'd remain Henri Detré until I was certain it was safe to be a Verzat. And if that happened, I'd tell Geneviève. First, I'd be elected a deputy.

54

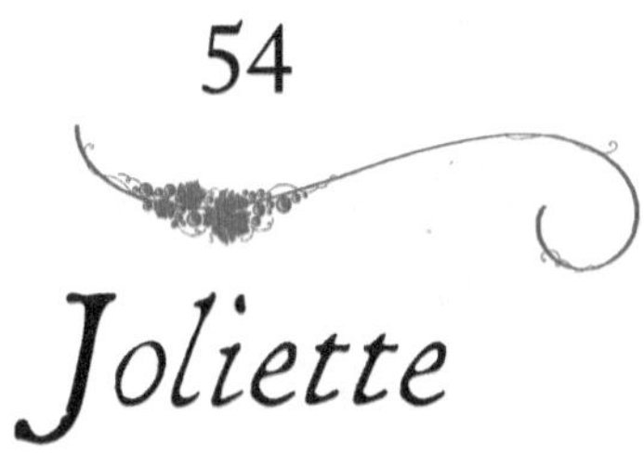

Joliette

Paris
May 1, 1790

I CLOSED THE VENDANGES account book and paced
before the fire.

Marquise de Bourran rubbed the silver swan's head atop her
walking stick. "What vexes you?"

"Although the shipment to New York has arrived, the merchant has not ordered more wine. Despite the drought, the
vigneron is expecting the vintage to be better than average. I
must find other merchants and increase sales."

Jacques delivered an invitation, and my breath caught. The
fleur-de-lys design replicated the gate surrounding Versailles—
the image now burned before my eyes as if the sun glared off
the paper. As there was little chance of being ostracized from
a Court diminished by its fleeing courtiers, I corresponded

with émigrés, hoping to be recommended to more merchants. I tore it open. "Marquise de Condorcet has invited us to tea."

"Condorcet?" The Marquise tapped her chin. "Oh, yes, the young wife of the Marquis. His ears were forever full of wig powder before he met the sweet young Sophie de Grouchy."

"I have always found her refreshing—ever since she helped a maid who fell at Court. She ran over, declared the maid could not walk, and commanded one of the Queen's own footmen to carry her to her quarters." I laughed. "Courtiers were horrified. I have not seen her since last summer." I tapped the card. "An odd residence, the Hôtel des Monnaies."

"Actually, the Marquis's position as Inspecteur Général allows them apartments above the mint." She picked up her embroidery hoop and needle. "You know the purpose of this invitation is political discussion?"

"I welcome it." I closed the accounts book. "I hope the new American Minister attends. If so, I will entreat Monsieur Short's rumored paramour to introduce me. What better place to meet people who might assist me in finding merchants than at Condorcet's salon?"

"You may find you must defend the royal family." The Marquise pierced the cloth. "Increasingly, that is a dangerous position to be in."

"The Queen has refused both our requests to visit her. I suspect it is her way of protecting us, but I would still defend her."

"As would I." She tugged a thread. "Are you ready to enter the fray?"

I ran my hand over the gold letters of the account book. Exporting wine could be equally dangerous—for a woman.

Gunfire on the Queen's staircase pounded in my mind, pulling me back to that day at Versailles. I closed my eyes, smelling gunpowder. Nothing could be as dangerous as what I had already lived through. I pressed my mouchoir to my nose. "Care to join me?"

55

Joliette

Paris
May 2, 1790

As Minister to the King, Papa attended His Majesté every day at the National Assembly. I asked Guillaume to escort us to Marquise de Condorcet's salon.

He arrived wearing a white sling to brace his healing arm and holding two square beribboned boxes, he bowed.

"Let us leave immediately." I was eager to start my search for people who could recommend me to potential buyers in America.

"This will take just a moment."

I tapped my fan. "Very well."

"I am grateful to you both for saving my life." He held out a box. "To you, Comtesse, for your ingenuity, astonishing bravery, and excellent aim."

My face warmed as I accepted it. "It was—"

He put up his hand, bowed before the Marquise, and presented the box tied in lilac ribbon. "Madame la Marquise, I owe my life a second time to your knowledge and brave use of the maggots."

She began to speak and again he put up his hand. He stood between us and looked at the floor. A slight shudder moved through him. "I owe you my life, and I humbly thank you." He looked up at the Marquise, then me, "I hope you know, should you need me in any way, I shall be at your command." He took a step back and lifted his hand. "Please, open them."

The Marquise drew out a mouchoir embroidered with aubergine-colored silk thread. Her eyes grew wet. "The butterfly, the metamorphosis of life?"

He blushed. "The seamstress did not understand the larva or maggots."

He gazed at me as I untied the dark green ribbon. Nestled in the silk-lined box lay a fine white mouchoir. Embroidered in pale green silk thread were the words: Mon coeur est tien.

I looked up at him. The sunlight streaming into the room made his eyes a vivid green. He placed his hand over his heart. His heart was mine. Mine was his. I pressed the mouchoir to my chest.

My heartbeat raced when he held my hand and led me to the carriage. The Marquise sat next to me and raised a brow. I pressed my lips together to stop smiling. I had to concentrate on the business of finding more buyers.

We arrived at an imposing, columned, tufa-stone building facing the Seine. A valet led us through grand rooms with marble floors, wood-paneled walls, crystal chandeliers. A queasiness moved through me. The night Soubrier attempted to humiliate Guillaume at Versailles still haunted me. I hoped she was groveling for a position at an Italian court.

Guillaume's eyes sparkled, taking in the splendor of the gold candelabra and silk wallpaper. Although Guillaume trounced the cunning Soubrier with éclat, I prayed courtiers here would be kinder to him. I placed my hand on his arm.

A footman requested our names at the ballroom entrance and announced us. I did not recognize any of the guests, dressed far more somberly than courtiers had at Versailles. Sophie de Condorcet hurried to us. I presented Guillaume, and she welcomed him as if he were the guest of honor. Because of her warm acceptance, I knew she saw Guillaume as I did, not a Garde Nationale, not a mere baron without property, but as an equal. She, not her maid, poured glasses of wine and presented them to us.

"I see someone I know. Please excuse me." The Marquise headed for a table laden with pastries.

Sophie tucked one hand in the crook of my arm and the other in Guillaume's and led us into a salon decorated in shades of yellow and gold.

"Have you invited the Duchess de la Rochefoucauld?" I asked.

"She sent her regrets." Sophie smiled, rather impishly. "Might you be interested in speaking with Minister Short, Comtesse?"

I gripped my fan. I had been found out.

Sophie patted my hand. "Worry not, Comtesse. Everyone knows you sent Verzat wine to Monsieur Jefferson."

I fluttered my fan. How did everyone know? Guillaume seemed as surprised as I.

"The Minister is not coming, but there are some women, powerful women, like you, whom you might like to meet."

Guillaume's eyebrows rose.

I did not feel powerful. I felt exposed. Grandmaman had been powerful, and she would want me to act as if I were. I would concentrate on not fidgeting.

Sophie led us toward a group of women who wore gowns of drab colors without ribbons, ruffles, or furbelows. The men with them wore plain cuffs and jabots that were pleated rather than trimmed in lace. She presented everyone, whether a Garde, comtesse, or commoner, with the same charm, grace, and respect. The ladies fussed over Guillaume, inquiring about his injury and insisting he tell them every detail.

Sophie steered me away and whispered, "I understand you wish to export Verzat wine to America?" Her eyes were bright.

Did everyone know of my failure? My mouth opened, but I had to push my voice. "Are you mocking me?"

"No! But I find it is nearly impossible to conduct business as a woman, do you not?" Her smile resembled a pink satin bow. I nodded. "There are ladies here who help one another. Like the chocolatier, Pauline Léon."

She pointed to a petite woman with a long straight nose, soft brown curls, and eyes the color of the bonbons she crafted. "Her widowed mother owns the shop on rue de Grenelle. Should her mother die, despite her expertise, Pauline will not inherit the shop. She can only do so through a husband." She tapped her fan against her wrist. "As she has not yet met a suitable spouse, we can only imagine the kind of chocolat he would make if he were a wig maker." She giggled like a girl behind her fan.

My throat tightened. Had Henri any idea he would inherit the château, the mansion, and the vineyard, along with all the money needed to run them? He was willing to sign contracts for me, but there was no guarantee he would support my decisions. Could I trust him? Did Papa? I had to rely on him when I wanted to rely on myself. If I were not married and Papa passed, I would be at Henri's mercy. I drank the rest of the wine and returned the glass to a servant.

Sophie pulled me toward a plump woman wearing a gown of aqua silk. Her blonde hair, styled to resemble a wig with tight ringlets, framed her round face. Aquamarine gemstones hung from her neck and her ears. She sat on a sofa next to the Marquise, who pulled me to her. "Comtesse, you simply must meet Madame Robert!"

Sophie laughed. "My work is done. I shall leave you now."

What did Sophie mean? Had she wanted to introduce me to this woman?

Guillaume returned to my side. "I have narrowly escaped." He smiled down at me. "Please do not let them take me from you again."

"Do not fear." I cupped both my hands about his arm.

The Marquise snapped open her fan. "May I present la Comtesse de Verzat"

Madame Robert's eyebrows lifted. "I tried to meet you at Versailles, but you were in Paris that day. It is my pleasure." She rose and curtsied.

I dipped. "My pleasure as well, Madame Robert." I presented Guillaume and searched the Marquise's face for clues, but she tapped her fan to her jaw in delight, keeping a great secret.

"I understand you wish to ship Verzat wine to America, Comtesse." Madame Robert straightened her bracelet.

"Yes!" My heartbeat raced.

"As I have heard." She sat back down next to the Marquise.

Another flush of embarrassment rolled over me. The rumor must have spread beyond Versailles. Had I been invited here for everyone's amusement?

"Perhaps we might strike a bargain." The corners of her eyes crinkled.

My jaw tightened. "What sort?"

"You do not know my business?" She tapped her fingernails on her fan.

I wanted to rub the silk cords of my réticule, like a frightened child, but I inhaled and straightened to my full height instead. "No. Pardon."

"I have a wine depository here in Paris. I distribute wine not only throughout France, but also Europe." The shine in her eyes matched the glittering gems at her ears.

My breath caught. "It is *your* business? *You* run it?"

She nodded. "*Your* shipper refused to store Verzat wine in my depository, I suspect because I am a woman." She adjusted her necklace and looked up at me.

She did not know that I had fired Jaupart and hired a new distributor. My cheeks blazed. "Madame, forgive me. I was unaware of this."

She laughed. "I thought so."

"My vintner does not speak for me. You can rest assured our storage facility and distribution partner will soon change." I cleared my throat. "How is it that you have contracts, Madame?"

"Although my husband relied upon me to manage the business, my signature was worthless, much like yours. Now that I am a widow, my signature is binding." She smiled up at Guillaume, but her eyes were moist. "It is a terrible price to pay, and I doubt you would wish to pay it."

Guillaume's smile faded with mine. He straightened his sling.

"Of course not. I am so sorry for your loss," I replied.

She nodded. "It was a long time ago. But I also do not wish to remarry, for if I did, I would no longer be allowed to run my own business. An unjust law, would you not agree?"

"Exceedingly unjust." Guillaume's voice was firm.

"It encourages a widow to take lovers and not remarry." She laughed, and the Marquise joined her; both women fluttered their fans.

Guillaume's face reddened, and he looked at the floor.

My stays pinched as I inhaled.

"I run my late husband's business quite efficiently. All my customers are pleased with my terms and delivery. I would like to suggest," she tilted her head, "we consider conducting business as women. That we accept one another's signature as binding. That is, if you agree to allow me to distribute your wines, not only in America, but also in Paris, the rest of France, and Europe. Would you like to visit my warehouse?"

My heart beat as if I were on a galloping horse. "I would be delighted."

56

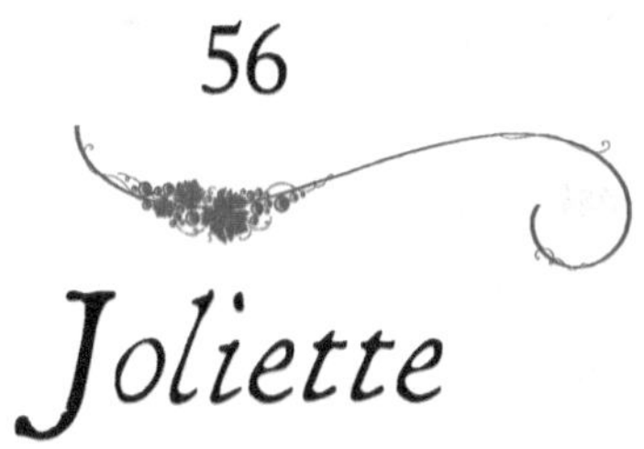

Joliette

Paris
May 2, 1790

I FOUND PAPA IN the library, pacing before the fireplace.

"Papa, I met a woman—a wine distributor. Did you know that oily shipper, Jaupart, refused to conduct business with her because she is a woman? An outrage!" I removed my gloves and tossed them on the account book. "She can guarantee shipment to America and accept my signature." I sat at the desk. "I shall inform Joseph immediately." I pulled out a sheet of paper.

He stared at the fire.

"Papa?"

He turned. "You know that your maman wanted me to arrange a marriage for you?"

My back stiffened. "Yes."

"The Duc de Lillers has requested I consider his proposal for you."

My chest seized. "He married Cécile. They live in Koblenz."

"I am sorry, ma chérie, but Cécile passed…a fever…only months after the wedding.

"No." I fell back against the chair. Cécile was my age. How could the Duc still live, yet she was dead? "I received a letter from her just last week."

"I received the news today. Along with the Duc's request for your hand in marriage."

I lurched to stand. The room spun. "She died only a few weeks ago." I fell back. "He was my best friend's husband." She had not wanted him; she had cried that morning at Versailles. She had no choice, and now *she* was dead. "He is ancient, his breath atrocious."

"He is a Duc and in need of an heir."

The image of his gnarled ancient hands on my friend…on me. I swallowed against a building nausea. Was he not too old to perform? I squeezed my eyes until tiny flecks of light spun. I inhaled to calm myself. "Papa, I would be widowed before he could complete the task."

Or, like Cécile, I could die. I stood, heat thrumming down my arms. "But at least then my signature would be worth something."

"Joliette, you know I have your best interests at heart. I realize the Duc is inappropriate, but most nobles have emigrated. The Duc de Gaumont has written from Italy. He would be willing to meet you there and marry you. You would be safer in either place. You must agree."

"It is in my best interest to marry a man I do not love and

leave France? Leave you and my home?" I drummed my fingers upon the desk. "Is that the *happiness* you wish for me?"

"Neither is the best match. But at your age, most women are married."

"Is there a law regarding this?"

"It is *customary*…and it is time." He pressed his lips together and turned away. "I refused the Baron Pricaud this morning."

My breath caught. "Refused him what?"

"Permission to court you." He steepled his hands.

I held onto the desk. Guillaume must have met with my father before he accompanied us, yet he never let on.

"He did not speak of this to you?"

I withdrew his mouchoir from the sash at my waist. "No."

He grunted. "At least he is a man of honor." He turned toward me. "But that means little. He is not appropriate for you, Joliette."

I pushed myself away from the desk. "My dear Papa, is this not hypocritical of you? You tossed aside feudal laws the day your father died. You run your estate like the American democracy. You encourage equality at the Assembly, and yet you reject Guillaume because he is not appropriate—below my station?" My legs trembled. I did not want to speak it, but I could not stop myself. "You have an illegitimate son." His face fell, and I instantly regretted my words. "I apologize. I love my brother." I held the back of the chair. "You cared for Guillaume like he was a son when he was ill."

"Your maman did not speak of titles."

"Duc de Lillers is totally inappropriate *except* for his title. For the sake of Duc de Gaumont's title, you would have me leave France? Never!"

"You are a strong woman; you will need an equal as a husband."

"You see strength in a doddering sixty-year-old or an emigrating coward?"

"Their spirits are strong. Both are noblesse d'épée."

"Guillaume is strong." I picked up the account book and pressed it to my chest. "And he believes a woman's signature should be respected as any man's. He believes the current laws are unjust to women. He understands me!"

"I forbid you to marry the Baron. I promised your maman."

I gripped the book. "I forbid you to accept any proposal." My stomach knotted around itself. "I shall never marry. Henri will inherit everything, so I do not need to marry. I only hope he will allow me to continue to run the winery and live at the château. I hope you trust he will not abandon me."

His mouth dropped open. Anger would have flashed in Maman's eyes. Papa's filled with sorrow.

I had never raised my voice to him. My eyes burned, but I lifted my chin. "If you truly believed in equality, I would not need your—or any other man's—permission for anything—least of whom I love and marry." I picked up my skirts and swept upstairs to my chamber. I would meet Madame Robert alone.

57

Henri

Paris
May 3, 1790

T HE ODOR OF wet wool and perspiration filled the chilly
dark Salle du Manège. Clerks argued with one another. People
in the gallery shouted insults to deputies and ministers below
them. With a clerk's badge, I could sit on the benches that
stepped down to the main arena. I would have to write furiously to complete Tinville's report and the article I promised
the printer—both due by the end of the day. I'd never worked
so hard at University.

I sat in the back for a good view of all the deputies and
spotted Papa, wearing a frock coat and breeches of olive green,
in a front row. He leaned back and regarded the lack of pro-
ceedings with amusement. The President and other officers
of the Assembly sat at a desk on an elevated stage, arguing

amongst themselves. Tricolor bunting festooned the podium.

I caught a glimpse of Geneviève wearing a gown the color of a fawn in the balcony that hung over the rear entrance and served as a gallery for spectators. She wiggled her fingers. I waved back, leaned into my seat, and hoped she'd stay all day.

A man with bushy eyebrows and an enormous nose ascended the steps to the speaker's podium. He clapped his hands for silence and began speaking about the exact measurements of the boundaries of the departments of France—every name of which I raced to write down. A hum gathered among the spectators. A stevedore in the gallery yelled out, "Why do we waste time with this when there are important matters to discuss?"

Papa laughed. A tall thin man, wearing an old-fashioned wig, stood to the side of the deputies with his arms crossed over his elaborately embroidered yellow waistcoat and stared at Papa. In my mind, I heard Papa's voice whisper: *Thin as an asparagus spear. I never trust people who do not eat.* Cassard was supposed to be in England. Had he escaped the debtors' prison?

An officer rose and clapped his hands. "Quiet!"

The people in the gallery stilled. He glared at the speaker. "Get to your point."

There was much grumbling. The tall man, the only person not wearing fashionable drab colors, stared only at Papa.

"There should be," the speaker droned, "according to my geographic calculations, eighty-three departments. Not eighty-one."

The people in the gallery stomped. A market woman hurled potatoes at him. A fusty stink erupted as they hit the stage.

Papa picked up his tricorne and climbed the steps. The tall man slid across the back row toward him.

I squinted. His wig covered his ears. He slammed on his hat and strutted quickly after Papa. A squirming crawled in my stomach. Cassard. It had to be. I dropped my folder and quill on the bench and ran outside.

Papa climbed into his carriage. Cassard descended the side stairs and hailed a diligence. It took off, following Papa's carriage.

Sweat burned my eyes. The tunnels were faster. I had to warn Papa before Cassard reached him.

58

Joliette

Paris
May 3, 1790

"**T**AKE THIS BONNET to the milliner's shop on rue Saint-Honoré and have her replace the velvet ribbon with satin of the same color. I handed the hat to Marie. "Wait for it to be sewn on before returning. Please tell Jacques and the others I do not wish to be disturbed."

She dipped a curtsey. "Yes, Comtesse."

I waited until the door closed and no longer heard her footsteps before pulling the dung-colored servant's gown from the bottom of my trunk. I tied the skirt at my waist and laced the bodice. I needed Madame Robert's wisdom. I needed to feel that someone understood me. I needed Grandmaman, for I knew deep in my heart she would agree with me and not Papa. I wrapped a shawl around my shoulders and shoved my pistolet into my réticule.

The clock ticked in the grand hall. I crept down the steps, into Papa's library, and shut the door. I grabbed two candles and lighted one before easing the lever down and entering the secret chamber.

Dressed as a maid, I traveled the Paris tunnels without the encumbrance of a chaperone, but when I emerged onto the streets, it was impossible to hire a diligence. Madame Robert's warehouse was on the quai, and, as I neared the river, a group of dockworkers sat on a wall, passing a jug amongst themselves. I slowed. They watched me like hungry dogs.

Gripping the gun, I quickened my pace. The biggest man grinned, pulled a rat by its tail from inside his tunic, and set it down. The rat scurried toward me.

I pulled back my shoulders. I would not give him the satisfaction of screaming. Picking up my skirts, I stomped about the ground to keep it away.

"Hey!" the man roared.

The other men guffawed.

I swung my leg, and the animal ran for cover. I dropped my skirts, turned, and smiled to myself. Walking as if I knew where I was going, I searched for the warehouse.

The odor of must and stale wine emanated from a worm-eaten wooden door. I walked past it and searched the building for a public entry, but it had no other door or windows on the ground floor. Turning, I came face-to-face with a filthy man, his long graying beard streaked yellow. I backed away, but he leaned toward me. His smile revealed no teeth. He dragged his arm across his nose. "You're a pretty one."

"Merci, Monsieur. Excuse me, I have business to attend."

He reached for my shawl. I slapped his blackened hand.

He held his hand to his chest as if I had broken it. "I'm hungry."

The dockworkers still watched me, passing the jug, laughing, and hooting at the man who lost his rat.

"If you wait while I am inside, I will give you money when I return."

He nodded, ran to the door, and knocked.

I stood beside him. The door opened, and a footman looked from the man to me, then began to close the door.

"Monsieur, I am Comtesse de Verzat here for my appointment."

The footman nodded and closed the door.

"Monsieur!" I shouted, but the door remained shut. I banged on the door and kicked it.

The beggar looked me up and down, his eyes as sad as a lost child's. "You don't act like a comtesse."

The dockworkers left their jug and walked toward us.

Grandmaman, Maman, help me.

The door bounced open. "Comtesse, please forgive my doorman. Come in." Madame Robert reached for my arm. "Such a disguise!"

The beggar removed his hat. "I'll wait right here for you, Comtesse."

"Merci, Monsieur."

Madame Robert lifted a brow.

"I promised him coin in the hopes he will keep the others away."

"Excellent strategy, Comtesse."

We entered a huge wood-timbered room the size of a Versailles ballroom. Stacks of barrels of all sizes reached the rafters.

I breathed in a familiar moldy odor. "You distribute all this wine, Madame?"

"I have distributed wine for the past ten years, and each year, the number of barrels increases." She fanned herself.

"Is there room for Verzat wine?"

She laughed. "Plenty. I've three more warehouses."

"And you ship wines to America?"

"I will."

I turned. "But you have not?"

She held her hands before her. "We both take risks, Comtesse. I risk accepting your signature, and you risk my shipping to America—something I, like you, have yet to do."

Her smile was rather smug for such a risky situation. A wriggling in my stomach cautioned me. At the salon, she implied she shipped to America, but she never had. She had not lied… but I had not asked specifically. I would in the future. I adjusted my fichu.

She bade me follow her to a stack of smaller barrels with the crest of a Bourgogne vineyard burned into the casks. "I am holding these for a shipper who will pick them up next month and deliver them to Monsieur Jefferson."

Bright sunlight streamed into the room, illuminating a storm of dust motes. Her cleverness made me smile. "And if you can assure Monsieur Jefferson that you can deliver…."

She laughed a deep throaty laugh. "We women think alike."

"Yes." I laughed. She was as much an opportunist as I. "Bien.

If you will accept my signature on the contract, Madame, I shall write our vintner this afternoon, explaining our contract, authorizing you the new distributor of Verzat wine."

She held a bottle of Verzat wine aloft. "The contract is in my office, awaiting our shipping dates and your signature, Comtesse."

I laughed. The legacy was in my hands, now, and Papa was under no obligation to arrange a marriage for me. I could marry whomever I loved. I would run through the tunnels and surprise Papa in his library.

59

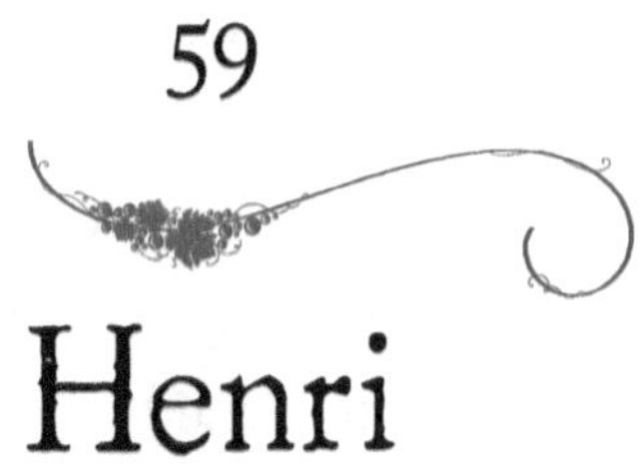

Henri

Paris
May 3, 1790

I CLIMBED THE STEPS through the secret chamber, unlatched the bookcase, entered the library, and pressed the bookcase back into the wall until it clicked closed. At the far end, candles burned in the candelabra. There were no sounds of servants moving about. The quiet was deafening.

I withdrew my pistol. "Papa?"

The back of my neck prickled. Scanning the shadows, I crept toward the light, my thumb on the pistol's hammer. My foot struck something.

Papa's sword smeared with blood.

My shoulders coiled. Had he killed Cassard? My heart hammered as I scanned the room, looking for the bastard.

Just beyond the couch, Papa lay face down before the fireplace. My breath stopped.

"Papa!" I knelt and rolled him on his back.

He began to smile. "My son." His breath was ragged.

I dropped the pistol and grabbed hold of him. "Where are you hurt?" I patted his body, seeking his injury.

His lips twisted in pain.

"Where, Papa?" My fingers reached a stain of blood spreading through his waistcoat. "Jacques! Get a surgeon," I shouted. A handkerchief lay next to Papa. I grabbed it and pressed it to his chest. He winced. "Cassard did this?"

"He will leave you alone…now…" He lifted his hand, but it fell back upon the rug. "Promise…"

"Yes. Anything." The handkerchief grew wet with blood. This was my fault. I shouldn't have taken the tunnels. I should've gone after Cassard. He promised to kill *me*, not Papa.

"America…" he gasped for breath.

I kissed his hand. "I wanted to make you proud." I held his hand to my cheek.

"Proud…." His other hand fluttered over his heart.

My chest throbbed. He wanted to hold Maman's portrait. I pulled it out and gently wrapped his cold fingers around the locket.

"Yours." He pushed it back. "Take Joliette…America. Promise…" His eyelids fluttered. Bloody foam dripped from his mouth. His chest collapsed with a terrible gurgle.

"Papa." I pulled him into my arms and pressed him to me. "I promise, Papa. I promise." I gripped his limp cold hand. I gripped harder and harder, willing my life into him. "I have only begun to know you. Please, Papa, please."

A cold draft swept my back. Cassard? I reached for my pistol. The secret door creaked.

"Papa! I have signed a contract!" Joliette called out.

Papa wouldn't want her to see him like this. I laid my father down and wiped my face and pushed myself up and ran to her.

"Henri! How lovely to see you. I have such good news. Where is Papa?" She hurried toward me. I put out my arms. She jolted back. "You are bleeding!"

"No. I'm not hurt." My chest heaved.

She looked about. "What has happened? Where is Papa?"

I swallowed against a pressure building in my chest. "Cassard followed Papa from the Assembly."

"Cassard who? You are frightening me. Where is Papa?" she cried.

I reached for her. "I took the tunnels, but I…"

She pushed past me. I grabbed for her, but she skirted me. She screamed. Her body buckled.

I caught her. We sank to the floor beside Papa. She grasped his arm. She curled onto him and moaned like a wounded animal.

Her sobs broke loose the tightness in my chest. A terrible hollow sucked my breath from me. He had only begun to teach me how to be a man. I wanted to fish with him, to argue politics, to feel his pride in me, embrace his love.

I was not yet man enough to fill my father's shoes.

60

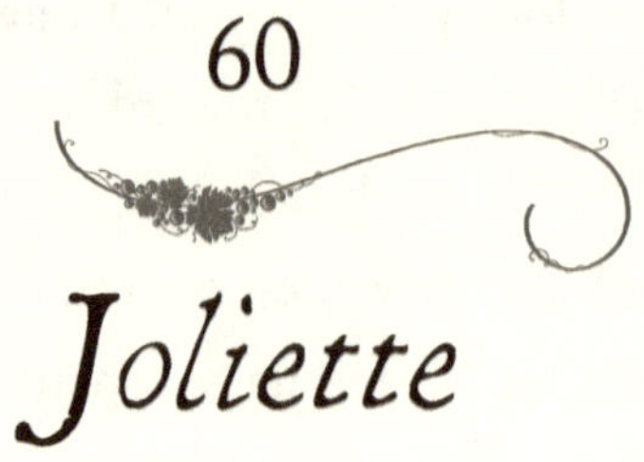

Joliette

Château de Verzat
May 6, 1790

GUILLAUME SAT NEXT to me on the stone bench. Mourners walked down the road, winding through the vineyard. A breeze spun the grape leaves.

I closed my eyes, seeing myself sitting beneath the chestnut tree, remembering. Grandmaman and Maman sat on a chaise longue, embroidering. Papa stood reading *Molière* aloud. Cook served glace au citron with raspberries. A cool breeze brought the scent of the muddy river and fish, and I inhaled deeply, feeling my childhood wrap around me like my father's arms.

Henri stood with his hand resting on the gate of the mausoleum. I looked past him, seeing Papa's coffin. How could that flimsy white box contain Papa? His laughter alone would splinter it. I could be happy that at least Maman and Papa were together again.

My brother wiped flecks of rust from his hands. "Joliette, Papa's last words—"

"No. I do not wish to hear it." I clamped my hands over my ears.

Guillaume gently pulled my hands into his and kissed them. "Let Henri tell you, please."

Guillaume's eyes were so kind and tender. My hands warmed in the heat of his. "The last thing I said to Papa was so unkind. I never spoke to him like that." I swallowed at the tightness in my throat. "I was disrespectful. I shall never forgive myself."

"I am certain Papa forgave you, Joliette. He asked me to protect you." Henri's voice was soft and tender, sounding like Papa's.

I nodded.

"He extracted one last promise." Sunlight reflected off tears, sitting in his eyes.

"How selfish I have been." I reached out and touched his sleeve. "You spent only a few days with Papa over the past few years. I lived my entire life with him. I am so sorry, Henri."

He dragged his hand over his eyes. His lips pursed, and he blew out a slow steady breath.

"I often asked my parents for a brother." My words surprised me.

Henri looked at me. The tiny muscles surrounding his mouth quivered. "Papa made me promise to take you to America."

"No." I shook my head. "I shall never leave."

Henri's mouth contorted, and I was afraid he would sob,

but he inhaled and gripped his hands in prayer. "I promised," he whispered.

"I did not promise." I stood and the vineyard whirled about me. I held onto the fence. "Maman and Papa and Grand-maman are here. I need to be here. I must be here. I promised Grandmaman I would continue the legacy. And I will."

"Papa wanted you to be safe. The only place you can be safe is America."

"France is my home. I shall never leave." I picked up my skirts and ran. I had the vineyard to oversee and wine to export.

61

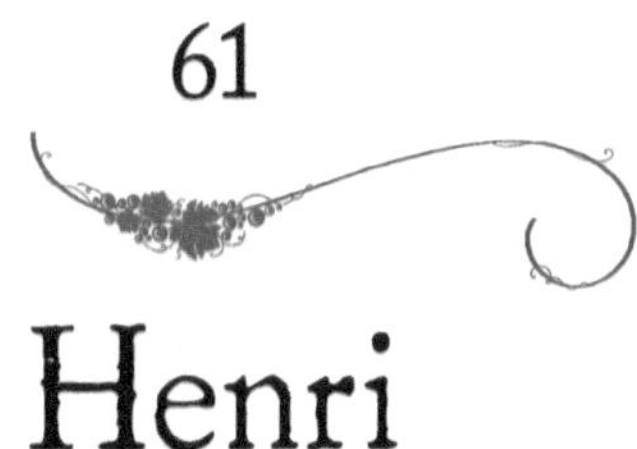

Henri

Château de Verzat
May 7, 1790

I DEEPLY REGRETTED NOT meeting the châtelain and learning how to manage the château, for that was my responsibility now—without Papa's guidance. The lingering scent of cloves led me to his chamber. The moss-like carpet and dark green bed curtains silenced the room, like I was in a forest. Did his favorite color comfort him? I'd never know.

A life-size portrait of Joliette and her mother hung above the fireplace. Both Joliette's mother and mine were beautiful in a fine, fragile way, like delicate pieces of porcelain. How divided Papa must have felt before my maman died.

In the drawer of the bedside table, I found a small, framed portrait of my mother, in the same pose as the painting at the Comédie. A bundle of letters tied with a green ribbon lay beneath it, the first dated the week of my birth.

My Dearest Love,

Our child is anxious to make his entrance upon the greatest stage. Yes, "his," for I have no doubt this little one who kicks with the strength of a lion, is much like his papa. My greatest hope is he will have the same generous, kind heart. And if he should make me laugh half as much as his father does, I could not be happier. I await his arrival and yours, my dearest.

Your Abrielle

I sat on the bed and touched my mother's words. *I hope he is with you now, Maman.* I struggled to inhale. The room closed in around me, like I was lost in the tunnels without a torch. I shook myself, re-tied the bundle and replaced it.

Beyond his ornate desk, a door to another room stood ajar. Inside, stacks of breeches, stockings, and waistcoats lined shelves. Frock coats hung on pegs. Below, a battalion of shoes—red-heeled shoes. I spotted the ones Papa wore the day we met, remembering how I'd thought the ornate buckles were silver lace. I put them on. How strange they made me stand, pressing my weight forward, pushing me off balance. I returned them.

I put my arms through the sleeves of a dark green frock coat and stood before a tall pier glass. I inhaled to fill the coat, but my breath caught. "I'm sorry I did not get there sooner, Papa." I pressed my face into the velvet, smelling his cloves. *You will grow to be tall like me.* I looked at my reflection. We resembled each other, and, I didn't want to admit, I had the nose I thought to be so crooked. His great laugh rumbled around me, and I felt small, like the day we'd met.

I replaced his clothes and returned to his chamber. Beyond the open windows, the vineyard was a stark contrast to the cloudless sky. Everything, as far as I could see, was now mine. Papa had invited me to the château to learn how to run it. Now who would teach me? I ran my hand through my hair, pulling it. I'd have to teach myself—how to be a man and how to run an estate. I'd start by questioning the châtelain.

Someone knocked. "Yes?"

Jacques, a thick white bandage wrapped around his head, stood with his hands at his side. "The Baron Pricaud awaits you in the library, Monseigneur."

"Is your head feeling better?"

"Yes, Monseigneur. Thank you."

"Thank you for risking your life to save Papa's."

He bowed. "It is my duty, Monseigneur."

Even though a servant, he had the courage of a Noble of the Sword. "Where *is* the library?"

He bowed his head. "If you will follow me, Monsieur le Comte."

Walking in my father's shoes was uncomfortable enough. Living up to his title was impossible. I scratched my neck. "Would you please call me 'Henri?'"

Jacques turned. "Etiquette would never allow such a thing, Comte."

Democracy would take some time.

"Please tell the châtelain I wish to speak to him before supper."

"Certainement, Comte."

In the library, the Baron stood gazing at a small portrait of Joliette upon the mantel. He turned and bowed. "Comte, thank you for seeing me."

I shook his hand. "Please, call me Henri."

"If you will call me Guillaume?"

"Of course. Let us have some wine." Before I could ask, Jacques entered, holding a carafe.

I sat on the sofa and opened my arm toward the chair opposite. "You no longer wear the sling. Your shoulder is healed?"

He rubbed his arm. "I cannot wield a weapon yet, but soon."

Jacques served the wine.

"Good." I brought up my glass. "Let us drink to the memory of my papa."

"I have never known so fine a man, Henri." He cleared his throat. "I am terribly sorry for your and your sister's loss."

I took a gulp to fill the hollow in me. The wine burned my raw throat.

He set the glass down and leaned forward. "You should know that when I asked the Comte, he refused my request."

Why had he told me? I rubbed the sleeve of Papa's frock coat, smoothing the velvet, but as I ran my hand back, it was rough.

"Monsieur le Comte said he had made a promise to Joliette's maman."

Although dusk brought a cool breeze, my father's coat was heavy and hot. "What is it you wish to ask?"

He bowed his head. "I humbly ask permission to court Joliette."

"Court? Do you not wish to marry her?"

He stood up, his eyes wide with shock. "It would not be proper etiquette. First, I must prove myself during courtship."

I rubbed the back of my neck. "It's obvious you love each other."

"Forgive me. My intentions should not be so obvious."

His awkwardness was so much like mine. I took a sip of wine, and now its warmth soothed me. "Please sit down, Guillaume."

He sat rigidly, staring at the floor.

"You did nothing wrong loving my sister or showing her your affection."

He jerked his head up.

"I made no promise to Joliette's maman or papa." I leaned forward. "But I cannot give you my permission."

His head dropped so his chin rested upon his neckcloth.

"Because it is not mine to give." I set down my glass. "It is Joliette's."

"Are you not her guardian?"

I shrugged. "I suppose I am. But, in any case, her permission is owned by her, not me. You must ask Joliette." I smiled. "I'm certain she will grant it."

He jumped up and extended his arms and, for a moment, I thought he might embrace me, but he caught himself and stood, smiling rather lopsidedly.

He was very much like me. "And when you do, rather than ask permission, ask her to marry you."

He rested his hand upon the hilt of his sword. "I fear that might be too forward, but should she give me permission to court her, I will take your advice within a fortnight." He smiled and extended his hand. "I cannot thank you enough, Com—Henri."

I stood and shook his hand.

"I must return to my regiment. Will you please ask the Comtesse to forgive me and tell her I will call upon her when she returns to Paris?"

"But you have not rested for three days. Please stay."

"If I do not leave immediately, I will not return on time, and I will be punished." He withdrew his gloves from his belt and bowed.

"Thank you for being here for Joliette, for comforting her."

"I would risk my life for her."

"I don't doubt it. Have a safe journey, Guillaume."

He bowed and left. The room was so quiet. A breeze dragged the curtains along the rug.

"Monsieur le Comte?"

I turned. "Jacques, my father was Comte. Won't you please call me Henri?"

His face paled to match his white bandage. "No. It would not be at all possible, you are Monsieur le Comte now." He bowed. "The châtelain, Monseigneur, has arrived."

Papa's frock coat was stifling, but wearing it made me feel closer to him. I had to learn to manage the estate and help Joliette with the vineyard. Then I had to get back to being elected a deputy. "Send him in, please."

62

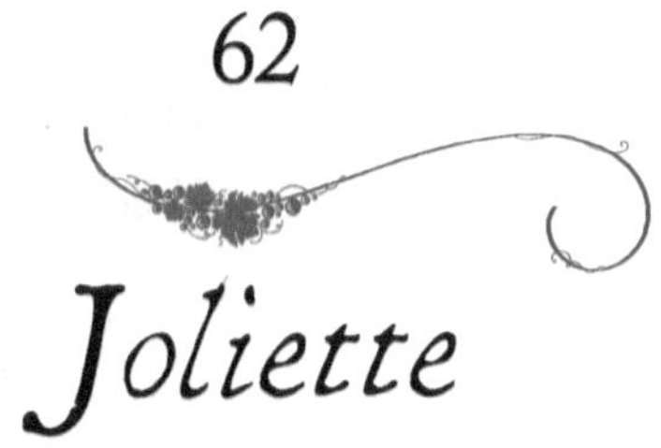

Joliette

Paris
June 24, 1790

"Papa wanted you to live at the mansion, Henri. He would especially want you here, now." I pressed my palms along my gown, trying to banish the image of Papa lying on the carpet in front of me. "It is your home."

"The Marquise and the servants are all here, and I have hired a rather large footman, who is armed, to attend the gate at all times." Henri loosened the knot of his jabot. "You will be safer from Cassard if I do not live here. He will continue to hunt me."

"If Cassard is looking for you, you would be safer here."

"He does not know Papa acknowledged me, does he?"

"Papa's avocats know." I straightened my lace cuff. "Once

the properties are transferred to your name, members of the Court will know."

"Court. I am more worried about the Assembly." He looked up at the ceiling and blew out a breath. "Well, Cassard will not find me here if I continue to use the tunnels."

"Which you could do if you lived here." I pushed the ledger across the desk. "You must be here to manage the accounts."

"I thought you did that." He picked up Papa's porcelain box and opened it.

The scent of cloves snatched my breath. Henri looked to me, sadness filling his eyes. He snapped the box closed.

"No." I pushed my voice. "I conduct all the wine business. Papa managed the accounts for the mansion and estate, both of which he wanted you to learn, if you remember?" I rubbed at the ink stain on my finger.

"I reviewed the accounts with the châtelain before returning to Paris."

"Without me?" My voice sounded shrill. I wanted to pull it back.

"You did not wish to be disturbed. I can have the châtelain send a copy of the ledger, so you can review it." He sat in Papa's chair. "I paid the taxes."

"What?" The word flew from my mouth. "And now that the estate is yours, you will have to pay an inheritance tax!" His jaw pulsed. I paced. "I do not have to worry, but you will. Where are the funds to pay the expenses here?"

He shrugged. "If you don't know, how would I?"

"The account you drew from is the only account. If you paid all the taxes owed, there are no more funds."

"How was I to know that?" He leaned across the desk.

"Did the châtelain not tell you?"

"Well, yes, but if the total was due, what choice did I have?"

"To continue paying a portion every month—with the money we have coming in from the wine business—as Papa did!" I threw up my hands. "How could you not know?"

"How *should* I have known?"

"Not only do you attend the Assembly where the laws change daily, but it is also basic economics." I slapped my skirts. "Basic budgeting. Basic common sense."

His face reddened. "For a noble, perhaps, not a commoner."

"You are now a Comte!"

"In title only. I am, and always will be, a commoner." He raked his hands through his hair. "The Assembly is in the process of abolishing titles of nobility—all of them." His shoulders hunched.

Our lives were so different. He had no idea how to be a comte. Papa never taught him. Shame burned my face. "I apologize. I should not have snapped."

He shook his head but did not look at me.

I gazed up at my father's portrait, towering above the fireplace. A dark green ribbon crossed his broad chest, chin raised, hand resting upon the hilt of his ancestor's sword. "Papa was so proud of being a noblesse d'épée," I whispered. "So was I." I eased myself down onto a pouffe.

"Yes, he was." Lines pulled at the corners of Henri's eyes.

"I am sorry. Regardless of titles, we are all still nobles of the sword, and you will always possess, if not use, your title."

He huffed a laugh. "I suspect my life will be longer without it."

"Then that is true of mine, as well." I opened the hidden

compartment of Papa's desk, removed a blue leather box engraved with the Verzat crest, and held it out. "I believe Papa would have given this to you himself."

He stood with his hands stiff at his sides.

I set it on the desk. "I believe it belonged to your maman."

His hands shook as he opened it. He nodded slowly. "She wears it in a portrait that hangs in the Comédie Française."

The guilt of having searched through Papa's chamber seeped through me. "She was an actress?"

He fingered the gems. "The Marquise told me she never missed one of my maman's performances."

"Will you show me her portrait at the Comédie one day?"

"If you like." He held out the opened box. Sapphires and diamonds sparkled. "They would not look good on me." He smiled. "They belong to you."

"I have Grandmaman's emeralds and Maman's diamonds, which we can sell should the need arise."

Specks of light danced across his face as he gazed at the jewels. "These shall pay the expenses for the mansion. Do you know who will buy them?"

"You should keep them for the wife you will have one day."

He laughed. "I cannot imagine marrying a woman who'd wear such things."

I fingered the pearls circling my throat.

"I'm sorry. I…we were not brought up in the same surroundings. I did not mean to insult you." He closed the box. "Can you arrange the sale?"

I nodded.

He grabbed his tricorne. "I must return to the Assembly

and discover if the decree passed. I will come tomorrow, and we can develop a budget, together."

"Together?"

"The Verzat legacy is our responsibility. Should we not work together?"

I smiled. "Papa would be proud of you, my brother. I am."

He reached for the lever to the secret chamber.

"Henri, I left a maid's gown down there. If I should have to flee, I would escape as a commoner."

"Excellent plan, Comtesse. Better put one in there for the Marquise as well." He grinned and closed the bookshelf behind him.

I walked to the dining room and gazed up at my mother's portrait. "You need not worry about me marrying beneath my title, Maman—in the eyes of the new France, we all shall be equal."

I sighed and rubbed my eyes. Even if titles were abolished, women still would not be equal to men. I would have even less power without my title. Guillaume and Henri thought us equals, but only Madame Robert accepted my signature. I would continue to dishonor the inequitable laws, as Grand-maman would want me to, and fight to change them.

63

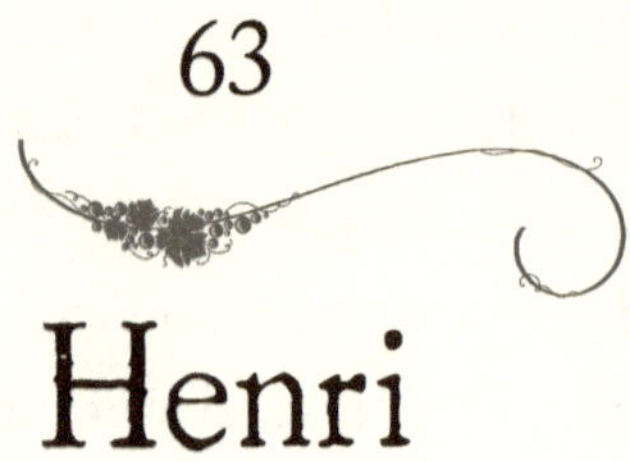

Henri

I SLOSHED THROUGH MUDDY puddles toward the Tuileries. I hoped Geneviève would understand why I'd hidden my nobility and still accept me. I had to word my explanation carefully. Papa acknowledged me and confirmed me as his rightful heir in his will. The only people who knew I was Henri de Verzat were Joliette, the Marquise, Guillaume, Rap, the servants, and the avocat, who'd been sworn to secrecy. I blew out a breath. And everyone on the estate—nearly a thousand people. I had to tell Geneviève before she found out.

Torrents of rain stained the Decrees tacked at the entrance to the Salle du Manège. The Assembly had abolished hereditary nobility and commanded that every French citizen use only the surname of his family.

Was I obligated to take Papa's last name? I had yet to apply for those identity papers—but without them, I'd be unable to claim Papa's property. If I didn't, everything, including the wine business, would be lost. Lost by Joliette. I had to claim my inheritance, if for no other reason than to save Joliette's legacy.

I entered the hall and searched the gallery for Geneviève. She spotted me, jumped up, and raced for the steps. I stood outside, my heart thumping and arms aching to hold her.

"Where have you been?" Geneviève, dressed as Pierre, stood before me, squinting beneath her tricorne.

I wished she'd worn a gown. "I sent a message to your father."

"I couldn't ask him about you, could I?"

"I'm sorry." I reached out and remembered myself. "I had no way of getting word to you. I don't know where you live."

She leaned against the column, the shoulder of her frock coat buckling from the lack of muscle that should've supported the padding. Her mannerisms were masculine, but her feminine physique gave her away. I exhaled trying to slow my heartbeat.

"Where were you?"

"My father died." My chest burned. I had never said it.

She crossed her arms. "You said you didn't know your father."

"I'm a bastard. I didn't know he was my benefactor."

"I'm so sorry, Henri." Her arms dropped to her sides. "I mean, sorry that he died. It doesn't matter to me if you're ille-gitimate."

I wanted to touch her cheek, pull her hat off, caress her hair.

"How did it happen?" she whispered.

A lie squirmed. If I told her the truth, she'd be one more person who knew my real name, and one more person I'd put in harm's way. Yet, carrying the secret exhausted me. "He was murdered."

She pulled back. "What?"

"You must promise to keep what I tell you a secret. Do you promise?"

"Yes. I'd never betray you." Her eyes were innocent, like a dove's.

"My maman died giving me life." I sighed. "Her husband killed my papa."

Geneviève slipped her hand into mine. "I am deeply sorry, Henri."

I ran my fingers over hers, so soft, small. "The man has sworn to kill me."

"You must tell my father!" Her voice wavered.

"He is slippery—escaped the law here, weaseled his way out of a London debtors' prison, and returned here under an assumed name and false papers."

She grabbed me. "Ask my father to have him arrested."

"I don't know his assumed name." My arms hung limp. "He does not know who I am, only that I exist. And that I have a half-sister, who is in greater danger than I, for he knows her name and where she lives."

She let go of me. "But why is she in danger?"

"Vengeance."

"It's not enough to kill the man who wronged him?" A curl stuck to her wet cheek.

A familiar hollowness sagged in my chest. I wanted to defend my father, for he loved my maman, but Geneviève was right, he had wronged Cassard. "I am the one who killed his wife."

"You know that's not true." Redness flamed her cheeks.

"He'll not stop until he's killed the people my papa loved."

She leaned close. "He'll not get you, Henri, if my papa has him arrested."

Her flowery scent drew me closer. "If I learn his assumed name, I will tell you." Her breath warmed my neck.

She gripped my hand and pulled me toward the river.

I stood my ground. "I cannot be late on my first day back at my duties. I have many articles to write."

"Tonight? Pont Neuf?"

I nodded. Rain bounced off the stone steps as I climbed back to the Assembly and abruptly stopped. I'd still not told her the entire truth. My chest sagged. Telling her could endanger her. Nonetheless, she'd be angry when she learned the truth. I wiped rain from the back of my neck. I'd rather face her anger than put her in danger.

Taking my father's name would identify me as a former nobleman, which was not nearly as safe as being a commoner from the poorest faubourg in Paris. Becoming Verzat would make Cassard's search for me an easy one. Maybe I'd let him do the hunting, as this time, I'd be doing the killing.

64

Joliette

I CLOSED THE ACCOUNTS book. Although I fought constant reminders of Papa's murder, I felt his presence the strongest in his library. It was also the safest room in the mansion should we need to suddenly flee. "When Papa surrendered his feudal privileges, he did not make provisions for paying tax on property that tenants inhabit, without rent, for eternity."

Henri stood with his hands behind his back looking up at Papa's portrait. "If tenants are forced to pay the tax on land they do not own, they may starve." He faced me. "I don't think either one of us wants that, nor would Papa."

"There has to be a solution." I paced. "What are we not seeing?"

"There is something risky, but that risk might save the château."

I tapped my nails against the accounts book. "Want to share the secret?"

"When nobles emigrated after the Bastille, they abandoned their land and châteaux, which they cannot reclaim. Right now, the château and all the land are Verzat property." His eyes sparkled. "What if we sell parcels of the estate to the existing four hundred tenants at a price they could pay over the course of twenty years? That way, we would receive enough funds to pay taxes on the majority of the property now, and the tenants would be responsible for the taxes on their small pieces of property. In the event we must emigrate, we could assign the rest of the land to the tenants and put the funds to pay the taxes in trust. Then the land would not be lost to those who might not be loyal to Verzat. When we returned, we would buy back the property at the price we charged: ten livres per year."

In my mind, I saw the Verzat crest carved in stone above the wine cave. I wrapped my arms around myself. "I think I would rather sell Maman's jewels." I swept my skirts aside and stood before him. "Every summer, when we arrived at the château, Papa told the same story about how François I awarded the land to his great, great—I do not know how many greats and neither did he—grand-père. He was never as proud as when he was telling that story. To sell even a parcel of it?"

"Those loyal tenants would be holding the land for us, like insurance." He gently gripped my arm and walked me back to the sofa. "I want you to think about something that may happen."

I closed my eyes. *Maman, Papa, give me patience.*

"Already in the Assembly, there is talk of ridding the nation of Royalists."

His voice was so soft I could barely hear him, and I leaned forward.

"Both you and Papa served the King and Queen. There may come a day when those actions could be considered a crime."

"What?" I leapt up.

"The royal family may try to escape."

Dizzied by the thought, I collapsed into the sofa.

"Yesterday, ministers to the King were dismissed from the Assembly." He dragged his hands across his eyes. "There may come a time when we must leave France, Joliette. Papa foresaw it, and he told me to take you to America."

I rested my head back on the sofa. Jacques softly cleared his throat. "Comtesse, the Baron Pricaud has arrived."

Henri smiled and bobbed his head as if amused.

"You have another secret, brother?"

He looked at the carpet and scratched his jaw.

What was he up to? I turned to Jacques. "Please have him wait in the salon and ask the Marquise to join us."

Jacques bowed.

"Jacques, I am glad to see you are recovered." Henri walked toward him. "Tell me, can you remember anything more of the man who attacked you?"

Jacques squeezed his eyes and tilted his head. "His black wig was askew. He had gray hair. Half his right ear was missing. He was thin."

Henry reached out and touched his arm.

Jacques froze. Tears welled. None of us had ever touched

him. He mourned Papa—as we did. He was suffering, terribly, yet he took care of us.

"That is most helpful, Jacques. Anything else?"

His eyes shone. "He was taller than me, Monseigneur."

"I know it's painful for you to recall that day." Henri patted him on the back. "Thank you, Jacques."

"I regret not having protected the Comte."

"Cassard did not give you a chance. You are not at fault."

He bowed and left us.

Henri looked down at the place where Papa's body had lain. I shivered, shaking off the image. "Think about the possibility of what we discussed. I will consult Papa's avocat." He lifted the lever and the bookcase swung open. "Please give my warmest regards to the Marquise and the Baron." He left me.

I blew out a breath and regarded the portrait. "I know I asked you for a brother, Papa, but why did you give me such a troublesome one?"

I found the Marquise embroidering and Guillaume standing at the window, a shaft of sunlight deepening the green of his eyes.

"Thank you for accompanying us, Monsieur le Baron."

"Comtesse!" His smile banished my frustrations. He held a small posy of muguet, the little bell-shaped blossoms shivering.

I inhaled. "They are my favorite. Merci."

He brought out another nosegay tied with a lilac ribbon and handed them to the Marquise. "And some for you, Madame."

She blushed. "Oh! I have not received flowers since my dear

husband passed." She stood. "I shall take these to my chamber so that their fragrance fills it. Excuse me for a few moments."

Guillaume held my hand and kissed my fingers but did not let go.

My heartbeat raced.

He cleared his throat and opened his mouth but uttered no words. A blush crept from his white jabot to his hairline. "I asked Henri for permission to court you, but he told me he could not give it."

A prickling ran up my back. "I would not have expected my brother to be concerned with a person's station." I blinked back tears.

He coughed a laugh. "He said your permission was not his to give. As it is *your* permission, you are the only one to grant it."

My anger snuffed like a candleflame. "I?"

"May I court you, Joliette?" He watched me as he opened my hand and kissed my palm.

I clasped his arm, for I feared my legs would fold beneath me. "Yes." The word flew from me like a bird taking flight. His smile drew me, and I leaned into him. His lips were warm upon mine.

The sound of a light tick tack of a walking stick broke us apart. I pressed my hand to my bosom to slow my breathing.

The Marquise took her time entering the salon and kept her eyes on the Aubusson rug. "Guillaume will your regiment allow you to join us for dinner?"

"It would be my greatest pleasure, Madame."

As it would be mine. The music of the night we met in the ballroom of Versailles echoed. I began to hum along, and Guillaume smiled at me.

I abruptly stopped. Guillaume also served the royal family, and if Henri's prediction proved true, both of us would have committed an unimaginable crime. I would speak to Madame Robert. If I could arrange shipping from the château, perhaps we would all be safer there.

65

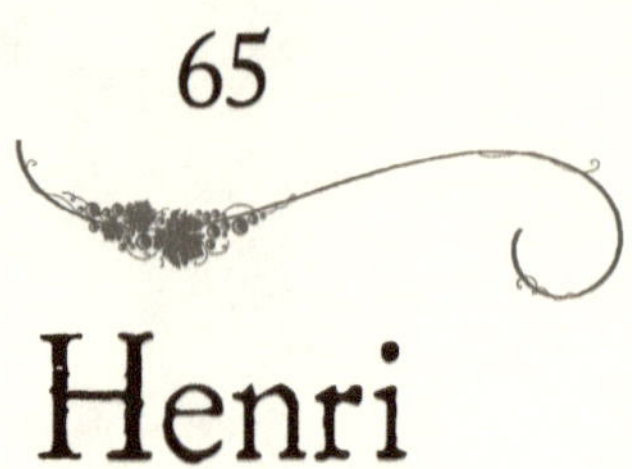

Henri

Paris
December 12, 1791

My neck grew sore from scouring the face of every peddler, coachman, news crier, gendarme, chimneysweep, tanner, stevedore, charwoman, lacemaker. I had no doubt Cassard would stop at nothing to disguise himself, despite Papa's assurance Cassard would leave me alone. The bastard was in Paris. I felt his presence like moisture in the air.

Geneviève, dressed as Pierre, met me at the Pont Neuf. Her waistcoat gapped between the buttons and the image of her bare breasts roused me. I feared she could hear my heart thundering. Her gray eyes drew me, and I took a step closer, reached out, caressed the backs of my fingers along her cheek. Her breath smelled of mint.

"It's a warm evening. Shall we walk along the river?"

She gazed beyond me and pointed. Streaks of pink and purple clouds hovered as darkness crept over the city. Flashes of golden light reflecting off the water danced across her face, sparking in her eyes. I took off my hat and, holding it up to shield prying eyes, I leaned in and kissed the tiny naked space below her ear and above her neckcloth. Dressing as a man was illegal for women, but her father might not prosecute his own daughter.

"Would you do that if I were wearing a gown?" Her voice was low.

"A gown would allow me to kiss more of you." I leaned in. "And I would."

"I will be sure to wear one tomorrow." She pressed her hands against my shoulders.

"You must come with me to the Jacobin Club, tonight."

She pouted. "Why?"

"I predict the Jacobins will take over the Assembly. And..." Did I want more attention should people learn my real name? I swallowed. "I will apply to be elected as a deputy there."

"The gown can wait." She laughed.

"I want to show you something that could save your life." I held her arm. She tipped her head. "Come." I led her down stone steps to a tunnel entry, pushed open the wooden door, and pulled her forward.

She resisted. "You want me to go into the tunnels?"

"I know them like the inside of my purse. I won't let anything happen to you."

She jumped back.

"You're shivering like a cornered rabbit."

"I'm frightened."

"Of what?"

She scuffed her boot. "It's dark."

"You forged your father's signature and dressed as a man to attend University and you are frightened of the dark?"

She turned away. "I knew you wouldn't understand."

"Try me."

She brought her hands behind her neck and looked at her boots. "I was four years old. I awoke. The candle had burned out and the nurse was gone from her pallet. I ran to my mother's room and stood beside her bed. Her arm was hanging down, and I clasped her hand. It was cold. I climbed in beside her and cried, but she didn't stir. My father came and locked me in my dark room."

I swallowed. "She died?"

Geneviève nodded. "Ever since that night, I cannot abide the dark. Silly, I know, but…"

I drew her to me. "It's not silly. It's understandable."

"It is?" Her eyes were pinched.

"Yes. The catacombs terrify me because my maman's bones might be there. I not only avoid the catacombs, but also the tunnels around them."

She blew out a breath. "I don't think the tunnels are for me."

I squeezed her fingers. "Would you try one trip with me? I have spare torches hidden, and I always carry an extra candle, flint, steel, and box of char cloth." I encouraged her with another squeeze. "Just one?"

The muscles around her eyes flinched.

"If you are ever in danger, knowing that you can escape through the tunnels could save your life."

"How long would we be down there?"

"Fifteen minutes."

She grasped her trembling hands in prayer.

Challenging her would be effective in every other conversation, but not this one. I had to win her over. "Ten, if you hold onto me every step of the way, and we hurry." I reached out my hand.

She studied my palm like it was a sleeping snake.

"Geneviève," I whispered. "I won't let anything happen to you. I promise."

She heaved a sigh and gripped my hand. "I pray I won't regret this."

"I'll ensure you don't."

When we surfaced on rue Saint-Honoré, Geneviève giggled so hard, her waistcoat buttons popped open. She bent over, slapped her legs, and laughed a great big long laugh.

"I didn't know you enjoyed it so much. Would you like to go again?"

She stopped her laughter and stood, straightening her waistcoat and neckcloth. "No."

A couple strolled past us, looking us up and down. When they were out of earshot, I patted her shoulder. "Well done. You were very brave."

She cleared her throat. "Now let's see how brave you are when you voice your intent to the Jacobins." Her smile challenged.

I wiped sweat from my brow. I was on my way to becoming a deputy. God help me.

66

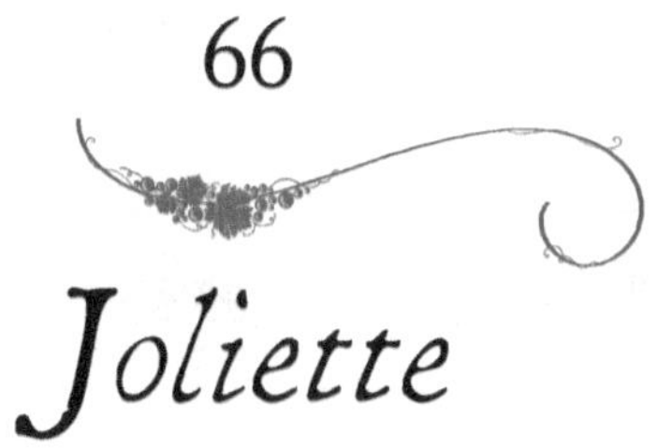

Joliette

Paris
December 21, 1791

SINGING FLOATED INTO my bedchamber: "Ça Ira." Fine? Everything will *not* be fine. I slammed a shutter and reached for the other when a chill ran down my arm. They changed the words: "Aristocrats to the lamppost, it'll be fine, it'll be fine, it'll be fine. The aristocrats, we'll hang them, it'll be fine, it'll be fine, it'll be fine."

"You will not be sending anyone to a lamppost." As I checked the flint in my pistolet, a banging on the front door made me run to the top of the stairs and look down into the grand hall.

Beneath the chandelier, a poissarde, wearing a bloodstained apron, thrust her long thin knife at Jacques. He held his arms up, fingers fluttering like leaves in a strong wind. Five other women—each brandishing a knife, all wearing bloodstained aprons—surrounded the leader. The shouts pounded in my head. What had they done to the huge footman? I grabbed the balustrade and hid the pistolet behind my skirts.

The Marquise entered the foyer from the salon and whacked her walking stick. "What is the meaning of this outrage?"

My heartbeat thundered. I ran halfway down the steps and pressed my thumb to the pistolet's hammer.

The poissarde did not loosen her grip on the knife at Jacques's throat. "Give your jewels to the Republic, and we shall leave without hurting anyone."

I straightened. "Can you not see this woman is in mourning?"

The leader jerked her head toward me and back at Jacques. Her knife wavered dangerously close to his jaw. The other women looked up at me.

"She wears no jewelry." I prayed the Marquise had hidden her diamond bracelets. She had already removed her necklace.

The leader gestured with her knife "Her jewels must be in her...*boudoir*?"

Descending a step, I aimed the pistolet at her. The woman pressed the tip of her knife into Jacques's throat. The poor man's eyes bulged.

"She left them at Versailles." I drew back the pistolet's hammer. "Your predecessors must have found them."

The leader cackled. "We must have missed those!"

The other women laughed nervously. I trained my gun on the leader. The stink of gunpowder, blood and sweat made me sway. I widened my stance.

The leader lifted her chin. "And yours, Mademoiselle?"

Sweat trickled beneath my arms. "Back at Versailles."

A woman of about thirty years with a red blotch spreading across her right cheek cried, "You said we'd get food. I'm not letting my children die of starvation while you demand jewels for the Republic." She backed up toward the door, her eyes on my gun.

I steadied my voice. "Jacques, please help Cook bring flour, bread, and eggs from the kitchen." I pointed at the leader. "Let him go, now."

The leader withdrew the knife and looked from me to the Marquise, who held her walking stick as a cudgel.

Jacques—hands fluttering, eyes on the knife—backed up all the way to the door and looked up to me. I nodded. He turned and left.

The woman with the birthmark yanked the leader's arm. "Food for our starving children, *not* jewels for the Republic."

The leader shook her off.

"Your children have died; have pity upon ours." Tears streamed down the scarred woman's face.

My heart thumped wildly. What would Papa do? His words raced, *Give them a way to feed themselves.* But there were so many.

The birthmarked woman placed her knife in the sheath at her waist and looked up at me. Dark circles surrounded her sunken joyless eyes. "My children have not eaten in days, Mademoiselle. Merci."

I lowered the pistolet a bit. "I am so sorry. How many children have you?"

She jerked her head as if suspicious. "Three."

"Does your husband have a trade?"

Her hands clasped in prayer. "Barrel cooper, but there's no need."

"I have a need."

Her hand trembled against her stained cheek.

Keeping the pistolet aimed at the leader, I called out, "Madame Bourran, please go to my desk and write a note to our vintner at Château de Verzat." I turned to the woman. "What is your name?"

"Gois, Laure Gois, Mademoiselle."

"Tell him I recommend Monsieur Gois as cooper for the vineyard."

The Marquise nodded and hurried into the salon. I turned to Madame Gois. "If your husband agrees to work at the vineyard, you will have a house, a goat, chickens, and a small plot of land you can farm, at no cost to you, other than your husband's labor. You are free to eat and sell whatever you grow and raise. Your children will attend school there. Is this acceptable to you?"

Madame Gois's neck blushed as red as her birthmark. She shook with her nodding. "Yes, Mademoiselle. I promise you, yes."

The leader tapped the flat of her knife on her apron and frowned.

The Marquise glared at the leader as she passed her and handed me the quill and paper on a silver tray. I signed and held out the paper to Madame Gois. "Are we agreed?"

She grasped the paper to her bosom, fell to her knees, clutched the hem of my gown, and kissed it. "Merci, merci. A thousand mercis."

I offered my hand to help her up. "There is no need,

Madame. We are equals. And if your husband can assist in my business, I am grateful."

She smiled and wiped tears away with her bloodied apron.

The leader grabbed the tray from me. I let it go. She fell back, surprised at my lack of resistance. She righted herself and hugged the tray to her breast.

I smiled. "It will be useful for carrying the food."

Her eyes were wary, but her posture softened. In unison, the other four women turned their eyes toward me.

"Madame Bourran, please bring the silver présentoirs for the others."

She hurried into the dining room and returned with four wine bottle coasters and distributed them.

Jacques and Cook, arms laden with food, emerged from the hallway. The leader and other poisssardes swarmed them, grabbing at whatever they could claim, and fled.

My chest grew as empty as their stomachs must have been. Jacques secured the door. Cook patted her apron to her forehead. Madame Gois stood clutching my note, her arms empty.

"Cook, please bring Madame Gois food for her family." I put my gun in my hanging pocket and held out my hand. "I am Joliette Verzat. I am pleased to make your acquaintance." She grasped my hand. "Do you have a daughter, Madame?"

She smiled broadly. "Three."

"They shall all go to school." I laughed and glanced at the Marquise.

She stood at the doorway, not leaning on her walking stick as if she needed it, but holding it as a weapon. A tear ran down her face. "Mademoiselle is much like her father, a brave, kind, and generous man. He would be most proud of her."

A tear slipped down my cheek, and my hand trembled as I wiped it away. I hoped I would continue to make my father proud. But Henri's words rang in my mind. Being a noblesse d'épée could get us all killed. I could not give everyone in Paris a position at the château.

But I could give Révolutionaries a reason not to burn Château de Verzat. I had to export more wine. They would not dare destroy a business that employed so many people and paid taxes. Perhaps Henri's idea should extend to the château. If every tenant owned a piece of it, they would protect the entire château.

67

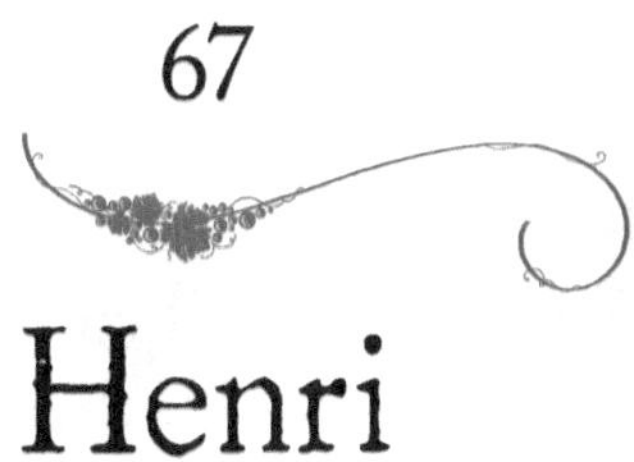

Henri

Paris
January 5, 1792

I RIPPED OPEN THE letter. *The Président de l'Assemblée Législative, Claude-Emannuel Pastoret, congratulates the Député de Faubourg Saint-Antoine: Henri Detré.* I ran around my lodgings, shouting and laughing. I folded the letter and tucked it in my waistcoat, grabbed my hat, and headed for the market. Maman and Madame Françoise would be most proud and join me in a celebration. Geneviève and I'd celebrate later, alone.

There were fewer stalls and less food for sale. I found a shriveled ham, a cabbage, and a few half-rotten potatoes. I stuffed everything in a sack and went into a wine shop. "Have you Château de Verzat?"

The proprietor, a rotund man with black hair and eyebrows

that stuck out like thorns, laughed. "Where'd you think you are? Versailles?" He slapped the counter and laughed.

"I'm sure whatever you have is good."

He grabbed an empty bottle, thrust it under a spigot from a large cask, filled and corked the bottle, and slid it across the counter. Flecks of something swirled in the liquid. I hoped it wasn't flies.

"Fifteen sous."

"For wine that will turn to vinegar by this evening?"

"My mistake." He leaned over the counter and pinned my hand. "Twenty sous."

His paw could crush my bones. "It must be a very good vintage."

He crowed another laugh and slapped the counter again, releasing his hold on me. I threw my money down and grabbed the bottle. No sense fighting with him, I was representing the idiot.

I slowed as I arrived at rue du Faubourg Saint-Antoine and the market. Vendors crowded the street, shouting their wares: brooms, candles, rabbits, lanterns, firewood, baked apples, toy windmills. A man with an animal pelt tied atop his tricorne and a plague of dead rats hanging from his staff, cried out, "I kill the rats—they die, Mesdames!" People scurried around him.

I turned the corner and skidded in the muck. Before a window two buildings away stood a tall, thin man with yellow-gray hair hanging over his shoulders. *Thin as an asparagus spear.* Blood whooshed in my ears. I shoved the wine bottle under my arm, pulled out my pistol, and pressed into a doorway, waiting for Cassard to move, repeating my promise to Papa: *I will avenge you.*

He stood as if interested in the wares in the window, chewing his fingernails and spitting the trimmings in the gutter. He rubbed his fingers against the sleeve of his ox-blood colored frock coat, though I saw he was not as interested in the hats displayed in the shop as in using the reflective glass to observe passersby. He kept his head still, but his eyes roved.

Juggling the wine and food as I hid my pistol, I tilted my hat to shadow my face and crossed the street. A coppersmith rattled his pans toward me. "Buy a pot, a spoon," he called, then bent his neck and leered, "or a bed warmer for your lovely wife, Monsieur?"

I stared beyond the man's pots and saw the man I took for Cassard speak to a gentleman and tip his hat. Half an ear.

My throat closed. My finger thrummed on the trigger.

The gentleman stopped, peered in the window, spoke, and pointed. As he did, Cassard lifted the flap of the man's pocket, pulled out a leather pouch, and tucked it into his waistcoat, all the while nodding and smiling at the gentleman.

My mouth opened. I snapped it shut.

The men laughed. Cassard clapped the man on the back and strutted away.

A prickling moved through me as the image of Papa bleeding on the rug flooded my vision. Staying on the opposite side of the street, my thumb pressed the pistol's hammer as I stalked Cassard. Three street boys surrounded him, their filthy hands clutching at his frock coat. He waved the purse above his head, and the boys jumped. Cassard opened the purse he'd just stolen and pulled out a shiny coin. The boys lurched. "One at a time," he shouted.

Looking from one to the other, the boys backed off. They extended their hands, and he placed a coin in each. The boys whooped and tore down the street. Cassard tucked the purse into his waistcoat. A French Robin Hood. I spat.

A horse drew a diligence past, blocking my view. "Stop! Thief!" a man's voice shouted. The man who'd been robbed must have figured it out.

People scattered. The horses spooked. The driver stood to gain control.

I forced myself to walk calmly, fearing I'd be mistaken for the thief. On the other side of the street, Cassard strutted into an alley.

Something savage reared up in me, and I flew across the street, clutching my pistol before me. I ran down the alley, around a stack of broken baskets, crates, barrels of stink, and into a courtyard. I pressed my back against the cold stone of a building, scrabbling for breath. Had there been other doors along the way?

I pressed the wall with my palm. Think. A breeze billowed sheets, hanging from poles protruding from the upper windows, casting shadows over the yard.

Unless he'd hidden in the garbage heap or had a key to one of the two doors beyond the yard, he was here, close, hiding, watching me. I tilted my hat to keep my face in the dark. A rat scurried between my feet. The wine bottle slipped. I grabbed it before it shattered. The rat's tail snaked in the muck.

A panting came from behind. I flicked my eyes to a mangy dog hunched and snarling, ready to pounce. He growled. I aimed the pistol. The wine bottle smashed on the stone. The dog yelped and lunged at me, fangs dripping with slobber.

A shadow moved out from behind the garbage heap. A barrel toppled and rolled toward me. The dog barked. I jumped back as the barrel pinned me to the wall. Cassard fled.

I threw the ham into the courtyard. The dog ran after it. I shoved my way around the barrel, my boots squelching in the filth. Cassard knew now, for certain, I existed. He knew I was seeking revenge. He knew what I looked like. And I knew he'd find me again.

My legs quaked. I collapsed back against the wall. I'd be ready.

68

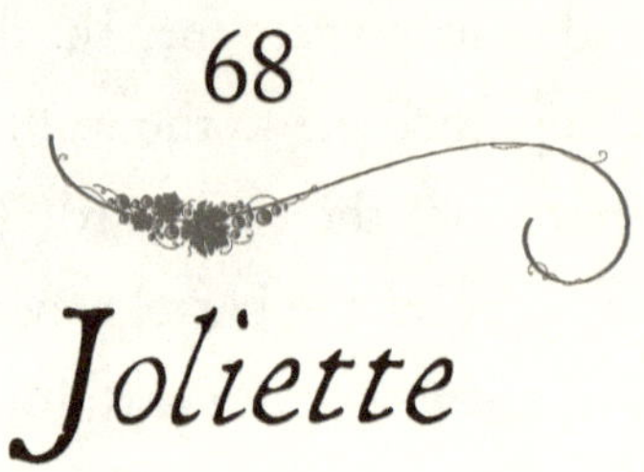

Joliette

Paris
February 1, 1792

"FIFTY-THREE FROZEN TO death in their sleep!" A news crier's voice was the only sound in the muffled world enshrouded by snow.

Even with the warmth of the fireplace, I wore fingerless gloves and placed a fur throw over my lap while I worked on the accounts at Papa's desk. Henri was late. My hands shivered, spitting ink as I wrote. Would my brother be as accepting of my news as he had been when Guillaume asked his permission to court me? Papa smiled down at me from his portrait. "I know you would not be happy, Papa. Forgive me."

I heard a soft scratching noise, followed by the bookcase swinging open. I stood. "Henri, welcome."

"Good day, sister." His face white with cold, he removed his cloak and laid it on a chair. "Sorry to be late, but the tunnels are filled with people taking refuge." He blew a breath into his hands and stood close to the fire.

"I will have Jacques put more wood on."

He put up his hand. "I can do that." He picked up a log. "He is an old man. Let him rest." He added it to the fire and stood.

"Jacques lives to serve."

"He'll live longer if he rests more." He turned his back to the fire and smiled. "It's rumored the Seine may freeze over."

"The last time that happened, Papa...." The ache in my chest stabbed like a knife. I pressed my hand against my heart.

Henri's eyes were dark and sad.

I sipped in a breath. "He wanted to distract the royal children from the impending death of their brother, the first Dauphin, so Papa took us ice skating on the Grand Canal." I stood and extended my arms, imitating Papa. "He was so serious, his voice low. 'The important things to remember are, keep your knees bent and your weight over your toes. I shall show you how to start.' A servant walked out onto the ice and held out his hand. Papa put one foot on the ice, turned and flung his arms out wide. His skates scraped and slid. The servant grabbed for Papa, but he hit the servant in the chest, knocked him over and sent him spinning across the canal. Papa's arms whirled as he slid away from us, his feet flew up, and he dropped like a stone onto his back. He lay looking up at the sky, his arms and legs whirling above him."

Henri laughed.

"Louis Charles said he looked like a giant beetle." I laughed a sob. "And he did." I swiped tears. "Louis Charles clapped his hands and begged, 'Do it again, Comte! Do it again.' With his most serious face, Papa attempted to skate across the Canal. Whether he could actually skate or not, I do not know because with every one of Louis Charles's requests he slipped and spun along the ice, his arms and legs flailing above him. For the next week, Papa brought a pillow with him wherever he went." I was laughing and crying, my mouchoir no longer of any use. "I miss him so."

Henri gave me his mouchoir. I sat next to him. He held my hand and stared at the fire. The light flickered over his face, deepening the lines, making him look much older, much more like Papa.

"Sometimes," he began, stopped, struggled, "when I pause in the tunnels…deciding which way to go…" He drew in a breath, held it, blew it out in a slow steady stream. "I feel his arm about my shoulders and a nudge to the right or left." He snorted a laugh to cover a sob. "Perhaps it's my imagination." He wiped his eyes.

"Do you think he is with us right now?" I asked.

"Don't you smell the cloves?"

I squeezed his hand. "Thank you for coming. I am glad you are here. Would you like a tisane?"

"Brandy."

"I shall join you." I poured us both a glass from the decanter on Papa's desk.

"Before you tell me your news, we must discuss another law the Assembly has passed that affects us." He took a sip and set down the glass.

I sat at the desk and slapped the accounts book. "I am exporting as much wine as we produce."

He put his palms up. "That is good." He sat opposite me. "But I am here to discuss Papa's last wish. I think he foresaw what is coming."

"You promised Papa, but I shall never leave France." The brandy burned its way down to my stomach.

He raised his hand. "In the event we must, as émigrés, we could lose our property."

I ran a finger over the crest in the glass. "A good reason not to leave."

"There is no reason to lose one's life, Joliette. Should we lose our lives, the legacy would end. And that is what Papa feared and why he wanted me to take you to America."

"There is no reason now, so why discuss it?" I stood, plucked up the fur, and draped it over his shoulders.

"Thank you." He wrapped it about himself tightly. "The Comte de Provence has been recalled. If he does not return, the state will confiscate his property and holdings. The same could happen to us."

"Not if we do not leave."

"We must prepare, should the need arise."

I sat down and leaned over the desk. "You know the irony of this? That law is much like a lettre de cachet."

He stifled a laugh. "If we must flee to save our lives, we've got to have a plan in place so that we don't lose the Verzat château and legacy. You don't want to lose control of the vine-yard and the distribution of wine, do you?"

"Did you investigate selling the land to the tenants who already live on the estate?"

"Possible, but not the best option. No matter how loyal the

tenants have been to Papa, there is no guarantee they will remain so under a new Republic."

I tapped the quill on the accounts book. "The Marquise?"

"As a former member of the nobility and servant to the royal family, she is in as much danger as we." He gazed at the fire. "Do you trust the châtelain?"

"I do not know him well enough to make that judgement. However, he has been at his post since Grandmaman managed the estate."

He sipped his brandy. "You remember Papa's tutor, Monsieur Rapineau? He was my tutor, also."

"Yes, he is a delightful man. He taught me English when I was young. I called him Oncle Albert. He wore a funny straw hat that made him look like a scarecrow. He made me laugh almost as much as Papa."

"Are we speaking of the same man? He never made me laugh."

"You were probably not as good a student as I, so he was firm with you." I laughed. "I know Papa loved him. But he is old."

"Perhaps we could have more than one person, in the event of one not being able to act as owner." He drained his glass.

"Monsieur Rapineau and the Marquise?" I poured more brandy.

"Both are old."

"Is there anyone else you trust?" I asked.

"My milk-mother."

I tilted my head. "Of course, you trust her, as do I. But would she understand the responsibility?"

"She cannot read, but she is as loyal to me as we are to Papa, and much younger."

"But do you think she could comprehend the risks?"

He smiled. "She would do anything for me."

"Would she mind leaving Paris?"

"Mind not working her fingers to the bone washing other people's laundry sunrise till sunset?" He gave me a funny frown that reminded me of Papa, and I missed him all the more.

"Would Oncle Albert, the Marquise, and your maman all live there?"

"I will check with Papa's avocat, but you will not need the Marquise living here as chaperone much longer."

He spoiled my surprise. Heat flashed up my neck. "Why do you say such a thing?"

"The Assembly decrees marriage ceremonies must be civil not religious."

"And why do you tell me this?" My voice screeched. I regretted speaking.

"Guillaume is a National Guardsman. Obeying the law before it is passed would put him and you in good standing with the Republic."

I spun around. "You assume he has asked me?"

His smile gleamed. "You are ready to burst with the secret."

I pressed my lips together. I wanted to shout it to the world.

"I am so relieved he did not ask me for your hand."

"Is my hand not mine own to give?"

He laughed. "Of course, my sister."

"You toy with me."

"No, Joliette. I could not be happier for you."

"As my guardian, you must sign. Will you?"

"Of course. Guillaume is a good and honorable man." He

leaned across the desk and whispered, "After the civil ceremony, I can arrange for a religious one with the bishop at Saint Séverin."

"Would you? A church wedding would make Maman so happy." I lied. Nothing about my marriage would make my mother happy. But a church wedding would make Guillaume and me happy. We needed God's blessing.

69

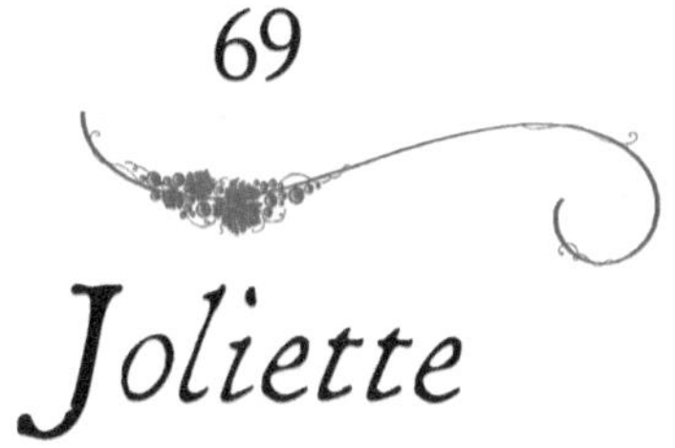

Joliette

Paris
February 12, 1792

A WEEK LATER, THE Marquise stood behind me, smiling at my reflection in my dressing table mirror. I willed myself not to cry. She had become a Maman to me, nearly as dear as my own.

I picked up Maman's diamonds, glittering in the morning light. "She expected me to wear them on this day."

"Not if it means risking your life." The Marquise placed her hands on my shoulders. "You can wear them at dinner."

Although the civil ceremony would be cold and official and being married in a church was illegal, I was determined to make our special day a joyful one. I asked Cook to prepare a celebratory dinner and Marie to fill the salons with fresh greenery and candles.

She placed a fan on the table. "Here is something you can carry."

I spread open the fan, revealing a hand-painted scene of Versailles upon fragile cream-colored silk. "It is lovely."

"I carried it at my own wedding." Her hands were warm on my shoulders, reminding me of Maman's tender touch. I would not cry.

The Marquise gazed out the window as if watching herself on her special day. The ruffles and lace of her lilac gown were limp and worn, but she was no less regal than if she were wearing brand new silks.

"Were your parents happy with your match?" My voice caught.

"*I* was." She shook her head. "Only the bride and groom must be happy." She squeezed my fingers. "And I know you and Guillaume are." She placed a white lace fichu over my shoulders. "You are beautiful in your mother's gown."

I stood and ran my hands over the stiff taffeta skirt. "Maman always wore white, the color of mourning, but I never asked her why." I inhaled her lavender scent, still clinging to the fabric. My heart ached. I exhaled slowly and tucked the mouchoir Guillaume gave me into my dark green sash.

The Marquise and I joined Guillaume and Henri in the salon. I squinted at the brilliant white of Guillaume's crisp waistcoat and breeches, and brass buttons and epaulettes. The cutaway of his dark blue frock coat emphasized his broad shoulders. He rested his hand on the pommel of his sword and grinned. His smile matched his dazzling uniform.

My heartbeat quickened as it had the first moment I met him. I smiled, and his hands captured mine. He kissed my palms. "Mon coeur est tien."

His face was haloed by my tears. "And my heart is yours, my love."

"Joliette?"

I turned to face Henri. He must have had Papa's dark green velvet frock coat altered because it fit him perfectly. He looked even more like Papa. *Maman, Papa, I wish you were here with us.*

Henri held out a small circle of gathered blue, white, and red ribbon. "Wearing this will put you in good standing with the Republic. It's a cockade and complements Guillaume's uniform."

I kissed Henri's cheek and pinned it to my bodice. "You think of everything."

We four donned cloaks and traveled through the bitter cold in Papa's carriage to the Hôtel de Ville. The Grand Hall wore a resplendence similar to Versailles with its crystal chandeliers, parquet floors, marble steps and balustrades. An acrid stink of gun smoke burned my nose. I gripped Guillaume's arm.

He patted my hand. "What is it, my darling?"

I would not let the memory of the slaughter on the Queen's staircase ruin this day. I shook my head and smiled.

I expected the ceremony to take place in one of the salons, but we were directed to a back office without ornament. Filthy windows let in mottled sunlight. Taupe colored paint flaked from the rough walls. Documents were nailed to wooden beams supporting the low ceiling. The fireplace held cold ashes. We kept our cloaks on.

A tall official, wearing all black except for the cockade upon his lapel, greeted us. "Citizens, one of the first duties to the Republic is marriage."

I sighed. If I was not obeying my parents, at least I was obeying the Republic.

Guillaume repeated, "I declare, as a free man and good citizen, I take Joliette Verzat as my friend and my wife."

The official removed my title, and Catherine Alisson Françoise Baumere, and the *de* before Verzat. I felt as plain and powerless as a peasant. I was more attached to my title than I thought.

I repeated, "I declare, as a free woman and good citizeness, I take Guillaume Pricaud as my friend and my husband."

Both our signatures were required, and mine was legal on this document. I gazed at the drying ink. Our signatures were equal. Our vows were equal. We were equals. I smiled up at Guillaume. His eyes glistened. I dabbed at my eyes and gathered my cloak tightly around me.

The official stamped our document and dismissed us to make room for the next couple.

We hurried through the Grand Hall and returned to the mansion.

As we stood before a roaring fire in Papa's library, Guillaume held me to him, kissing my hair, my face, my lips. "What is it, my dearest?"

I had not realized I was crying. His voice and concern were so kind. I released a sob I had held within me since the day he asked me to be his bride.

The lines around his eyes deepened. "Are you not happy?"

I nodded. "I am so happy."

The Marquise sat on the chaise longue. "I am thrilled you are husband and wife." She clapped.

Henri joined us. "Jacques, please bring the special bottle of our wine to celebrate the first ceremony and ask Cook and Marie to join us."

Jacques brought a tray of wine and glasses. Cook and Marie stood, worrying their aprons.

Henri opened the bottle. "Three more glasses, please."

I smiled. Henri treated the servants as equals. Jacques returned with the glasses, Cook dabbed her apron at her eyes, and Marie stifled a giggle. Had they ever tasted Verzat wine?

Henri filled all the glasses and raised his. "I honor Joliette and Guillaume and toast to a long life filled with love and joy." Our glasses clinked.

Guillaume's eyes did not leave mine as we drank. When we finished, he leaned close to me and whispered, "I shall never leave you, my dear wife."

My heart pounded. "Nor I you." I prayed our religious ceremony would be as beautiful as our love.

70

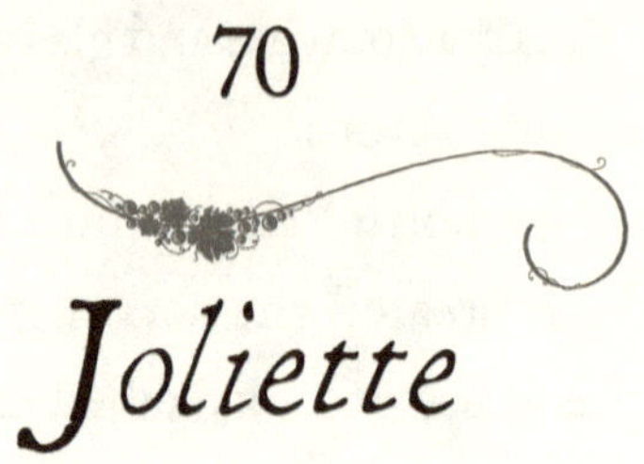

Joliette

Paris
February 12, 1792

As dusk fell, the Marquise, Guillaume, and I arrived at Saint Séverin. We crept through the courtyard and along a path to an unmarked door. Trembling moved through me. If we were discovered, we would be arrested. It would be all my fault. The door creaked open. Henri, holding a candle, his jacket smudged with the chalky white of the tunnels, urged us to hurry.

He motioned us along the side aisle of the empty Saint Séverin, the same aisle he walked the first time I saw him. He had become a brother to me as surely as if I had known him all my life.

A priest waved us into a chapel and closed the door. As

many times as Maman and I had visited this church, we had never entered this chapel. Her echoing soft prayers calmed me.

To the right of the altar, a statue of a peaceful and loving Virgin stood above a clutch of flickering candles. In her arm, she cradled the Christ Child. Her other hand held a piece of her veil, as though to dry her baby's feet. She smiled tenderly at him. My mother knew the Verzat legacy was held by me, but it had nothing to do with wine. The Verzat legacy would live on in the children I birthed. I blessed myself and kissed Maman's rosary.

Guillaume and I stood before the small altar. Henri stood next to me, the Marquise next to Guillaume. Guillaume's touch steadied me. I inhaled Maman's scent of lavender. *Please be happy for me.*

The priest opened his book and asked us to quickly whisper our vows. He spoke of the holy state of matrimony and the importance of faith and fidelity.

Guillaume repeated his vows, all the while smiling, nodding, and caressing my fingers.

I repeated mine as quickly but faltered.

"Do you promise to love, honor, and obey?" The priest peered over his book.

My mouth moved, but nothing came out.

The Priest cleared his throat. "Madame?"

Guillaume's eyes softened. He understood me. He would never ask me to obey. He knew it was not in me.

"I…" I inhaled. "I promise to love, honor…and obey."

Henri released a sigh. The Marquise let out a little cry.

"I now pronounce you husband and wife." The priest smiled.

Guillaume embraced me. We held each other in the flickering candlelight until Henri whispered, "We must leave now."

Although it was not the ceremony Maman would have wanted, I was married in the eyes of God and my parents and Grandmaman. Something weighed heavily in my chest, and I feared it was their disappointment.

Guillaume pressed me to his side as we returned to the carriage. His heartbeat strong and steady. I clung to him. Yet a nagging pulled in me. I promised to obey my husband. From deep in my heart, I knew I would regret it.

71

Henri

Paris
April 25, 1792

I LEFT THE SALLE du Manège in disgust. Though I and many other deputies voted against, the Assembly declared war on Austria. There was enough war *within* our country. If I weren't a deputy, I'd be conscripted. I'd no sympathy for the Queen until now. Wasn't her marriage to the King of France supposed to prevent a war with her home country? If she sent a letter to her family, she'd be accused of treason. Maybe that was the point.

I also voted for the use of the guillotine, a more democratic way of execution. I thought it more humane and an improvement over other tortuous methods. I also thought it my duty to see it in action.

Wind ripped along the streets. I clutched my cloak and took

narrow alleys. Rounding the crumbling medieval wall of Saint-Julien-le-Pauvre, I stopped and stood dumbfounded. A square wooden door was embedded in the wall. To the side, a leather latch. At the bottom, a wooden-handled lever.

A baby-wheel.

Maman had threatened to take me to the baby-wheel when I misbehaved, but I'd never seen one.

I shivered, imagining a mother pulling the latch, the door opening, her placing the baby inside, shutting the door, pulling the lever, leaving. How many hesitated, grabbed the baby back before pulling the lever? How many returned, pounded upon the door, yanked the lever to an empty wheel?

Papa could have left me here. If he had, he'd never have found me. I'd never have known him or Joliette. I could have become a thief, on my way to the guillotine. *Thank you, Papa.*

I stomped, shook myself, and crossed the river as it began to rain. People streamed around me, toward the Hôtel de Ville. I couldn't take another mob.

"Orange, sir?" A girl of about fifteen years stood beside me, the piece of fruit balancing on her outstretched palm.

I reached into my pocket for a sou.

She took the coin, tossed the orange, and caught it. "Don't you want it?"

"Oh." I pushed the orange into my waistcoat.

Rain dripped from her bonnet onto her face. I wanted to wipe it away, touch her cheek, but I thought of Geneviève. I hoped she was warm and dry in her father's office.

The girl tilted her head back catching raindrops with her tongue. "Isn't it wonderful?"

"The rain? I guess."

She laughed and jerked her head toward the Place de Grève. "Another execution, but not like any we've seen before."

I shook my head. The equality of the guillotine seemed lost on her.

"Come. You've got to see it!" She pulled my arm.

Dragging my feet, I reminded myself I might be called upon to vote on an execution, so it was my duty to witness it. In the center of the square, standing upon a platform built above the height of a man, were two narrow wooden beams, connected by crosspieces, shuddering and swaying in the gusting wind. I pulled my hat down. At the top, suspended between the beams, angled a gleaming metal blade, sharp as a noble's sword. Shards of light flashed, and I bent over, inhaling deeply.

I slowly straightened. A boy selling firewood unloaded his basket, and a few men built a fire at the edge of the square. Around the perimeter, carriages drew up and, on the seats meant for drivers, ladies and gentlemen in silks and furs perched. Children wearing little more than rags begged. An acid taste filled my mouth. The atmosphere was more like a carnival than an execution.

I scanned the crowd for Cassard. He'd attend, not only to find me, but also pick pockets.

Someone tugged at the back of my cloak. A boy, about Simon's age, looked up, eyes blinking, mouth open, looking like a fledgling fallen from its nest. He wore torn trousers and tunic, no cloak or shoes or hat. His plight could have been mine had I been left at the baby-wheel.

I pulled out the orange and gave it to him. He bit into the skin. His lips puckered a moment and then he grinned. Before I could explain about the peel, he fled. Something like a stone sat in my stomach. It might be the first time he'd taste the flesh of an orange rather than peels from the gutter.

The girl held her empty basket above as a shelter from the rain. "A quick painless death even for those who can't afford to pay the executioner to sharpen his blade."

I could not return her enthusiasm, but I felt obligated to inform her. "The National Assembly passed the law—equality even in death."

She squinted. "You a Jacobin?" Her question sounded more like an accusation.

"Me? I—" Was I an anti-royalist? I didn't agree with the Jacobins' extreme measures, but if not a Jacobin, then what group did I belong to? If my true name was discovered, people would think me a Royalist. I didn't want to belong to any group, but people liked to put you into them.

A drumbeat sounded. The crowd hushed. The largest man I'd ever seen stood to the side of the contraption. The prisoner, wearing a red tunic, hands bound behind his back, was led up the ladder by his jailor, who forced the prisoner to kneel behind the guillotine. The jailor placed a basket before the machine. "Nicolas Jacques Pelletier, you are sentenced to death for the crimes of robbery and murder."

A charwoman, her bonnet black with ash, cried out, "Now you'll get what's coming to you!"

Silence fell. Drumbeats thudded. Rain pounded. A rolling pulled in my gut.

The executioner pushed the prisoner onto the bench, pulled up the top of the crosspiece, and shoved the prisoner's neck onto the lower section. He dropped the top half of the crosspiece which held the prisoner's neck and forced him to face the basket. The executioner reached for the rope, running along the side. I clamped my eyes shut. A whistling cut through the silence and ended with a chop, like a butcher's axe against the block.

I opened my eyes. Blood spattered the faces of a priest and a mother and her baby. The priest gasped. The mother screamed. On the platform, the executioner reached into the basket, grabbed the hair of the head, and waved it above him. Blood rained down on the crowd. A roar erupted.

I swallowed against the urge to vomit and inhaled deep breaths.

The girl yanked my sleeve. "That's all? We should bring back the gallows."

"Over in an instant!" the charwoman shouted. "What kind of punishment is that for a thief and a murderer?"

A butcher thrust his fist. "The rack! That's what he deserved. The rack!"

"Better the wheel," boomed a rotund man in a flour-covered apron.

A low rumbling moved through the crowd.

The girl's eyebrows pinched together. "Why should he have a painless death when the people he murdered suffered?"

Perspiration covered me like mist. "It's legislated: equality in death."

"Well, it's not very satisfying, is it?"

I tilted my face into the cool rain. The girl joined a group of men stripping the corpse. I shoved my way toward her, grabbed her arm, and spun her around. "Execution is entertaining to you?" She pulled back, but I held her. "Is equality not more important to the living?"

"Let me go."

I loosened my grip. She snatched up her basket and fled.

I stood in the rain watching people celebrate. It was not France Joliette and I'd be escaping, but the guillotine and the people who wielded it. I spat on the bloodstained cobbles. Now that we had equality in death, what about equality for starvation?

Would my neighbors understand what I was trying to show them? Would they fight for equality without violence? I hoped I could persuade them.

72

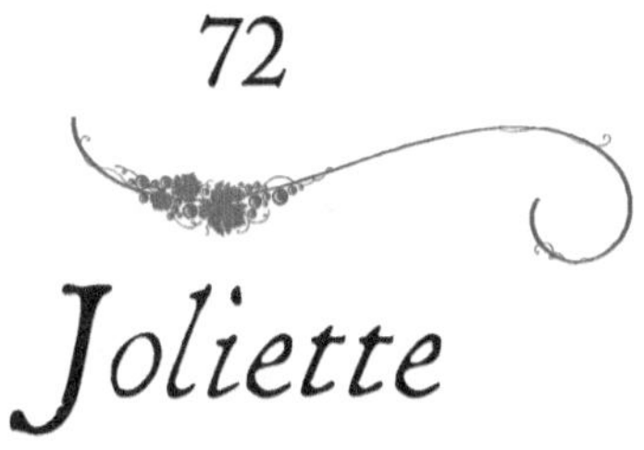

Joliette

Paris
August 1, 1792

I WAITED FOR HENRI in Papa's library. Papa's faint odor of cloves, the walls echoing his laughter, his smiling portrait, comforted me. My last words to him clattered up at me like a flock of crows, snatching my breath. I bent over. "I am so sorry, Papa." I folded over, resting my forehead on my knees.

"Are you all right?" Henri knelt before me.

I wiped my face. "Yes. I am missing Papa."

He poured a glass of brandy. "I have those moments myself."

"I did not mean to cause you worry." The brandy's heat warmed me.

He brushed the tunnel dust from his frock coat. "What can I do for you?"

"The Marquise is ill and needs to convalesce at the château.

Would your maman be willing to go with her and keep her company there?"

He wrapped his hand around the back of his neck. "As a nurse?"

"A companion. The Marquise should not travel alone. The châtelaine will tend to her once they arrive."

He stretched his head to the side. "I lost a friend at the Bastille. His wife and son are near starvation. They live next door to Maman. She would not leave them. Could we give them jobs and a place to live at the estate?"

I recalled the day the poissardes threatened us. The smile and relief in the face of the cooper's wife were what Henri wanted for his friend's family. His kindness, so much like Papa's, touched me.

"Madame Françoise is a fine seamstress. She has altered Papa's coats to fit me. I am sure she and Simon would help with the vendanges. They would earn their keep."

I shook off the memory. "Of course. They could all live at the estate. Simon could attend school."

He laughed. "I thank you, but Simon won't."

"You are a kind man. I hope to become as generous as you."

He shrugged. "I don't know if we can afford it. More taxes are due."

"How can that be?"

"As a deputy, I should know, but the tax situation is so complex, I don't understand how they calculate it." He sipped his brandy. "There is talk of increasing export taxes, and that will affect the wine business." He turned to me and sighed.

"At least the Marquise, Maman, and Bertrand's family will be out of danger. I wish you would go with them."

"First Guillaume, now you." I stomped my foot. "Are you both against me?"

"Are you feeling all right?" He put down his glass.

I paced before the desk, rubbing my temples. "Yes. I am fine." Why had I erupted? "You both speak of my leaving. If I did, the wine business would falter, and then where would we be?"

He shook his head. "I'm sorry. We're both concerned for your safety. We didn't consider the business."

"Obviously." I sighed. "Forgive me. I have been upset. Guillaume may be called to the front."

He stood. "But he is a National Guardsman."

I did not want to cry. I clasped my hands and pressed them to my stomach. "They need leaders."

He placed his hand on my arm. "I am sorry."

I nodded. "I apologize for being so irritable."

"I understand. Will you be all right?"

I nodded.

"I must return to my duties." He unlatched the bookcase. "Should the people riot again, take the servants into the secret chamber and wait for me there." He left.

A chill cut through me. Guillaume and Henri were protecting me from something—but what? I would pay a visit to Madame Robert. She might know.

73

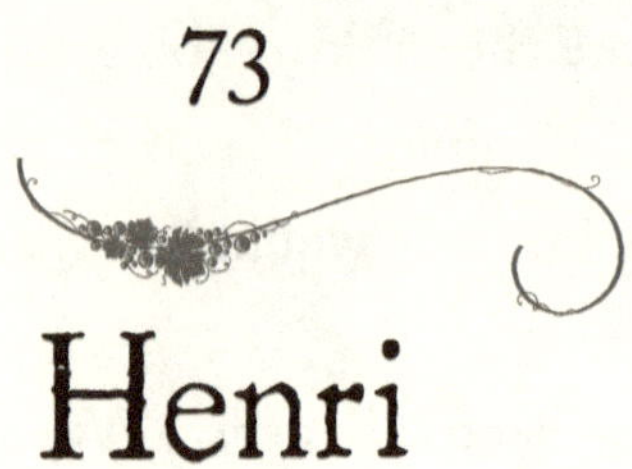

Henri

WHEN I OPENED Maman's door, no smell of damp or taste of soap hung in the air, no cauldron bubbled, no laundry hung from the rafters. Maman wore a new cloak the color of a fawn. A crisp white bonnet framed her worried face. A bundle of clothes and bread sat on the table. "The château… is far away?"

"It's in Saint-Étienne-de-Chigny—three days by carriage— along the Loire. It's a beautiful journey. You'll rest at inns in the evenings."

"Since you were born, you've always been nearby." She rubbed her fingers. Her hands would no longer crack or bleed. The calluses would soften. "Will you visit?"

I didn't want to disappoint her, but when would I have time? I drew my boot across the stone floor. "Do you remember how the laundry dripped and puddles froze in the winter when the fire burned low?"

She crouched down and stooped in the cold fireplace. With both hands, she reached up and pulled down a large stone and set it on the hearth. Holding out her apron with one hand, she scooped piles of gold louis onto the fabric.

I blinked, not believing my eyes.

She set the bulging apron on the table. "If you need money, you have it."

My mouth moved until I found my voice. "Where did this come from?"

"Your papa. I raised you on the money I made doing laundry, so that you would have this one day, should you need it."

A thrumming in my chest ebbed into my arms. She'd washed other peoples' clothes, when she didn't need to, and hoarded money for the past twenty years—all for me. "I cannot. It's yours."

"I saved it for you." Her lips screwed up into a half-smile, tears fell.

I wiped her face with my handkerchief and gave it to her, then I packed the gold louis into her leather pouch. "Tie this at your waist, under your skirts." She pushed my hands, but I captured them and placed the pouch in them. "I promise that if I need it, I will ask you for it."

She nodded but her eyes wouldn't meet mine. I gently pinched her chin, so she had to look at me. "Do you know how many times you did this to me?" I wanted to hug her forever.

My birth-mother was a beautiful actress, but my milk-mother's love could not be more generous or kind or beautiful.

She laughed. "Too many times. You were such a rascal, so many tall tales you told, my son." She laughed and sobbed. "My son."

I held her close. "I will always be your son, Maman. You will be safer at the château. You will love it there."

"I don't want to lose another son." Her body shook against mine.

I held her, rubbing her back like she soothed me when I was a boy, until she calmed. I stepped back. Her eyes were soft and loving, like a puppy's, yet so fearful. "You'll never lose me. I'll come to visit. I promise."

She swiped the handkerchief. "Eat your bread before you go."

I broke off a chunk and shoved it into my waistcoat. Always, I had to eat my bread. "I mustn't be late for the Assembly. Nobles have been causing trouble, and there's been much shouting from the gallery."

"I am so proud of you, my son." Her face glowed. She was beautiful.

"Wish me luck. I hope to speak out for equal education for all children. Girls, too."

"Your papa would be so proud of you, Henri."

I nodded. "Don't be late for the Marquise. You'll like her. She's funny."

"I'll be on time. Be careful." She kissed me and pushed me out the door.

I turned to her. "I love you, Maman." Her mouth opened.

She blinked. I kissed her again. "I'll see you soon." I closed the door behind me.

Standing on rue de Cotte, I imagined her face when she first glimpsed the château. A weight lifted from my shoulders, like I'd set down a yoke of water buckets. Maman, Madame Françoise, and Simon would all be safe, no longer in danger of starving or freezing. I wished Joliette would join them, but that battle I did not want to fight. Although I dreaded it, fighting with the other deputies was far easier.

74

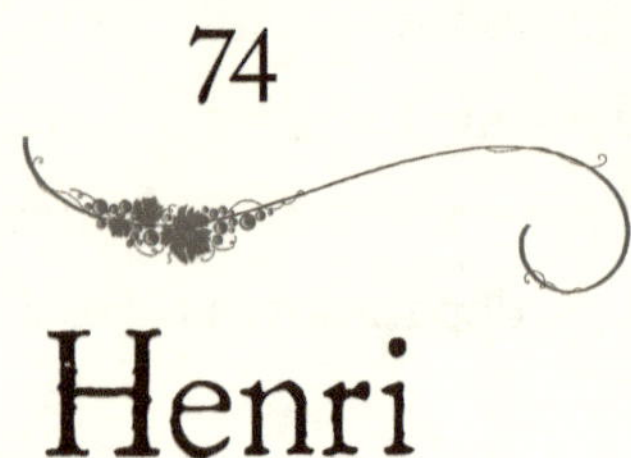

Henri

Paris
August 9, 1792

EVER SEARCHING FOR Cassard, I headed for the Salle du Manège and bumped into a market woman who shoved a red hat in my face. "Wear the bonnet rouge. Show you are a true Patriot!"

I pointed at the blue, white, and red cockade pinned to my frock coat and skirted her. The tricolor cockade was worn by all, and Cassard was certainly among them, though not because he was a patriot. My hand jittered as I patted my pistol. My determination to kill Cassard tested my commitment to non-violence. For him, I'd make an exception, not only for revenge, but also to defend Joliette and self-preservation.

Pushcarts of fruits and vegetables stood in a haphazard line, forming a makeshift market. "Ribbons and laces for the ladies," a peddler cried out, as an overladen wagon rumbled through the muck. Rotting pig guts and vegetable leavings squelched beneath my boots.

The buildings closed in around me, blocking the sunshine. I slowed. A prickling moved across my skin. Cassard was watching me.

I turned, scrutinizing the ears of tall thin men passing beneath an arcade on the opposite side of the square. A figure dashed behind a column. Never taking my eyes from the column, I slipped between people until I stood under the arcade. Keeping my back to the building and my hand on my pistol, I edged to the column, brought up the pistol, pivoted around the corner.

A little girl, her legs splayed over the stack of crates she sat upon, squeezed a doll of rags to her chest.

I dragged my sleeve over my face as running footsteps echoed the length of the arcade. He was taunting me.

Shoving the pistol into my waistcoat, I worked my way around the market. He would not surprise me like he had Papa. Something pulled in me. Had Papa been surprised, or had he expected Cassard, even lured him? Did Papa believe he'd wronged the man, and dying was the noble way to right a wrong? Were Joliette and I in such great danger Papa sacrificed his own life? Would I do the same? I hurried away from the image of Papa bleeding upon the floor.

As I walked along the Seine, a thin column of smoke rose over the middle of the Pont Royal. A crowd gathered, chanting "Liberté!" Two dockworkers dangled a man, dressed in fine silks and plumed hat, from a pole over the river.

I jolted. Freedom was not permission to kill. I reached for

my pistol. One of the dockworkers brought a torch to the hanging man's feet. I shoved and pushed my way through sweating stinking men. Flames engulfed the man, devouring his legs.

I stopped. Wiped sweat from my eyes. Flesh would not burn so rapidly. The man was made of straw. Smoking chunks of it fell into the river. A cheer went up from the crowd and echoed along the riverbanks.

I spat over the bridge. I was ashamed of the vicious animals who were my neighbors.

Men bumped and shoved me deeper into the crowd. I choked as smoke billowed. Grime streaked the face and hands of a chimneysweep who wielded an iron bar. "Sharpen your pikes to exterminate aristocrats!"

The men behind me chanted, "Death, death, death to the rich."

The hot current of people, jamming the boulevard and chanting "Liberté," trapped me like a fish in a net. I panicked. I was wearing the wrong clothes to be anywhere near this mob. How would I get through them to the Assembly? They'd take me for an aristocrat. At least I had the foresight to pin Papa's fleur-de-lys on the inside of my waistcoat. They'd hang *me* over the Seine if they saw it.

Two white horses pulling a carriage came to a stop at the crest of the bridge. Parisians, carrying pikes, scythes, pitchforks, and a few muskets, stood in a line across the bridge and chanted, "Death, death, death." From behind them, a rotund woman hurled a rock. It hit and bounced off the coach. Others stooped, grabbed stones, and threw them. They surrounded the coach. "Death, death, death, death, death." The horses whinnied and stomped. The footman jumped atop his bench at the back of the coach and held a whip at the ready.

Whoever they were, the people in that coach had done nothing, so why was the mob attacking? I pushed forward. Laborers surrounded the carriage and rocked it from side to side. The horses reared. The driver strained to keep the horses from trampling a woman who'd been pushed to the cobbles.

"Stop." I shoved my way through the people. "Stop!"

The crowd fell back in a wave. I pushed the retreating people out of my way. "Death to you, you servant to the rich," a woman screamed.

A rock smashed into the footman's head. He toppled down onto the cobbles. I pulled the woman away. She raised another rock. I grabbed it and held it above her head. "He has done nothing to you. Be gone." She fell and scrabbled away.

I reached down and turned the man over. Blood smeared his face, but he was breathing. I picked him up, opened the carriage door, placed him at the feet of two terrified women, and closed the door. The driver pulled the coach around, snapped the whip, and the carriage shimmied down the bridge.

Bending over, I pressed my hands into my legs, and heaved. Wiping sweat from my face, I stood to hate-filled eyes and glinting pike blades.

A poissarde thrust up her filleting knife. "Kill the aristocrat!"

I put up my hands. "I am no aristocrat. I live in Faubourg Saint-Antoine."

A hulking mass of a man advanced, carrying an animal organ dripping blood from the tip of a pike. "This is what we do to the hearts of aristocrats!"

My legs tensed to run. Papa would stand his ground. "I am

a Deputy of the Assembly. Deputy Henri Detré." I pulled out my badge and held it up. "I serve the people of Faubourg Saint-Antoine. People like you."

"How've you helped us?" The poissarde waved her knife in my face.

"I petition for free education. For everyone. Your sons *and* daughters."

"The Assembly approved this?" She cackled. "All they do is talk and veto!"

"The Assembly does much discussing, it's true." I lowered my hands. "We are trying. But violence won't convince deputies. I've seen violence kill people like you. My best friend was a vainqueur."

A porter took off his hat and placed it over his heart.

The butcher nodded. "The King's the one who vetoes."

My legs vibrated with the urge to run, but I stared at the man's eyes. I could not deny it, but to affirm it could be a death sentence. The guillotine was frightening, but these people would take pleasure in killing me. Sweat stung my eyes. Papa stood proud in the portrait. I was obligated to act the Comte de Verzat. Whether or not anyone knew it, I knew it.

"Louis le faux pas!" the butcher yelled. People roared with laughter. He grabbed my arm. "We'll stop his vetoes. Come, Deputy Detré, to the Assembly!"

The crowd swept me and the butcher through the gates. Never letting go my arm, the butcher pushed me into the main floor of the Assembly. I searched for Geneviève but did not see her. At the center of the low stage, an enormous man shouted and waved a paper at the President, requesting permission to read his petition.

The butcher raised his axe. "Deputy Detré has something to say."

The trembling in my legs shook all of me. Had Papa ever been this frightened when he was brave? He'd been born with his title; I was growing into it. The mantle of nobility seemed far too large for my shoulders.

The man crept off the stage. The President stood.

The butcher shoved me forward. "Allow Deputy Detré through."

Men jumped from my path as I stumbled forward. What were the words I'd written? Another shove pushed me to the edge of the platform. I cringed, knowing I had told them everyone deserved a free education. I believed in it but convincing the Assembly could take a lifetime. I stepped up and faced the Assembly. The crowd quieted.

I gripped the edge of my waistcoat, felt Papa's pin beneath it. My father had been a minister to the King of France. Now I had to be a minister to the people of France, my people, even if I was ashamed of them. "My..." I cleared my throat. "My maman's hands are scarred and callused, just like the hands of many women here." I looked up at the gallery. "Are they not?"

Hundreds of women raised their hands and yelled out, "Yes!"

I looked back at the deputies. "For, without education, what else besides laundry can a woman do to feed her children?"

"She can whore!" A cackle came from a woman in the gallery.

I nodded. "You laugh, but it's true." Whispers ran through the gallery. "Rousseau said that a woman's place is the home. Many women are at home." I looked up. "Watching their children starve."

"Both my children starve!" called out another woman.

I lifted my arm. "Some Assembly members voted for schools to teach girls home arts. Did any woman of the Third Estate *not* learn home arts as soon as she could walk?"

Shouts of agreement and stomps rattled the chandeliers.

"If women were educated, they'd have other ways to feed their children besides laundering and whoring."

Cheers filled the hall.

Buoyed by their reaction, I turned to face the President. "You may say that there are many seamstresses and lacemakers and glovemakers, and you are correct. Seamstresses prick their fingers from dawn till dusk, stitching the clothes you and I wear, and are paid thirty sous a day." I looked back at the sea of deputies. "Could any one of you feed a family of four on thirty sous a day when one loaf of bread costs twenty?"

Stomping rattled the gallery floor.

I pointed at a deputy wearing silks. "Monsieur, how much did you pay for your frock coat?" His face reddened. I pointed at another. "And your jabot, Monsieur?" I pointed again. "Your stockings, Monsieur?" The men remained silent. Papa's laughter would have filled the place.

I stared up at the women in the gallery. "If women are to emerge from beneath society's restrictions, they must know how to cipher, so they can charge fairly for their work. They must be able to identify letters to become type-setters, so they can help spread the news of *your* laws." I pointed at the deputies. "They must be able to read to become responsible landlords, so they can feed their children and pay their taxes, Messieurs."

High-pitched cheers rained down.

I raised my arms for quiet and turned to the President. "I call for education for all children. I call for education to be paid for by the state." I faced the crowd. "If educating women would improve their lives and their children's lives, would not educating women also improve France?"

Stomping, shouting, cheering rattled the windows. Chaos.

I imagined Joliette's beaming face. *I would greatly appreciate your campaigning for equal rights for women when you are elected député.* I hoped I could change things for her and Geneviève. I scanned the gallery.

The President banged his wooden hammer. "Who are you, Monsieur?"

"Deputy Detré, of Faubourg Saint-Antoine." I bowed.

"Imposter!" A voice from the back of the hall called out.

I jerked up. A sinking feeling pulled in my chest. A rumble moved through the room. It could only be Cassard. No one else knew. From the back, Cassard walked down the steps, heading for me.

"He is no commoner." He flung his arm out toward the gallery. "He is the Comte de Verzat! A noble!"

Shouts shook the walls. To accuse him of murder would make *me* the liar. My legs burned to run. I should stand my ground, as Papa would. But would he?

"He's a noble," screamed Cassard. "Seize him!"

The butcher, his axe raised, ran down the aisle toward me.

I ripped my dagger from its sheath. Arms grabbed at me, tore my sleeve, yanked my hair. I brandished the dagger at them all. I backed out, turned, and ran, dodged, slid, stumbled out through the hall, into the gardens, jumped over bushes, scattered gravel, charged across the courtyard to the bridge.

From the far end, a group of stevedores stood, their hooks raking the air. Behind me, the crowd ranted, "Kill him!"

Not caring if I was a noble coward, I jumped upon the abutment. The muddy Seine swirled below. I dived.

Plunging into icy darkness, I pulled myself down deeper. The shadow of the bridge darkened the water, and I swam for its cover. My chest burned, but I forced myself to slowly surface and sip only a breath of air, then I dove again and fought the current, searching for a toehold. I gripped the slimy rock supporting a column and brought my face above the water.

Bits of pink scum and a few turds floated by. Waves slapped and pushed. I choked and clung and stared at the shore, looking for Révolutionaries. Downstream, sailors thrust poles into the water from a barge, sitting low in the water from a towering load of firewood.

Hope burned in me like an ember. The barge was headed north. The mob wouldn't search the water upstream. If I could swim under water and grab onto a log, they'd tow me, unaware. But where would I go?

A rock hurtled down and splashed within an arm's length. I sucked in air, dived, and powered myself across the current for what felt like an hour. When I surfaced, the barge was still yards away and farther upstream. Screams echoed across the river. I plunged and willed myself not to surface until I was under the barge.

Clinging to an overhanging branch dragging in the water, I sucked in a breath and submerged again. I was able to rest and think. I couldn't go to the mansion; Cassard would find me there. And Joliette was in danger—if Guillaume wasn't with her.

I needed fresh gunpowder and flint, but a dripping man would attract attention. I'd have to wait until dark to emerge from the river. I had to reach the mansion before Cassard. I scanned the shore. *Papa, protect Joliette.*

75

Joliette

Moonlight poured around the drapes, casting an eerie glow over my chamber. Guillaume lay next to me, his arm cradling my head, his hand cupping my breast, our skin glistening from lovemaking. How would I convince him to leave the National Guard? He would never abandon his duties, even for me. Perhaps the Queen would dismiss him if I wrote to request it.

I turned on my side and slid my leg up over his hip. One wiry hair sprung up from the perfect arch of his eyebrow. I ran my thumbnail over it, coaxing it into line. Translucent blue crescents sat beneath his eyes, earned by worry—for me, the royal family, the future of France. I traced the curved silver scar running over his shoulder and down his arm. Gunfire from that day echoed, and I nuzzled close and breathed in his scent. I would request an audience with the Queen and ask her to release him.

Saint Séverin's bell rang. I willed it to stop at three strikes, but it continued, past six, twelve, eighteen. The humidity dulled the clang of the tocsin, and I hoped Guillaume would not hear it. I wanted him to stay with me forever.

Guillaume mumbled, thrashed, and called out. Again, he dreamed of the Versailles battle. I pressed my hand over his heart. "You are with me, my darling."

He let out a shout, heaving for breath, grasping the crumpled bedclothes.

I pulled him close. "Hush. I am here."

"The tocsin." He sat up and flung his legs over the bedside.

I had lost count of the bells—it was the call to arms. Our warmth leached from me. "Do not leave. It is not yet daylight."

He closed the drapes. The sonorous vibrations came slow, steady, unrelenting, like waves lashing the shore. "Get dressed."

"But—"

"We are already at war with Austria and Prussia." He plucked up his crumpled tunic. "You must be ready to flee." He tossed my chemise to me.

"Flee?" The terror of Versailles swept through me. I snatched up my dressing gown and shrugged it on.

He sat next to me, held both my hands. "Henri warned me. The fédérés and sans-culottes, who belong to no army but fight nonetheless, will attack the Tuileries and overthrow the monarchy."

"Why did you not tell me last night?"

He smiled. "You did not give me the opportunity."

I gripped his fingers. "Stay. I will request the Queen release you."

He kissed my hands. "I must report for duty. Not to the royal family."

"Guillaume!"

He dropped my hands and tugged on his boots. "Henri told me, should they attack, he will come and take you to the château." He knelt before me. "You must go with him. He will protect you. You must trust in him, as I do."

"I will not leave you." I shivered in the heat.

"I am sorry I must say this, my darling. On our wedding day, did you not promise to obey me?"

Dread seeped through me. The muscles in his neck were taut with worry, which I could not make worse. I had dreaded this moment, but I forced myself to nod.

"I ask it of you now. Go with Henri to the château. I will meet you there in a week. You must send the servants away, to protect them. Command them, Joliette. If the sans-culottes find them, they will kill them. Henri has asked the bishop at Saint Séverin to hide them until it is safe for them to travel. Give them money to get there. Sew your jewels into your skirts and take all your papers. Wait for Henri in the secret room."

A cold wave burst over me. "You are terrifying me! I will not leave you."

He gripped my arms. "I want you to be safe. This is the only way. Do you promise me you will do this?"

More bells clashed. I trembled. I wanted to clutch onto him, yet I knew it would make leaving more difficult for him. He was going to face the sans-culottes, and he would fare better if he did not worry about me. "You told me to go back to my apartment at Versailles, but had I not been there, you might have been killed."

"And you might have been killed as well." He tucked his gloves into his belt, then pulled me to him, tugging the ribbon from my hair. I longed to surrender and fall into him. He kissed the ribbon. "Tie this about my wrist. I will wear it until we are together again."

My fingers trembled. Tears spotted the pale green silk. He held me tightly, caressing my back. I wanted to melt into him, become part of him.

His chest expanded with his breath. He straightened and held me at arm's length. "Promise me, my dearest."

The thick air filled my throat. I nodded.

"Say it." His eyes gleamed, like sunlight on water.

"I—" I pushed my voice through my tight throat. "I promise."

He pulled me close and whispered, "I will always be with you, I will always love you." He let go of me and strode to the door.

Wrapping my gown around me, I ran down the steps after him.

He stood in the grand hall, sliding his sword into its scabbard.

"Guillaume." I had to shout above the bells' clanging.

He looked up and smiled his bright smile.

"I love you. I will always love you." My arms ached to keep him with me. "My heart is yours."

"And mine, yours. I will always love you, my dearest, always. Trust Henri."

"Yes, my love."

He closed the door.

The cacophony of the bells rumbled in the hall, and through me. I stared at the empty space for several long moments, then raced to my desk to write a message to the Queen.

76

Henri

Paris
August 10, 1792

A PUTRID STINK WAFTED from the east. The piss and shit of the tanneries and dyers on the Bièvre River poured into the Seine. The barge finally moved toward the shore. Hôpital de la Salpêtrière loomed above.

I emerged from the river in quiet darkness lit by a half moon, near a garden. Prepared to be imprisoned for theft, I pulled leeks, radishes, carrots, and devoured them and the dirt that clung to them. I brushed my clothes, but I looked a pauper.

On the other side of the garden, a candle glowed in the window of a church. I crawled toward it and found a mound of hay. I lay on my belly and shoved myself into it. Papa would be ashamed of me. I'd acted as a coward. But, I was alive. My flight from the mob, the swim in the stinking river, my terror of escaping Cassard—all had exhausted me. I'd rest until my clothes dried and wouldn't attract attention.

A bell clanged, waking me. I choked on the dust of hay. No light penetrated the dark, yet the bells rang, ceaselessly.

One by one, candles illuminated windows. I sat in the hay and pressed my hands over my eyes. Were they looking for me? I shivered. Of course not, the tocsin sounded only during emergencies.

My breath caught. There'd been talk of overtaking the King at the Assembly—he hadn't been present for weeks. With the mob tossing me before the deputies, I'd forgotten.

If I am called to defend the King, promise me you'll take Joliette to the château. Guillaume's voice was so clear, I looked about for him. Joliette was in danger, especially since Guillaume would be answering the tocsin's call, leaving her alone. I pulled out my pouch of gunpowder, useless mud. How could I get to her, unarmed?

I fell back into the hay. I was depleted of strength. What little courage I had, I'd spent. *Papa, I have shamed you. I did not stand my ground. I did not accuse your murderer.* I pulled the fleur-de-lys pin from my waistcoat. *I don't deserve to wear this.* I threw it in the dirt. His voice thundered, *You have the blood of a noblesse d'épée. And as a noble of the sword, I expect you to behave as one.*

"How, Papa? Show me!" I wiped my face, picked up the pin, and shoved it in my pouch.

A door creaked open, spilling a sliver of light across the garden…like the secret entrance to Papa's library. Papa stored his pistol, gunpowder, bullets, and sword in his library. If Joliette already waited for me in the secret chamber, she'd be armed. I had only to reach her, and I could do that through the tunnels. Where was the nearest entrance? In my mind, I searched the map I'd memorized, but I was unfamiliar with this faubourg.

The clanging intensified, joined by the church bells of Faubourg Saint-Marcel. My muscles pumping as the answer came to me, I jumped up. In the cellar of Hôpital de la Salpêtrière. I felt for the keys around my neck and nearly cried when my fingers touched them.

I ran to the tunnels.

77

Joliette

Paris
August 10, 1792

I STITCHED GRANDMAMAN'S EMERALDS, and Maman's diamonds, and my pearls into the seams of a servant's gown and filled a leather purse with gold louis. I dressed, loaded my pistolet, and secured it in my hanging pocket.

I stood as if frozen to the staircase, the purse heavy in my hands. Before me, Marie gripped Cook's hand, both crying. Jacques stood tall and reverent. "The sans-culottes will punish you for having served me." I tried to sound like Papa. "I want you to leave immediately."

Cook gripped her apron. "I cannot, Comtesse!" Her warm arms reached for me, and the smells of the kitchen wrapped around me. I patted her back, wiped her tears, and looked at each of them. I could not cry anymore. Guillaume had taken my tears with him.

"You will not be able to leave Paris today. Go to Saint Séverin. Tell the Bishop, Henri sent you. You will be safe there until the barriers open again and you can take a coach to the château. Keep your papers with you at all times. You will be arrested without them."

Jacques refused the purse. "I shall not leave you, Comtesse. I have been servant to your family before you were born. It is my honor to protect you."

I embraced him, feeling his heart beating wildly. He remained stiff. I handed the money to him. "I order you to go." He placed the purse at my feet. *Papa, please give me courage.* "I will not allow you to endanger your life for mine. We are equals now, Jacques—all of us—citizens. But as we both honor King Louis, in his name, I order you to leave." I picked up the purse and held it before him. Jacques would never dishonor the King.

He brought his hands to his face and shook his head. I would miss him, even for a few days. "We will be together again at the château." I pushed the money into his hands. "Go now. Your safety is my heart's desire."

With the elegance of a disheartened royal, he walked away. Marie and Cook followed, weeping.

I stood in the grand hall until the sound of their footsteps faded.

Echoes of voices chilled me. I had never been alone in the house. I wrapped my arms around myself. Shouts outside grew louder and more frequent, punctuated by gunshots. An explosion made me jump.

Rushing to the library, I shoved all the account books into a leather satchel and buckled the clasp. Maman's thimble. I would sew it into my hem. I ran back to the salon and threaded a needle. My hands shook so, I could only stab at the fabric, hoping the uneven stitches would hold.

I thought I heard footsteps in the hall, but it was unlike Henri to make any noise. "Henri, I am in the salon." I knotted the thread and bit it off. "Henri?"

"I am André."

I jumped up. How did he get in? Did he attack the servants?

A tall, thin man in worn silks and plumed tricorne, holding two swords, stood at the door. "André Cassard." His eyes, his smile, his countenance—viperous.

I planted my feet in a wide stance. "How did you get in here?"

"Alas, your very large footman is no more." He flicked the short, blood-stained sword. "Enchanté, Comtesse."

He'd killed another man. My hands trembled, but I did not reach for the pistolet. I had to surprise him. "You do not enchant me, Monsieur. You killed my father."

"A fortunate event." His tongue sucked at his teeth. "Let us wait for your brother." He sat on the chaise longue and waved the short sword for me to sit opposite him.

The church bells rang and rang and rang.

I walked toward the table of wine. The sound of my blood pulsed in my head. I gripped the neck of the decanter. *You will be dead long before my brother arrives.*

78

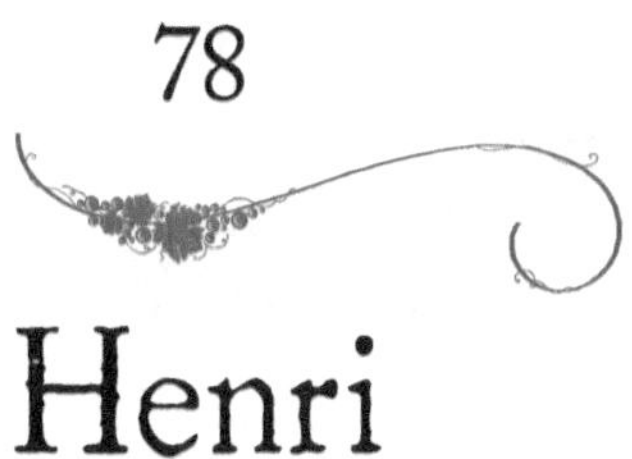

Henri

Paris
August 10, 1792

T HE AIR HUNG heavy in the vacant library. A large leather satchel lay open on the desk. I took Papa's pistol from the desk drawer, checked it, and tiptoed to the grand hall. The murmur of voices stopped me. With pistol drawn, I inched toward the salon.

"You had your revenge with my father. What do you want with me?"

My throat closed. Cassard! I peered around the door.

Joliette stood with her back to me. Opposite her, Cassard gripped a short sword in his left hand, in his right, a rapier. I'd studied this lethal strategy: distract the prey with the rapier and move in for the kill with an upward thrust of the short sword.

I aimed the pistol.

He advanced, whisking the air with the rapier, closer and closer to Joliette's face. Yet, she stood her ground.

I could not get a clear shot without risking my sister. She stood tall and appeared calm.

"You are the bait, Mademoiselle." He sneered. "Your brother shall arrive in time to watch me kill again." The rapier quivered. "He was too late last time."

She jerked up her chin. "He attends the Assembly."

"I exposed him at the Assembly yesterday. He is wanted for treason." He waved the short sword. "And so will you be, Comtesse."

I pulled back the hammer, muffling the click with my sleeve.

Holding a crystal decanter, Joliette edged her way around the table, toward the window. Cassard followed her every move. "Would you like a glass of wine while we wait?" Cassard swished the rapier nearer her face, but she did not blink. She poured a glass of wine and held it close to her chest. I tensed, knowing she'd never allow him to drink from a wine glass bearing the Verzat crest. She was going to throw the wine in his face. My sister possessed the courage of a knight.

I crept into the room.

Cassard swiped the rapier. The glass shattered in her hand. Shards flew. She cried out, grasping her bloodied hand. He lunged at her.

"Let her go!" I rushed him.

In one step, he dropped the rapier, grasped Joliette around the waist, and brought the short sword's tip to her throat. She scratched at his arm.

"It's me you want, Cassard. Let her go." I aimed the gun.

He used Joliette as a shield. Her eyes flashed bright with panic.

"This is between you and me." I aimed the pistol at his head.

He ducked behind her and laughed an oily laugh. He was mad, beyond reason. "Drop your gun," he ordered.

Joliette blinked, signaling me to do what Cassard wanted. She calmed, letting her hand drop alongside her skirts and slide into her pocket, then she rested her head back on him. Her lack of resistance unbalanced him. He shifted his weight. She let her body sag, like an unstrung puppet. He brought up the short sword and pricked her neck, a drop of blood swelled at the tip.

Rage thrummed in me. My finger pulsed on the trigger, but I held up my left hand and slowly placed the gun on the table, beyond his reach. He wore Joliette like a second skin.

I took a step closer to the fireplace, where great grand-père's sword hung. I had to direct his rage toward me.

"I killed your wife," I whispered.

His eyebrows hooded his dark eyes.

"She died giving me life." I forced my voice to be cruel. "I killed her."

His face reddened. "You lie. The Comte killed her because she wanted to come back to me," he shouted. "She loved me!"

Joliette blinked some signal I could not decipher.

He flicked the short sword out, aiming it at me. "She loved me!"

"She despised you." I stepped closer. "She loved my father." My voice was like a caress.

His face crumpled. "She loved—"

"The Comte de Verzat. She loved the Comte de Verzat," my voice taunted.

He shifted the sword, pointing it at me.

"And she loved me," I whispered.

A gun fired. I started toward them. A trickle of blood dripped from Cassard's gawping mouth. His eyes bulged. His body pitched forward.

Joliette threw herself to the side. Cassard thumped to the floor.

I grabbed my pistol from the table and ran to her. "He is not dead!" she cried.

Cassard's shaking hand pulled a pistol from inside his waistcoat.

"Stay down!" I shoved her across the room and rolled behind a chair.

The pistol wavered in his hand. His breath was ragged.

Keeping the gun aimed at his heart, I stood. Fired.

Blood sprayed. I'd shot him in his ugly face. His gun dropped. The acrid stink of burned gunpowder filled the room. I bent over and retched.

Joliette put her hand on my back. "Knowing he killed Papa will keep the nausea at bay."

I dragged my hand over my sweating face. I imagined Papa, and a terrible hollow gaped in my chest that even Cassard's death could not fill.

Joliette stood next to me, trembling. The trickle of blood on her neck had dried.

"Are you badly cut?" I examined her hand, picked out tiny

glass shards, wrapped my handkerchief over the cuts, and tied it under her palm. "You are the bravest person I have ever known, dear sister."

She pushed stray curls from her face. "What should we do with…?"

Blood pooled around his body, seeping into the rug. A ringing filled my ears, but it wasn't the echo of gunfire. People were shouting in the streets. "We must escape now. Sans-culottes are breaking into homes and murdering people. We've not a moment to lose."

She pressed her hand to her stomach. "I do not want his body defiling Papa's house."

"I'll drag his body into the tunnels. Bring your papers and meet me in the secret chamber. I promised Guillaume I'd get you to the château."

79

Joliette

THE TUNNELS SWALLOWED us. I clutched Papa's satchel to my chest. My bandaged hand throbbed. Sweat soaked my bodice, despite the chill air. If Cassard's body was found, we would be executed. A clamor of metal striking metal and shouts assaulted us. A herd of drunken sans-culottes bearing torches, arms loaded with silver candelabra, trays, and serving dishes, stormed toward us. Henri pulled me behind a column as they whooped past. I had never wanted to be at the château so much.

"Why are there so many people down here?" I whispered.

"Révolutionaries attacked the palace."

I jolted. "I sent a messenger to the Queen, requesting Guillaume's freedom, this morning."

He gripped my hand. "Let us hope the messenger never arrived."

I stumbled. If the messenger was caught by the sans-culottes, they had my name and Guillaume's. We would be killed as Royalists. We ran through the darkness for what seemed like hours.

Henri reached along the rock. "We're beyond the city barriers now."

The chill had entered my bones. I shivered. If the Révolutionaries did search beyond Paris, there would be no place to hide during the journey to the château. Although I wore Marie's gown and cap, my brother passed for a commoner far better than I. My husband was in far greater danger. *Please, Guillaume be careful.*

Taking his key from around his neck, Henri climbed a stairway and opened a wooden door. I inhaled a yeasty scent, taking me back to the flickering warmth of Cook's kitchen. But the clattering of pans and voices shouting orders reminded me of dismissing the servants that morning, and the warmth drained from me.

We crept upstairs and out into a shaded alley, littered with rotting food and feasting rats. I pressed my mouchoir to my nose. I stomped and Henri kicked at the rats as we charged out into a market with people dancing, laughing, cheering, singing *La Marseillaise. Guillaume, I pray you are safe.*

Squinting, Henri led the way through the market stalls. He stopped an old farmer—wearing a straw hat and reminding me of Oncle Albert—loading empty crates onto a wagon.

A roar of laughter burst through the market. A group of

red-bonnet-wearing drunkards stumbled through the stalls, grabbing at fruit and women.

The man waved us into his stall. Henri and I stood in the shadow of his wagon, willing the drunkards to leave. The man stood before us, his arms crossed over his chest. When the drunkards' voices faded, he turned. "You are safe now."

"Thank you." Henri tipped back his hat. "Where does the coach to Tours stop?"

The man wiped sweat from his eyes and looked Henri up and down. "No carriages from Paris today, barriers closed."

"Is there an inn?" I asked.

"In Montrogue? Not where a lady would sleep." He scooped a plum from one of the boxes and held it out. "Very sweet."

I accepted it, thanked him, and savored its juice, until I realized he had called me a lady. Juice dripped down my fingers.

Henri reached into his pouch. "How much?"

"No charge." He scooped a few more, offered them. "I haven't sold 'em."

Henri thanked him but did not take any. "Which is the road to Tours?"

The man laughed. "It's two days by carriage. Many more by foot!"

Henri straightened his shoulders. "We must."

"Why're you traveling on such a dangerous day?" He bit a plum.

I scanned the market people, constructing a plausible story. "We were visiting relatives in Paris and received word our poor mother is ill."

The man shrugged. "My farm's two hours away. I'll give you a ride."

"Monsieur, that is most kind," I replied. I wanted to cry.

"We can pay," Henri said.

The man shook his head. "Help me load and unload the wagon. That'll be payment enough." He put out his hand. "Étienne Chastain."

Henri shook it. "Thank you. Henri…Saulnier. And this is my sister—"

"Madame Pricaud. Thank you, Monsieur, you are most kind."

"Call me Étienne."

"Étienne." I smiled. "Please call me Joliette and my brother Henri."

Étienne nodded. "Hide those curls of yours, Madame." His eyebrow arched. "Else people will take you for the aristocrat you are."

Even my hair gave me away. I shoved it into Marie's too-small bonnet.

The wagon loaded, Henri helped me up to the bench, and I sat between the two men. Leaving the village, we passed through an eerie quiet that hung in the air like fog. No people or animals were about, and the shutters and doors of the houses were all closed. I was afraid to ask about Guillaume's troop, but I had to know. "Have you heard news of Paris?" I asked.

Étienne's hands were scarred and gnarled as old grapevines, and so large the reins looked like ribbons in his fingers. "Citizens of Paris killed the King's Guards."

My breath stopped. "The Gardes Nationale?"

He shook his head. "The Swiss. The Gardes Nationale joined the sans-culottes in their slaughter."

I gripped the bench. "Certainly not all of them."

"The royal family took refuge at the Assembly." He stared ahead. "Criers say fédérés burned Swiss bodies. Sans-culottes killed aristocrats in the street."

I gripped Maman's rosary. *Grandmaman, Maman, Papa, please protect Guillaume.* Henri leaned forward, rested his arms on his legs, and stared out over the valley. Workers climbed trees in an orchard and tossed fruit to women below who held out their aprons. Insects hummed in newly harvested fields. Far in the distance two chimneys protruded from the rubble of a château. Étienne stopped and turned toward a hilltop where a piece of rope dangled in the breeze from charred gallows. He made a sign of the cross.

"What happened here?" I asked.

"After the August Decrees, we all refused to pay our feudal dues."

Henri sat up. "That was within your rights."

Étienne nodded. "The Marquis demanded huge rents for our shacks. None of us had money, so we set fire to his château, his gallows, and him."

Was that how Guillaume's father died? I smelled the roses in the Versailles Gardens, heard birdsong, saw Guillaume's face lined with sorrow.

"When I was a boy," Étienne wiped his brow, "the Marquis hung my father—Papa was châtelain."

"But why?" I asked.

"For giving the Marquis's extra grain to starving vassals." Étienne shook his head. "My papa was kind, too kind. The Marquis forced my maman and me to watch." He snapped the reins, and the horse plodded past the ruins.

My stomach cramped. He had no other choice. "You like living here?"

Étienne shrugged. "Come winter and no food to sell, I won't be able to pay the taxes, and somebody'll buy the land."

I rubbed my wrist. "Could you take us to the château de Verzat? We will pay for feeding the horse. In return, we would give you a plot of land and a house—rent-free, on the estate— if you help work the vineyard and harvest the grapes."

Étienne slowed the horse.

I held my breath. Would he report us as Royalists?

"Would you like to live on the Verzat estate, Étienne?" Henri asked.

"Château de Verzat? The one that produces the finest wines in France?"

Still holding my breath, I nodded.

"You work there?" Étienne asked.

I looked to Henri. "We…manage the estate."

He ran his hands down his face. "Yes, I would, Madame Châtelaine."

I exhaled and smiled. "Then you will take us there?"

Étienne snapped the reins. "If the old nag can't make it, I'll pull the wagon myself."

80

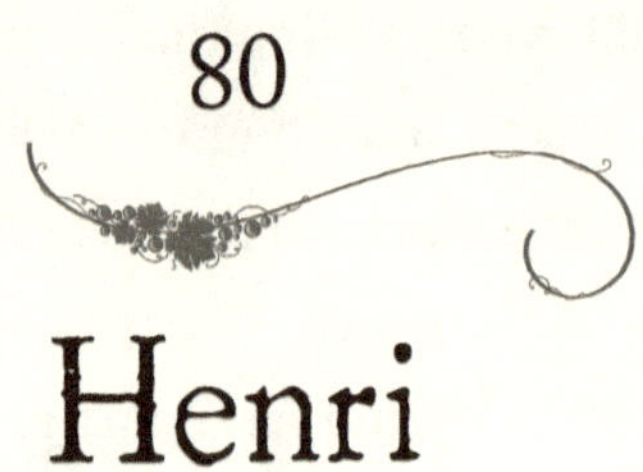

Henri

THE CICADAS SCREAMED. I never thought I'd miss the sounds of the city. Instead of searching for Cassard, I now searched for sans-culottes. In the early afternoon, the mare slowed as she climbed a hill.

"I have a bad feeling. Let us take the other road we passed," Joliette said.

Étienne clucked at the horse. "It's too narrow here to turn around."

I took off my hat and drew my arm across my forehead. "Étienne, should anything happen to me, will you promise to take Joliette to the château?"

He placed his hand over his heart. "Upon my soul, I swear it."

"Thank you."

He snapped the reins. We crested the hill. On the other side of the valley, a uniformed man on horseback, surrounded by a regiment of red-capped men, blocked the road. Keeping my eyes on them, I reached into the leather satchel resting on the floorboard.

"Étienne, do you have your identity papers and a passe-avant?" I asked.

"Identity papers. No passe-avant."

"Do not give anything to the soldiers." I handed Joliette two sets of the papers I'd had the printer forge. "Your name is Henri Saulnier, you were born in Paris, on the sixth of February in 1750, your wife's name was Abrielle Renée Lenogue Saulnier, and she died in 1773, the year your daughter, Joliette Saulnier was born on the eighteenth of June in 1773. Both of you memorize this."

They nodded.

"Memorize it until you can repeat it with confidence."

"Where are you—"

"Hopefully, they will come after me and not bother you. I'll meet you at the château. Don't worry." I jumped down and fled.

The regiment broke ranks and dispersed. A few dropped to their knees and aimed their muskets. I raced through fields and the sounds of gunfire toward a bridge arcing over a wide river. I crested a hill and began to cross the bridge. A Garde galloped on a horse from the other side.

Jumping down the embankment, I plunged into the water. The current shot me through a narrow gorge. I didn't fight it. I swam for my life.

81

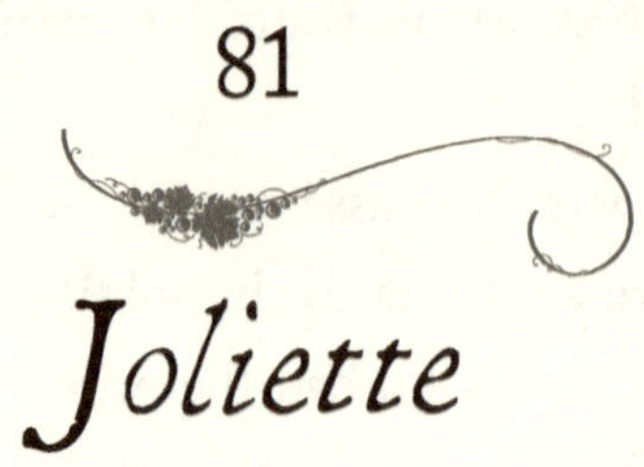

Joliette

Loire River Valley
August 11, 1792

I PRAYED, *PAPA, PROTECT him*, as Henri raced across the hills to the Loire.

Étienne touched my arm. "We'll all be safer if you don't watch him."

The men might kill him. If not for Étienne, I would be alone. The troops spread out, but the officer rode steadily toward us. I gripped Maman's rosary but could not pray.

"We must remember what Henri said. Your name is Henri Saulnier, born in Paris, sixth of February 1750, your wife, Abri-elle Renée Lenogue Saulnier, died 1773. I am your daughter, Joliette Saulnier, born Paris, eighteenth of June 1773." We repeated it as a group of men advanced.

The Officer—his white uniform without a trace of wrinkle or

stain, his moustache perfectly trimmed, his hat shading eyes—raised his arm. Étienne brought the mare to a stop. "Papers." The officer swung his stiff arm out at us.

I picked up the satchel, dug around a bit. "I know they were here when we left."

"No time for stories." The officer snapped his fingers. "Your papers."

"Excuse me, Officer." I pulled out our identity papers and passe-avants.

Without acknowledging me, he examined them. I dropped some of the account papers, hoping I looked a silly fool. The Officer gazed at us, down at the papers, then Étienne. "Who're you?"

Lines creased Étienne's forehead. He pointed. "Her papa."

The Officer blew out a sigh and whispered, "Crétin." Lines about his mouth deepened. "Your name, Monsieur?"

"Oh!" Étienne laughed. "É—" He shot a look at me.

I tilted my head to where Henri had been sitting.

"Henri." He nodded and smiled. "My name is Henri."

"You have another name? Or are you called Henri the Idiot?"

I dug my nails into Étienne's leg. "Saulnier." I smiled like I was eating sugared almonds. "His name is the same as mine, Officer. Please forgive Papa. He grows forgetful in the heat." I patted Étienne's shoulder.

"You were born?" He looked to Étienne.

"The eighteenth of June."

"Papa, that is my birthdate. Yours is the sixth of February. I recently celebrated mine with champagne. I love champagne. Do you like it, Monsieur?"

The Officer's eyes hardened. "Only aristocrats can afford champagne."

Sweat coursed down my neck. Stupid, stupid, stupid. This man was as stubborn as the first shipper I had met. "Did you read my papers, Monsieur?"

"Mademoiselle, you will be quiet, or I will take you to prison."

Étienne tugged my arm, frowning.

I straightened. "Our papers are in order and the passe-avants allow us to travel without hindrance. You have no right to stop us."

"Enough." Étienne flicked the reins on my legs.

My breath caught. How dare he? A peasant.

"She lost her maman and, because of this, she thinks she is the boss of everyone." He pressed his hand on my arm. "Apologize to the Officer."

The Officer glared.

My nobility was a danger, not an advantage. Tears rose, angering me more. I sputtered. The image of the Queen's staircase and François Varicourt's head atop a pike stopped me. My heart raced as if I stood amidst the battle. If I acted as the noble I was, I would get us both imprisoned.

The Officer arched an eyebrow. "You have a right to travel… *if* the papers are authentic." He shoved our papers into his waistcoat.

"Forgive me." Tears burst. "I humbly apologize. Papa's right. I boss everyone, including Papa. I…I put on airs. I've never tasted champagne… I'd like to…but we…since Maman died…" I sobbed. I sobbed for Grandmaman, Maman, Papa, for Guillaume. I sobbed for Henri.

Étienne patted my back. "You see, Officer, she's a good girl at heart, but her mother was overbearing, and my daughter takes after her."

I wiped my apron over my face and bit into the cloth before I bossed us into prison.

The Officer ran his tongue over his teeth and made a sucking sound. "Having two overbearing wenches is more than any one man should endure." He tossed the papers to Étienne. "Good luck."

"Thank you, Officer." Étienne put the papers inside his tunic and snapped the reins.

The Officer galloped away.

"Forgive me, Madame," Étienne whispered. "I could die of shame."

I placed my hand on his arm. "No, Étienne, I ask your forgiveness. You saved my life, and I am indebted to you. I *was* overbearing. Thank you."

He nodded, but his face was crimson.

82

Joliette

Château de Verzat
August 12–13, 1792

I PROMISED TO MEET Guillaume at the château. I could not break that promise by risking my life and being a stubborn noble. I had to act like a helpless woman to be believed. Now that Henri had escaped, I had to trust Étienne to get me home.

After changing horses, Étienne and I followed the silver ribbon of the Loire throughout the night. As the sun rose, a blanket of morning mist lay over the water. It drifted away exposing a long line of barges vying for the one thin navigable channel left by the receding water. One barge, loaded with sacks of grain, stood stranded on a sandbar. Villagers ran down the steep bank and began unloading the boat.

I pointed. "Are they lightening the load, so they can push the vessel into the current?" The peasants ran with the sacks back up the bank toward town. "What are they doing? That is stealing."

"They feed their families."

I closed my eyes. Had I ever known how fortunate I was? I had taken everything, our life at Versailles, the Paris mansion, the château, all as normal. I believed I deserved it all because I was a noblesse d'épée. The sun's heat reflected my shame.

I remembered the abundance of Cook's dishes, served at every meal. Never once had I felt guilty for all I had when so many had so little. No wonder the peasants were so violent. I prayed the château would not be a victim of their rage.

We rode for hours through screeching cicadas. Abandoned boats littered the banks. Among the reeds, boys hunted frogs. One brought up an eel and held it wriggling above his head to the cheers of his friends. I silently clapped for him.

We passed the city of Tours without being stopped. "We should arrive within an hour."

A sudden breeze brought an acrid scent. Across the river stood the smoldering skeleton of a château. Hawks circled above. The blackened stubble of crops surrounded the charred vineyard. How stupid. "Why would they burn food?"

Étienne slowed the horse. "It's so dry, when they set the house afire, the fields caught."

From the west, a pillar of smoke rose like a building storm cloud. *Please, Grandmaman, Maman, Papa, protect our home.* "We must hurry."

As we rounded a bend, smoke rose from another estate, charred and burned like the first. I prayed Maman's rosary as we passed it.

At the crest of a far distant hill, the afternoon light struck a château, making it dazzle like an amber brooch. A honey-sweetness filled the air. It was early to harvest, yet peasants moved through the vineyard, cutting the clusters, and placing them in the baskets strapped to their backs. I feared my chest would burst with joy. "Take that turnoff."

"We've arrived?"

"Yes. I am home." I pressed my fingers to my lips until, at the sight of the old chestnut tree, I calmed myself. "Merci, Étienne."

"This is paradise."

"Yes, it is paradise." I looked back, hoping to see Guillaume and Henri. A low cloud of dust hung over the road. "And I shall never leave it again. Never."

83

Henri

Loire River Valley
August 12–13, 1792

I SWAM THE RIVER until night fell. Exhausted, I crawled to a beach and slept fitfully until I woke at dawn. Mist rolled down the hills and sat like a cloud over the river. Papa had hidden me my whole life, and now that he'd acknowledged me, and Cassard was dead, I was still hiding. Would I ever stop?

I knew of only one safe place to be Henri de Verzat—America. How would I get Joliette there? I'd promised Papa and Guillaume. I had to find a boat sailing for America, and the port of Nantes wasn't too far from the château.

In the distance, the ancient palace walls of Amboise rose through the mist. Guards would check papers at the city gate, as they had when we'd brought Papa home for burial. Grateful for the mist's cover, I ran down the hill. Walking along the river's edge, I trudged through the sand, stumbling in the deep groves, considering swimming. Aided by the current, I could make Saint-Étienne-de-Chigny by midmorning. But I'd walked and swam for two days, and I was so exhausted I feared I'd drown. I sighed. At least I trusted Étienne to get Joliette home.

Sunlight reflected on the looming walls and towers of the palace on the hilltop. I'd have to travel far inland to skirt the city walls. I searched for an easier way.

Hidden among a stand of trees, a small boat lay on its side. I overturned the boat. I could be hanged for stealing, but I'd have to be caught first. I leaned over for the oars. Someone pushed me. I fell over the boat, face first into the sand. Please, not a soldier, I prayed as I scrambled to my feet.

A muscular, barefoot fisherman, wearing pale blue trousers and tunic, held a branch like a club. He spat to the right of my face. "Thief."

"I can pay." I pulled out a silver écu. It gleamed in the sunlight. "If you'll take me to Saint-Étienne-de-Chigny."

He tapped the club on his palm.

"I'm not a thief. I was going to leave this money."

He advanced.

"Please." I extended my hand. "I must get to my mother before she dies."

He ran his hand along the length of the club. With two fingers, I offered the coin. He grabbed it and shoved it into his pocket. "You row."

He jumped in as I slid the boat into the river. I sucked in the scent of brackish water, dipped the oars, and pushed off toward the current. My relief fueled my sore arms.

After we passed Amboise, I rowed for two hours until the walled city of Tours rose in the north. "Don't you have to join the army?" I asked the fisherman.

"Have to catch me first."

"They nearly caught me."

He looked up at the towers and then grabbed the oars. "I'll row."

I lay down under the nets so that if any guards saw the boat none would see me. With his rhythmic pulls and the swift current, we sped past the city and the remnants of a bridge as strong sunlight broke through the mist.

The sun was directly overhead when we came upon two men standing waist-high in the river, flinging a fishing net out over the water.

"Is Saint-Étienne-de-Chigny far?" I shouted.

"Around that bend."

I laughed in relief, but it was short lived. I prayed Joliette arrived and was safe. Then we had to find Guillaume.

Workers in the vineyard stopped picking and hurried to help me to the château, glimmering at the top of the hill like a jewel. I understood why Joliette would never want to leave this place, but she had to.

Joliette and Étienne greeted me, and we all feasted in the château's kitchen with Maman, the Marquise, Madame Françoise, and Simon. I ate a bit of soup and bread before I began nodding at the table.

Joliette whispered, "Come, you need rest."

84

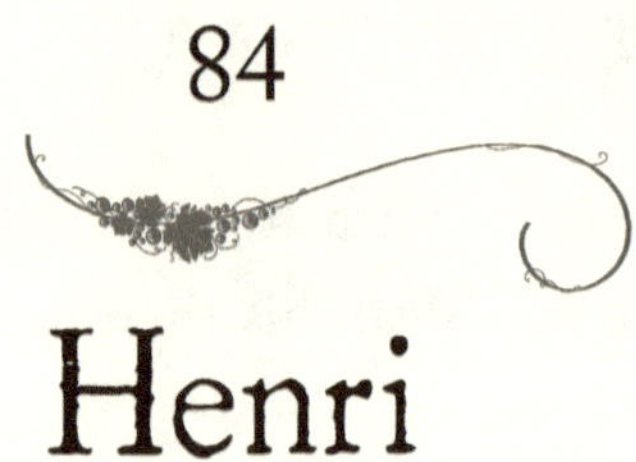

Henri

Château de Verzat
August 14, 1792

I AWOKE IN A sweat. The screams of sans-culottes piercing my ears. If Geneviève saw me jump into the river, she might fear I drowned. I hoped her father did not punish her when he learned my true identity. If it was safe to send a message, the châtelain would know who I could trust.

Like Étienne, he was tall and muscular, but he wore boots, breeches, and a silk waistcoat. A crescent scar marked his right cheek. "This is your papa's stallion. Fast as the wind, gentle as a lamb. Would you like to ride him?"

I nodded. "But first, do you know of anyone I can trust to deliver a message in Paris?"

"You can trust everyone on this estate, Comte. But do you wish to risk any one of their lives?"

I blew out a breath. "No." I'd find another way. When Guillaume arrived, he'd have more news and insights. When Joliette and I departed, we'd need every single person to remain loyal to us. Étienne was just the person who could ensure that. He'd already proved himself by delivering Joliette. He'd lost everything to a feudal nobleman. He'd convince those on the estate the benefit of loyalty to the Verzats.

Étienne and I walked through the vineyards and crossed a stream that stood at the edge of a meadow where sheep and lambs grazed. "This is your farm."

He approached a weather-beaten shack and smiled. "Thank you."

"That's the shed for your lambs." I pointed to a tufa-stone house with a slate roof, chimney, and three windows. "That's your home."

He crept toward the building as if hurrying would make it disappear. Standing at the threshold, he removed his hat and blessed himself. I gave him a gentle nudge. "This is your home, Étienne."

Clutching his hat, he took a step, paused, and took another. He turned in a circle, taking in the fireplace, iron cooking pot, crockery, the long wooden table, bench, two chairs. I opened the white curtains, and sunlight spilled across a woolen blanket covering a pallet surrounded by a carved wooden frame. "The family that lived here sailed to New France."

His cheeks quivered. "I've never had such a bed...such a fireplace..." His breath caught, and he swallowed. "Such...a home." He turned away, his shoulders rising and falling.

He shook himself and walked back out into the meadow. Waving his arm in a circle, he shouted, "This will be the garden. And you and Joliette are welcome at my table every day."

I'd no doubt Étienne would ensure Château de Verzat's safety. Now I only had to get Joliette to America.

85

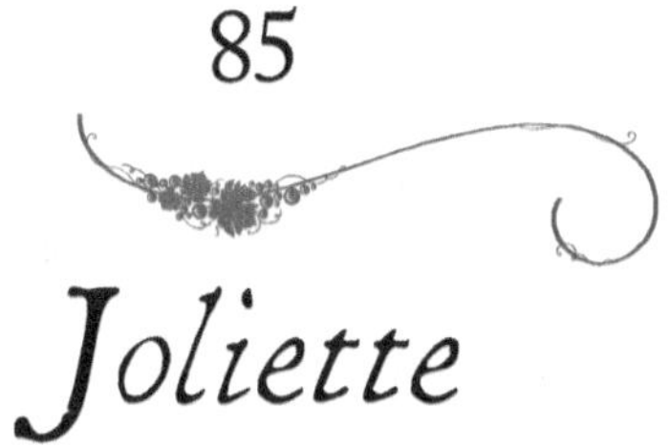

Joliette

Château de Verzat
August 16, 1792

HENRI STRODE ACROSS the fields, his walk so like Papa's. I wanted to cry at this, but I smiled. "Come, I want to show you some things you will need to know. We must expand the vineyards to keep up with the exportation."

"Joliette, I promised—"

I put up my hand. "The Verzat legacy is *our* responsibility, now."

"But I know nothing of it." He put out his hands as if they were useless.

"Neither did I. But it is in your blood. You have the Verzat palate, like I do. You tasted the lavender in the wine."

The corner of his mouth twitched, but he did not give in to a smile.

Around us, the canopy of leaves—many yellowed, some already brown curls—fluttered in the breeze. The air hummed with the gentle whirring of insects drawn to the grapes' nectar. A burst of dust rose with each step we took. "Do you smell that?"

He looked about and shrugged.

"The earth," I urged.

He bent and brought a pinch of dirt to his nose. "It doesn't stink like the filth in Paris."

I picked up a few pebbles. "You saw the cliffs along the river? They and the château are of the same tufa stone." I shook the rocks together. "I smell a mineral scent. Do you?"

"Like when striking flint?"

"Yes."

"Sorry, no. But the tunnels have such a smell."

I tossed the rocks aside. "Perhaps in time, you will smell it here. I taste a hint of minerals in some of the white wines." I picked a bunch of grapes, removed the withered ones, and offered some. "They are small, but their juice is intense. Tell me what you taste."

He placed a few in his mouth, chewed, and paused. His eyes watered, and I feared he might have bitten a tart berry. "It's the most delicious thing I've ever eaten." He picked a bunch. "How did the wine get the taste of apricots?"

"Grandmaman would be so proud of you. Look about you, see the fruit orchards on those distant hills? The sweetness you smell usually indicates a robust, complex flavor, and it only occurs during years of scant rainfall. I believe this year will be an excellent vintage." I brought my arm up and turned. "Everything—the fruits, the insects, the flowers in the meadow—everything is a part of the terroir, the soil, the climate, the conditions."

"You're as much a part of it as any of those things."

"You are right." I smiled. "I shall never leave my home. Never." The sunset tinged the clouds amber-pink, and the sky turned violet. "Is this not paradise?"

He dipped his head and his shoulders rolled forward. "Joliette—"

"The vendanges is early this year." I studied him. He seemed troubled. "What is it?"

"Both Papa and Guillaume made me promise to take you to America."

I stiffened. "Guillaume said he would return by tomorrow."

"I will discuss it with him, but I am sure he will agree. It is too dangerous for you to remain here."

"Do you wish to go?" I whispered.

His eyes swept over the vineyard, past the river, along the horizon. "Papa wanted to go to America. He told me of his conversations with Benjamin Franklin. He warned me to study English." He laughed. "I wish I'd listened to that advice." He ran his boot along the earth. "It was Papa's dream, and I think he dreamt it for us, too."

The clouds shifted from violet to rose to gold. "Bring Guillaume back?"

His eyes squinted in the fading light. "If he doesn't return tomorrow?"

"Yes. I know it is a huge thing to ask. But I beg you, please bring him home."

A dark line formed between his eyes. Was he remembering Papa? Or all we had been through, killing Cassard, and dragging his body into the tunnels, escaping the army, walking, and rowing all the way here?

"Forgive me for asking this of you—" Something broke in me, and I inhaled to steady my voice. "I am so worried. Something is wrong. I feel it." I pressed my fingers to my mouth, held them there until I could speak again. "I cannot lose him, too."

Henri placed his hand on my back.

"Besides, how can the Verzat legacy continue if Guillaume and I do not have children?" I wiped my face. Golden light shone behind Henri's profile, accenting his crooked nose. "You look so much like Papa."

He ran his finger along the length of his nose and frowned. "Truly?"

I laughed. "Truly."

"I will leave at dawn. Do not worry, I will probably meet Guillaume along the road."

"Merci." I kissed his cheek. "I know you are right."

If Guillaume insisted I leave for America, I would convince him to go, too. I would not leave without him.

86

Henri

Paris
August 18, 1792

I RODE THROUGH THE day and night, stopping only to change horses—ever on the lookout for soldiers. In small towns, I listened to news criers. The royal family had been taken to the Temple prison. As Guillaume had served them, he could have been one of the slaughtered guards. He was a brother to me, and I did not want to deliver another corpse.

In Montrogue, I learned the barriers were still closed. I stabled the horse, bought flint and torches, and entered the tunnels.

The damp stench of death seeped into my tunic. When I came upon rats feasting on a pile of decomposing bodies, I fell against a wall, praying Guillaume's body wasn't one of them.

Hoping to find the Verzat servants, I ascended through Saint Séverin but found it empty. I hoped they'd not returned to the mansion. The city was quiet, too quiet. I took back alleys to the Palais-Royal.

"The Assembly has abolished the monarchy!"

Idiots. Did the news writers think the King could rule from a prison?

"Insurrectionary Commune to be established at the Hôtel de Ville." The criers out-shouted one another. "Military Tribunal to judge traitors within!"

I snatched a broadsheet and read that Danton issued a warrant for Lafayette's arrest. I swallowed a bitter taste. Guillaume was loyal to all his commanders, Lafayette and the King. Did that make him a traitor?

I stopped a man in a red cap. "Where are the Gardes Nationale?"

His laugh stank of stale wine. "If they're not dead, they're at the border or at La Force!" He slapped a pamphlet at me and marched off.

I smoothed the paper, *L'Orateur du Peuple*. Fréron called all citizens to hold the families of émigrés hostage, burn their châteaux, and sow desolation. The paper shook. A direct order to destroy the Verzat estate.

Every Royalist was a traitor. A Royalist was anyone who served the royal family. Joliette was in grave danger, and Guillaume knew it. Smoke and a stink of burned meat hung like a cloud over the Tuileries.

I headed for Place de Grève on my way to La Force. Gossiping crowds were sure to swarm the execution site. The guillotine no longer cast its shadow, and the square was now a bustling market. I stopped a broom peddler. "Where's the guillotine?"

He plucked a straw from one of the brooms and wedged it between his teeth. "Moved it to Place du Carrousel. Bigger square. Bigger audience."

I flinched. I would never understand the entertainment of execution. I headed for La Force.

When I reached rue du Roi de Sicile, I entered the cobbled courtyard of the former château. Iron grids covered the windows. Wiping sweat from the back of my neck, I approached a battered wooden door.

A red-capped corpulent man, wearing a too small uniform, looked up and spat just beyond my boots.

"Is Guillaume Pricaud imprisoned here?"

He rubbed his fingers against his thumb. I gave him a sou. He belched.

I pulled out a livre. As he grabbed for it, I pulled it away. "Is Guillaume Pricaud here?" I fluttered the livre.

He ran his finger down a page in a book, grinned, and reached.

"Do you give me a pass?"

He jerked his head toward the entrance across the courtyard.

"Thank you." I crumpled the livre in my fist and left him with his empty hand.

Two young guards, wearing uniforms of the Gardes Nationale but also the bonnets rouges of the sans-culottes, stood with their pikes crossed before the gate. Another guard sat at a battered desk. Sweat soaked my tunic and puddled at my waist. I stood before them and prayed they wouldn't ask for papers. "I wish to visit Guillaume Pricaud, please."

"Twenty sous." He held out his hand, took my livre, stamped a pass, and gave it to me. "Take this one to Pricaud!"

The gate opened and a gendarme, pimples crowding his greasy forehead, stomped his pike on the cobbles. "This way."

He led me through a warren of passages. I memorized every turn. The odors of moldering hay, dried blood, and urine soiled the air. We climbed a spiral stairway for three floors and entered a windowless corridor. He marched to the second door, took out a ring of keys, and unlocked it. "Visitor."

A pallet of straw lay to the side. A stinking wooden bucket sat in a dark corner. A small square window several feet above cast a patch of light upon an escritoire in the middle of the straw-strewn floor.

I entered and peered into the shadows. Guillaume stood against the far wall, tall and straight, his hands clasped behind his back. Although ripped and torn, his uniform had been brushed. Streaks of black cinders and dried blood marked the once pristine fabric. Whiskers covered his strong jaw.

"Ten minutes." The creak of the door, the scratch of the key, the thunk of the lock, and I was as much a prisoner as Guillaume. The guard's heels clicked against stone.

My mouth went dry.

Dark hollows sank beneath Guillaume's eyes. "You took her to the château and, when I did not arrive, she sent you."

I nodded. 'Why are you here?"

"My troop escorted the King to the Assembly, but doing my job marked me as a Royalist. I am a traitor."

I started. "How can you be a traitor if you were protecting the King?"

He huffed. "All those who protected the King are a part of a royal conspiracy, and that makes me a traitor to the Republic."

A pricking ran across the back of my neck. "Who says this?"

"The Insurrectionary Commune." His face appeared carved of stone.

I hadn't believed the news criers. "What of the Assembly?

"More than half the deputies have fled. The Assembly has no power against those who have claimed it."

Could I have helped change things had I not fled? I was caught in the same current that trapped Guillaume. I was back swimming for my life, but I'd escaped. I didn't want to hear the answer, but I had to know. "What's to happen to you?"

"A fellow Garde, Louis-David d'Angremont, has been sentenced for leading the royal conspiracy. He is to be guillotined this evening."

I pressed my hand against the wall. "And you?"

"I am accused of the same. I am to face Madame Guillotine tomorrow."

My heart pounded. "We have to get you out of here."

"There are no tunnels for me."

I jerked toward him. "But there is an entrance not far from here."

He brought a letter out from behind him. "You promised your papa to take Joliette to America. I ask the same."

A pressure built in my chest. "She will not leave without you. Nor will I."

"More than a thousand people have been imprisoned—

suspected of being part of the conspiracy—including all who served the royal family. Joliette is not safe—anywhere in France." He leaned toward me. "If they discover *your* noble identity, you will beat me to the guillotine."

"Cassard exposed me at the Assembly. My nobility is known."

He stepped closer. "You are risking your life being here. Why?"

The tightness in my chest gave way. "She will not go." My voice sounded like a little boy's. He held out the letter. His hand did not shake, yet my whole body trembled.

"Henri, they questioned me, demanded to know where she was. I told them she emigrated. She saved my life at Versailles, and now I save hers—but only if you take her to America. This letter reminds Joliette that she promised to obey me in her wedding vows, and I command her to go to America." His eyes brightened when he spoke her name. He stood before me, a courageous man, a noblesse d'épée in the truest sense of the word, accepting his fate. I wanted to cry, but I could not. I had to be brave—for him.

I tucked the letter into my waistcoat. The muscles in my arms pulsed. My rage could get us all killed. "I wish I could be as courageous as you." I pressed my lips together, to be strong for him. My arms hung, throbbing, useless.

He clasped me and drew me close. "You have been a brother to me. I could not have asked for a more loyal or courageous one."

I embraced him, overwhelmed with my love for him. Yet, helplessness sucked a hollow in my chest.

"I know you have the courage to keep your promise." His voice was calm.

The click of the guard's boots sounded on the stone corridor.

He clapped my back, as Papa had, and whispered, "I will be with you both." He looked into me. "Tell Joliette she must go to America and not let me die in vain. Tell her I shall love her forever."

"I will." My words stuck in my throat.

The door opened.

"Leave immediately. There is no time to lose." His eyes held alarm.

I placed my hand over my heart. "I will, my brother."

I stumbled out into the courtyard. The gate slammed behind me. My eyes burned in the stark light. I pulled my hat down low, the stench of the prison sour in my mouth.

A woman stood in the center of the courtyard, selling citronnade. I paid her, drank deeply, and returned the wooden cup. At her feet, a boy sat placing stones atop one another, building a wall. He looked up, offering a stone. I added it to his barrier. He handed me another. I squatted down, took a coin from my pocket, gave it to him, and whispered, "For your Maman."

He grinned, put it atop his wall, and clapped. The coin glinted.

I forced myself to walk calmly. Every bit of me wanted to run all the way to the château.

87

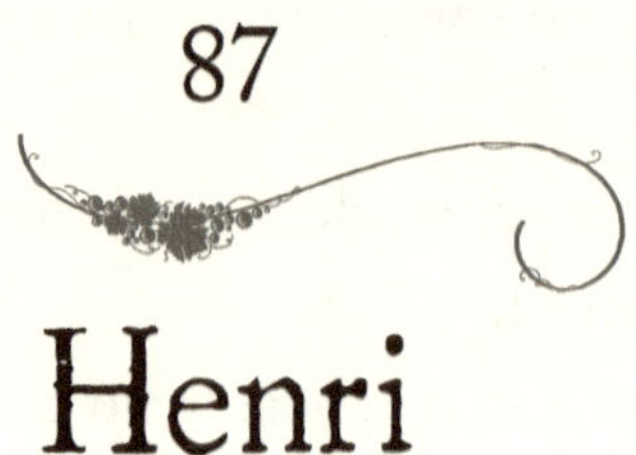

Henri

I HAD TO FIND Geneviève without being caught by the sans-culottes. A carnival-like atmosphere filled the streets. Drunks sang, men and women wearing red hats danced, children aimed sticks, pretending to shoot one another. I skirted the Place du Carrousel and hurried to the Salle du Manège.

The noise level made me think the salle would be crowded, but only a quarter of the deputies sat on the benches—the noise came from the packed galleries. The moment I looked up, I saw Geneviève, wearing a dove gray gown and bonnet. She ran to the back of the gallery, and I caught her in my arms before she reached the last step. I embraced her, breathing in her vanilla scent, burying my face in her softness.

"Are you mad? If anyone recognizes you, they will send you to the guillotine."

I put my fingers to my lips and led her outside.

"I feared you'd drowned. I've searched and searched." She trembled.

"I'm sorry. I'm here now. Hush." Her tears seeped into my tunic.

She pulled away. "Where were you?"

"Come." I hurried her toward the river. Dried pools of blood stained the gravel paths, and thick clouds of black flies hovered over them. Scraps of blood-stained cloth littered the brown grass.

"Do you not know what happened here?" Geneviève squeezed my hand.

"I fear I am desecrating the ground where brave men died."

"People were killed all over the city. I do not think you can avoid it."

The river was low. Two bodies were snared under the docks on the far bank. Barges, carrying cattle, sheep, barrels of wine, plied the Seine. Although the city barriers were closed, the river was not. Hiring a boat would be faster than the tunnels. I pulled Geneviève down the quai. Except for the river traffic and birds, we stood alone, watching the slow muddy water.

I held her shoulders. "I wanted to tell you earlier."

She closed her eyes, opened them. "Yes?"

"My father...was the Comte de Verzat."

"The Minister to the King?"

I nodded.

"It's true then. You're a noble." Her eyes darkened.

"Illegitimate. He recognized me, but I did not take his title."

"It matters not. And—your sister—she served the Queen!" Alarm seeped into her eyes. "The sans-culottes will hunt you down—both of you."

"I know. That's why…" The garden whirled. I pulled her to me and held her tight. "Will you come with me to America?"

She backed away and blinked. "America?"

"Joliette and I must leave. Will you come with me?"

"As what?" She pulled away. "Your mistress?"

"No. I…."

"Do you love me?"

I pulled her close. "I admire you, your courage, your strength, your audacity! How could I not love you?"

"Then you wish to marry me?"

"Someday." My tunic stuck to my back. "I mean, Geneviève, I have no way to support you. I have no job. Maybe, one day in America, but not now."

Her mouth opened, and she pressed her hand over it.

"I promised both my papa and my sister's husband, I'd take Joliette to America."

She crossed her arms. "I was frantic with worry that you were dead."

"I'm sorry I frightened you. I had to get Joliette out of the city."

"Where have you been?"

"At the château, in Saint-Étienne-de-Chigny, on the Loire."

Her arms dropped to her sides. "And you came back for me?"

I nodded and dragged my fist over my lips. "Also for my sister's husband."

"Did you find him?"

I shoved my toe through the mud. "Yes."

"Is he going to America with you?"

"No." I looked back at the palace. "He goes to the guillotine, tomorrow."

She jolted and gripped my arm. "I am sorry. Why? When?"

"Tomorrow. As a Garde Nationale, he is accused of being part of the royal conspiracy."

"Your poor sister."

"Geneviève, it is not safe here. Come with us."

"You did not come back for me." Her smile was sad. "I am safe." She held my hand, her skin so soft. "But you must go, Henri." She leaned in and kissed my cheek. "We will see each other again when you return."

My heart hammered. "I am sorry—"

"Hush." She placed her fingertips on my lips. "You will write?"

"Of course."

"What is your sister's husband's name? Where is he?"

"Guillaume Pricaud." My throat was raw. "He is at La Force."

"I will visit him. He will not be alone."

"My sister and I thank you."

She squeezed my hands. "I hope you have a safe voyage and France will be at peace soon." Tears dripped from her chin. "So, you can…return." Her face looked rumpled, like when Maman cried about not losing another son. She dropped my hands.

I clutched her arm. "Wait. Should you need to escape Paris, go to the Verzat château, in Saint-Étienne-de-Chigny. They will hide you and care for you."

She shook her head and stared at the blood-spattered ground.

I had to make her feel useful to convince her. "Joliette needs a vigneron. You would be helping her."

"I know nothing of wine."

"You will learn." I pulled the key to the tunnels from my neck. "This key opens all the doors in the tunnels of Paris but one. Even if you are afraid of the dark, the tunnels can save your life. Use the key."

She wrapped her fingers around it, kissed my cheek, and ran.

I wanted to stop her, pick her up in my arms, and carry her to America. I dragged my foot. What did I have to offer her but danger? Terrible danger.

I walked downriver, looking for a fisherman who'd take me beyond the city barriers. I had no time to lose in getting Joliette out of France.

88

Joliette

Château de Verzat
August 18, 1792

I RAN TO THE cave, searching for Joseph. "Madame Robert wishes us to ship the wine directly." I waved the letter. "We must take two hundred barrels to the barge she has arranged to port at Langeais. It will take the cargo to the ship moored in Nantes." I stopped to catch my breath. "Can we get them there in two days?"

He removed his straw hat and wiped his sleeve across his forehead. "We will be taking pickers away from the fruit, and it is ripe, Madame."

I looked out across the vines. The breeze ruffled the leaves into alternating patches of pale and dark green. The sun poured heat upon my face, and I tilted the brim of my bonnet. I remembered the day Grandmaman began my studies. She had done everything in her power to educate, prepare, encourage me. My greatest desire was to grow the legacy of Verzat wine to be the greatest in the world. I grabbed a pair of secateurs. "I will help. I will ask the women at the château to pick. We cannot lose this opportunity."

He gave a small bow and then smiled. "You are like your grandmaman, Madame."

I rushed to the château. Even Simon and the Marquise could help. When Guillaume and Henri arrived, I would put them to work. I would never leave France. Never. I would convince Guillaume. He had to understand.

89

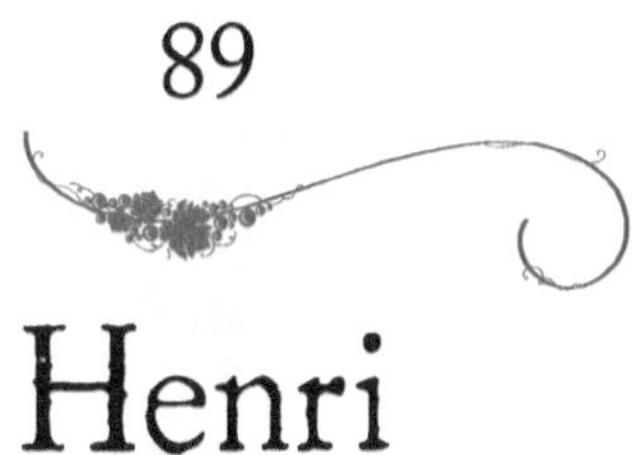

Henri

Loire River Valley
August 20, 1792

AFTER TWO DAYS of riding without rest, my vision
began to blur, but I kept on. Joliette did not yet know Guillaume was dead. How would I tell her? He'd been there for her
when Papa died. Now, she had only me. I wasn't up to the task.

Between Amboise and Tours, smoke rose like an angry
wraith from a burned château. Hawks and buzzards screamed.
The sans-culottes wasted no time in *sowing desolation*. I spurred
the horse.

A golden aura shone in the western sky as I crested the last
hill. I'd thought it was mist rolling down the Loire, but across
the river flames arced through clouds of smoke. Dozens of
men carrying torches ran through the fields lighting the vines.
Waves of fire swallowed the outlying orchards. The men tossed

their torches onto the dried grass and ran along the riverbank heading for the bridge—the bridge that reached the Verzat estate. Flames followed the men and swallowed the wooden span. The air cracked as flames devoured everything south of the river.

I gripped the reins. "François I gave this land to my ancestors, and you'll not destroy it."

I galloped through the Verzat vineyard, yelling at the workers, "Sans-culottes are attacking! Sound the alarm!" I whipped the horse and raced to the porte cochère. Maman hurried out. "Send Madame Françoise to tell Joliette she must hide in the cave and not come out until I come to get her."

She ran as Étienne and the châtelain led workers, carrying rakes, scythes, hoes, pikes, secateurs, horse whips, muskets over the hill. The châtelain directed the workers to circle the house. "We must protect our land and the château!" He looked to me. "And the Comte de Verzat." The workers cheered.

I gripped the reins. *Papa, give me the courage to fill your shoes.*

Estate women and children streamed out the doors of the château, lugging wooden buckets of water. Madame la Châtelaine smiled up at me. "We will not let them set fire to your papa's home, Monsieur Henri."

My heart pounded. Papa was there next to me, his arm about my shoulders. *You have the blood of a noblesse d'épée, my son.* The horse spooked, and I ran my hand along his neck.

The red-capped sans-culottes moved up the hill like a herd of goats. The leader, a swarthy man with the shoulders and arms of a blacksmith, brought his torch to others, who touched theirs to more—a wall of torches blazed and snapped. "Who're you?"

I steadied the horse. They wouldn't have heard I was wanted.

I needed to intimidate them. I patted the two pistols I wore. "Député Detré of the National Assembly."

"We come for nobles," the leader said.

"The Comte and Comtesse are dead." I reached for the butt of my pistol.

A middle-aged woman dressed in trousers and a bonnet rouge stepped forward. "We want the Comtesse. Don't deny she's a noble, Monsieur." She swayed her hips. "I saw her playing with the royal children at Versailles."

"We are all citizens, Madame. And Mademoiselle Verzat is not here."

The leader sniggered. "We saw her in the vineyard." He waved his torch. "Best not lie, Monsieur. We hang nobles *and* liars—even if they *are* deputies."

The woman cackled. "We're hungry."

"If you hadn't set fire to the crops, you'd have food!" I shouted.

The woman cupped her breasts and rubbed circles around them. "The Comtesse's breasts simmered in cream would be so tender."

The men roared with laughter.

People from the estate crowded around the château, protecting it with their lives.

I pulled out my pistol and sat higher on the horse. "I told you, she is not here!"

Murmurings buzzed among the men, and then a terrible silence thickened the air. The mob pulsed with hate.

"We'll see for ourselves." The leader waved his torch. Men ran to the doors.

I shot my pistol into the sky.

The men staggered. Torches flickered against a blood-red sky.

I brought the horse within an arm's length of the leader and aimed Papa's pistol. "The citizens you see before you have owned the farms on this estate for more than twenty years. Because they own the land under the château, they own it." I cocked the pistol's hammer. "They, and I, will defend it to the death."

The leader raised his torch to one of the columns supporting the porte cochère. The dry wood beam caught, and flames raced across the other beams, heading for the château. He stepped back to watch, his grin spreading.

I grabbed the gun barrel and slammed the butt into his head. The man dropped, sprawling in the gravel. I righted the pistol and aimed it at the mob.

The estate women ran toward the fire, their buckets slopping water. I pulled my horse near the column and helped a man climb up onto the roof of the porte cochère. Women formed a line and handed up buckets. Children raced back to fill them.

The workers moved as one. Men aimed their muskets, pushing the marauders back.

A thick silence fell, burning torches crackled, smoldering beams hissed.

"Look around. There are far more of us." I aimed the pistol at the crowd. "We will defend our home to the death—your deaths. You wish to try again?"

Shadows flickered over defeated faces. A woman stepped out from behind the leader. "Forgive us, Monsieur." She blessed herself. "We are so hungry."

The châtelain spoke softly. "If you need work, the grapes need picking."

A man dressed in the tunic and frayed trousers of a farmer stomped on his torch, removed his hat, and bowed his head. "I need work, Monsieur." Others followed the farmer's plea until the leader, holding his hand over his bleeding head, nodded.

"Come at sunrise. We will have bread and cheese before we begin picking." The châtelain rested his whip over his shoulder.

I held back a smile of admiration. A wise man, the châtelain. He'd ensured the safety of the estate and the harvest. Papa trained him well. I could assure Joliette the estate would be safe and protected.

I spurred the horse toward the cave.

90

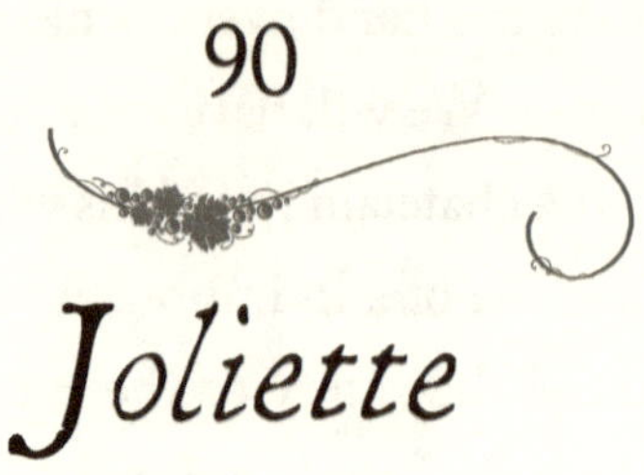

Joliette

Loire River Valley
August 20, 1792

I GREW DIZZY FROM the fumes of the cask I crouched in. I hugged my knees and rested my head against the staves, my chest as hollow as the barrel I hid under. If Guillaume was with Henri, someone would have told me. *Please protect him, Grandmaman. I need him. Please.*

Scuffling footsteps startled me. I prayed they were not Révolutionaries. "This one," Joseph shouted. "Crouch down, Madame."

I pushed my head between my knees. Cool air whooshed in as the fake lid of the barrel lifted. Torches made the moist walls of the cave glisten.

"Joliette!" Henri and Joseph lifted me out.

"Where is Guillaume?"

Henri tried to embrace me.

I shrugged him off. "Tell me!" I screeched.

He withdrew a letter, shaking in his hand. "I am sorry." He reached for me.

I pushed his hand away. "Don't." I snatched up the letter and pressed it to my breast. I sank to the floor, darkness rushing over me.

"Joliette, listen to me." He crouched down and held my hand.

I pressed my heart. "If I do not hear it…it will not be true."

"Read his words."

"I do not have the strength." My hands and the paper were wet.

He pulled me to him. "I give you my strength." He coaxed my hands, guiding them to open the folds. Curled inside lay the hair ribbon I had tied around Guillaume's wrist. The words blurred.

"Do you want me to read it to you?"

Guillaume's voice whispered, *I will love you forever.* I blew out a breath. He would want me to have the courage to read his words. I shook my head.

My Dearest Joliette,

I was not alive until the day I looked into your eyes and touched your fingertips. You always thought it was you who missed a step, but my darling, it was I who caused it. I was so taken with the beauty and kindness that glow from within you~a radiance and generosity that outshine the sun itself. Since that day, I have not taken a breath without the thought of being with you. The hap-

piest day of my life was the day you became my beloved wife, my partner, my world. Every moment I have spent in your company has been a day in paradise, my love.

If it were in my power, I would never leave you. As you feel the beat of your heart, so feel my love for you. You need only look to the sky, feel the wind on your face, hear the song of a lark to know I am with you, always.

Go now, with Henri, so that he can fulfill the promise he made to your papa and me. Know that my greatest wish is for your safety, my angel. Know I will be with you always.

My heart is yours through the tides of time,

Your devoted husband,
Guillaume

I curled around the letter.

Henri picked me up, carried me in his arms, sat me at the tasting table. I was a doll of cloth, my neck unable to support my head. The Marquise waved a vial of vinegar. I gagged.

A small travel bag sat on the table. Madame Detré shook out a vine worker's gown—covered in white tufa dust, stained with sweat and grapes. "I wish we had time to wash this, but it is a good disguise." Her tear-stained face embodied my brother's kindness. She was losing her son, yet she was here for me.

The Marquise held out Maman's silver thimble, and for a moment, I was next to Maman, her fingers stitching stories with threads, her dulcet voice and laughter, ringing. "I removed it and your jewels from your other gown."

I ran my finger over the filigreed edge.

She placed Maman's thimble and rosary into my hand and curled my fingers around them, then held out a leather purse.

"Never let anyone take this from you. All your jewels are in here. Keep it hidden." She wrapped the leather straps of the purse around my waist twice and knotted them.

I ran my fingers over Guillaume's words, feeling the gentle warmth of my husband's hands. The two women pulled the gown over my head, tied the laces, and placed a shawl over my shoulders. When they finished, the Marquise embraced me.

I held out the ribbon I had tied around Guillaume's wrist. She tied it around mine and kissed it. "Be safe, my dear. Trust Henri. She handed me the pistolet. "It has been cleaned and reloaded."

I could not look at her. Guillaume would want me to be brave. Papa would demand it of me. I shoved the gun in my hanging pocket.

"Joseph told me of the wine shipment to America." Henri's face was lined and dirty. What had he been through?

Guillaume wanted me to trust my brother, despite my doubts. "We shall join it in Nantes?"

Henri nodded and led me out into a moonless night. "The Révolutionaries are convinced you are here. You must hide."

In two days, I would sail across an ocean. I looked up at the hill as moonlight shifted across the château walls. I would never again see my home.

Outside the cave stood a large wagon and, beyond it, three more with teams of four horses harnessed to each. Women pulled ropes around wine casks standing on their metal-banded ends and lashed them together. Twenty men sat on horses—holding torches, carrying muskets, and wearing swords. Étienne sat on the driver's bench of the last wagon. They all wore the trousers, tunics, and straw hats of the vineyard workers, as did my brother. How could we possibly leave these people, who risked their lives to protect ours?

Henri led me up onto the last wagon, not yet fully loaded and through an aisle between the casks—each one with the Verzat crest burned into its side and top. "You must remain hidden, until we reach the barge."

"The barge?"

"It is safer to travel on the river. They will not look for us there."

"We will keep you both safe." Joseph's fraying straw hat shadowed his eyes. I opened my mouth to thank him for saving me, but nothing came out.

Beneath the driver's bench lay the green velvet quilt that covered the chaise longue in my father's study. The Marquise smiled. I thanked her, collapsed upon it, and pulled the scent of cloves around me. Henri set the travel bag next to me. My thundering heart quieted as I heard Guillaume's voice. *Know I am with you, always.*

Wood screeched against wood as the men loaded the last of the casks, encasing me in a muffled darkness. *This could be my coffin.* I inhaled slowly.

The horses' traces jangled, the barrels groaned, and gravel crunched beneath the wagon wheels as they rolled.

In the tunnels, there had been at least a bit of torch light. Here, I saw nothing. Except my husband's face. Henri reached down from the bench above me and brought the quilt up over me. I shivered. "I am…frightened." The word stuck in my throat as if barbed.

"We all protect you."

A thumping came from the side of the wagon. "We can

hear you. You must be silent." Joseph's voice was sharp as the sword he carried.

The horses quickened their pace. The wine sloshed. The barrels could crack with the juddering. Muffled shouts came from a distance. We rolled to a stop.

I held my breath. *Guillaume, protect us.* The horses pawed. Shouts were exchanged. Casks jostled. I reached for Henri's hand. He gently squeezed mine.

"Let us pass," Henri shouted.

"Royalist wine! We take it all." A man's voice retorted.

My legs tensed. Wood scraped against wood. A cask was being removed from a wagon. My heart clogged my throat. Metal clanged against metal.

"This is wine of the Verzat Estate," a deep male voice boomed.

"Death to the rich," another man shouted.

A gun fired.

"The Verzat Estate is owned by the tenants," the châtelain shouted. "If you steal this wine, you steal from your neighbors' mouths." His words rang in the silence. "You will not live as Révolutionaries. You will hang as thieves."

The horses shifted. I pulled the quilt up, remembering Papa thanking a family for harvesting the grapes, and the farmer replying, *We are proud to pick for the greatest wine in France.* Papa ensured our safety long ago.

Remember, you have the courage of a noblesse d'épée. It is in your blood. A whip cracked, and we traveled farther from home. I feared I would need the courage of ten thousand noblesse d'épée.

91

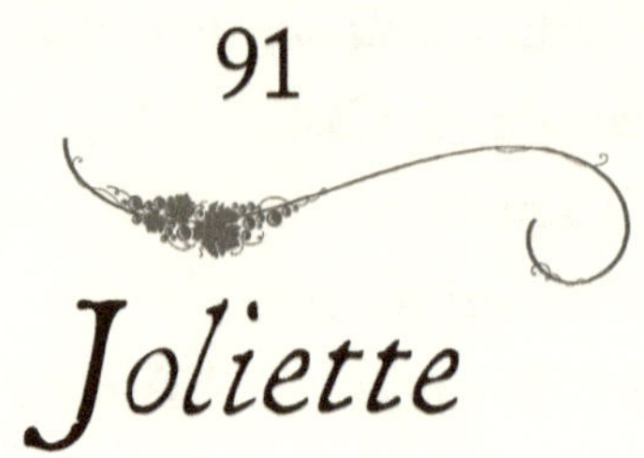

Joliette

The Loire River
August 21, 1792

I AWOKE TO BIRDSONG—CRYSTAL clear, like the playing of a flute. I reached for Guillaume, then jerked. The rocking wagon poured the terror of the night over me. I choked on tufa dust that crusted in my mouth and nose and eyes.

Panicked, I searched for Papa's scent of cloves, and then Guillaume's letter. I ran my fingers over the soft paper. *I am with you, always.* I would not cry. There was not time for such a luxury.

The wagon lurched and tilted as we descended. The bench above creaked. I imagined Étienne pushing his feet against the floorboard and pulling back on the reins. If the horses stumbled and Étienne lost control of the wagon the casks would crush me.

Bringing my legs up, I braced my feet against the staves. The casks slid. I pushed my hands and feet against them. They slid until my knees pressed my chest. One of the horses stumbled, and I dug my fingernails into the wooden slats. The top metal bands of the casks screeched beneath the bench above. The wagon slammed to a stop.

Someone above breathed hard. My knees pressed into my chin. I tried to calm myself and realized the sound of liquid sloshing was not the wine. The lapping was rhythmic, waves hitting the shore. I exhaled but was not calmed.

"Joliette, we're at the barge." Henri's voice was close.

The wagon shook as the men unloaded the wine. A crack of light spilled through, and in rushed the river's sweet scent. A symphony of frogs and crickets and burbling water brought images of halcyon days spent under the chestnut tree at the château with Grandmaman and my parents.

Men dislodged the casks from the bench. I swallowed against a sickening rising in my stomach. My legs numb, I leaned heavily on Henri as we walked into a mist-enshrouded dawn.

Along the shore, reeds shot up straight as pikes. Moored at the end of a short dock, I spotted a gabare, a barge as big as four wagons with a mast so tall it pierced the fog. At the rear, a boy of about twelve years, held a tiller attached to a black rudder shaped like a giant bat's wing. Our men rolled the casks onto the deck and lined them up along the railing.

"Where are we?" I asked.

"Langeais." Étienne walked down the dock and motioned Henri and me to the front of the vessel.

I clasped the ribbon at my wrist and followed. The leather pouch was heavy against my thigh.

We boarded and entered a small shack at the front of the barge, where a man with a face the color and texture of a withered grape sat beside a small iron stove. He wore trousers, wooden sabots, a blue tunic and cap, and a red neckcloth. He shoved a chunk of bread into his mouth and drank from a metal cup. Holes acted as windows in each wall. Charts covered a table.

"Our men loaded the wine," Henri said. "We'd like passage to Nantes."

The boatman stood, and the chair fell back. The long thin blade of a dagger glinted in the weak light. "I take cargo, not people."

Henri held up a leather purse. "We'll pay."

The boatman spat. "I'll not be hanged for helping Royalists escape."

"We are citizens, like you." Henri crept closer to me.

The boatman's eyes were flat, lifeless as a dead fish. "Révolutionaries will believe that as much as I do."

Henri stacked a fistful of louis d'ors on the table. "If you deliver us and the wine to the ship in Nantes—safely—this is yours."

The boatman slid a look at the money, chewed at the corner of his mouth, looked up. The boy stood at the door. His pale blue eyes shone like ice between his sun-bleached eyebrows. He slapped a large hook, like those used by stevedores to drag crates, against his other hand and leered at me.

I reached in my hanging pocket for the pistolet.

Henri pulled a pistol from beneath his tunic. "You can risk your boat being scuttled by men who do not know this river, or you can pilot us safely to Nantes. What do you say?" Sweat streaked through the dust on his neck.

The air hung thick. I wrapped my finger around the pistolet's trigger.

The boatman did not raise his eyes. "You pay me now."

"We give you your life now. You'll be paid when you deliver the wine and us." Henri's voice was calm, as if he were accustomed to pirating boats.

"My son will steer." The boatman grunted, and quick as a heron striking a fish, he threw the dagger. I jumped. It struck the wall, a few inches from me.

Henri smacked his pistol against the boatman's head. The man collapsed. "Étienne, bring ropes and tie him up."

I grabbed the handle, pried it loose. "I will keep this safe, Monsieur."

His son laughed.

I aimed the pistolet at the boy. "I have already killed two men, do not make it three." My arms and legs were steady.

The boy's leer faded, along with the light in his eyes.

Rows of barrels filled the deck. The men ran about, securing the casks with ropes tied to the railings.

At the edge of the dock, Joseph held his hat in shaking hands. "Forgive my earlier abruptness, Comtesse." He bowed, and I smiled at him. "I will protect your home and vineyard with my life." His voice was so soft I leaned closer to hear him whisper, "Until you return, Comtesse." I touched his leathery cheek. He kissed my hand, turned, and strode to the wagon.

All those years he served Grandmaman and advised me. Gratitude swelled in me. How would Henri and I survive without all the people who helped us, protected us, loved us?

Henri stood before the pilothouse with his gun trained on the boatman. Étienne untied the moorings and coiled the ropes on the deck. The boatman yelled to raise the sail. The barge shifted. A chill breeze moved over us.

I gripped a rope tied about a barrel and twisted it so tightly my palms burned.

On the shore, our men stood silently, hats tucked under their arms. They made the sign of the cross and knelt in prayer.

Regardless of their blood or station, every one of them had the courage of a noblesse d'épée.

I knelt, blessed myself, and put up my hand to them, staring until they were tiny dots.

I had no more tears. I prayed for courage. I got to my feet and turned to face our journey.

92

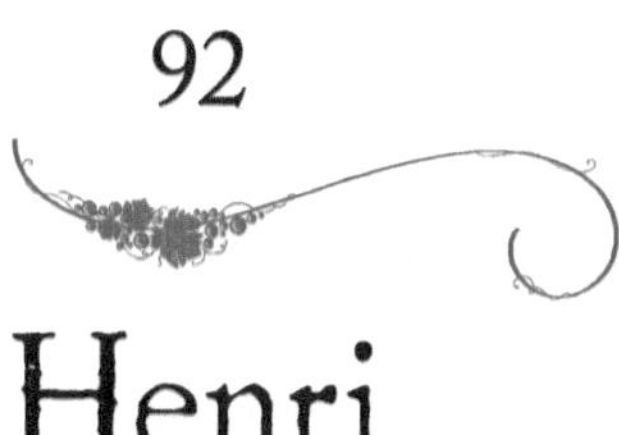

Henri

The Loire River
August 21, 1792

WITH THE BOATMAN trussed to a barrel at the bow, his son pushed his weight into the tiller and steered us into the current. After a few hours, we sailed into a section of many islands that disrupted the current. The son handled the rudder with the same agility that Maman used churning her laundry paddle. When would I see her again?

As the sun rose, the river widened, the wind lessened, and the sail sagged. With two hundred barrels of wine on board, the barge sat low in the water, already shallow due to the drought. The boy might purposefully steer us into a sandbar. I jumped up on a barrel to watch for them.

The barge shuddered. Étienne leaned over the bow. "She's run aground."

When had the sail been lowered?

"I'll push her off." Étienne jumped into the water, which came up to the middle of his chest. "Turn the sail."

The boy grinned. "Sure." He turned the sail and secured it, then returned and leaned against the tiller, holding it fast. The brat had aimed for the sandbar. I pulled out the pistol. "Turn the barge into the current."

He shrugged. "No current here."

I swiped his cap and tossed it. It splashed onto the water and began to bob away from the barge. "Follow that—it'll show you the way!"

The boy's smile grew wide as he yanked the tiller. "Sure."

A prickling ran across my back. "Étienne, get out of the way of the boat!"

With a grunt, Étienne shoved his weight into the hull. The sail caught a breeze. The barge rocked and floated toward him. I leaned over and gripped his arm as the boat began to sail right over him. His hand slipped, and he gasped for breath.

Pulling off my pistol and dagger, I jumped over the other side. Mud sucked me down to my knees. I pulled at my thighs to yank my feet free. The barge moved toward me. I shoved myself away from the hull and felt my boots pull free of the muck. I dived beneath it, my arms sweeping in the silt.

My lungs burned. I surfaced, and dived again, my arm hitting Étienne's leg. I pulled and heaved him to the surface. He gasped and choked. Blood trickled from a gash in his temple. I held his head above the water. A gun fired.

Joliette held her smoking pistolet in one hand and aimed my pistol at the bargeman. He shouted at his son to drop anchor. The barge slowed and stopped about fifty feet away.

Étienne coughed and gagged.

"Can you make it if I help you swim?" I asked.

He nodded.

I turned him on his back, grabbed the collar of his tunic and towed him. As we neared the barge, Joliette commanded the boy to help.

"Let out a rope," I called. "I'll not trust him again."

The boy attached a piece of rope to the railing, but as he began to toss it, Joliette grabbed and tested it. The knot loosened and fell from the rail with her pull. She dropped it on deck and cocked the pistol she aimed at the boatman. "If you wish your father to live, you will tie a secure knot."

The boy did so and tossed me the end. I caught it and hauled us back. Étienne lay on deck, coughing up water and trying to catch his breath. Joliette handed me the gun and ripped a piece of her apron to wrap around Étienne's wound.

The boy gnawed at his lip. I handed Joliette the gun. "Hold this on the boatman while I tie up the son."

The boatman's bushy eyebrows hooded his dark eyes.

The boy pulled his hands away. "How'll I steer?"

"I'll steer." I grabbed his arm and spun him around.

"You won't make it. You don't know the currents." The boatman wiped his tied hands across his forehead. "You'll scuttle her and kill us all."

I tied the boy's hands behind him and yanked the rope so tight the boy sucked in air. "Should've thought of that before your son tried to kill us." I shoved the boy onto the deck. "Stay out of our way."

"Joliette, hold the tiller until I pull up the anchor." With the anchor and its rope in a heap safely on deck, I took over.

North of the shore, the city of Angers stood in the distance, the keep to a castle and a cathedral spire the only things rising above the sloping farmland. As we passed the city, the water grew choppy as another river poured into the Loire. The current rushed with renewed force.

Étienne stood. "We should take advantage of that wind."

"Are you rested enough?"

He raised the sail.

Later in the afternoon, clouds darkened the sky like a spreading stain. Joliette jerked her head toward the north shore. Dust billowed as a gang of pike-wielding men on horseback advanced upriver.

I tasted the dust. "We'll outrun them with this wind."

A gust hit, snapping the sail. I ducked below the pole as it swung across the deck. The barge rocked, and water sprayed over the railing. The boat was headed for shore—right toward the mob of pike-wielding men. *Papa, show me what to do.* I grabbed the tiller, trying to push against the current.

"Drop sail!" I shouted at Étienne.

The boy sniggered. The canvas whooshed down, yet the barge didn't slow; it continued straight toward the men who now thrust their pikes and jeered. I threw my weight into the tiller, but it didn't budge. We crossed the center of the river, now only fifty feet from shore.

My shoulders burned from pushing against the tiller.

The barge grazed a sandbar, making the barge tip so violently Joliette fell. A barrel escaped its rope, and another rolled right toward the boy. He jumped out of the way, but he lost his footing and fell into the roiling current.

Joliette screamed.

I clung to the tiller, holding it fast.

"Jean!" The boatman, his hands tied before him, ran from the bow, jumped atop a barrel. "Jean!" He turned. "Drop anchor!"

"Help!" The son popped above the surface, but he was already a barge-length away.

I pulled the tiller, hoping to turn the barge back to get the boy, but it slipped in my sweating palms. The barge lurched, and I grabbed with all my strength. *Don't drown.*

"My son." The boatman held out his tied hands. "I must save my son!"

Joliette grabbed the dagger and sliced the rope at his wrists.

The boatman dived and his mighty arms thrust through waves as the boy went down. He dived under the chopping water.

Étienne worked the sail, and I pulled the tiller as we glided into a calm patch before some reeds along the opposite shore.

"Drop anchor before we're grounded," I yelled.

Étienne heaved it over the stern and the rope followed it. Étienne grabbed at it, screaming as the rough cord burned through his hands. The barge slowed and bobbed. Joliette stood next to me, mouthing a prayer. I scanned the water. If I spotted the boy, I could dive for him, but neither the father nor his son reappeared.

"Is there nothing we can do?" Joliette's voice trembled.

Étienne blessed himself. "Pray."

The current spun the barge around the anchor line. The red-capped men shouted on the north shore.

"Still, they wait for us." Joliette blessed herself.

Near the south shore, the father rose from the water, pulling his coughing and flailing son. "They're alive!" I pointed.

Joliette let out a cry.

"We must keep going." Étienne returned to the anchor.

I shouted at the boatman. "You'll find your barge and the payment in Nantes." Étienne hauled the anchor, and I steered back into the current. The men on horseback rode in the same direction, keeping to our speed.

Joliette stood at the stern, watching the bargeman and his son. "How will we get to the ship?"

"Don't worry." The river would take us to the port, where the ship had to be. But how we'd find the ship, I'd no idea. I'd figure it out. I held the tiller, and we charged toward Nantes.

Far in the west, cathedral spires glinted in the late afternoon rays and poked through black clouds. The river widened, and the wind picked up again, spraying water across the barrels. The barge dipped and rose with the regularity of a pendulum. Both Étienne and I leaned all our weight against the tiller to keep the vessel from running into one of the many islands.

So large a city had to be Nantes. Like the Île de la Cité in the Seine, a large island sat in the middle of the Loire. A huge stone bridge with many arches spanned the river, and on the north shore, buildings towered above the bank. We passed under an arch as rain splatted.

"The ship we must find is *Soldat Patriote*!" I shouted.

Joliette opened the door to the pilothouse. "I will get the spyglass."

The current raced. Past the tip of the island, the river widened. Rain stung my burning arms. Silhouetted against the graying sky, dozens of ship masts pierced the blackening clouds. On the horizon, a frigate pitched, her cannons trained on the harbor.

Joliette pointed. "The largest one, straight ahead!"

I breathed a sigh of relief and inhaled worry. How the hell would we board her? How the hell would we stop this barge?

The ship's three sails were furled against the downpour, but her flag snapped brilliant blue, white, and red. Étienne held the tiller fast. I pushed aside the tangle of ropes and dropped the bow anchor. Its rope snapped taut.

The barge did not slow. "The anchor's not holding," I yelled. "Drop the stern anchor!"

Joliette ran out into the downpour. "You threw the anchor, but a loop of rope caught!"

My stupidity. "Damn!" I scrabbled to let out the rope and headed for the stern. The ship loomed.

We'd crash apart when we hit its hull. I threw the anchor. "Hold on!" I grabbed Joliette.

The barge turned thirty degrees and grazed the ship. Screeching and cracking split the air. The barge knocked against the ship with each surging wave.

Men above shouted and cursed. A dozen musket barrels aimed down on us. Lines and a rope ladder spilled over the side of the ship.

Rain needled my face. They'd throw me in prison, then serve me to the guillotine.

An officer climbed down and jumped onto the barrels.

He aimed a pistol at me. "You attack the *Soldat Patriote!*"

"No! It was an accident."

"You don't know what you're doing!"

"The anchor didn't catch."

"This is not your barge." He cocked the hammer of his pistol. "Pirates!"

I held my palms out. "No. We hired the boatman and his son to deliver wine to your ship. But they were knocked overboard, and we had no other choice but to sail it."

He looked me up and down, then Étienne, then Joliette. Keeping his eyes on her, he shouted, "Whose wine?"

"Château de Verzat, finest in France and the world." Joliette stood proud.

"And how would a wench like you know?"

Her lips were pursed so, I feared she'd spit at him.

"The barrels bare the crest," I shouted.

His laugh taunted. He motioned to the sailors, who lowered their guns. Nets unfurled over the side of the ship. Sailors scrambled down them, jumped onto the barge's deck, and rolled the barrels into the nets. They steadied them as men on the ship hauled them up onto the deck. They raced in the increasing wind and rain. The water darkened, and waves foamed white. Now lighter, the barge pitched and rolled.

I gripped a rope tied to the railing, as the waves sprayed from three directions. How would I convince the captain to take us? I patted the purse hanging at my waist. If he didn't take the money, then what? *Papa, we got this far. Help us.*

When the last few barrels were hauled up, I motioned the officer into the pilothouse. Joliette sat near the cold stove, shivering in the gloom. I gripped the table. "Along with the wine, we wish passage to America."

Water streamed from the officer's tricorne. "She's not a passenger ship. She's cargo."

"We're exporting it to America, and my sister and I want to go with it."

"We don't go to America." His sharp jaw pulsed.

My stomach turned. "Where do you go?"

"Saint-Domingue. The wine's shipped to America from there."

"Then we'll take the same route," I shouted over the storm.

He stared at Joliette, shook his head. "We cannot take a wench."

Joliette sighed. "I am accustomed to lack of comforts."

He ran his fingers over his moustache. "Having a *lady* onboard might make a more interesting voyage."

A blast of wind plastered my wet clothes to my back. Joliette gripped the hilt of the dagger and glared at the officer. In my mind, I saw her firing her pistolet into Cassard. She could protect herself but keeping her out of trouble would require every second.

"Will you take us?" she demanded.

The officer's smile reminded me of Cassard's, when he thought he was about to kill us. "Le Capitaine will decide." The officer left us.

My hands, my arms, my shoulders burned. But that was nothing compared to the prickling alarm running down my back. Rap's voice drummed in my head. *French ships are an integral part of the triangular trade—molasses, rum, and slaves.* I shuddered. The officer said the ship was headed for Saint-Domingue, but Africa was on the way. Even if the captain agreed, how could I subject my sister to this journey?

Joliette holstered her dagger, wrapped her arms around herself, and leaned against the wall.

I wiped water from my eyes. We will be sailing aboard a slaver. God help us.

93

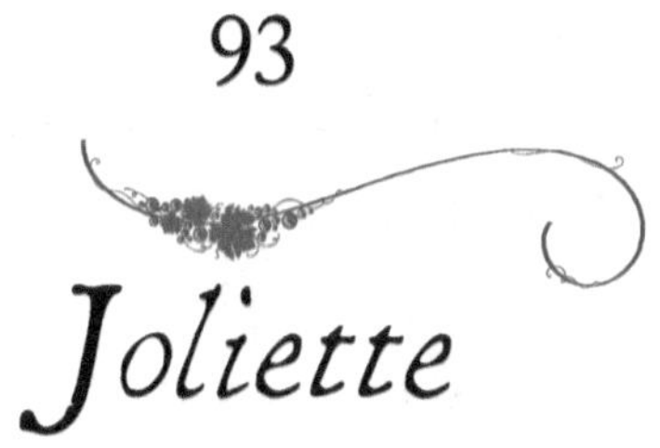

Joliette

Nantes
August 21, 1792

HENRI'S SHOULDERS WERE high and tight as I followed him from the pilothouse. I shivered in my wet gown, plastered to my skin. A gust yanked my bonnet, and I was too tired to grab for it. It flew into the night like a bird.

Henri handed a leather purse to Étienne. "Wait on the barge until you see the bargeman and his son on shore. Put this on the table and leave the barge before they arrive." He handed him more money. "Hire a horse and return to the château." Étienne nodded.

I touched his arm. "Again, I thank you, Étienne. I wish you a safe return."

He pressed his fist to his heart and nodded.

The officer clambered up the ropes to the ship's deck fast as a monkey. A few lights from the ship blinked and shimmered against the choppy water. The sky was indiscernible from the water. Darkness, as deep as that of the tunnels, fell. Within that darkness I had left my home, my husband, my grand-maman, my parents…nearly all of myself. I could not return any more than I could leave.

Étienne emerged from the pilothouse holding a torch, its flame struggling against the storm. Henri whispered to Étienne and turned to me. "You must climb the ropes. I will be above you, and Étienne will be below you."

Everything stopped—my breath, my heart, my thoughts. The wind stirred a cacophony of waves crashing against the hulls. Cold spray drenched me. I stared at Henri's eyes, dark and pinched.

"Climb…to the ship?"

He tied a rope around my waist and the other end around his own. He put out his hand. "Hurry. Before the storm worsens." My mouth would not open. Henri's fingers wrapped around my wrist. He stepped onto the rope ladder.

Étienne held out the bottom rung. My feet were part of the deck, as if rooted to it. Étienne took my other hand and coaxed, "Do not look down. Only up, at Henri."

The makeshift ladder swayed above. Waves leaped through its rungs. Henri's foot slipped, but he caught himself. "The first step's the most difficult, but you're braver than I am." He gently tugged me.

Like Papa. They both knew I could not resist a challenge. I

pressed my feet to the deck, lifted my foot, then grasped the side rope. A wave crashed, and the deck dropped from below me, leaving my foot pawing the air. I screamed but did not hear it. I clung to the side rope. Étienne's hand pressed my foot to the rung. I panted for breath and pressed my forehead against the ship. Cold, black waves jumped and swallowed my foot.

"Keep looking up!" Étienne shouted.

My legs vibrated so I pressed all my weight into my foot as soon as it found a rung. A sliver of pale light spilled over the ship's deck. I wanted to fly to it.

The wind skirled, twisting the rope and me around so I faced out over the harbor. Like a giant hand it pushed me away from the ship, then slammed me back against its hull. My breath burst from me. I lost my grip. Henri held me tighter, and another hand grasped my flailing arm. My legs pedaled. Hands gripped my arms and hauled me up over the rail and onto the deck, landing me like a fish. I lay on my stomach, gasping as the world spun and rain thundered.

Henri draped a woolen blanket over me. He crouched down, helped me to sit up, and rubbed my back.

As if by magic, a pair of tall, shiny black boots appeared before us. The man's uniform was spotless, all white, trimmed in red and blue, with brass epaulettes broadening his shoulders—le Capitaine. He looked down. Water streamed off his tricorne and puddled onto the blanket.

"You wish passage?" His voice was rough as the wind.

Henri stood. "Yes, Monsieur, le Capitaine."

The man chuckled. "*With* a woman?"

Feeling like I still clung to the rope, I pushed myself up

with the words searing my mouth. "I arranged for the wine shipment—"

Henri gripped my arm and pulled me back.

Le Capitaine let out a grunt, turned, and walked away. "We sail when the tide turns."

94

Joliette

Nantes
August 22, 1792

Neither my brother nor I wish to be aboard this ship. We are sailing down the Loire River, leaving the port of Nantes and the shores of France. We both know we shall not return. But we hope.

Henri stands at the bow, staring at an endless ocean. I have never seen it, and I am curious. But as I stand at the stern, listening to the buffeting wind and watching the river, green as my husband's eyes, I caress the ribbon at my wrist.

The yellow light of dawn glitters across the water. The image reminds me of the summer when Grandmaman, Maman, Papa, and I spent our days in the shade of an immense chestnut tree, watching rainbows arc and shimmer along the water's surface as the fishermen towed their bulging nets onto their boats.

The ship bucks and rolls as the river's current battles the ocean's tide. Waves slap the hull. The sounds remind me of Papa's laughter rumbling along the Grande Galerie—entertaining the Queen and shocking courtiers at Versailles. His laugh made horses whinny, servants grin, and nuns shudder. His laugh is one of the things I miss most.

Henri tells me he was born because of Papa's laughter, but he has not yet told me the entire story. There is time.

We have a long journey ahead.

THE END

ACKNOWLEDGEMENTS

UN GRANDE MERCI À

Dr. Berry Edwards who often resorted to speaking French to drag me back from the eighteenth century. Thank you for making me laugh. You are my chevalier.

Aunt Di for your love, support, laughter, and craziness.

Mireille Belt without whose generous gift of two weeks in her Paris apartment this book would not have been conceived.

Teachers and coaches: Susan Penberthy-Nowak for instilling in me a love for the French language and culture, Priscilla Long, Don Maass, and Lorin Oberweger and Brenda Windberg of Free Expressions.

Attorney Matthew Dresden, Dresden Law PLLC, for his generous time and counsel. And Washington Lawyers for the Arts https://www.thewla.org/.

Librarians everywhere. In particular, the Bibliothèque Nationale de France, and Art at the Lionel Pincus and Princess
Firyal Map Division of the New York Public Library.

The gracious and generous Monsieur Thierry Sarmant, con-
servateur en chef, Cabinet Numismatique, and the very kind
and helpful staff at Musée Carnavalet, Paris, France.

The gracious staffs at the Château de Brissac, Château de Che-
nonceau, Château de Meung, and Château de Versailles.

Critique partners, first readers, and editors who asked the right
questions and demonstrated great insight, patience, humor,
and honesty: Allison Basile, Dr. Marty Blalock, Cynthia Blair
(Cynthia Baxter), Sandy Bremser, Tiffanny Brooks, Chris Butler,
Julie Cooper, Kate Dane, Bill Dickett, Vaughn Entwistle, Ejner
Fulsang, Lea Galanter, Lisa Glasgow, Gabi Herkert, Bharti
Kirchner, Joanne Khuns, Susan LeMiles, Marylee MacDon-
ald, Jody McCoy, Jill MacGregor, D.R. Ransdell, Ed Ratcliffe,
Jane Sutherland, JoAnne Tompkins, Jennifer White, Robin Yak.
And the late Richard Askern and John Zobel.

Subject matter experts: Charlotte Rose Basile, Lana Bortolot,
and William A. Edwards III.

My gracious and helpful French hosts: Dominique Cale-
gari-Jehl (Côte Sud—chambres d'hôtes village troglodyte,
Troo, France), and Julie and Jeremy Kolbé (Les Rosiers Loire
Valley Gite, Monteaux, France). Concierge, Estelle Hoglund,
at Paris Marriott Hotel Champs Elysees.

Cultural events and websites helpful to my research and cultural understanding:

- *Emilie* and *The Revolutionists*, plays by Lauren Gunderson https://www.laurengunderson.com/
- Alliance Française: https://afusa.org/
- Bonjour Paris https://bonjourparis.com/
- Courtney Traub's Paris Unlocked https://www.parisunlocked.com/
- Dani Belau's Girl's Guide to Paris https://girlsguidetoparis.com/
- France Magazine https://francetoday.com/
- France Today https://francetoday.com/
- Gallica, the digital library of the National Library of France and its partners. https://gallica.bnf.fr/
- Irene Levine's More Time to Travel https://www.moretimetotravel.com/
- Janine Marsh's The Good Life France https://thegoodlifefrance.com/
- Kristin Espinasse's French Word-A-Day https://www.french-word-a-day.com/

Communities in which I have participated with many generous writers: Community of Writers at Squaw Valley, Free Expression's Inner Circle, Historical Novel Society, Hugo House, Sisters in Crime, Women fiction Writers Association.

SOUPE POIREAUX-POMMES DE TERRE

Leek & Potato Soup

INGREDIENTS

2 large leeks

1 pound baby Dutch (or yellow) potatoes

Extra virgin olive oil

Sea salt & white pepper

1/8 cup dry white wine

1–1½ quarts chicken or vegetable stock

Dash cayenne pepper (optional)

Chopped fresh parsley

DIRECTIONS

1. Thoroughly clean leeks, chop the white parts, and allow to dry on towel.

2. Dice potatoes (do not peel skins for extra texture), rinse, and keep covered in cold water until ready to add, then drain and pat dry with towel.

3. Heat heavy-bottomed pot on medium. When hot, add enough olive oil to cover bottom, add leeks, and stir. Reduce heat to low, stirring frequently, do not allow leeks to brown.

4. When leeks are wilted, add potatoes, and continue to stir. Keep heat low so that nothing browns.

5. Add salt and a few grinds of white pepper.

6. When potatoes are a bit tender and leeks have melted, add wine.

7. Let mixture simmer for a few minutes, then add enough stock to cover vegetables and cook until potatoes are done. Remove from heat.

8. Allow mixture to cool.

9. Add batches to food processor and process until mixture is smooth with a few chunky bits.

10. Taste the mixture. If it needs flavoring, add a dash of cayenne pepper and a bit more salt.

11. Return mixture to pot, and heat on low. Add as much stock as you prefer for the consistency and texture of soup you like. (The soup will continue to thicken as it heats.)

12. Serve and, if you like, sprinkle parsley on each before serving.

Note: This recipe may be doubled or tripled for a crowd.
It freezes well.

© Debra Borchert Author,
Her Own Legacy

DISCUSSION QUESTIONS

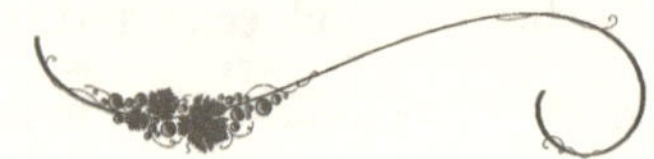

1. By law, Joliette cannot inherit property or own a business and her signature is not accepted on contracts unless she is widowed. During the French Revolution a law passed in 1790, which made women, along with illegitimate children, equal inheritors of property. Did this solve Joliette's problem or complicate things?

2. Do you think Joliette should have obeyed her father and married the man the Comte chose?

3. Had Joliette married the man the Comte chose, what do you think would have happened to Château de Verzat, the families who lived on the estate, and the Verzat legacy?

4. Henri feared he could not fill his father's noble shoes. Do you think Henri became the man he wanted to become? How are Henri and the Comte similar and different?

5. The Comte explains red heels on his shoes means one has presented at the Court of Versailles. French fashion designers Christian Louboutin and Yves Saint Laurent went to court to battle for the trademark of red-soled shoes. Did you notice any other eighteenth century fashions that have been popular during modern times?

6. A lettre de cachet was the King's power to lock anyone in the Bastille, without trial. The Revolutionary government declared if émigrés did not return immediately, the state would confiscate their property and holdings, and, should they return later, they would be executed for treason. Joliette comments, "You know the irony of this? The new law is like a lettre de cachet." How are the laws similar? Is the revolutionary law democratic?

7. Were you surprised to learn the reason Comte de Verzat had not acknowledged Henri? Did the Comte do the wrong thing for the right reason? Have you ever faced a decision to do the wrong thing for the right reason?

8. Henri thinks people do not take responsibility for the parts they play in their own misery, such as when people burn wheat fields and then complain there is no bread. Are there other examples of people contributing to their own demise in the book? Are there any parallels to this in today's world?

9. Henri's neighbor, Madame Françoise, is forced to join the march to Versailles. How would you feel if you were forced to protest something you did not believe in?

10. Who was your favorite secondary character and why?

11. What do you think Joliette and Henri will do when they arrive in America? What must Joliette do to create her own legacy?

ABOUT THE
AUTHOR

Debra Borchert has had many careers. She debuted, at the age of five, as a model at a local country club where her crinoline petticoat dropped to her ankles in the middle of the runway.

Since then, she's been a clothing designer, actress (starring in her first television commercial with Jeff Daniels for S.O.S. Soap Pads www.youtube.com/watch?v=m5SjByjwjs4), TV show host, spokesperson for high-tech companies, marketing and public relations professional, and technical writer for Fortune 100 companies.

Her work has appeared in *The New York Times, San Francisco Chronicle, The Christian Science Monitor*, and *The Writer*, among others. Her short stories have been published in anthologies and independently.

A graduate of the Fashion Institute of Technology, she incorporates her knowledge of textiles and clothing design in writing historical French fiction. She brings her passions for France, wine, and cooking to all her work. The proud owner of ten crockpots, she is renowned for her annual Soup Parties at which she serves soups from different cultures.

Debra's debut novel, *Her Own Legacy,* is the first in a series that follows headstrong and independent women and the four-hundred loyal families who protect a Loire Valley château and vineyard, and its legacy of producing the finest wines in France during the French Revolution.

She lives in the Pacific Northwest with her family and standard poodle who is named after a fine French Champagne.

SPREADING THE WORD

Word of mouth is the best way to discover books, so if you'd like to help spread the word, please share your review. Your feedback is greatly appreciated.

WWW.AMAZON.COM/AUTHOR/DEBRABORCHERT

WWW.GOODREADS.COM/DEBRA_BORCHERT

If you'd like a complimentary e-story or a recipe,
visit my website:

WWW.DEBRABORCHERT.COM